Nocturnal Lies

Linzi Carlisle grew up in Dartford, Kent, in the UK, before moving to South Africa where she met her husband. They lived in Zambia for many years before settling in South Africa in the beautiful town of George, part of the Garden Route, nestled between the Outeniqua Mountains and the Indian Ocean – the perfect spot for writing her books. They share their home with their two beautiful cats.

Blogger: www.linzicarlisle.blogspot.com
Instagram: @linzicarlisleauthor
Facebook: www.facebook.com/linzicarlisleauthor
Goodreads: goodreads.com/linzicarlisle

Also by Linzi Carlisle

Revenge Plan
Village Lies
Graphic Lies
Old Lies
Skipping Christmas in Holly Crescent
The Little Cat who thought she was a Dog

Nocturnal Lies

Linzi Carlisle

With thanks to my loyal readers
*Your public support and encouragement mean more than you
will ever know*

CONTENTS

THE MAIN CHARACTERS

Sasha Blue, *Private Investigator*
D.S. Tony Palmer, *C.I.D. Kensington*
Eric Latimer, *Sasha's ex-fiancé*
Zoe Pullman, *Sasha's best friend*
James Birch, *Zoe's boyfriend*
Rowan Penrose, *'Red', Eric's friend & business partner*
Harry Reddingham, *'Shuggy', Eric's friend*
Warren Porterhouse, *'Franco', Eric's friend*
Vernon Abaoke, *'Ham', Eric's friend*
Drew Merton, *'Dealer', Eric's friend & work associate*
Quentin Thomas, *'Rain Man', friend of 'Franco'*
Max Canning, *business associate of 'Rain Man'*
Kay Saunders, *writes Kay's Killer Blog*
Staff at Freedom Hotels: Rachel, Soreena, Mrs Carter, Samantha, Fran, Donna, Henry, Alfredo, Stefan, Mrs Mason, Giulianna, Neil
Alex Green, *secretary at Latimer & Penrose*
Dillon Brown, *barman at Bar Simone*
Rick Turner, *Dillon's friend from Seattle, US*

PROLOGUE

'There's so much blood... it's everywhere... you've got to help me...'

Eric's words played on a loop in her head as Sasha left Parva Crossing behind and headed back to London, nocturnal darkness waning as the sun began its inexorable rise, bringing with it light and warmth.

There were two things she could rely on, she thought, Eric's propensity for getting himself into trouble over women, and the daily sunrise – the one guaranteed to cause her pain, the other to lift her spirits... except today her spirits remained steadfastly somewhere in the depths of her despair.

Three days, she thought bitterly, three bloody days was all it had taken for Eric to go from being her fiancé to spending the night with a woman who'd been stabbed to death in his bed.

'There's so much blood... it's everywhere... you've got to help me...'

The words started again, and she clicked on her playlist, selecting a song by The Clash. Blinking back tears, she yelled out the lyrics as the song played, its bleak message perfectly reflecting her mood, as if, by drowning them out she could drown out her own emotions. London was calling her, for good or ill...

'I DIDN'T DO IT, I SWEAR'

Winding her way down from Cromwell Road, Sasha followed the one-way streets until she reached Hogarth Road, stifling a yawn and squinting in the bright sunlight as she crawled along looking for the hotel. Taking a swig of tea, she grimaced, realising too late that it was cold, had probably been cold for the last half an hour. She felt queasy, the oily bacon breakfast roll she'd picked up earlier not sitting well in her stomach, especially when combined with her nerves, knotted as they were into a twisted mass of anxiety. Bloody Eric. Why did he have to wake up next to a woman who'd been stabbed to death?

There it was. Indicating, she half-pulled in behind a police car, noting the forensics van partially blocking the road ahead. *Freedom – what kind of a name was that for a hotel chain?*

'Sorry, love, you can't park here.' The police officer tapped on her passenger window, bending down to address her through the glass.

'I'm here to meet D.S. Palmer, he's expecting me.' She looked hopefully at the officer as he shook his head.

'I'm going to have to ask you to move along.'

A movement at the door of the hotel caught her eye and she craned her neck upwards, spotting Tony Palmer walking towards a vehicle, mobile phone to his ear.

With an apologetic glance at the officer, she opened her door and stepped out. 'Tone, over here.' Waving frantically to get his attention, she yelled louder, 'Tone, it's Sasha.'

D.S. Palmer looked up, lifting his arm to acknowledge her as he changed direction and headed her way.

'Sorry, Sarge, this lady refuses to move on.'

'That's alright, officer, I'll deal with it.'

He turned to Sasha. 'Sasha, babes, how are you? Good drive back? You look like crap.'

Talk about state the obvious. 'I feel like crap too. Good to see you, Tone. What's happening? Where is he? Can I see him? What did he tell you?'

'Whoa, slow down, hold on a sec.' Tony held his hands up. 'He's being taken in, sorry, babes, you'll be able to speak to him once he's been processed.'

'But–' Her eyes picked up movement again, this time a group of three men leaving the hotel– Eric, flanked by two officers.

As if sensing Sasha's presence, Eric looked around, the sun catching his blonde hair as his eyes met hers across the cars.

'Sash,' he called desperately. 'You've got to help me. Please, baby. I didn't do it, I swear.'

'Leave it.' Tony held her arm. 'Let my men take him.' He turned her to face him, his eyes serious. 'It's not looking good for your boyfriend, Sash, I have to be honest with you. Walk away, babes, trust me, it's the wise thing to do.'

'He's not my boyfriend, not anymore. Not since he told me with great satisfaction how he had a choice of two women when he cheated on me last week. We were engaged. Can you believe it?' She swiped a hand across her eyes, looking mutinously at Tony. 'But I can't just walk away. No matter how much of a stupid bastard he is, I don't believe he's a murderer. Look, can I just–? Could you just show me the room where it happened, at least?'

Sighing, Tony Palmer gave a whistle, catching the attention of one of the scenes of crime officers. 'Chuck us over a couple of suits, will you?'

They walked into the hotel foyer as Tony expressed his distaste at Sasha's defence of Eric. 'Let him rot, babes, you deserve better than a cheating wanker like him. I can't believe he expects you to stand by him now, not after what he's done.'

Her eyes took in the wall-sized image of a smiling couple clinking glasses as they sat on a bed. *Free to be yourself. Free to indulge. Free to enjoy. Freedom – the hotel brand of choice for life's pleasure seekers.* Well, that explained the stupid name. Maybe Eric had sought a little too much pleasure last night, and freedom might be the one thing he lost as a result, she thought bitterly.

They took the lift to the third floor and Sasha followed Tony along the carpeted corridor, stepping under the police tape as he held it up for her. He stopped at a doorway manned by an officer. 'Suit up and wait here for me, yeah?'

Impatiently she zipped up the white coveralls and slipped the paper shoes over her sandals, peering into the room and straining to hear what Tony was saying to another white-suited individual. Her eyes fell on the bed, taking in the shape of a person lying beneath the duvet – a white duvet stained with crimson in a number of places – towards which the other man was now lifting and driving his hand down at repeatedly.

Tony nodded, his face grim, as he turned and saw Sasha staring through the open doorway. He shook his head at her, holding up his hand to indicate that she should wait, and nodded at two other white-suited officers who removed the blood-stained duvet and bagged it, before moving a wheeled trolley beside the bed. As the body was bagged and transferred to the trolley, Tony returned to Sasha.

'Once they've removed the body, I'll take you in. The photos are all taken and the SOCOs are bagging up everything else. Two minutes only though, okay?'

She nodded. 'Was she stabbed through the duvet?'

'Yep, at least half a dozen times.'

Standing aside as the body was wheeled out, she resisted the crazy urge to reach out and unzip the bag – she just wanted to know what the woman looked like. Who was she? How had she and Eric ended up at this hotel? *And, more to the point, how had she ended up dead?*

'Who was she?' Her voice was barely a whisper.

'We don't know yet, there was nothing of a personal nature to identify her in her bag, no purse, no bank cards, only a mobile phone. We'll work through the phone's call history and contacts, see what we can discover, but there are none of the expected names or message threads at first glance.' He cleared his throat awkwardly. 'She, er, well, her bag contained quite a few condoms, as well as a bottle of lube and another of mouthwash.'

'So, she was a hooker.' Her voice was croaky and she cleared her throat.

'Let's go in.'

They stood together beside the bed, looking at the blood-soaked sheet. Tony turned to her, his expression sympathetic.

'She was dressed in provocative clothing, a low-cut dress with a front zip, sexy undies, stockings, that kind of thing. But we can't jump to conclusions, maybe she was just spicing things up for the pair of them. Mind where you step.' He took her arm as she wobbled.

'You can bag that,' he said to the officer beside him, 'it was hidden by the overhanging duvet.'

She averted her eyes from the used condom as it was picked up by the man's latex-clad hand, feeling sick.

'Stockings, you said? On a warm summer's night? Yeah, she was a hooker,' Sasha said bitterly. 'But someone must have seen her come into the hotel dressed like that? I suppose they turn a blind eye.'

'These particular hotels are known for their discretion apparently, hence the name. They don't have a manned reception, just a couple of tablets on stands for guests to check themselves in with and slots to receive their key cards. There's a floor-walker, or something like that, who hangs around and helps out if needed, but most of the time guests just come and go unnoticed with no human contact, unless they go into the bar or restaurant, of course. At least they haven't switched to bleedin' robots yet, that'll be the next thing.'

'How many were there?'

'You what?'

'How many used condoms did your men find?'

'Just the one.' Tony paused. 'Which I thought was a little on the odd side of things, considering the set-up, you know, sexy bird, plenty of booze, but then we found torn-off corners of two other condom wrappers, so one of 'em got rid of the wrappers, as well as the other used bad boys. Must have flushed 'em down the loo – nothing in the rubbish bins, not a bleedin' sausage.'

Sasha watched the scenes of crime officer bag an empty champagne bottle from the floor beside the rubbish bin, moving aside so that he could do the same with another identical empty bottle on the nightstand.

'Expensive champagne, that's typical Eric,' she said.

'Only one glass, which is weird. Two empty bottles and a third, almost full, on the floor beside the bed. We only found it when we moved the duvet.'

Sasha walked carefully around the room, checking in the bathroom and noting the two clean water glasses next to the basin, before stepping out onto the balcony. 'Those are Eric's cigarettes and lighter. Looks like he smoked a few cigarettes out here, judging by the ashtray, and–' she indicated the long ash on the cigarette lying on the floor, 'he didn't finish that one.'

'Beats me why he'd get himself a prostitute, I mean, he's a good-looking bloke, I don't suppose he's ever had any trouble picking up a bird.' Tony shook his head, mystified.

'Oh no, Eric was particularly good at picking up birds,' she said caustically. 'The good old Eric charm, so good he could charm the knickers off a nun if he set his mind to it. I suppose getting a prostitute was just another thrill for him.'

'Seen enough?'

'Yeah, let's go, this whole scene is making me feel sick.'

I didn't do it, I swear. How many times had she heard Eric say those words? It should be carved into his headstone, he'd said it so many times. Well, maybe this time he did do it. And maybe she wouldn't stick around to help him wriggle out of it. Except...

'Tone, you said she was dressed in provocative clothing. D'you mean she was fully dressed or her clothes were found in the room?' She tugged at the zip of the coveralls, pulling the suit down and stepping out of it.

'Fully dressed. Doesn't mean anything though, maybe he wanted her to keep her clothes on. Different strokes and all that. Oh, and she had a sort of light coat or mac beside her in the bed, that and her bag. Chuck your suit and bits in here.'

'So, she was in the bed, fully clothed, with her bag and coat beside her? And, what? The duvet was pulled up over her? Don't you think that's a bit weird?'

Tony Palmer stopped mid-way along the corridor. 'Maybe it's weird, babes, maybe it isn't, we see all sorts in this business, but the simple fact is that they were the only two people in the room and she's the one who ended up dead. No signs of anyone else being there, only one room key card, and your fella covered in her blood. Like I told you earlier, it's not looking good for him.'

'But he called me.' She hurried after Tony as he strode to the lift and jabbed impatiently at the button. 'Why would he call me and ask me for help if he did it?'

'In you go.' He stepped into the lift behind her, hitting the button for the ground floor. 'Clever ploy, maybe?

Make you believe he's innocent? Muddy the waters and all that?'

They stood silently as the lift returned them to the foyer, stepping out and heading outside.

Tony turned to look at her, his eyes sympathetic. 'You look pale, you sure you're feeling alright, love?'

'I'm just a bit knackered, I'd only been asleep for a couple of hours when Eric called, and I grabbed my stuff and left Parva Crossing to drive here. I didn't even say goodbye to anyone.' Fleeting thoughts of Cal appeared unwelcomingly in her head. *Maybe we could have lunch or something? Try again?* Why did life have to be so complicated?

'Tell you what, meet me at the station and I'll make you a cuppa, you look like you could do with it. Then you can have a few words with him, but unofficially, keep it between us, alright? You can't be involved in this investigation, Sash, sorry, babes, but you've got a personal connection to our suspect. You get it, right?'

'Yeah, I get it. Thanks, Tone,' she said, hugging him. 'I'll meet you at the nick.'

~

'The custody sergeant will let me know when we can see him, alright, babes? He's just being processed, won't be long. Come on, I've got cups of tea coming from the beautiful Audrey, our very own tea aficionado. There she is, right on cue, don't know what we'd do without you, Audrey my darling.'

Audrey, the tea lady, simpered, her cheeks pinking up as she patted her tightly permed hair. 'Oh, you are a one, you really are. Here's your tea, and one for the young lady. Oh, and I popped some biccies on the tray for you, but don't you go telling the others, they'll be accusing me of favouritism and we can't have that.'

'And there was me thinking I *was* your favourite, Audrey. Bet you say the same thing to all the boys.' Tony winked at Sasha, picking up a Jammie Dodger and waving it at her, as Audrey tutted happily and bustled out.

'Little bit of flirting with old Audrey and I get all the best biscuits.' He popped the whole biscuit in his mouth, munching it as he indicated that Sasha should do the same.

Smiling, she took a biscuit, savouring the sweetness and the sugar rush.

'Wow, this tea's good, you weren't wrong about Audrey.' She gulped half of her mug of tea down thirstily, before putting it down and looking anxiously at Tony. 'D'you think they've finished processing him by now?'

'Finish your tea and take a minute to catch your breath, you walk in to see him looking all end-of-the-world wide-eyed like you do and he'll collapse on the spot. And listen, Sash, this is a big favour I'm doing you so not a word, yeah? If my D.C.I. finds out about it it'll be my guts for garters.' He looked up at a tap on the door and nodded. 'Right, let's get you in to see lover boy before his solicitor arrives. Oh, and, Sash? You have to prepare yourself – your boy's guilty – has to be.'

Tony led the way, stopping outside a door to an interview room and glancing up and down the corridor. 'Make it snappy, okay? I need you out of there pronto. And no telling him anything I've told you.'

She stepped inside the room, closing the door behind her, as arms clutched her, a sour smell hitting her nostrils.

'Sash, thank God you're here. You've got to get me out of here, baby, I–'

Wrestling free, she pushed him away, stepping back slightly and surveying him coldly.

'And why exactly am I here, Eric?'

'Come on, baby, I told you, I need your help. I didn't do it, I swear.' He grinned suddenly. 'And look at me, in this bloody awful grey tracksuit, I look like a real prat. I need to get home, take a shower, and put some decent clothes on – you know grey was never my colour...'

Trust Eric to mess around even at a time like this.

'Then I'll take you out for a splash-out meal and as much of the best champagne that you can drink. I know, I'll take you to this amazing spot in Soho where you press a button at your table for more champagne, how does that sound? I ate there yesterday with Shuggy, you remember him, I took you to his wedding? I'm telling you, Sash, caviar, oysters, truffles in everything...'

She blinked, shaking her head in disbelief. 'Eric, stop talking. STOP.' She put her hand on the door handle. 'I'm going to leave now, I can't believe I was stupid enough to come here. You can't help yourself, can you?'

'What?' Eric's expression was a picture of confusion. 'What did I do? What did I say? Last night – that's all a big misunderstanding, baby, the cops'll sort it out. You'll help them, you're good at all that detective stuff – don't I always tell you you're the best? I didn't kill anyone, you know that. I'm the victim here, you know, ask your mate outside, one of his cronies has nicked my wallet and the two hundred quid that was in it, as if it isn't enough to accuse me of murder, they're pinching my cash.'

'Is that where you picked her up?' Her voice was soft.

'Picked who up?'

'The prostitute, Eric – who d'you think? Did you pick her up in Soho after you'd had your nice meal with good old Shuggy? Who I've never met and whose wedding, incidentally, you did not take me to – you must be confusing me with one of your other girls. Was it after you'd drunk your fancy champagne in the restaurant? Did you take her to the hotel and order more champagne because you just hadn't had enough at the restaurant?' She was shaking now. 'And then, did you screw her bloody brains out until you ran out of condoms and then kill her?

And then call me to get you out of your mess? I must be the world's biggest idiot.' Her hand began to turn the handle of the door.

'Wait.'

Eric's shoulders drooped as he held his hands out in supplication. 'I've been an idiot, I've treated you badly, I've upset you, and I admit it – I'm the world's worst boyfriend, but I'm begging you to help me out here, Sash. I don't even know how I ended up with her last night, it's all just this big blur. All I can remember is being out with Shuggy and then getting bladdered with a few of the guys. There was me and Shug, Rowan, of course, Ham, Dealer, and a couple of other blokes I didn't know – not sure how they ended up with us.' He sank onto a chair, leaning his head in his hands. 'I was covered in her blood, I was lying next to her, next to a dead body. I could smell it, like metal. Oh God.' His eyes were huge in his white face as reality kicked in. 'They're going to say I did it. They're going to charge me and I'll be found guilty and I'll spend the rest of my life in prison.'

Sasha started at the hammering sound on the door and dropped her hand as the door shot open.

'You have to get out now, Sash, right now, hurry.' Tony grabbed her hand and pulled her from the room.

'She said she was leaving. Why was she in the bed? She kept saying she had to go, that she wasn't allowed to talk to me. Sash?' Eric's voice rose in panic as she turned back to him.

'I've got to go. I'll try and speak to you again.'

'Let's go,' said Tony, glancing up and down the corridor. 'Your solicitor's here, I'll bring him through, but calm it, Latimer, none of that shouting, alright? And no one nicked any money from you, just for the record. You came in without a wallet and you'll leave without one – if you're telling the truth about the girl, that is.' He slammed the door and pulled Sasha along with him as he rushed for the stairs.

'Speak to Shuggy.' Eric yelled through the closed door. 'Ask Shuggy, he'll tell you what happened.'

What had he yelled at her? Something about Shuggy – ask Shuggy, maybe? Ask him what, though? What he and Eric had for dinner? How pissed Eric was on champagne? Whose idea it was to go in search of prostitutes? 'You can let go of my hand, Tone, it's going blue.'

'What? Sorry, it's just, the super's on the prowl. Can I leave you to head on down on your own? You know the way. Let us speak to him properly once he's seen his solicitor, alright, babes?'

'You'll give me a call? Once you've looked at everything? Tell me how bad it looks? I mean, stuff like if his fingerprints are on the murder weapon, that kind of thing?'

'Er, yeah, course I will now go.' Tony turned her to face the stairs. 'Go and get some rest,' he called as he pulled open the door to the corridor they'd just left.

'Wait!' She grabbed the door. 'What aren't you telling me? It's about the murder weapon, isn't it?'

'What murder weapon?' Tony raised his eyebrows, tapping the side of his nose. 'Now get out of here.'

She walked down the stairs and out of the police station deep in thought. Was Tony telling her that they didn't have the murder weapon? That in a locked hotel room, with Eric and the dead woman its only occupants, they'd found no murder weapon?

'Here she is.'

'Over here.'

'Are you the girlfriend of the suspect?'

'It's her, Sasha something.'

'Did he do it?' A phone was held in her face and she turned her head away.

'What's it like to be engaged to a murderer?'

'How many prostitutes has he killed? Is this really only his second victim?'

'I have no idea what you're talking about. Excuse me.' She pushed her way through the small group of reporters, ignoring their questions and doing her best to keep her head down. The last thing she, Eric, or Tony, needed was a photo of her leaving the police station. Fumbling for her keys, she opened her car and sank into the driver's seat, her knees feeling weak. She felt desperately thirsty and had a sudden overwhelming desire to bawl her eyes out. A tap on her window prevented her from giving in to the tears and she started the car, driving out and away from the small group.

Wait. She slowed as the words of the last question registered in her brain – is this really only his second victim? *Whose? Eric's?*

KAY'S KILLER BLOG

Sasha drove around the block and parked her car in the same spot as before, hurrying from her car as her eyes searched for the young woman who'd asked her the question. Who was the first victim and why did the reporter think it was connected to this murder?

'Excuse me.' The group had dispersed and the last two were walking off as she called to them. 'There was a young woman with you, er, darkish hair? Wearing a white shirt?'

'That was probably Kay – she's gone.' They turned away, not interested in someone not prepared to give them any information.

'Have you got a last name? Anything?'

'It kind of works two ways, you know.' The older of the two men turned back to her, his tone peevish.

'I'm sorry, I've got nothing to tell you, I–'

The younger man nudged his companion. 'You alright, love? You look a little peaky.'

Relenting, the older man spoke again. 'Check out Kay's Killer Blog.'

'Thank you, I appreciate it.' She smiled her thanks as they nodded and walked off, before getting back into her car and tapping the name of the blog into her phone.

Kay referred to herself as the unofficial expert on murder in the capital and, at a cursory glance, appeared to have reported on about seven murders in the current month. *Free to be murdered* was the title for her latest entry – a brief paragraph below giving very little information about the actual murder other than the fact that there appeared to have been a murder at the Freedom Hotel, Kensington. A photograph of the body bag being wheeled out accompanied the short article with the caption *Is she the serial killer's second victim?*

Having expressed inner admiration at the title of the post, Sasha scrolled down quickly until she reached the beginning of the year, then slowly scrolled up through the posts, scanning the titles for anything that might be prostitute related. A drive-by shooting in Stratford in January was alleged by Kay to be gang-related and a drugs turf war and, according to Kay, a man named Raymond Pinner, who was found stabbed to death in a hotel room and relieved of his wallet, in the City of London during the same month, was quite possibly connected to the gang in some way due, in part, to the viciousness of the attack – he'd been stabbed seven times in total – and to the fact that he'd had a small amount of cocaine in his possession which could potentially be linked to the larger quantity found on the shooting victim. Sasha smiled to herself, Kay had quite the active imagination. His widow, Jennifer Pinner, had denied the drugs connection, Kay had informed her readers.

Her eyes continued to scan the titles, rejecting the stabbing to death of Linda Brown in Hackney by her husband, Derek Brown, as well as, in February, the murder of Susan Tilman in a supermarket car park in Hampstead who, although described by Kay as a part-time stripper, had been run over in what appeared to be a particularly nasty episode of car park rage. She moved onto March, where a shopkeeper had been stabbed in Finsbury Park, and a young woman had died after an incident outside a pub in Soho– Sasha paused, reading Kay's post. Tiffany Palmer worked as a model for a small agency in Soho and had apparently complained to the police about someone stalking her. Kay alleged that the incident outside the pub had occurred when the model confronted her stalker and that he had pushed her into the road, where she had died after being hit by a motorbike courier. She shook her head, no, not what she was looking for.

March had been a busy month, murder-wise, there'd been two more shootings; a man had been pushed from a window on the fourteenth floor of a hotel in

Hammersmith – possibly a disagreement between staff, said Kay; there had been three deaths by stabbing – one, in Bermondsey, was a woman killed by her lover's wife; one was a man, Adrian Harking, killed and robbed in his hotel room at The Luxe, Camden, in quite a frenzied attack resulting in a number of stab wounds, for which Kay had been unable, even with her active imagination, to come up with an explanation for, other than to say that he appeared to have spent many of his evenings entertaining clients in bars and restaurants, and had perhaps therefore offended an unstable character who saw him as a sinner indulging in too much alcohol, expensive food, and women – which would account for the number of stabbings, she'd proffered, attempting to draw an analogy with the famous film about the seven deadly sins starring Brad Pitt and Morgan Freeman; and one was the death of a performer in a magic show in Covent Garden – the unfortunate man having stabbed himself in the stomach with his knife which, contrary to his belief, was not the spring-loaded prop he expected it to be, but a real knife. Kay asserted that the exchange of knives had been done by a rival street performer although the man was never arrested.

Sasha carried on scanning Kay's posts, finding the overall blog quite entertaining, even if it was about murder. She passed through April and May and, frustratingly, found what she'd been looking for in June.

There it was, a prostitute found murdered at the beginning of June, round about the time they'd all got back from their holiday and just after she and Eric had become engaged – the shortest engagement in living history, she thought sadly – about three weeks.

Bleak photos of where the woman's body had been found accompanied the account, which raised questions about the safety of female sex workers and whether this was the start of a new killing spree by a serial killer inspired by Jack the Ripper. It was unfounded nonsense designed to alarm and attract readers, Sasha decided. If Kay had spent even a moment checking her facts she would have known, indeed should have known, that Jack the Ripper's victims had had their throats cut and were brutally and horribly mutilated. Aside from that, to declare the possible presence of a serial killer after one murder was nothing more than scare-mongering.

This woman, identified as Sonia Clark, had been strangled and her body, heavily bruised, left in an alleyway leading from Old Compton Street, between the back entrances of a fish and chip shop and a massage parlour, in Soho. An employee from the fish and chip shop had found her body when disposing of rubbish in the bins in the alley.

Clearly, the two murders were completely different, not only in the method used, but in the area where the body had been found – one in Soho, an area once renowned for its sex trade, now less so, and one in Kensington, an upmarket area known for its expensive boutiques, embassies, museums, and hotels. And a palace, of course. One body had been dumped unceremoniously in an alleyway and the other had been found in a bed in a room of a moderately expensive hotel.

These murders couldn't possibly be connected, nonetheless, she'd still like to speak to Kay as the girl seemed to have a knack for finding out information, she decided, as she rummaged in her glove compartment and found a container with two Tic Tacs remaining. She tipped them into her mouth, grateful to have something to suck, and pondered her next move. What she really wanted to do was to go home, shower, and fall into bed for a couple of hours, but the buzz of the mystery was growing and wouldn't be satisfied with such a move.

There was no contact number for Kay, only a contact page where a message could be left. She tapped out a quick message asking the woman to call her and made a decision – she'd head through to Eric's office and speak to his colleague and partner, Rowan, in the hope that he'd be able to put her in touch with the mysterious Shuggy.

~

'Er, hi, is that Discreetly Elite? Great, um, I'm not exactly sure how this works, but I've got one of your cards...'

Dillon listened to the voice at the other end of the call, nodding as he looked around to make sure that no one was listening.

'Yeah, okay, well yes, I've got something written on the back of the card, is that it? Right, it says VIPMR09. Yeah? Oh, great, so, er, how much is it per hour?' He gave a silent whistle at the cost, calculating the approximate amount for a hotel room plus drinks. 'Yep, not fussed, they're all top class, right? That's fine. It's for Saturday night, say, eleven o'clock? Er, a bottle?' *Rick's tipple of choice had been Rum, hadn't it?* 'A bottle of Rum will be perfect. How's two hours?' *Might as well allow enough time for plenty of fun.* 'Er, yeah, Dillon Brown, my card details? Yep, hold on a sec.' Making a mental note to tell his bank that he'd moved and forgotten to update his address – *it had been a year, but no need to tell them that* – he gave his card details, grinning as he placed his phone down, this was going to be highly entertaining. Looking up, he smiled as a man approached him. 'Yes, guv, what can I get you?' He handed over the pint of lager before crumpling the card up and dropping it in the bin, whistling as he wiped over the bar counter.

~

Sasha drove up Kensington Church Street, along Notting Hill Gate, and made her way up Pembridge Road, before picking up the Great Western Road a little further on. Crossing the railway lines, she headed over the Grand

Union Canal and picked up the Harrow Road, driving past shops and takeaways, her stomach grumbling as the smell of food wafted in through her open window. She needed sustenance and a loo break and, seeing a parking spot ahead, pulled in, heading into the nearest coffee shop where she devoured a small baguette stuffed with halloumi and avocado. She used the loo and sat back down to finish her cup of tea, using her phone to confirm exactly where Eric's office was, it having been a long time since her one and only visit about a year ago. When she was ready to leave, she picked up a bottle of water, paid, and returned to her car for the short drive to Portnall Road and West Kilburn.

The office of Latimer and Penrose, property development specialists, was through a doorway squashed in between a kebab shop and a dry cleaners and accessed via a steep flight of stairs which Sasha climbed before giving the door a tap and entering. Trying to ignore the smell of onions permeating the room from the kebab shop below, she called out.

A giggle sounded from a back office and a girl walked through, smoothing her blouse and tucking her hair behind her ears. 'Can I help you?' she asked, sitting down at a desk and looking at Sasha expectantly.

'Yes, I'm looking for Rowan, is he in?'

'Ro?' the girl yelled, before smiling at her, shrugging her shoulders.

'No need to shout, Alex, it's unladylike, for one thing, and it's the last thing I need with this killer headache threatening to explode my skull.' Rowan appeared holding three used coffee mugs. 'Wash these up for me, there's a darling.' He noticed Sasha, and smiled, his brown eyes puzzled for a moment before recognition struck. 'Sasha, isn't it? Eric's fiancée? It's been a long time, I always say to the old dog, where are you hiding that woman of yours? I suppose he wants to keep you all to himself, can't say I blame him.' His eyes involuntarily flicked over her body before returning to her face. 'He's not here. Are you supposed to be meeting him? Not sure what's happened to him today, not a peep, and we had a meeting this morning with a potential client. Hangover probably, you know what he's like...' His sudden guffaw petered out as he took in Sasha's pursed lips and slightly frosty demeanour, and he cleared his throat, shifting awkwardly on his feet.

'Can we speak privately?' Sasha looked pointedly at the girl he'd called Alex.

'Er, sure. Alex, wash these up and put the kettle on, there's a good girl. Come into my office.' He waved his arm, indicating that Sasha should go ahead of him. 'Take a seat. How can I help you?'

'Eric's been arrested for murdering a prostitute.' For some reason, she enjoyed the momentary shock that registered on Rowan's face.

'He's what?' He ran his hands through his unruly mop of red hair, leaving it even more untidy than it had been previously.

'He's been arrested. A woman was stabbed to death in his hotel room last night at the Freedom Hotel, Kensington. And, just for the record, I'm not Eric's fiancée, we broke up after his last little escapade with two women he met at The Woolly Sheep in Covent Garden.'

Awareness flashed in Rowan's eyes for a moment and Sasha realised that he'd probably been with Eric that night as well.

'I'm sure you know all about it, Rowan, after all, you were out drinking with him last night, weren't you?' *As if the rank odour of his beer breath wasn't enough evidence.*

'There's got to be some mistake, I mean, yes, we were out having a few bevvies last night, but... bloody hell, they're saying he murdered a prostitute? Eric? No way, we were all totally hammered when we parted ways. I doubt he was capable of finding his way home, let alone carrying out a murder. What's he supposed to have stabbed her with? His credit card?' Rowan leaned back in his chair with a braying laugh, wincing slightly at the pain in his head.

'I'm glad you think it's funny. Eric's a stupid twit and a complete bastard, but I can't quite see him as a murderer, can you? The trouble is, though, the police can so, if you can curb your amusement for a moment, can you tell me what happened last night so I can get on with trying to clear the stupid bugger's name? It might be in your interest, seeing as he is your business partner and, presumably, your friend.' This guy was irritating the hell out of her, he was like Eric, but worse.

'Sorry.' Rowan said sheepishly. 'And sorry about you and Eric, I didn't know, he said you'd just had a little tiff, that it would all blow over. Of course, I want to help, it's just, well, to be honest, I can't remember much, like I said–'

'You were all totally hammered, yeah, I get it. Eric can't seem to remember anything either. But you must remember something? Who were you with? Where were you drinking? Did you go to the restaurant with Eric and someone called Shuggy? Somewhere in Soho?'

'Oh, that's right, old Shug was with us. No... no, I didn't eat with them, we just met up at the pub, not sure which one though, we went to two or three. There were a few of the guys there, um, Franco and Ham, if I recall, and Dealer, he's a good guy, we've done some great work with him. Have you met him? No?' He frowned in effort. 'There were a couple of other blokes there, never met them before, nope, no idea of their names, sorry.'

What was it with this lot and their inability to use actual names? 'Rowan, I'll need their names, and contact numbers if you have them, I mean – Ham? Dealer? And

Shuggy? What are they, Muppets? And where did you start drinking? Was it in Soho? Can you remember anything?'

Rowan suddenly snapped his fingers. 'Soho, yes. We did start off there, some pub or other, too many men there, not enough birds, if you get my drift... Old Compton Street, that was it, that was where we started.'

Old Compton Street – where the strangled prostitute had been found, according to Kay's blog... 'Names, Rowan, can you give me the guys' names? And numbers?'

'Right, right, let me have a look.' Rowan picked up his phone and scrolled through his contacts. 'I do remember something, we were mucking around, not sure how it came about, but there was some bird there, at one of the pubs, and I know Shuggy kept saying Eric was spoken for. He said he was as good as married, course, he meant you. Eric never told us you'd broken up, he'd said something about an argument but that was a week or two ago, so as far as we were concerned, he was out of the running, you know, for birds and stuff. I don't think she was a prostitute though...' He shook his head. 'No, one of the guys must have just been chatting her up. Not Eric,' he said quickly. 'Okay, here are the numbers. What's yours? I'll send them to you.'

'Thanks.' She took out a pen and notepad. 'And their real names? I'm assuming they do have them?'

With names and numbers secured, Sasha thanked Rowan and said she'd be in touch with him soon. She couldn't stand another minute of sitting in his office, of the smell from the kebab shop, or of the smell from his heavy night.

'When d'you think he'll be back at work?' Rowan's voice reached her as she thanked the girl and opened the door to leave. 'He'll be alright, Eric always is.'

'I'll be in touch,' she called out in reply, letting the door close behind her. She rolled her eyes as she descended the stairs, pushing the door to the street open and drawing in a large gulp of fresh air tinged with traffic fumes. Rowan certainly wasn't taking Eric's plight very seriously.

~

Kay walked along the pavement outside the Freedom Hotel, glancing casually towards the entrance. It was no good, there were still police hanging around – she'd never get in, not unless she had a booking, and right now that was way more than her budget could afford. She could say she was getting a drink in the bar, she supposed, but then she'd have to buy one and no doubt that would set her back a few unnecessary quid. It would have to be the staff entrance – but where was it? She continued on, her eyes scanning the entrances between the buildings, looking for anything promising. A laundry van pulled in ahead of her, turning into a narrow lane, and she picked up her pace, maybe it was down there.

By the time she reached the lane, the van had disappeared, but a couple of minutes later she arrived at an open gate, its sign stating its use as the service entrance to the hotel. She walked through purposefully, nodding at a couple of staff taking a smoke break, and caught sight of the van again, its doors now open. A rail of pressed uniforms stood outside the van and, as she hesitated for a second, was rolled to a door by a young man and taken inside. She hurried down the slope after him and found herself inside the basement of the hotel, corridors leading off in various directions with signs affixed to the walls indicating the various cogs which turned the wheels of the machinery that kept the hotel operating smoothly.

But where should she start? The sound of voices reached her from the corridor on the left and she walked quietly along, straining to hear the conversation.

'That the lot, Arthur? Busy day?'

'You can say that again, yeah, that's all of it. What's going on with all the coppers everywhere then?'

'You'll never believe it, we had a murder here last night, woman got herself stabbed to death. We're not supposed to talk about it though so you can't breathe a word.'

'Blimey, that's a turn-up for the books, made an arrest, have they?'

'Well, I wasn't on duty, but Alfredo's been going off on one like you can't believe. He reckons the husband did it, says they booked in for a romantic night and had a bust-up and then he stabbed her. But listen to this – he reckons the man stabbed her with one of his knives, Alfredo's, I mean.'

'You what?'

'I know, you couldn't make it up, could you? He says the man took a knife from the kitchen, stabbed her, then put it back.'

Well, this was interesting. Kay crept closer. But he wasn't the husband, not from what she'd overheard the police officer saying this morning, and had subsequently based her blog post on. He was the client, and that only meant one thing – she was definitely the second prostitute to be murdered.

'You're turning my stomach, you are. Imagine ordering your steak and chips in the restaurant and your steak's been cut with the murder weapon.'

Kay grinned to herself. *Gross.*

There was the sound of giggling.

'Hold up, though, if the knife was put back how did Alfred what's his face know it was taken in the first place?'

Raising her eyebrows thoughtfully, Kay nodded. *Good point.*

The girl giggled again. 'You should be a detective, you should. You better get going, Mrs Carter will be along in a minute.'

'Oh blimey, not the old dragon. Fancy a drink tonight? What time d'you get off?'

'Wouldn't mind, I'm off at eight. Where you taking me then?'

'Only the best when you have a drink with Arthur. How about bringing your friend along, what's it? Sorry, I can't remember?' Arthur cackled.

'Pack it in, Arthur, you know her name's Soreena. Yeah, I'll ask her, why though?'

'Thought I'd get Femi to come with us, he fancies Soreena something rotten, don't blame him neither, she's got the looks, ain't she?

Careful, Arthur... Kay waited for the girl's response.

'Yeah, well, she looks alright, if you like that foreign look. Femi's good-looking, I'm surprised he's single.' There was a challenge in the girl's tone.

Touché. You asked for that, Arthur.

'Can I help you?' The stern voice came out of nowhere, making Kay jump.

'Quick, it's Mrs Carter, you better go.'

'I was just looking for the, er...' *The boy was saying something, the name of the pub – what did he say?* 'Er, the loo?'

'Afternoon, Mrs Carter. Just dropped your clean uniforms off, all pukka. I'll be off then.'

'Yes, thank you. Well, don't just stand there, Rachel, get these rails through to the changing rooms.'

Kay took the gap, slipping away and hurrying out after the boy, who jumped into the waiting van and was gone. Squinting in the bright sunlight, she smiled to herself. She'd got enough to write another post on her blog and if she could somehow get chatting with the girl tonight at the pub then she might be able to get a bit more out of her. But what was the name of the pub? The Earl something? No, it was plural – it would come to her – she'd check online and look at pub names in the area. She walked back along the lane at a brisk pace, playing with ideas for her title in her head, eager to get back to her flat and type up her new post.

Her phone pinged and she opened the e-mail sent via her blog, her mind still on a catchy title for her next post – it was her, Sasha Blue, the girlfriend of the murder suspect – she wanted to talk to her. *Well, this was unexpected... her day just kept getting better and better...*

~

Sasha glanced at her phone's screen as her ringtone sounded, pulling into a parking space when she saw the name, her hand reaching for her notepad to find the list of names that Rowan had given her.

'Hello?'

'Is that Sasha? My name's Vernon, Vernon Abaoke, Rowan Penrose left a message asking me to call you.'

'Er, yes, Vernon, um, they call you Ham, is that right?'

The man chuckled good-naturedly. 'Afraid so, a throwback from school days. I graced our good school's stage as Hamlet, many moons ago – add in the tights and the chaps never let me forget it. What can I do for you? Rowan said something about Eric having been arrested? What's the silly bugger gone and done now?'

'Thanks for calling, yes, well, he's being held for questioning but he could be charged at any time. As for what he's done – something interminably stupid is the phrase that comes to mind. I was wondering if it might be possible to meet for half an hour if you're free, maybe today or tomorrow?'

'It'll have to be today, that's why I called. I'm going out of town on business for a few days. Where are you now?'

'I'm on my way to Shepherd's Bush, should be there in about half an hour, tops, but I can meet you anywhere.'

'Alright, how about Notting Hill? There's a coffee shop on Portobello Road, near the so-called famous travel book shop – d'you know it? Some name like summer or winter or something?'

'Yep, I'll see you there, Seasons, that's its name, and thanks.'

She pulled back out into the traffic, running her tongue over her teeth absentmindedly. She could do with brushing her teeth, and a shower wouldn't go amiss, it felt like it had been a horribly long day already.

~

Kay pressed publish on her post. She'd been careful to use wording such as *allegedly, an unnamed source*, and, *unconfirmed reports*, and was satisfied that she'd covered her bases – just enough to keep her readers coming back for more…

She turned her attention to an online map of the area around the hotel, searching for the pub where the unlikely lothario, Arthur, was meeting the girl called Rachel. The Three Earls – that had to be it, nothing else jumped out at her. She'd buy a soft drink and make it last, then all she had to do was hang around near the two couples and eavesdrop. Rachel would probably visit the loo at some point and that's when she'd get her talking.

She sat back, clicking on her blog and gazing at the title of her latest post proudly. *The hotel of ill repute? Hooker's night of horror at hands of London's latest serial killer – The Street Cleaner.*

The last line of her post was guaranteed to bring her readers back for more: *What happened to the murder weapon? Kay reveals all tomorrow!*

She picked up her phone, tapping in the number left in the message from Sasha Blue. She was really ahead of the game on this one – maybe it would be her big break, she thought excitedly.

~

Sasha was at Seasons, the coffee shop, before Vernon, and ordered herself a drink as her phone rang.

'Sasha? This is Kay, you left a message on my blog for me to contact you?'

'Hi, Kay, thanks for calling. I wondered if we could meet up for a chat? I'd like to talk to you about the prostitute killings you've been writing about.'

'Yeah, I'd love to meet up. How's tomorrow? Maybe late morning?'

'How about lunch? On me? You name the place.' She smiled at the man standing in front of her mouthing her name, indicating that he should take a seat.

'Costa Coffee, Old Brompton Road, got it. One o'clock alright? Perfect, I'll see you there.'

'Vernon?' She put her phone down, turning her attention to Eric's friend.

'Yep, and you must be Sasha, nice to meet you at last, albeit under rather difficult circumstances. I gather we all rather let ourselves down last night and Eric's ended up in a spot of bother?' He turned to the waiting server. 'I'll have a double espresso, please.' He turned back to Sasha. 'Maybe that'll take the edge off this hangover, something needs to, I've got a long drive tonight and an early business meeting tomorrow. Right, what's he done?'

'Didn't Rowan tell you? About the murder?' At Vernon's blank expression, she continued. 'At the hotel last night? The woman who was stabbed?'

'Hold up, Eric was at a hotel last night and a woman staying there was stabbed? Why wasn't he at home? So, what, they're just interviewing everyone as witnesses, is that it? I thought he'd been arrested for being drunk and disorderly – about time they nabbed the old chap, I said to myself.' Vernon laughed, his eyes regarding Sasha thoughtfully.

'No, I'm wrong,' he said slowly. 'It's about the woman...' Nodding his thanks to the waitress, he took a gulp of coffee. 'You'd better tell me everything.'

Five minutes later, Sasha had finished telling Vernon the little that she knew of Eric's situation, and she watched him as he leaned back in his chair and let out a low whistle.

'I'll help in any way I can, of course, but I have to be honest with you, we got totally smashed last night, hence my need for this.' He picked up the small cup and gulped the last of his double espresso. I can't remember where we went or where we parted company, and I certainly can't remember Eric going off with a woman. A prostitute, you say? You're sure?' At her nod, he continued. 'And Rowan can't remember anything? I'm surprised, he usually has more stamina than the rest of us put together, he can drink a whole bar and remain standing. What about the other chaps? There were a few of us, he told you that?'

'Yes.' Sasha ran through the list of names to make sure she had everyone.

'There were a couple of others, you'll have to ask Shuggy or Franco, see if they can help you with names.' He checked his watch, looking at her apologetically. 'I'm really sorry, I have to go. I could stick a knife in Eric myself, what an idiot. I mean, how the hell did he go from being engaged to you, to paying a prostitute for a night in a hotel? That's never been his style, you know what he's like, old Mr Charming, he could always get the girls – I suppose that was half his problem, and probably all of yours. You say you'd broken up, funny though, I don't recall him mentioning it. Maybe it was some rebound thing?' He shook his head. 'Not much help, am I? Can I at least pay for your drink?'

'No, it's on me, thanks for meeting me, Vernon.'

She left the coffee shop, having paid for their drinks, and walked back to her car, feeling despondent. So far, she had found out nothing of any use. It was time to give it up for today and go home. She'd drop her stuff at her flat, have a shower, and walk to her corner shop for basics – and then order a pizza later, pizza always made her feel better.

~

It was a quiet news day in London and once Kay's latest blog post caught the eye of an eager newspaper reporter working for one of the tabloids, it wasn't long before articles began appearing on several newspapers' online versions. These, in turn, were picked up by TV news channels and radio stations and, within hours of Kay having pressed the publish button, the news of a serial killer of prostitutes was all over London, with one particularly sensationalist newspaper displaying Kay's name for the serial killer – *The Street Cleaner* – in huge letters.

Blissfully unaware of the hijacking of her story, Kay had taken a leisurely bath and then prepared herself an early meal of beans on toast, which she took to her small dining table and began tucking into, switching on her laptop as she did so.

'Bloody bastards, they've nicked my story.' She put down her knife and fork and stared at her screen in dismay. Rapidly clicking on headlines, she scanned the articles, relieved that no one appeared to have further information, and then, nodding in pleasure, she noted that two or three had provided links to her blog page. This was good, it was better than good, she smiled to herself, they were now using her name for the killer – she was going to be right famous! And she was the only one who had an inside connection at the hotel. Well, okay, the girl, Rachel, didn't know it yet, but she was her contact and would be able to give her valuable details. And, best of all, she had Sasha Blue. She just needed one more murder to totally substantiate her claim of a serial killer...

ALL GONE

'Sasha? Drew Merton here. Vernon Abaoke gave me your details. I'd like to help if I can. Buy you a drink? Hilton Kensington? I'm finishing up a meeting in the next ten minutes so will be here for a while. Otherwise, give me a call.'

She replayed the message to catch the caller's name. Drew Merton. Referring to her list from Rowan, she matched the name to his and Eric's business associate – the man that they had both referred to as Dealer. Oh, what the hell, it was on her way home, practically on her doorstep, she might as well meet him and see what he could tell her. Jumping into her car she headed for the Hilton.

~

'Yes, Maria, I'll come straight home, stop worrying. I told you, last night was strictly business. No...' he sighed into the phone. 'I'm not up to my old tricks, as you so eloquently put it. When are you going to start trusting me again? Yes, I'll be home in time for dinner.'

Rowan put the phone down, staring out of the window as he contemplated his visit from Sasha. Murder... not what he'd been expecting... it had been as much as he could do to not throw up right there all over his desk for a second. Had he convinced her that he knew nothing? Hell, if Eric couldn't remember anything then there was no point in muddying the waters, was there? He'd been careful not to use his own name so there was no reason for the cops to come knocking on his door, not unless... How much was Max likely to give away? How much would Max even remember? He'd been as trolleyed as the rest of them. No, he'd be alright, he decided, he hadn't given Sasha Max's name – he wasn't actually sure who Max was or how he'd come to be drinking with them, all he knew was that the bloke had turned out to be extremely generous – and his carefully worded messages to the guys should give them the heads up to all stick together.

He opened his top drawer, removing the small business card and stroking his thumb over it. They must be bloody busy, they'd only been able to provide one escort – she'd been perfect though, lucky old Eric. Still, he thought, with a small smile, all that talk of 'We're single, he's the married one' had attracted some equally desirable attention at the pub, resulting in two very sexy ladies for him and Max to use to make up the numbers. They hadn't been too pricey either, according to Max. Pity he hadn't asked them for their cards. One thing he knew for certain, he wouldn't be spending any more nights with escorts when Max was around...

He took a last look at the card, tempted to keep it for future use, but the cops would no doubt be sniffing around this particular escort agency before too long and it was better that he had complete deniability. He crumpled the card in his fist, dropping it into the bin.

'I'm off home, Alex. Empty the bins, would you? There's a good girl.' He headed out, resignedly – his dear wife would no doubt have a romantic dinner for two planned for them, complete with a bottle or two of wine, candles, and soft music, all in aid of her ongoing quest to make their marriage more interesting. When would she realise that bird had flown the nest long ago? And after last night he wasn't sure if he had the energy for her small talk and suggestive glances. He left with Alex's affronted response ringing in his ears.

'What am I? The flaming cleaner now?'

~

Sasha made her way into the bar at the Hilton as a group of three men were standing up, shaking hands, and saying their goodbyes. One of them remained behind, checking his watch, and she took an educated guess.

'Drew Merton?

'Yes, and you're Sasha? Thanks for meeting me at short notice. Can I get you a drink? I don't know about you but I'm ready for something stronger than sparkling water. There's only so much of the stuff I can drink in all these meetings. Plus–' He checked his watch. 'The working day's officially over.'

She smiled. 'Thanks, I'll have a glass of white wine.'

Once they were seated with their drinks, Sasha opened the conversation.

'I'm not sure exactly how much Rowan told you about Eric's situation?'

'Not much, but Ham filled me in, so I know enough to know it doesn't sound good. He woke up in a strange hotel room with a murdered woman lying beside him, is that right? And he can't remember anything about it?' At Sasha's nod, he continued. 'Eric's not a killer, whatever happened there's got to be some explanation behind it. I've known him for about three years now, it started off as just business but we've become friends and I'd like to think I know him pretty well. Vernon asked me to call you, he said he'd met with you but hadn't been any help and felt bad. I've done a little business with Vernon, but mostly with Latimer and Penrose – Eric and Rowan, of course. We were partly celebrating the acquisition of a new property that we've lined up for mixed-use development, shops, offices, a couple of flats, that sort of thing. Rowan and I decided to go for drinks and Eric said he'd join us later as he'd made plans to dine with his old friend, Harry.'

'Er, and Harry is...' Sasha consulted her list. 'Shuggy? Is that right? Harry Reddingham?'

'Yep, he's Shuggy, and don't ask me why, you'll have to ask them, all boys together, the old school tie and all that.' He smiled. 'I'm not, and never was, part of all that.'

'And yet both Eric and Rowan referred to you as Dealer. Why's that?'

'I don't think they can help themselves, everyone has to have a nickname of some kind, and for me it's Dealer. I assume it's because I've come to them with a couple of great deals. I kind of like it, I suppose. Look, Sasha.' He paused, looking awkward. 'I'm aware that you and Eric are engaged, is that right?'

'We were, not any more. I'm guessing you know what Eric's like? How he can't help himself when there's an attractive woman around? I gave him one chance too many. I suppose I hoped he'd changed, but it'll never happen. No, I'm involved in this purely as an old friend with connections, and as a private investigator, which is my line of work, in the hopes that I can help him. Eric's an idiot – something I think I'm going to be saying to a lot of people over the next few days – but he's not a killer, I firmly believe that, and he needs my help.'

'I'm sorry, it must have been hard for you. Right, let's see if I can remember anything that might help the idiot out. Okay, so Eric, Rowan, and I finished up at the site and Rowan suggested having a few pints to celebrate our new deal. Eric went off to dinner at maybe half past seven or so, and I decided I was just going to have one or two pints with Rowan and then head home as I was feeling quite tired. We were close to Soho, and Eric had said he was eating there, so we kind of gravitated towards it.

'And here the trouble starts. We walked into what should have been obvious was predominantly a gay bar, not that either of us was bothered by that, but Rowan had ordered pints and about four shooters before we realised, which we then downed rather rapidly so that we could go somewhere with *a bit more totty* to repeat his eloquent phrasing. Next, we went into The Golden Lion, I think it was, and Rowan ordered the same as before, before looking round and deciding that the clientele wasn't to his taste. Translated from Rowan speak into English, I think he meant there was no one there that he fancied. So, this meant we had to down our drinks again – I'm no lightweight but two pints and four shooters each, in about fifteen minutes or something, is not the best way to start the evening on an empty stomach.

'We were both nicely warmed up by our next round in the third pub we visited, and I'd forgotten all about my plan to have a couple of pints and go home. I think this was when Eric joined us, no, not Eric, it must have been a couple of the other guys. Bar Soho, I think it was called, it was a bit of a party place. Yes, that's when Warren and Vernon arrived. The drinks were going down nicely and then Warren's mate turned up, chap called Quentin, with his work colleague. I'm afraid I can't remember his name. We left as a group, I think and went on to... well, another pub, maybe someone else can remember the name...'

Sasha was frantically trying to match the names to her list but gave up, for the time being, she could figure that all out later, she decided. 'So, after Bar Soho, you went on somewhere else and Eric and Shuggy joined you?'

'Yes, this is where it begins to blur a little, I'm afraid. It was a cocktail bar more than a pub, I think. There was quite a bit of loud-mouthed flirting going on with a table of women.' He shifted awkwardly. 'It was everyone, not just Eric. Lad talk, you know how it is. A few other women hovered around on and off, hot-looking, that kind of thing. One of the guys took the phone number of one of the women, who might have been, well, probably was, an escort. That's just my opinion, might be unfair, I was a little sozzled after all. The reason I'm saying that is because a few cards were handed round, couldn't say which of the women was handing them out, but there was a lot of talk about who was going to get lucky. Sorry.' He looked sheepishly at Sasha. 'The chaps were messing around with one woman, small, petite, blonde hair, saying this one or that one was married and couldn't partake, or whatever, this one was single – like the escorts were concerned with anyone's marital status.'

'I don't suppose you have any of the cards by any chance? Or remember the details on any of them? Agency names, maybe?'

Drew shook his head. 'Afraid not. It wasn't my thing and I took off at that point – home to a rather frosty reception from my girlfriend. Can't say I blame her, and on that note, I have to get going, a large bouquet of flowers needs to be purchased and reparation made for my neglect.'

'Well, good luck.' Sasha grinned. 'And thanks, Drew, you've been most helpful. You've given me a lot more information than Rowan did. And thanks for the drink.' She drained her glass and they walked out of the hotel together, each going their separate ways.

~

What had she learned so far, she pondered, as she drove the short distance towards her flat, pulling over for the flashing lights and siren of a fire engine, before slowing down as cars gradually ground to a halt in front of her.

Rowan was a little shifty, Vernon and Drew seemed genuine, the guys had gone on a bit of a bender, and escorts had been sniffing around them. The escorts had given out their cards and Eric had obviously decided to follow through. Had any of the other guys, she wondered? Would Eric remember anything further now that the initial shock of waking up next to a murdered woman had worn off and he'd had time to recover from his night of heavy drinking?

She huffed impatiently, craning her neck to see why the traffic had stopped, watching the second fire engine wind its way past, through the cars, as its siren whooped and its lights flashed, a slight sense of foreboding crawling through her as a police car shot past. Her eyes scanned the sky above the buildings, picking up a spiral of smoke. That wasn't good.

The traffic began to move again in stop-start fashion and, eventually, a policeman came into her view, his arms directing the cars to the left. She leaned out of her window to speak to him as she reached the front of the queue, spotting the barrier erected behind him.

'I live in Warbeck Road. What's happening, officer?'

'House fire, miss. Warbeck's closed currently. Sorry, you'll have to double back further along.'

After a convoluted series of turns, she finally pulled into a parking space in Devonport Road, a couple of minutes' walk from her flat, and hurried off on foot, the thickening smoke plume filling her with anxiety.

Groups of onlookers were gathered at various points as she walked along, straining to see through the billowing smoke obscuring the street ahead, and she quickened her pace as she neared her flat, the acrid smell of the smoke filling her nose and mouth, the sound of flames crackling angrily filling her ears, together with the shouts of the firemen.

Oh no. Please, God, no. The smoke had thinned for a moment, offering her a little visibility. She stopped in the middle of the road, aghast, her legs feeling weak. Her flat was gone.

~

The Three Earls was in Hogarth Place and only a ten-minute walk from Kay's flat in Kempsford Gardens. Nevertheless, she set off early, at around seven o'clock, deciding that she may as well be there as at home, and if her source got to the pub earlier then all the better.

The pub wasn't crowded, which didn't surprise her, it being rather gloomy, its wood-panelled walls grimy, its carpet sticky underfoot, and its velvet-covered banquettes somewhat threadbare. Good choice for a double date, Arthur, she smirked to herself, you really know how to impress a girl.

She sat nursing her Coke and checking on her blog stats – her readership had gone up quite a bit since her serial killer articles – while keeping an eye on the door and was pleased with her decision to come earlier when Arthur walked in with his friend.

Once they'd got their pints and selected their table, Kay casually moved to the table next to them and awaited the arrival of the two girls. She was now perfectly positioned to eavesdrop on their conversation but didn't expect to hear anything useful while the four of them chatted. No, she needed to corner her source in the ladies, and find out what she could about the murder weapon. Excitement wriggled through her stomach – she could be the one to break the case – to actually break the case! Before the police. How could they not know about the knife? She tuned into the banter at the table next to her.

'Alright, Soreena? You're looking nice tonight.'

'Yes, I am alright, thank you for asking, Femi, and thank you for the compliment.'

Arthur sniggered. 'He don't mean are you alright, he's saying hello, ain't you, Fem?'

'You English and your funny ways. Why do you not just say hello, then?'

'Fem ain't English, look at him.'

'Course he's English, Arthur. You're from Lambeth, aren't you, Femi?'

'See? Rachel knows. Blimey, Arthur, how long have we worked together?'

'Yeah, alright, but Olufemi ain't exactly English, is it?'

'Ooh, listen to old Sir Arthur over here, with his posh English name. So, where are you from, Soreena?'

'I am from Romania, but we came here when I was a young girl, so now I am English.'

'And a very lovely English rose you are, too, Soreena.'

Kay watched, amused, as Rachel cast an irritated glance at Arthur.

'Drink up, ladies, it's my round. Same again?' Femi drained his pint glass and stood up. 'Give us a hand then, Soreena?'

'What's up with you? You got the huff or something?'

'Yeah, maybe. D'you fancy her or what?'

'What? Me fancy Soreena? She ain't a patch on you. Come 'ere.' Arthur snaked his arm around Rachel's shoulders and she snuggled into him.

'Alright, I'll let you off then. Oh no, look, he's only gone and got shots. You trying to get us drunk, Femi?'

'Maybe I am.' Femi winked at the girls, who giggled as they threw back their shots, wrinkling their noses.

Just over an hour later, Kay had watched the table of four consume four shots each, together with the same number of pints for the guys and vodka and lemonades for the girls. She was beginning to despair of Rachel ever needing the loo, when, to her relief, the girl stood up and jokingly announced her intention of going to powder her nose, to much amusement from the others, especially when she staggered slightly as she left the table.

This was perfect, it would be like taking candy from a baby, she thought to herself as she stood up and made her way to the ladies.

She waited for Rachel to flush the loo, and quickly ran the tap, washing her hands as the girl appeared beside her.

'I really like your top, where's it from?' She smiled at the girl's reflection.

Rachel preened slightly. 'Thanks, got it down the market, didn't I?' She groaned. 'I've drunk too much, bloody Arthur.'

'He your boyfriend, is he? Good looking bloke you're with?'

Pleased, Rachel flicked her hair. 'Yeah, sort of, I spose.'

'Didn't I see you at the hotel earlier? Rachel, isn't it? Alfredo was going on, wasn't he? Something about his knife? He's such a drama queen.' *Careful, Kay, don't get carried away...*

Rachel narrowed her eyes, trying to place Kay. 'Yeah... were you the one he was arguing with about the vegetables?'

Rolling her eyes, Kay nodded, laughing. 'That's me, the vegetable girl. They don't pay me enough to be dealing with the likes of him. It can't be true though? He reckons the murdered woman was stabbed with a knife from his kitchen? And the killer put it back? I bet you know all about it?'

'Might do.' Rachel applied some lipstick a little haphazardly, pressing her lips together and wriggling them. 'We're not supposed to talk about it though.'

'Yeah, I was told the same thing. But it's alright for us to talk, isn't it? So, why d'you reckon he thinks it was his knife?'

'Obvious, innit? It was in the wrong place and all sticky. When he'd finished biting Stefan's head off for not washing it up properly, he started complaining about missing one of his chef's jackets, or something. Kim told him to take it up with Mrs Carter, but I said to leave it, next thing Arthur would be getting into trouble.'

Rachel cupped her mouth with her hand in an exaggerated manner. 'Between you and me, I had a look for it as I was worried about Arthur – those tight fists over at Laundry King dock their wages if their count's down, did you know that? And what with Alfredo being a bit spiteful sometimes, well, I thought, if I can find it, I can put it in the laundry bin and there'll be nothing to get Arthur into trouble about.'

'And? Did you find it?' Kay felt almost breathless with suspense as she waited for the answer.

'Yep.' Rachel nodded smugly. 'It was filthy dirty, someone had made a right mess, disgusting it was. No wonder they chucked it. I bet it was Stefan, he probably dropped a saucepan of spag bol all down the front of it and didn't want to get in trouble with Mrs Carter. But that's all very well but he didn't spare a thought for Arthur and his laundry count, did he?'

Kay shook her head. 'No... and, er, so where did you find it? Where had Stefan chucked it then? Arthur's lucky he's got you, you should tell him that.' She threw in the little buttering up to keep the girl on side.

'Yeah, I should.' Rachel laughed. 'It was in one of the food waste bins, you know, all the peelings and the scrapings off the plates, and stuff. So, I took it outside and gave it a quick shake and then I stuffed it in the bottom of one of the laundry bins – too late for today's collection, but they tally up each week so Arthur'll be fine.'

'And Alfredo never told the cops about the knife?'

'No, why would he? Next thing they'll say he done it.' Rachel looked more closely at Kay. 'It wasn't you in the kitchen, I've remembered now, it was that Veronica girl who takes the fruit and veg order. What did you say your name was again?'

'Kay. Yeah, I was there with Veronica.'

'Yeah? Who does Veronica work for then?' Rachel snapped her bag shut and turned to face Kay. 'You're lying. Why are you asking me all these questions? What are you, a reporter or something?'

'No, I promise. I'm a rep and I was there talking to Alfredo about new products. Veronica showed me the way to the kitchen. I was just interested, that's all.' *Had she convinced her?* She tried one more tactic. 'Kim was really helpful, she told me where I'd find Mrs Carter...'

'Yeah? Funny that, seeing as Kim's a bloke. How d'you know my name?' Rachel was backing out of the ladies. 'You better not repeat any of this. It's entrapment, I've seen it on the telly.' The door swung shut behind her.

Sighing, Kay left the ladies and snuck out of the pub. That hadn't gone quite how she'd planned it, but she'd got plenty to put on her blog, enough to stretch to two more posts, she thought happily.

Hugging herself with excitement as she walked back to her flat, she replayed the girl's words in her head. 'I bet it was Stefan, he probably dropped a saucepan of spag bol all down the front of it.'

Oh, Rachel, that wasn't spag bol all over the chef's jacket, it was blood.

~

'Sure you don't want another cup of tea, love? You're still looking very peaky.' The concerned faces of the kindly couple who lived further along her road studied her across the coffee table from their position on the settee.

'No, honestly, you've both been very kind, but I think I'm alright now.' She removed the blanket the woman had placed around her shoulders, folding it and laying it over the arm of the chair. 'I should get going.'

'But where are you going to go? You poor thing. Have you got someone to go to? Somewhere to stay? You're welcome to stay in our spare room.'

'Thank you, but I have people that I can go to.'

'Well, if you're sure...'

'I am. Thank you again.' Sasha stood up, relieved that her knees weren't feeling quite so weak, and hugged the man and woman before saying goodbye and walking slowly along the road to where her flat had been.

Red and white fire safety tape was stretched in front of the gaping, blackened remains of her building and its neighbour, and firemen were still hosing down the smouldering rubble. The crowds of onlookers had thinned now, with just a few bystanders remaining, as well as a couple of police officers, one of whom Sasha approached.

'Do you know what caused the fire? I lived in the first-floor flat in the building on the left. I'm Sasha, I gave my details to an officer earlier. Do you know anything about the other residents? Mike was on the top floor and Nicole and Saffron were below me.'

Having expressed her sympathy to Sasha, the police officer leafed through her notebook. 'I'm told that the top floor resident is away overseas, and the ladies in the flat below you are fine. They were both out at the time of the explosion and–'

'Explosion?'

'Yes, connected to the renovations next door, something to do with the gas pipe to the oven. Sounds like they tried to take a short cut instead of getting the gas people in, then one of the bright sparks lit up a cigarette. A couple of them are in hospital, but they're lucky, could have been curtains. Can you tell me who lived in the basement flat of your building?'

'It was empty, had been for some time.'

'Right, thanks, and do you have somewhere to stay? You'll need to get in touch with your insurance people, of course.'

'Yes, I do, and I will, thanks.' She took a last glance at what had been her home and walked back along Warbeck Road to her car.

It was a strange feeling, kind of weightless like she was floating, she thought as she drove off in no particular direction. She was now officially homeless, her worldly belongings having been reduced to the contents of her car – the few items that she'd taken with her to Parva Crossing for her investigation into Dorothy Newton's murder.

She was filled with an overwhelming urge to see her best friend, Zoe, to be enfolded in her arms and told that everything would be alright. So that's what she'd do, she'd go to Zoe's and cry into her wine, get completely pissed, and pass out in her spare bed in the box room. Feeling marginally better at the thought, she drove the short distance to Zoe's flat, parked, and rang the front door bell.

She must be out or working late at the gallery, she decided, heading round the side of the building to grab the spare key from the back garden and let herself in. She'd call Zoe once she was indoors. Except the spare key wasn't there in its usual place. Okay, a phone call it was then.

'Sash, hi, babes, are you still in Parva Crossing? How's it going? Hold on. It's Sash.' Murmurings could be heard, and then Zoe's laughing voice rang louder in her ear. 'James says hi. We're in Canterbury, I'm sitting on the terrace of our suite looking at the Cathedral – pics to follow on Graffic. He flew back into Heathrow this morning and had an urgent meeting down here, so he whisked me off for a romantic night away. We're coming back in the morning, after breakfast. When are you coming back home? Did you solve your case?'

'Hi, Zo, that sounds fabulous.' She injected enthusiasm into her voice, not wanting to spoil Zoe's night. 'Yep, I'm back and I solved the case, can't wait to tell you all about it. Listen, call me when you're back and we'll get together, yeah?'

'Definitely. How about tomorrow night? Girl's night, I'll tell James he's banned. Oh, I meant to tell you, I changed my locks, I know it sounds paranoid, but after everything that's happened... well, anyway, I've got a spare key so I thought I'd give it to you. Not sure that I'm too happy keeping a key hidden in the back garden anymore.'

'That's a good plan, and tomorrow night sounds perfect. Say hi to James and have a fabulous time. I'll check out your photos later. Love you.'

'Love you too. And, Sash? You sound a bit– are you okay? About Eric behaving like such a bastard in Parva Crossing, I mean?'

'I'm fine, I promise.' *Zoe didn't even know that Eric had been arrested, well, she wasn't going to tell her over the phone and spoil her night.* 'I'll see you tomorrow, babes. Have fun.'

She walked back to her car feeling flat. Her options of where to spend the night were now halved, the other option being Eric's flat – something she had not wanted to consider, associated as it was with so many happier times, before it had all gone wrong between them. But there was a problem – the spare key, which used to reside in Eric's back garden beneath the ugly garden gnome, had become her key when they'd become engaged and, as such, had moved to her own flat, where she'd kept it on a hook on the side of the kitchen cupboard, which meant... well, which meant it was somewhere amidst the blackened, wet remains of her life in Warbeck Road – which was quite appropriate, really, and the perfect analogy for her relationship with Eric.

Taking a chance, she drove the short distance to Kensington Police Station, pondering how best to find out about Eric's belongings which he'd had on him at the time of his arrest, acknowledging that even if she got hold of his key, she'd have to ask him if she could stay at his flat – after all, they certainly weren't a couple anymore.

Her dilemma was solved instantly, as the loud voice of D.S. Tony Palmer echoed across the parking lot. 'Yeah, alright, alright, give us a break, it was only the one time, but fair dos, I owe you a pint. But it ain't gonna be tonight, you cheeky bastard, I've got a girlfriend at home who's gonna give me a hard time if I don't get my arse home a bit pronto.' In response to something said by the other man, he laughed. 'Henpecked? Yeah, that's me. Come 'ere and say that, I'll show you henpecked, you little bugger.'

Scuffling and laughter followed, and the sound of cars being unlocked.

'Bleedin 'ell, Sasha, you nearly gave me an 'eart attack. What you doing 'ere, love?' Tony peered closer at Sasha. 'You okay? You don't look too good.'

She laughed, sounding slightly hysterical, if Tony's wary expression and step back were anything to go by. 'Well, between my ex-fiancé being arrested for stabbing a prostitute to death in his hotel room, to my flat burning to the ground this afternoon and me being homeless, I don't suppose I am okay, not really.'

'Alright, alright, come 'ere.' Tony pulled her close and squeezed her, before releasing her. 'There, feeling better? You've just been given the magic Tony hug. Not gonna cry now, are you?'

She sniffed, smiling. 'No. Thanks, Tone, but I do have a favour to ask you.'

'Name it, if it's in my power it shall be done. Unless you're asking me to break that twerp out of his cell for you.'

'No, he can stay in there for a day or two as far as I care. But I do need to ask him something, well, you as well. It's about his stuff, his possessions when you brought him in. Where are they?'

'They're with the custody officer. Why what's up?'

'I need to ask him if I can stay at his flat tonight.' She shrugged, looking embarrassed. 'It's the last place I want to go, but needs must, at least for tonight... and I've lost his key, you know, in the fire...'

'Walk with me and tell me all about your flat and this fire. I'll see if I can get you a quick word with him, but I won't be able to give you his key, sweetheart, all his bits and bobs are logged in, and old Barry's a stickler. We'll be at his flat first thing tomorrow, anyway, searching it.'

She told him about the fire as they walked into the police station and through to the cells, where Tony had a quick, huddled, word with the stickler, Barry, the custody officer on duty.

'Right, you can have a couple of minutes, but no more, and don't tell anyone about this. The love of my life is waiting for me to get home with a Chinese takeaway, and it's more than my life's worth to keep her waiting too long.'

She thanked Tony, and slipped in once the door was unlocked, much to Eric's surprise.

'Sash. Have you got good news? Am I getting out of here? Tell me they've caught whoever killed her?'

She sighed. 'Eric, they still think you killed her, nothing's changed, and it won't, not unless you can remember more about what happened.'

'But they're the police, that's their job. And you? What have you found out? You must have found something out by now, I mean, what have you been doing all day?'

Trying not to feel irritated by Eric's attitude, and acutely aware of Tony's hovering presence at the door as he tapped his watch meaningfully, she sighed.

'Eric, I've got about one minute, so listen carefully. I've been to see Rowan at your offices, and I've met with Vernon Abaoke and Drew Merton. I'll try to talk to the others as soon as possible, but the thing is, something's come up, well, happened, and I–'

'You've got to do better than that, I'm locked up like a guilty man while a murderer walks free. Whatever came up can't be as important as my life, Sash, come on...' Eric's whining tone hit a nerve but she tried to stay calm.

'My flat burnt to the ground today.'

'Yeah, well, sometimes, Sash, you just have to put your own– hold on, did you say your flat?'

Finally, he got it. 'Yes, it's gone, there was an explosion and I've lost everything, which is why I–'

'Good God, I'm sorry. How? Why?'

'There's no time to tell you about it. Listen, Eric, this is awkward, but I was wondering if I could stay at your flat tonight, only, I don't have your key, it's gone, like everything else that was in my flat, so I wondered if there's a spare anywhere? Maybe with Chris, your neighbour, or someone?'

A strange expression flitted across Eric's face. What was it, she wondered? He looked uncomfortable, embarrassed, even.

'Er, my flat? You can't, that is...' His eyes glanced away and back to her in a flash. 'There was a burst pipe, it's a mess. Sash, you know I'd let you if I could, but I wouldn't wish it on my worst enemy.' His eyes flickered, as if with sudden inspiration. 'That's why I had to stay in a hotel last night. I told the cops but they weren't interested.'

'A burst pipe,' she said flatly. He was hiding something, she knew it.

'And besides, I don't have a spare key,' Eric finished lamely, avoiding her eyes.

'Right, well, no problem, thanks anyway.' She nodded at Tony as he gesticulated that she should leave. 'I have to go now.'

'Will you come back tomorrow?' Eric grabbed her arm.

'Maybe, I've kind of got a lot on my plate right now.' She pulled her arm free and walked to the open door.'

'That's enough, Latimer, get some sleep.' Tony banged the door closed and turned to Sasha.

'I don't know what you ever saw in him, darlin', the bloke's a complete tosser, you ask me.'

'Neither do I, and he is. Listen, thanks, Tone, I'm sorry I had to delay you.'

'Any time, love. You'll be alright tonight? You've got somewhere to sleep? I've got to get these keys back.'

'I'll be fine, I'll see myself out, goodnight, Tone. Oh, one last thing, did Eric tell you he had to stay in a hotel last night because he had a burst pipe at his flat?'

'Nope, that's news to me.' Tony shook his head, frowning.

She walked to her car and drove off, Eric's words niggling away in her head. He was hiding something. *When wasn't he?* The question came from nowhere. So, the real question was, was he hiding something from her or the police?

A sixth sense made her drive to his flat and park outside where, to her surprise, lights were on and she could see someone moving around inside. She climbed out of her car and walked up the path to peer in the front window. A woman was sitting on the settee, drinking a glass of wine. *What the hell?* She rang the doorbell.

'Where've you been? I cooked you flaming dinner last night, you, oh–'

The two women stood facing each other.

'Can I help you?' The woman raked her eyes up and down Sasha.

'I'm looking for Eric Latimer,' she said. 'And you are?'

'Not that it's any of your business, but I'm his girlfriend. His rather pissed-off girlfriend, if you must know.' The woman lifted her hand, tucking her hair behind her ear as she regarded Sasha haughtily. 'And who are you, if I might ask?'

Sasha stared at her, dumbstruck. 'I'm an old friend,' she said when she'd found her voice.

'Well, he's not here.' The woman closed the door in Sasha's face.

Charming. She turned and walked back to her car, her mind racing. What the hell was going on? Was she living in some kind of parallel universe? And then a thought struck her. *The woman had been wearing her ring.* Her engagement ring – the one she'd thrown so unceremoniously at Eric only days earlier when she'd told him their engagement was off.

'Would someone please explain to me how I can break off my engagement with him on Sunday morning, how he can wake up in a hotel room with a dead woman beside him on Wednesday morning, and how he can have a girlfriend ensconced in his flat, wearing my engagement ring, on Wednesday night while he's locked up in a police cell?' she yelled into the void as she drove off with no idea of where she was going.

Well, there was nothing for it but to find a hotel for the night. She considered the irony of spending the night at the Freedom Hotel in Kensington – knowing her current spate of good luck, she'd probably be given the room Eric had spent the night in with his escort before he murdered her. Feeling guilty at even considering that Eric could be capable of murder – anything else, but not murder – she found herself driving down alongside Ravenscourt Park, recalling that there was a Premier Inn in the vicinity.

Relieved to have a plan for the night, Sasha pulled over before driving into the car park next to the hotel, reaching into her handbag for her purse in case she had to pay on entry. It was dark now and she couldn't feel her purse. She switched on the interior light, searching her bag in increasing panic. It wasn't there – unbelievable. Frantically she mentally retraced the steps of her chaotic day, trying to remember when she'd last used her purse. Not at the Hilton, Drew Merton had paid for her drink, so it must have been at the coffee shop where she'd met Vernon Abaoke. Oh crap. She pictured herself paying with her card at the counter, her mind preoccupied with unfolding events – but try as she might, she couldn't remember putting her purse back in her bag. Great, she couldn't even pay for parking, let alone a night in a hotel. Starting her car again, she drove off, fighting back tears of frustration.

She assessed her situation as she drove – no home, no bank cards, it was getting late, she was tired, she was also hungry, she desperately needed a shower and, most pressing of all, she needed the loo. A sign for fish and chips blinked to her right and she glanced in through the lighted window, hunger making her stomach rumble.

Oh, Halle-flippin-lujah – she had an emergency ten-pound note in her glove box, she remembered, grinning – talk about the small things making you happy. She pulled over and reached across to open the glove box, fingering the note thankfully.

Standing at the counter, she perused the overhead menu, mentally tallying the cost of a battered sausage, chips, and a soft drink – she had enough. She placed her order and used the loo before collecting her food and sinking gratefully into a plastic-covered bench seat at one of the Formica tables lined up along the wall, where she devoured her meal.

Wiping her mouth with the paper serviette, Sasha considered her situation, craving a cup of tea, something the chippy did not serve. She looked at her watch – half-past ten – and reluctantly left the restaurant to return to her car. She was out of options and exhausted, but drove along looking for a petrol station where she might be able to get a cup of tea with her remaining cash, deciding that she would park outside Zoe's and try to get some sleep until her friend returned home in the morning.

Well, she decided, as she tipped the cup back, draining the dregs of what had turned out to be a pretty good cup of tea, this had to be right up there with one of the shittiest days of her life ever – correction, this *was* the shittiest day of her life ever. She reclined her seat as far as it would go and closed her eyes, falling asleep almost instantly.

IT'S NOT A GAME

Rick Turner stepped out of the doors of terminal three at Heathrow and breathed in a deep lungful of early morning London air – filled as it was with the gentle fumes of traffic from the nearby motorways, with that sweet dewy freshness unique to England's green and pleasant land on a balmy summer's morning, with the heady mix of freshly brewed coffee in a passer-by's hand, and the scent of a freshly-baked croissant as it was messily consumed by a tired-looking fellow traveller standing nearby. Home, after twenty years. He turned to his driver. 'Let's go.'

His eyes hungrily devoured everything around him as he listened with half an ear to his driver, responding intermittently, more interested in absorbing the sights of his homeland as viewed from the back of the car as it made its way along the M4. Commercial enterprises and green parkland passed by, framed in his window – anything and everything was food for his soul, no matter how mundane. Two days of business meetings and then he could let his hair down with the lads. What would it be like, he wondered, seeing them all again after so long? Were they all married with kids? Divorced? It was hard to picture Mike with a wife and kids, he smiled to himself, he and Mike had been the worst two, always egging each other on with the girls. No, Mike, he decided, would still be a party animal, up for one-night stands and zero commitment, just like he himself was; and Dillon – good old Dillon – the only one he'd seen in the intervening passage of time, when he'd visited him for a riotous couple of weeks in Seattle, well, he'd made his way through a wife and a string of girlfriends and was now determinedly single. So that left Will, Jimmy, and Felix – Will, he figured, had to be married with a whole bunch of children, who would at least be mostly grown-up by now; Jimmy, he knew from Dillon, had unsurprisingly married Maggie after the two of them had spent their time at university joined at the hip; and Felix? Felix was a bit of a mystery man, not appearing to have been interested in girls, or boys for that matter, at school, but rather in getting regularly and horribly drunk whenever the opportunity arose. Dillon maintained that it was down to an unhappy homelife, and if he was right then Rick hoped that things had improved for him since he'd grown up.

They were a great bunch overall, and he was looking forward to it, knowing that the guys would spend half the time ripping off his 'Yankee' accent, which was, in fact, a mild Pacific Northwestern accent, but that he, in turn, would rip off their 'Brit' accent, and would no doubt, by the end of a long night of drinking, revert to his old 'Brit' accent himself. He nodded off, to be awakened when the driver announced they were at his hotel.

'Welcome to the London Henrietta Hotel Marble Arch.' The girl at reception smiled as she tapped away into her computer. 'Ah yes, Mr Turner, you're with us for three nights, checking out Sunday morning, is that right?'

'Sure is.' He smiled, accepting his room key card. 'Er, can I get breakfast still?' He had a sudden craving for a full English breakfast – fried eggs, bacon, pork bangers, baked beans, grilled tomato, hot buttery toast, and a huge pot of tea. That didn't take long, Ricky boy, he thought wryly, he'd been back in England for less than three hours and he was already reverting to his inner Brit.

~

Kay hummed as she sipped her early morning cup of tea, her eyes skimming through her new post as it sat proudly at the top of her blog. She should be a detective, she really should – no one else had mentioned a word about the killer stealing a knife from the hotel kitchen and using it to stab his victim to death, before returning it to the kitchen. Had it been used (and here she'd shamelessly nicked Arthur's overheard words) to prepare the steaks for your steak and chips in the hotel restaurant, she'd asked her readers?

She'd finished with a rather show-offy line about the killer having worn a hotel uniform to protect himself from the blood spatter while he'd viciously stabbed his victim to death – information exclusive to Kay's Killer Blog – with more revelations to come. She pondered the chef's jacket situation for a moment... It had to still be lying there with the other dirty kitchen uniforms, waiting to be collected by Arthur or Femi from the laundry service. She had to get hold of it before it was laundered. Quickly searching for Laundry King's phone number, she tapped in the numbers and cleared her throat, ready to speak in her posh voice, as she called it.

While she waited for her call to be answered, she figured out how she was going to retrieve it, excitement bubbling inside her as an idea popped into her head. *She was having the time of her life – what was it? Best days of your life? Well, these were those.*

~

Alex unlocked the door to Latimer and Penrose Property Development Specialists, smiling and waving at the man lifting the shutters of the business next door.

'Morning, Hasan, you're here early.'

'No rest for the wicked, Alex. Have a good day.' The man disappeared into the kebab shop, and Alex climbed the stairs to the offices, groaning as she remembered she hadn't cleaned up the night before. Resignedly, she took the vacuum cleaner from the cupboard and pushed it around the carpet, before flicking a cloth over the computer screens and keyboards, and wiping the desk surfaces. Having collected a couple of dirty glasses, she picked up the waste paper bin from beneath Rowan's desk, carried it through to the front office where she tipped the contents into her own bin, and returned it. Finally, she took her bin through to the small kitchenette, where she tipped the contents into the larger kitchen bin. A flash of pink caught her eye, and she fished out the crumpled card, flattening it on the counter to see what it was.

He couldn't get enough, could he, the dirty bastard? Escorts now, flaming charming, as if it wasn't enough to have his wife, Maria, waiting for him hopefully at home every night while he flirted with Alex at every given opportunity. Well, it was a bit more than flirting, if she was honest, she thought, remembering how Eric's ex had almost caught them in a bit of a clinch over his desk the day before. She'd been tempted to give in, she'd fancied him for ages, but his beer breath and garlic sweat had been more than a little off-putting. No, if she ever had a fling with him, he'd have to wine and dine her a bit first. Not quite knowing why, she took the card and slipped it into the bottom drawer of her desk, before switching the kettle on.

~

'Sash, wake up.'

Sasha came to with a start, the banging on her car window finally rousing her, and she grimaced as she shifted her stiff limbs in the passenger seat, staring at Zoe blankly for a moment, before remembering where she was and what a nightmare her life had turned into in the space of one day. She opened her car door.

'Zo, hi, babes.'

'Hi, babes, look at the state of you. What's going on? Please don't tell me you slept here all night?'

'It's a really long, really horrendous, and really crazy story.'

'That's a lot of really. Come here.' Zoe enveloped Sasha in a hug, finally releasing her and then watching her with concerned eyes. 'Are you alright? Does something hurt?'

'Everything at this moment.' Sasha's arms were wrapped across her chest. 'I'm just sore from sleeping in the car, I'll be okay in a minute.'

Half an hour later, and on their second cup of tea, Sasha had filled her best friend in on her situation, as well as Eric's, and Zoe was staring at her open-mouthed.

'I'm speechless,' she said, proceeding to disprove her statement immediately.

'I cannot believe that you didn't tell me any of this when you called me last night; I cannot actually believe that you've been running around trying to help Eric the rat, after what he did to you; I cannot believe that your flat's gone and I cannot believe that you lost your purse and had to sleep in your car outside my flat; I also cannot believe that Eric murdered a woman – although I could murder him myself for cheating on you for the millionth time, for spending the night with an escort, and for somehow managing to have a so-called girlfriend in his flat who's wearing your engagement ring; I cannot believe any of it, Sash, like I said, I'm bloody speechless.'

Finding herself smiling, despite her situation, Sasha put her cup of tea down. 'For someone who's speechless, that was quite a speech.'

Zoe grinned. 'Yeah, well, you know me. Right, you're staying with me, of course, for as long as you need, forever if it comes to it. Now – name of the coffee shop?'

'Wha–? Oh, Seasons, Notting Hill, next to the–'

'Next to the travel bookshop, yep, I know the one.'

A short couple of minutes later and Zoe had Sasha's purse located and secured safely for collection at Seasons. She then bundled Sasha off to the shower while she bustled around like a mother hen, organising Sasha's limited belongings in her little box room, and making up the bed. By the time Sasha reappeared, a plate of toast and a pot of fresh tea awaited her.

'D'you fancy some scrambled eggs to go with the toast?' Zoe waved a wooden spoon.

'Uh, no, I don't think I could hold eggs down right now. The toast will be great though, thanks, darling.'

Fresh concern crossed Zoe's face. 'That's not like you, are you feeling sick?'

'Just a little pukey. Honestly, Zo, I'm okay, it's just a stupid reaction to everything.' She spread some crunchy peanut butter on her toast and munched it gratefully, washing it down with tea. 'See?' She smiled at her friend. 'I'm feeling much better, thanks, babes.'

'You do look a bit better, but still, take it easy today, read a book, watch TV, sleep... and sod Eric, let him fight his own battles for once,' Zoe continued, as Sasha opened her mouth to speak.

'I can't, Zo, I've already got a lunch appointment, there's something I need to follow up on with a blogger. Listen to this, she reckons there's a serial killer going round murdering prostitutes. She's wrong, I'm sure of it, but she seems to have a bit of a knack for finding stuff out and she might be able to help.'

Zoe stared at Sasha. 'You're serious. I don't believe it. Babes, your flat burnt down and you've lost all your belongings, don't you think you need to get on to your insurance people and get the ball rolling? There must be forms you have to fill in and all sorts. Can you put yourself first, please?'

'I will, I can, yes, I'll give my broker a call and find out what has to be done, but then I'm carrying on with this. I just can't– I can't desert that idiot. I must find out the truth.'

'For him or for you?' Zoe asked shrewdly.

Sasha paused. 'You're right, it's just as much for me as for him. Maybe I need to know that I wasn't once engaged to a murderer.'

Unspoken between them was the unwelcome recollection that they'd each had a relationship with a serial killer by the name of Miles Bleak, or Blake Selim, to use his real name, in their not-so-distant past.

~

Kay studied her finished handiwork proudly, squeezing out a small air bubble from the sticky back plastic that she'd just stuck onto her homemade badge for Laundry King – copied from one of their photos on their website.

She moved to the mirror, studying her severe appearance. It should work, the chances of running into the girl, Rachel, were slim, hopefully, and with her hair tied back and her fake glasses, she looked pretty different to yesterday, she decided, smoothing down the skirt of her navy suit. Plus, for bonus points, the girl had had a few drinks the night before, although she'd still been with it enough to call Kay out over her lies.

But with a bit of luck, if she managed to find the laundry bins before the van arrived, she might not need to call on her acting skills and her disguise. Checking the time, she fixed the badge to her lapel, she'd need to hurry – according to the helpful person at the laundry service who'd answered her enquiry this morning, the bins would be collected at eleven o'clock.

She'd bring the jacket back to her flat, and then go and meet Sasha Blue for yet more exclusive information.

'I,' she said to her reflection, 'have got the best murder blog in London. I'm going to be flippin' famous.'

~

'No.'

The word sounded loud in the quiet of the room as eyes filled with disbelief took in the online newspaper's account of the so-called Street Cleaner's latest killing.

What was this? How had this happened? Everything had been worked out so meticulously – the plan was fool proof... wasn't it? Mistakes weren't meant to happen, couldn't happen, not after so many months of planning...

A finger clicked on a link to which the article accredited its information – Kay's Killer Blog.

Who was this girl? She was going to ruin everything. How was she finding out so much?

The words on the screen shot upwards as an angry hand directed the mouse, eyes scanning the titles of the posts to see what else had been displayed for all the world to see.

She'd connected Tuesday's murder to the prostitute murdered in June in Soho; she'd blabbed about the knife, about the hotel uniform – but how could she have known? Or was she guessing? She hadn't said what type of uniform, although her promise of further revelations was worrying... Could she know about the chef's jacket? Surely not, unless... Was someone feeding her information? Who could she have spoken to who could possibly know about it? Everything had been going so smoothly until now. There was no way this stupid little girl was going to destroy it all with her little murder blog. Next thing she'd be connecting other dots and if that happened it would all be over. An error had been made, there was no doubt about that, and it was something that was going to have to be analysed with great care. It couldn't be allowed to happen again, it could ruin everything.

She'd have to be stopped – there was work to be done – people needed to pay for their behaviour, it was the only way to make everything feel better.

The hand paused over the mouse, before slowly scrolling back to the latest post and the so-called big reveal coming soon regarding the hotel uniform.

What big reveal? Surely the girl hadn't actually got the chef's jacket? It should have been taken away by now, shouldn't it? She couldn't have it, couldn't be allowed to retrieve it.

It was quite simple. The jacket was either still there and had to be retrieved, or the girl had it, and if so, then the jacket would just have to be retrieved from the girl.

About to close the laptop, the hand was stilled by the sight of another headline on the homepage, and a few clicks later it became clear that the serial killer story was gaining momentum, with some stating that street girls were at risk while others insisted it was high-class call girls. Either way, the media proclaimed that another attack on a sex worker was imminent, and a quick check on the television confirmed that the TV news channels had the same message. It was almost as if they wanted another murder...

The laptop snapped shut. If that's what they wanted then that's what they would get...

~

Sasha thanked the owner of Seasons for the safe return of her purse, bought a cup of tea and took a seat at the counter in the window. She had some time until she met Kay, the blogger, for lunch, so she brought up Kay's Killer Blog on her phone and prepared to read through it again.

A message flashed up on her phone from Drew Merton, the colleague of Eric's and Rowan's that she'd met the evening before at The Hilton. He'd spoken to Franco and found out the names of the other two men who'd been drinking with them. She sighed, another nickname – Rain Man, otherwise known as Quentin Thomas – and added it to her list, together with the name of his business associate, Max Canning.

Cursing her distractions of the day before, she then caught up on Kay's post from the previous day, before turning her attention to the latest one, posted this morning. She had to hand it to the girl, she certainly kept the information flowing, and seemed to know just how to keep her readers coming back for more. She'd be making quite a name for herself at this rate.

But how was she finding out this stuff? What was this all about a knife from the hotel kitchen having been used to kill the woman in Eric's hotel room? Did the cops know this? Surely they did if it was true. Tony had implied they had no murder weapon but, according to Kay, the knife had been returned to the kitchen where, and at this, she had to smile, it had been used to prepare food for the restaurant diners.

Was Tony deliberately keeping her out of the loop? And what about this claim that the killer had worn a uniform from the hotel to protect their clothing from blood spatter? No, this was Kay's overactive imagination at work again, the kind of thing someone would come up with as a murder plot for a book or TV series, although, if it was true then it would help Eric, for why would he have gone to all that trouble only to get into bed beside the woman and end up with his own body, or any clothing that he had on, covered with her blood?

Well, she'd get some answers from Kay when she met her for lunch, and then she'd go and see Tony, it was time he was honest with her about what they knew. They'd be pretty incompetent if Kay had truly found out about the murder weapon and the clothing worn and the cops hadn't.

But Kay was playing a dangerous game, she had far too much to say and someone out there would not be happy if she was giving away their secrets, she thought, deciding that the girl needed a little advice in that direction.

~

This time, Kay walked purposefully into the service entrance of the hotel, her business-like folder in one hand, and her laptop bag – the closest thing she owned to a briefcase – over her shoulder, complete with a bin bag inside, in which to stow the chef's jacket. She followed the signs for laundry collection, pausing for a moment as the girl she recognised from the night before, headed into the room, her arms filled with dirty linen. Her heart sank as she realised how many bins there were.

'Wait please.' Putting on her best posh voice, she made a show of peering at the girl's name badge. 'Soreena, is it? I'm from Laundry King, doing a spot check. I need a count of the items in each bin immediately. Which bin was filled first?'

Soreena dropped her bundle of linen into the closest bin and turned to Kay, a perplexed look on her face. 'I don't know of this, Mrs Carter didn't–'

'Mrs Carter is not in charge of Laundry King, but I will be informing her of our visit once I have my laundry count, and I'll be sure to mention how helpful you were, she's always pleased to know which of her staff are performing well. I'll need you to hurry as our van will be here soon. So, which bins were filled first?'

'We always start to the left, so this one here. But I have to fetch more dirty linens.'

'You can fetch them in a moment, this won't take long, just tip everything out and count it as you put it back in.'

Shrugging her shoulders, Soreena tipped the first bin out, counting out loud as she returned each item to the bin, while Kay kept her eyes fixed on proceedings, surreptitiously slipping on latex gloves in readiness.

'Pass me that one, please.' She examined the chef's jacket and gave it back to Soreena. 'Continue.'

She was beginning to feel agitated by the time they reached the third huge bin, wondering when her luck was going to run out and she was going to get busted by the infamous Mrs Carter.

'Twenty-five, twenty-seven,' Soreena counted, before correcting herself. 'I'm sorry, twenty-six, twenty-seven.'

There it was, it had to be. 'Let me see that.' She grabbed the jacket from the girl, her eyes studying the mess of dried blood spatters beneath the shrivelled potato peelings still adhering to it. The strident tones of Mrs Carter reached her ears and she thought rapidly. 'You can go and fetch the rest of the dirty linen, I'll carry on. Thank you.'

As soon as the girl had left, Kay grabbed the bin bag from her laptop bag and shoved the jacked inside it, her heart racing. Peeling off the gloves, she slipped them into her pocket and had just put her fake glasses on as Mrs Carter entered the room, deep in conversation with another woman.

'It's so nice to see you, Fran, we always miss each other with you on nights and me only here during the day. And you don't mind travelling here, there, and everywhere, to help with the night problems? And you're coping alright, dear, since you lost Adrian?'

The other woman smiled as she replied, 'Yes, it suits me, I'd rather that than be at home on my own. It's hard, of course it is, but it's been a few months now...'

Kay tried to blend into the wall, sidling along it in hopes of getting out before Mrs Carter looked her way.

'Three months isn't long, but we all think you've been so brave.' Mrs Carter's eagle eyes latched onto Kay.

'Laundry King? Is there a problem? I'm glad you're here, actually, I've got a few things to go through with you, if you could come with me to my office.' She turned to the other woman. 'Come and have a cup of tea with me before you go. I don't know what can have happened to your glasses, last night, you say? I thought you meant the night before, but I probably got muddled with all your comings and goings. Well, if you think you might have left them in the kitchen, then you'd best speak to Alfredo.' The other woman smiled and assured her that she would do that, before looking at Kay a little quizzically, and smiling at her.

Mrs Carter turned imperiously to Kay. 'Come with me.'

Helpless to refuse, Kay hurried after the indomitable ruler of the lower echelons of the hotel, wondering how she was going to extricate herself.

Half an hour later, she escaped, having made pages of notes concerning incomprehensible matters related to bed sheets, pillow cases, and other housekeeping linens, and having assured Mrs Carter that she would make sure her requests were actioned as soon as humanly possible.

'You can ride up with me in the lift.' Mrs Carter was suddenly beside her, and Kay had no choice but to acquiesce, smiling awkwardly at the woman as the lift gave a gentle ping for the ground floor reception.

'Ah, Mr Penrose, I presume? I understand you believe that you lost something valuable in one of the rooms you and your colleague occupied two nights ago. I can assure you that our rooms are thoroughly cleaned after every occupancy and anything found is held in lost property if we can't get hold of the guest.' Casting an unhappy eye over the man waiting in the reception area, she turned to Kay as she sidled her way towards the exit. 'Thank you for dealing with that matter, Miss, er–'

'Kay, Kay Saunders. I'll be off then.' She smiled at Mrs Carter and the man, feeling slightly uncomfortable as his grey eyes flickered the length of her body before seeming to study her face for a second as he gave her an almost imperceptible nod.

Phew, that had been close. But she'd got it. She'd only actually got the bloody jacket!

She walked out triumphantly, as Mrs Carter continued to drone on about housekeeping and room key cards. *Poor bloke, he'd be lucky to escape without the third degree. Those eyes though... urgh, they were like... flat, dead eyes...* She shuddered, checking her watch – there was just enough time to drop the murder jacket at her flat before going to meet Sasha. *Was her life bloody brilliant or what?*

Walking rapidly, she dictated a voice note into her phone, detailing her visit to the hotel.

~

Sasha smiled as the girl rushed towards her, red-faced and puffing, and stepped forward to greet her. 'Hi, Kay?'

'Yes, hi, Sasha, we met yesterday, well kind of, and sorry I'm late, I've had a bit of a busy morning.'

'That's okay, no panic. I didn't realise you had a day job as well, are you on your lunch break?'

'What? No, I–' Kay touched her lapel, fumbling to remove the homemade badge she'd forgotten she was wearing. She grinned at Sasha. 'A little bit of undercover work this morning and I didn't have time to change. I don't normally dress like this.' She wiped her hand across her brow, pushing stray strands of hair from her face. 'Phew, is it just me or is it really hot today?'

Laughing, Sasha pushed open the door. 'It is pretty warm. Come on, let's get some lunch, you look like you need to sit down. Come and choose what you want and then find us a nice table. I'll wait at the counter.'

A few minutes later, both women were seated in the small comfortable armchairs that Kay had managed to secure.

'Thanks for this, I was starving.' Kay scooped the last of her mac and cheese into her mouth. 'Mmm, this was delicious.' She drank the last of her lemonade thirstily.

Wow, this girl could eat. Taking another bite of her cheese and tomato toastie, Sasha saw Kay surreptitiously glance towards the counter.

'D'you want something else? A sandwich? A cake? Another drink?'

'I am still a bit peckish,' Kay confessed. 'Perhaps a scone or a brownie, and I fancy the look of those frappé things... What about you, fancy a cake?'

'Oh, go on then, I'll have a brownie. You go and order the stuff and I'll come over and pay in a sec.'

Finally, Kay's voracious appetite was abated and they both leaned back, sipping on their drinks.

'Kay, yesterday you asked me if the dead woman from Freedom Hotel in Kensington was the serial killer's second victim, whether I thought he'd killed more women, and what it was like to be engaged to a murderer.'

Shifting a little uncomfortably, Kay gave an apologetic smile. 'Yeah, look, sorry about that, it's just the best way to get a reaction from people, you know, throw them off a bit, be a bit cheeky, and they usually blurt stuff out before they know it. But still, it must be hard for you, being engaged to him.'

'Who do you mean when you say *him*?' It was time to find out what she really knew and what she was just blagging about.

'Well, Eric Latimer, that's his name, isn't it? It's all over the internet if you look, ever since that kidnapping you and your friend were involved in. He was on television as well, there's a clip of it on youtube.'

Okay, so she'd done her research... 'Right, well, he used to be my boyfriend, and we were engaged for a brief period, but that's all ancient history now.'

'Phew, that's a relief, so you're not bothered about him and the escort then? I'd been feeling a bit uncomfortable about asking you about it.'

'Kay,' Sasha said with a smile. 'I don't think there's much that makes you uncomfortable, which is why you're so good at finding out information, but, no, Eric and I are just friends and I'm not involved in the investigation at all.'

'Thanks, I do have my ways.' Kay grinned. 'But if you're not investigating, why did you want to meet me?'

'Mainly to set you straight, to tell you that Eric's not a killer, that the murder of a prostitute at the beginning of this month has to be unrelated to Tuesday night's murder, and to warn you—'

'To warn me? What on earth could you need to warn me about?'

'You're attracting attention, and I know it's what you want, but links to your blog are appearing in other online news sites, and—'

'I know. I even got a mention in two newspapers this morning.' Kay leaned forward excitedly. 'My followers have, like, quadrupled since I started revealing stuff about the murder that no one else knows.'

'But that's the thing, your name's out there, and any minute now they'll mention you on TV, they'll post your photo and, Kay, it's not a game. Look, you're good, you've got a knack, but there's a real murderer out there, and if he hasn't heard of you yet, he will soon enough. Do you think he's going to be happy to have you giving away all his secrets? Sorry, that's my phone.' Sasha rummaged in her bag.

'Harry? Or Shuggy, maybe I should call you. Thanks for calling back, yes, that would be great, er, Franco, you say, hold on...' She pulled her notebook out, rifling through it for the page where she'd written down all the guys' names and associated nicknames. 'So that would be Warren?

Warren Porterhouse? Uhuh, yep, and it was Rain Man who called him? Yes, I got the same names from Drew Merton, or Dealer, as you all seem to call him.'

Kay listened, fascinated, sneaking glances at Sasha's notes while pretending to study her phone.

'Shuggy, hold on, let me move to a quieter spot.' She stood up, mouthing sorry to Kay, who nodded, frowning in understanding, before typing importantly into her phone.

'Sorry about that.' Sasha sat back down a minute or two later. 'One of Eric's friends wanting to help. So, where were we?'

'You were telling me how famous I'm becoming.' Kay grinned cheekily. 'No, I get it, Sasha, I do, but I'm fine. It's not like he's going to hunt me down and murder me, is he? I mean, it's prostitutes he's after. And all my posts, it's not like I've got any actual proof...' She crossed her fingers underneath the table. 'I could be way wrong about everything.'

'So, what about this knife theory? How did you come up with that? I was pretty impressed.' Sasha played to Kay's ego.

Unable to help herself, Kay preened. 'I snuck into the hotel the back way yesterday, didn't I? Heard one of the girls who works there going on about it to a bloke who... oh, I might as well tell you, I've got to tell someone or I'll burst.'

A couple of minutes later, Kay sat back, pleased with herself, having told Sasha all about Alfredo in the kitchen, about Stefan having got into trouble for not washing up the knife properly and replacing it in the wrong place, about Rachel's theory that Stefan must have dropped a saucepan of spaghetti bolognese down the front of the jacket and thrown it away. She told the whole story of Rachel finding the jacket in the food waste bin and putting it in one of the laundry bins and finished off with her adventures of the night before at the pub, where she'd pumped Rachel for the information she'd just finished imparting.

'Wow, that's amazing.' Sasha was genuinely impressed, the girl had done some good work. 'When I set up my Private Investigator agency, maybe you should come and work for me.'

'Really? I'd love that.' Kay beamed. 'But I'd still be able to write my blog, right? We could be an amazing team, I could set us up a website, do all the social media...' Her eyes shone as she pictured it all.

Amused at the girl's enthusiasm, Sasha nodded. 'It could work. I'm not ready just yet, but you'd be my number one choice, how's that? So, tell, me, what about the chef's jacket? Did you find it? I mean, I'm guessing your outfit and makeshift badge were a ploy to get back in and hunt for it, am I right?'

'Yeah, but...' Kay looked at Sasha wide-eyed. 'I was too late. Arthur or Femi must have collected everything. So that's it, it's gone, laundered and ironed and back on the rack ready to be delivered to the hotel tomorrow, probably.' She crossed her fingers tightly beneath the table again. *Her mum would say she'd go to hell with all this lying.*

'Listen, make me a promise, okay? Keep me in the loop. I'll do the same. We can pool information. But if you find out something helpful to the police, you should tell them – you can tell me, and we can tell them together, I've got a contact.'

They parted ways outside Costa Coffee, with promises to stay in touch, and Sasha headed off to Kensington police station in search of Tony – she needed to ask him about what Kay had told her, and she wanted to speak to Eric again. She found herself smiling about Kay – she'd seen her crossing her fingers under the table as she'd no doubt lied to her. *But lied about what exactly?*

Kay walked off jauntily, it had been a great lunch, and Sasha was cool, she liked her. She stopped suddenly, smiling and shaking her head as she realised something. Sasha was a crafty piece of work, she hadn't really shared any information with Kay – which had been why Kay had wanted to speak to her in the first place.

No, clever little big mouth Kay had blabbed just about everything to her, well, almost... she'd been dying to tell her about finding the chef's jacket, but had managed to hold it back somehow. She'd known that Sasha would insist on them taking it straight to the cops, and Kay would have missed out on writing her post that was going to attract massive attention the next day.

She hugged herself in excitement. She couldn't wait to take photos of the jacket with all its blood stains. Everyone was going to be looking at her blog tomorrow. Everyone.

And, she grinned, opening up her phone's photo gallery, Sasha didn't know it but she *had* shared something with Kay – her list of the ex-boyfriend's mates with all their weird names. She'd be able to look them up online and check them out – if Eric Latimer wasn't the murderer maybe one of them was. They certainly sounded like a suspect bunch of characters, she thought, glancing down the list. *Tut tut, Sasha, you shouldn't have left your notebook open on the table while you went to speak to Shuggy bear or whatever the hell his name was.*

She paused, looking at one of the names again – she'd heard it before, hadn't she? She walked off slowly, racking her brain trying to remember where.

GOOD OLD SOHO

The jacket was gone. Frustration was replaced by irritation, followed swiftly by a mixture of anxiety and anger. This girl was turning out to be a massive spanner in the works. Had she somehow located the jacket? Not possible. It was gone, safely disposed of, no one, not the girl, not the police, no one would find it now, so that just left the knife, which had, surely, been washed a dozen of more times by now, and been used to slice up countless raw steaks. Any human blood on it had been washed away or was safely mixed with animal blood – all quite revolting to think about – a thought that had never occurred until now, thanks to the girl and her ridiculous blog posts.

Putting the recurring thoughts aside, and alighting from the bus, which had followed the tube ride, which made the complete travel time about fifty minutes, Clapham High Street was reached on foot in a couple of minutes. Now all that was needed was to find the right kind of shop.

A little extra caution couldn't harm. The cheap lightweight hoodie from the rather smelly charity shop was slipped on in the public lavatory and the search continued.

Well, this was perfect, rather thin, and no doubt poor quality, but the pack contained a raincoat and trousers – adequate protection, although some kind of head protection would also be needed. Best to get two packs, just in case. A pack of three shower caps was easy to find, and then it was on to a supermarket.

Into the shopping basket went a plastic spatula, a wooden spoon, a large kitchen knife, a plastic chopping board, a small frying pan, half a dozen eggs, a couple of onions, a small packet of grated cheese, a loaf of bread, and a small tub of margarine. A pair of washing-up gloves were next, and the shopping was wrapped up with the addition of a loose pair of men's black cotton trousers and a black long-sleeved shirt, both found in the clothing section.

A cheap shoe shop further along the road provided a pair of plastic clog-type shoes, possibly for gardening, and once this purchase was completed the return journey was undertaken, this time with a variation.

The tube was taken to Embankment, where the station was exited and a short walk taken along the road. The supermarket shopping bag, minus the knife, washing up gloves, and men's clothing, was deposited on the ground next to a bench occupied by one of London's many homeless who, as soon as the coast was clear, purloined the bag and headed off along the embankment, delving delightedly into the goodies.

Steps were retraced to Embankment tube station for the final stretch of the journey home. It was time to get some rest.

The stage was set, as it were – it was annoying to have to go to all this trouble, but a detraction from the hotel killing had been necessitated – the police needed the murder of another prostitute to keep them running around in circles, and the media needed another prostitute to be murdered because they were hungry for it, baying like wolves at the smell of blood. Plus, it sold newspapers and kept their digital and TV viewers glued to their screens, their excitement disguised as anxiety, as they professed concern for London's women of the night, all the while hoping for another murder. The timing would be a little complicated, but it was manageable.

But, most of all, tonight's murder was required so that the next murder, already lined up, could be carried out with no risk of being caught. And the murder after that, and the murder after that...

~

'Sweetheart, I can give you five minutes tops, the D.C.I.'s on my case about this bleedin' murder now, thanks to some girl who's started the perfect bleedin' storm with talk about serial killers rampaging round London killing off hookers. I mean, where's she getting all this stuff from? She's making our job a million times harder, that's what she's doing, getting everyone in a panic, everyone talking about it. I've even had Latimer's bleedin' solicitor, Brian Trefoyle, telling me we have to let him go seeing as it's obvious that it's the serial killer who killed your bloke's escort.

'The whole world and his aunty's suddenly a detective telling us our job. I mean, she's announcing to the world that the knife was taken from the hotel kitchen and then put back there afterwards. And–' Tony paused to take a breath, 'she only reckons the killer wore some uniform nicked from the hotel. Next thing she'll be saying the chambermaid done it. Meanwhile, we've got Latimer on the scene, covered in the girl's blood, and not a French Maid's uniform in sight. Bit of a relief though, come to think of it, not sure I'm keen on the idea of Latimer dressed up like a French Maid.'

Sasha tried to dispel the image Tony had conjured up in her head. 'But you haven't got the knife?'

'What's that?'

'The knife – you haven't found it? Could she be right? She does say that the chef, who admittedly sounds like a bit of a drama queen, was furious about his knife being in the wrong place and not as clean as it should be. And–' She held her hand up as Tony opened his mouth to interrupt. 'Alfredo, the chef, was complaining about missing a chef's jacket.'

Tony narrowed his eyes. 'You know her. You know this girl and you've talked to her. I should have known, if you can't get involved one way, you'll worm your way in another. Sasha, leave it alone, the girl's making it all up, no one said nothing to our officers, and we've spoken to every single staff member from the kitchen to bleedin' housekeeping.'

'Kay, that's her name. I admit she sounds like she's got one hell of an imagination on her, but she's pretty wily and good at getting information out of people. Some of those hotel workers might be naturally suspicious of the cops, Tone, you know that but they'll gossip amongst themselves, and it only takes one to have a little too much to say after a few drinks. And Kay found that one person, and that's where she got her information. And from the little that I know her, I've got a feeling she might have found out a bit more than she's letting on so far. Which could place her in harm's way if she's not careful. You should at least pay attention to what she's said and get it checked out.'

Tony looked slightly uncomfortable. 'Yeah, well, got a couple of blokes over there now going through the kitchen utensils and checking out the uniforms as it goes. But don't you tell that girl, the last thing I want her doing is crowing all over the internet that she's the one giving the cops the leads.' His expression became serious. 'Sash, none of it's going to make a difference where Eric's concerned. We could find the knife that was used, and the uniform that was supposedly worn, but none of it changes the fact that he was in the room, covered in her blood. All it would mean is that he put the knife back in the kitchen, and did something with the uniform, I dunno, laundry maybe?' Laundry.' He snapped his fingers. 'I'll get the guys onto whoever does the hotel's laundry.'

'That would be Laundry King.' Sasha couldn't help grinning, even amidst the seriousness of the situation. 'Sorry, it's just that Kay, well, she mentioned their name to me earlier.' *Best not to mention that Kay had been impersonating a Laundry King employee in her quest for information that very morning.* 'I told you she's good at finding stuff out.'

An officer stuck his head round the door. 'Sarge, sorry to disturb you. We've got a name, it just came in – anonymous tip-off. Reckoned the murdered woman's name is Lisa Pennington – went by the professional name Chardonnay. We're trying to find out her home address right now.'

'Thanks, Simon, and keep it quiet, yeah? Not for the eyes or ears of our lovable press posse hovering around outside.' Tony nodded, dismissing his officer, and turned back to Sasha.

'Looks like you just got yourself some inside information. I don't need to tell you not to give this detail out to anyone, do I, babes?'

'No, you bloody well don't. Since when did you worry about whether you could trust me or not? How long have we known each other, Tone?'

'Alright, don't get your knickers in a twist, I trust you, alright? I'm just being cautious, what with stories everywhere and speculation running riot.' He reached down, pulling a folded newspaper from his bin. 'I mean, look at this piece of tabloid trash.'

Sasha took the paper, her eyes scanning the bold headline, before dropping to the first couple of lines below.

SEXY SLASHER VICTIM STABBED TO DEATH IN HER STILETTOS.

Are high-class escorts the slasher killer's target as he makes it his mission to clean London's streets, one sex worker at a time? Have the police got the right man, or is The Street Cleaner still out there, awaiting the arrival of his next victim in an anonymous hotel room, dressed up as a hotel maid, and ready to strike?

Was Tuesday night's victim, the sex worker found stabbed multiple times at the Freedom Hotel in

Kensington, his first, or have there been more? Are the police doing enough to keep female sex workers safe from this serial killer on the rampage?

She handed the paper back to Tony. 'Talk about rubbish reporting. Not one piece of actual information, just stupid questions.'

'Yep. Does the damage though, gets everyone up in arms and talking about it. We've got a bloke locked up but they're talking about a serial killer as if it's a bleedin' fact. They'll soon shut up when no one else is murdered.'

'*If* no one else is murdered. So, you're still sure that Eric's guilty?'

Tony shifted in his seat. 'Well, we're getting there. We've got until tomorrow morning to make our minds up. I suppose you want to see him? Come on then. If anyone asks, you're my consultant. I want to ask him about Lisa Pennington, or Chardonnay, as he probably knew her.'

As she hurried to keep up with him, Sasha asked, 'Can't you just let me have a peek at the crime scene pics and stuff? You must have everything up on boards by now?'

'You don't give up, do you? You're connected to our suspect like I said, and I don't want to have my D.C.I. reading me the riot act. If it was any other murder I'd have no problem with it, you know that. Right, here we are, let's see what sunshine's got to say about a girl called Chardonnay.' He turned, grinning, his hand on the door of the custody suite. 'Did you like that? I'm a bleedin' poet and I didn't know it.'

Sasha rolled her eyes, following Tony inside.

Eric looked up, his face expressionless. 'What now?' he asked flatly.

'Now, you're going to tell us all you know about a girl called Lisa Pennington, but you probably knew her better as Chardonnay.'

'Who's Lisa Pennington? Chardonnay? What are you talking about?' His puzzlement cleared gradually. 'Wait a minute, Chardonnay, I'd forgotten all about that. Yes, that was her name, I remember now because I made a joke about fancying some Chardonnay. Sorry.' He glanced at Sasha, who shrugged.

'Bet that was the first time she'd heard that one,' Tony quipped.

'Alright, so I was drunk, the quality of my jokes is directly related to the amount of alcohol I consume – as one goes up the other goes down. And I was certainly drinking a lot, we both were...' His eyes suddenly sparked for a fraction of a second.

Sasha saw it. 'What is it, Eric? Have you remembered something?'

'I think I have... I was plastered when I walked into the room. You might not believe me, but I have no idea how I got to the hotel or how I ended up with this woman. But I do remember this: there was a bottle of whisky on the table and I thought it was weird to put whisky in the room, so I poured myself a large glass. She didn't want any, or wouldn't have any, insisting she could only drink the champagne. That's all I remember really. She was on the champers, and I had a few whiskies, then shared the rest of the champagne with her, in between, you know.' He had the grace to look awkward. 'Which we finished and– she ordered another bottle, she must have because we drank that as well. And then she said she had to go, she might have said something about a last-minute call. That's all I can remember, she said something about having to leave, I said she should stay, but she said something strange like, you're the one who said it or something? I don't know, I was in a bit of a mess, room spinning and all that, I'm not sure what I remember and what I'm imagining, it all feels like it was dreamlike or something. I said something like have one more drink, but she said it was all gone and she couldn't drink the whisky. She asked me why I wanted her to drink the whisky when I'd said she shouldn't, or something crazy, and I think we both started laughing. Look, I was on a bloody high, alright? I felt like I'd taken a ton of drugs even though I hadn't, but I knew I'd overdone it when I started feeling dizzy and shaky. I suddenly felt really tired and I could hardly keep my eyes open, and the last thing I remember is going out to the balcony for a smoke. I think she'd gone by then.'

'Nice try, Latimer. She hadn't gone though, had she? She was stabbed to death in your bed.'

Eric held his hands out. 'I'm doing my best to remember what I can, I can't help it if it sounds like I'm making it up. Bottom line – we were both rat-arsed, and we were having a wild time, so I don't even know why she said she was leaving, in fact, the more I think about it, I don't think she wanted to leave at all, but she did. I sure as hell don't know how she ended up back in the bed as dead as a dodo.'

'Alright, we'll leave it there for now.' Tony stood up, indicating that Sasha should do the same.

'Who's the woman in your flat, Eric?' She threw the question at him, catching him off guard.

'What? Who? No one, what are you talking about?'

'The brassy bit staying in your flat, drinking your wine, and wearing the ring you gave me when we got engaged. The woman who says she's your girlfriend.'

Eric groaned. 'I said she could stay at mine for the night, that's all. She was supposed to have gone.'

'Which night?' Tony interrupted. 'What's her name?'

'Er, Sunday night, well, okay, Monday as well. I was drowning my sorrows.' He looked defensively at Sasha. 'You'd dumped me, in case you've forgotten, and I needed a confidence boost. She ended up at mine on Sunday night and asked if she could stay for one more night because she had a problem at her flat. I assumed she'd be gone when I got home Tuesday night.' He looked at Tony. 'Sadie something.'

Sasha shook her head slowly. 'You know, Eric, I'm done, truly. I tried to put everything that's happened between us aside so that I could help you, but you're past help.'

'She's right, you're a real piece of work, Latimer.' Tony's face was incredulous. 'I don't know whether to applaud your ability to go from being dumped on Sunday morning, to acquiring yourself a live-in girlfriend called Sadie something on Sunday night, and to stabbing an escort to death on Tuesday night, or whether to give you the award for prize plonker of the bleedin' year.'

'I didn't give her your ring, I wouldn't do that, Sash, she must have nicked it. I'll kill her.' He looked at Tony, aghast. 'I didn't mean that, I meant–'

'I'd zip it if I were you, Latimer before you dig yourself in any deeper,' said Tony.

~

The photos were brilliant, Kay thought, somewhat immodestly, as she scrolled through them on her laptop. The blood stains on the chef's jacket stood out, even amongst the food stains, as a dark reddish-brown colour. Nonetheless, to make her blog post look more professional, she would add some arrows pointing to the blood stains, she decided, proceeding to do so, feeling like a forensic scientist out of CSI Miami. *Eat your heart out, Lieutenant Horatio Caine.*

She checked her blog statistics, pleased to see that her numbers were still increasing. This post could wait, for now, it was going to get a lot of attention and she wanted to be able to milk it for all it was worth. She'd mess around with a draft of her interview with Sasha – which would need some creative thinking, seeing as Sasha had kept pretty shtum about everything, and then she had some research to undertake online regarding the list of names she'd swiped a photo of from Sasha's note book.

A couple of hours or so later, Kay put the draft aside and fetched herself a glass of wine from one of the bottles she'd picked up in Lidl, taking a sip and nodding approvingly. It wasn't bad for four bottles for under twenty quid. She rubbed her hands together and began typing in names on her laptop, rapidly scanning the results, and clicking on anything promising.

By ten o'clock or so she'd delved deep into the friends lists on Facebook, for four of the men on Sasha's list, including Eric, and had sent friend requests to a number of carefully calculated choices. Experience had taught her that those with ridiculously high numbers of so-called friends were click-happy when it came to accepting new friend requests, and would do so without bothering to figure out if they'd ever heard of the person. None of the four men was particularly active on the social media platform, but some of their online friends were, and by gaining access to their feeds, she was able to peruse vast numbers of photos, read the captions and build up a little information about the men, having received several acceptances in a short space of time.

Between those photos and other images gleaned from business websites and online articles, she finally compiled a document with the eight men's photographs and names, sitting back and gazing at it, not sure if her efforts would lead her anywhere. Maybe, maybe not, she admitted, but the fact that Eric Latimer was the suspect, and that the other seven were his friends and/or colleagues, *and* the fact that Sasha had seen some reason for having a list of their names, meant that it was an avenue of enquiry worth following up on. She hugged herself, imagine if she could figure it all out and clear Sasha's old boyfriend's name. That's if he was innocent, of course...

She picked up her remote, put the television on, and switched to a news channel, before turning to ice in excited shock. A prostitute had been found stabbed to death in Soho. Turning back to her laptop to close the document of the men's photos, she leaned forward, frowning suddenly. She'd seen one of those men before somewhere... It would come to her in time, no use trying to force the memory. She stood up and moved closer to the television, peering at the scene behind the reporter and taking note of the names of the businesses behind the woman.

This was him, without a doubt this was her serial killer up to his tricks again. It was exactly what she needed to fuel her story – it was almost as if he'd done it especially for her...

~

'About time. I can't get the damn thing to give me my room key card.' The man scowled, his fingers jabbing at the tablet ineffectually.'

Samantha looked at Fran worriedly. 'I tried everything, there must be some sort of glitch with the system, sorry.'

'No problem, I'll sort it out.' Fran smiled at the girl and turned to the man.

'I'm terribly sorry to have kept you waiting, Sir, I'll have everything sorted for you in just a moment.' She offered her best apologetic smile. 'Perhaps I can offer you a complimentary drink in our bar and I'll bring your room card through to you in a moment?'

'Do I look like I want to sit around in a bar? I'm exhausted, I've travelled in for an early meeting tomorrow. Why on earth you can't just have a receptionist who hands out room key cards like a normal hotel, I don't know.'

'Absolutely, I quite understand.' She sighed inwardly, feeling tired. 'The Freedom hotel chain strives to offer a state-of-the-art service to offer our guests anonymity and the freedom to–'

'Spare me the sales talk, love, and just give me my room key.'

'Here we are.' She smiled tightly, breathing a sigh of relief as the system unfroze. 'Mr... Anderson. And you're staying just one night? Did you manage to take in Soho's sights this evening?'

'So much for all that anonymity talk.' He snatched the key card from her, pausing and studying her for a moment. 'You'd better come up with me and make sure it works, I don't want to have to wait another half an hour if there's a problem.'

'Certainly.' Fran slid her card into the slot for the lift, the doors slid open silently, and the guest pushed past her, bumping her with his overnight bag. *Charming, another male chauvinist.*

'Your wife's not joining you then?' she asked, noticing his wedding ring, and feeling uncomfortable in the man's presence in the small lift.

'Who said I was married?' He smirked, leaning against the mirrored interior.

She led the way along the corridor on the first floor, stopping at a door and inserting the key card. 'Here you are, room ten.'

'After you.' The man stood back. 'You might as well check that the room's in order.'

Fran entered the room, aware of the man's looming presence behind her. She might look slightly built but her clothing belied her strength, she thought, thankful for the boxing classes she'd taken up the previous year.

'You know what? I think I'd like that complimentary drink after all. Why not order one for yourself as well? I think we got off on the wrong foot.'

They were all the same, couldn't help themselves cheating, she thought angrily. Her phone buzzed and she glanced at the message gratefully. 'I'll have one sent up for you, I'm afraid I have an urgent call at one of our sister hotels.' She edged past him and out of the door as she spoke.

Taking the man's drinks order as he shrugged, unconcerned by her brush-off, she hurried off. Tonight was going down as one of her most unpleasant nights, and she still had hours ahead of her.

She walked down to the basement parking and climbed into her car, setting off, anxious to get to their Chelsea hotel as soon as possible for the waiting guest. The Freedom hotel brand's computerised self-check-in system didn't always seem like the best idea, and having one staff member from the restaurant available each night to deal with problems wasn't working out very well. It certainly kept her busy as the only trained expert though, she thought, as she tapped her fingers on the steering wheel a few minutes later, watching the refuse collection truck in front of her impatiently, willing it to move on and get rid of its revolting piles of refuse so that she could get going.

~

'Babes, this was delicious.' Zoe wiped her mouth, smiling at her friend. 'I should have remembered that you like to hit the kitchen when you've got a lot on your mind.' Zoe waved her hand in front of Sasha's face. 'Earth to Sasha. Is there anyone at home?'

'Sorry,' Sasha said, smiling and turning her attention back to Zoe. 'How was the food?'

'Like I said, it was delicious, you make a killer lasagne. Let's take the bottle and sit out on the terrace. You can tell me which part of your slightly chaotic life has got you so distracted right now.'

Sipping her wine, Sasha leaned back in the garden chair, lighting a cigarette as she tried to organise her jumbled thoughts.

'Tell me it's not about Eric.' Zoe blew a delicate stream of smoke from her mouth, tapping her cigarette in the ashtray. 'Not after this afternoon's revelations about Sadie something in his flat. Christ, the man's unbelievable.'

'The thing is, it is about him, or rather the case. There's something a little off-kilter about his whole story, but I can't pin down what it is... It's something to do with the drinks, like, there was a bottle of whisky already in the room, he reckons. Course, he could have ordered a bottle when he got there and not remembered because he was so drunk already.' She shook her head, frustrated. 'I wish I could see the crime scene photos, something might jog my memory. Maybe it was to do with the champagne, he said they were both drinking it... Oh, that's it, Tony told me there was only one champagne glass. Don't you think that's odd?'

'Might be, unless he was swigging it from the bottle, you know what Eric's like.'

'True, he is rather uncivilised when he's drunk.'

Zoe snorted. 'You said it, babes.'

'But there was another thing, that's if he's to be trusted at all, he kept saying that the escort, oh, her professional name was Chardonnay, by the way—' She waited until Zoe had composed herself. 'She was implying that he'd set rules for her to follow, stuff like, only drinking the champagne, not supposed to stay, not to drink the damn whisky, which wasn't even there, come to think of it, so maybe he imagined all that...'

'The whisky wasn't there?'

'No... I'm almost certain there was no whisky bottle in the room...' Dammit, I need to see those photos.' She rubbed her stomach distractedly.

'Sore stomach?'

'Ate too much, I expect.'

Zoe studied her friend, her eyes worried. 'You were sore this morning when I hugged you, and you felt pukey, and now you've got a sore stomach. It's not the dreaded, is it?'

'My constant companion and best friend, apart from you? The lovely endometriosis? No... no, I'm sure it isn't – it doesn't feel like that at all. No, I'm fine, I promise you. Where's that bottle of wine? Another glass will sort me out.'

'I'll grab another bottle, looks like this one must have sprung a leak, it's empty already.'

'Pesky leaking bottles.' Sasha grinned, feeling better. This was just what she needed, an evening with her best friend and plenty of wine.

'Tell me about your stay in Canterbury with James.' She wanted to be distracted from thoughts of murder, of Eric, and of her burnt-down flat and settled down happily to listen to Zoe describing their suite, the view across the city to the cathedral, and their delicious meal.

It was a little after ten, and just as Zoe shivered, rubbing her arms and commenting that it was feeling chilly, that Sasha's phone rang.

She listened to the caller for a moment, before jumping up. 'Zo, we need to put the news on.' They both rushed inside and stared at the TV screen as Sasha spoke to her caller.

'I'm watching it now. Where are you? You're on your way? I'll meet you there. What's the name of the hotel? And, Kay, watch yourself, remember what I said, you've been stirring things up and someone out there might not be too happy with you. And, yes, I'm talking about the killer. I'll be there as soon as I can.'

She turned to Zoe. 'You know what this means? They'll have to let Eric go. Another stabbing of a prostitute, this time in a hotel in Soho? Too much of a coincidence to not be the same person. It looks like Kay was right about her serial killer, she was just a little premature in announcing it.'

'I'm coming with you.'

'No, Zo, you need to get some sleep, I'll be fine.'

'You're not travelling on your own on the tube at this time of night.'

'Alright, Mum. You'd better put a cardigan on, you'll be chilly otherwise.'

'Now who's being the mum?'

They left Zoe's flat a couple of minutes later and headed for the nearest tube station.

~

'What's that?' Franco shouted above the noise of the rock music belting out from the speakers, putting his pint back on the table.

'I said, where's Red gone?' Harry Reddingham tilted his glass. 'Another?'

'Yeah, cheers. Rowan's popped out for a smoke, I think, either that or he's trying his luck with the transvestite he was eying up earlier. Someone should have told him, I suppose.'

The two men laughed as Harry said, 'He's a big boy, he can look after himself. I'll get a round in and we can join him outside.'

They carried their pints outside, looking around for Rowan.

'Isn't that the chap who was drinking with us the other night?' Harry squinted through his glasses.

Franco looked towards the men huddled together, seemingly in deep conversation. 'Yeah, that's old Rain Man's colleague, isn't it? Max?'

Harry put Rowan's pint on the ledge, nodding at the man he was talking to. 'Max? Good to see you again.' At the man's slightly blank look, he reminded him. 'Harry, we had a few beers with you the other night.'

'Ah, they called you something else...'

'Shuggy,' Rowan threw in helpfully. 'Cheers for the pint.'

'How's Quentin? Recovered from our heavy night on, when was it, Tuesday?' Franco took a long drink from his glass.

'I haven't seen him.' Max smiled politely.

'Is The Ship your local then? Soho your neck of the woods, is it?' Harry enquired.

'Max was just passing, small world and all that.' Rowan gave a loud laugh.

'Not really. Sanitised Soho, not like it used to be. Like Rowan here said, I was just passing.'

'I remember the good old Soho,' Rowan said, grinning. 'Schoolboy's dream come true, all those birds with their bits hanging out, lurking in doorways, trying to tempt us in for overpriced lager and a bit of how's your father.'

'Not anymore,' laughed Franco. 'Family-friendly now, isn't it?'

'On the surface,' Max replied, tapping the side of his nose. 'If you know where to look there's still plenty of fun to be had.'

'Sounds like you're the man to know.' Rowan guffawed loudly.

'Anyone heard how Eric's getting on?' Franco asked into the lull in the conversation.

'Still banged up I expect, poor bloke. I had a visit from his ex-girlfriend today, quite a looker.' Rowan checked his watch as he spoke.

'What did he do?' Max looked from one to the other, enquiringly.

'Wrong place, wrong time,' said Harry, firmly. 'I've known the fellow virtually my whole life. He's the biggest fool out there. Only Eric could get himself caught up in a murder about which he knows absolutely nothing. I'm meeting his ex tomorrow for a chat, see if we can shed any light on the whole dratted thing.'

'Who'd he murder?'

Franco responded, surprised. 'He didn't murder anyone. It's been all over the news, haven't you seen it? An escort was murdered and he's got himself mixed up in it. We'll get it cleared up, cops will do their job. Which reminds me, I got your message, Red, thanks.'

He turned to Harry. 'Shuggy, you're meeting Sasha tomorrow, you said? Tell her I'll give her a call to arrange a meeting. Between us all, we should be able to remember something that will help him out.'

'Will do, I've already given her your numbers and passed on your concern.' Harry nodded, hesitating. 'You were the last ones left with Eric, weren't you, when I left the other night? Where was it, Bar Simone?'

'You're asking the wrong blokes, mate.' Rowan gave another braying laugh. 'Max and I were totally off our heads. And on that note...' he checked his watch again, slurping down the rest of his lager. 'I have to get home to the missis or I won't have a head to be off on.'

'I'll walk with you. Good to see you again.' Max nodded at Franco and Harry, before following Rowan into the night.

'Funny bloke, doesn't say a lot, does he? Not sure how he came to be tagging along with Rain Man the other night.'

'Drink up, it's just about closing time.' Harry downed the rest of his pint and wiped his mouth, looking up as the blue lights from a passing police car shone over them as it turned into Broadwick Street. 'I wonder what's going on? Thought I heard sirens earlier.'

'We can walk that way and have a gander,' suggested Franco.

THE STREET CLEANER STRIKES AGAIN

Kay slipped through the kitchen of the compact wine bar in Berwick Street, finding herself in a small courtyard loaded up with bins and a couple of old chairs and tables. She looked up at the rear of the hotel which had its entrance in Duck Lane, pondering her next move, before dragging one of the discarded tables over and placing it against the wall. Clambering onto it, she grabbed the top of the wall as the table wobbled precariously on a loose leg.

She dropped silently onto the ground on the other side of the wall and tried to figure out which fire escapes were which, as she looked up at the lighted windows. Movement in one of the windows caught her eye and she began to climb the rusted steps.

~

Sasha turned into Duck Lane with Zoe, slowing as she saw the police car up ahead, its lights flashing lazily as they illuminated the police tape strung across the passage. She scanned the small crowd of onlookers, trying to identify Kay, but there was no sign of her. Touching Zoe's arm, they stopped, and Sasha took out her phone.

'I'm in Duck Lane, where are you?' she asked Kay.

'I'm on the fire escape,' Kay whispered into her phone, craning her neck to see into the room. 'And I can see the crime scene. It looks like she's been stabbed quite a few times, there's loads of blood. Walk round to Berwick Street and go out the back of Eva's wine bar, there's a table by the wall that you can use to climb up on. Watch the leg though.'

'There's nothing wrong with my leg.'

'No, the table leg,' Kay giggled.

Sasha turned to Zoe. 'Are you sure you want to come with me? I have a horrible feeling this girl is leading me astray with her methods.'

'I'm game.' Zoe grinned. 'It sounds exciting.'

They walked round the block, following Kay's instructions, and entered the small wine bar as a grumpy-looking waitress nodded at them.

'Er, the ladies' loo?' Sasha asked. 'We're bursting. We'll order drinks in a sec.'

'Through the back,' said the waitress. 'But you have to buy a drink, it's not a public loo.'

'Two glasses of dry white wine, please, we'll be back in a minute.' Zoe smiled brightly as she hurried after Sasha. 'Sash,' she hissed, 'I'll stay here and get the drinks, you go.'

'Sure? Make it three glasses, I'll find Kay and try to keep her out of trouble. Thanks, babes.'

Shaking her head at what she was doing, Sasha clambered onto the table and over the wall, looking up at the back of the hotel as a hissing sound came from the fire escape.

'Up here.'

She waved at Kay and warily climbed the steps to the second floor.

'In there.' Kay stepped back, indicating that Sasha should squeeze past her to the window. 'I've taken some photos already,' she said gleefully.

Bracing herself against the wall, Sasha leaned over and looked through the window, spotting D.S. Palmer in the room. *Shit, Tony was here.* Her eyes took in the scene, the blood-stained duvet now laid aside to expose the woman in the bed, as well as some blood on the floor. She looked for other similarities to the scene at the Kensington hotel, seeing no champagne bottles or signs of any drinks at all. But of course, there wouldn't be, this was a cheap hotel, and it certainly wouldn't offer room service.

Her eyes travelled back to the dead woman. She looked older than the other victim, and low-class, in her thin black top and cheap red satin skirt, her outfit finished off with black stockings and red stilettoes. Probably not an escort, more likely a street prostitute, burnt out, if her long and straggly bleached hair and darker roots were anything to go by, she thought sadly. It looked the same as the other murder, but it didn't feel right – this looked rushed, as if no time had been spent in the room before the woman had been killed. Had the killer begun to stab their victim before she was in the bed? She stepped back from the window.

'Have you looked into any other windows?' she asked Kay.

'No, why?'

'I'm wondering if this is purely a good old-fashioned knocking shop, it's certainly a long way from Freedom, Kensington.' She looked up, seeing a light from the window on the floor above them. 'I'm going to look up there.'

Kay followed her, and together they peered into the room, before looking at each other, their eyes wide.

'Did you see what he was doing to her?' Kay squealed.

'Shh.' Sasha put her finger to her lips. 'Let's go back down, I'll take a couple of photos of the crime scene and then we'll go.'

She angled her phone through the window, clicking rapidly.

'Sarge.' The police officer's eyes locked with hers for a second. 'There's someone outside.'

'We've got to go.' She pulled back, but not before Tony Palmer had looked out at her, his eyes widening in surprise. 'Down, now, Kay.'

They scrambled down the fire escape as the sound of the window opening reached them.

'Don't move.' Sasha pulled Kay into the shadow of the wall, holding her breath, her heart racing. *This was ridiculous.*

'I can't see anyone.' Tony's voice was loud in the silence. 'It looked like, I could have sworn it was– Sasha, that better not bleedin' well be you,' he bellowed suddenly. 'Get down there and check out the back. Why the hell haven't we got an officer out there?' The window slammed shut, and the two women made a run for it, dashing back inside the wine bar to a waiting Zoe.

'That was close.' Kay's face was flushed with excitement.

'Too close. I must be mad. Kay, meet Zoe. Now drink your wine.' She pushed a glass towards Kay and picked up the other one.

'Cheers.' Kay grinned, lifting her glass.

'What did you see?' Zoe looked at them both expectantly.

'An extremely unpleasant murder scene, multiple stabbings to the body of a woman dressed like a sex worker – poor thing, she looked more like a cheap caricature than the real thing.'

'It's him, it has to be.' Kay brought up a photo on her phone, sticking it under Sasha's nose, as Zoe looked on in horror. 'Look at this and tell me it doesn't look the same as the murder at Freedom Hotel – you saw it, didn't you? I've only heard about it second-hand. And even if it's a bit different, who cares? Someone's got it in for prostitutes, this is the third one now this month.'

'Kay, slow down, yes, it is very similar to the Kensington murder, but neither of these murders bears any similarity to the murder you wrote about at the beginning of June. She was beaten and strangled, and–'

'Yes, but it happened just round the corner. What are the odds? Two female escorts getting murdered in Soho? I reckon someone's got it in for these women and goes prowling round this area at night looking for vulnerable ones.'

'You see, you've just said something important.' Sasha gulped a mouthful of wine. 'Two female escorts – the Kensington killing had to be a high-class escort, presumably booked and paid for through an agency, for two or three hours, but that poor woman lying sprawled in that room over there?' She nodded her head towards the back of the hotel. 'She was as far from being an escort as I am from being the Queen of England. She was a lowly streetwalker, and whoever killed her simply offered to pay her for sex, resulting in her willingness to accompany her murderer to the room.' She paused, considering. 'Maybe she always used the same place, if it is what it looks like – a glorified knocking shop hiding behind the facade of a barely-disguised bottom-feeder of an accommodation establishment – and if so, then sadly, she was the one to lead her murderer to the room she would be killed in. Drink up, ladies, we need to find a way to have a word with whoever the poor wretch is who mans the reception of the Duck Palace Hotel.'

'Or you could ask me, I suppose. Evening Sasha. Surprised to see me?' Tony Palmer pulled a chair over, sitting down and smiling at the three surprised faces. 'I'm not a detective sergeant for nothing. Now, who's going to tell me what all that was about?'

Embarrassed, Sasha mumbled a rambling explanation about wanting to establish whether the murder had the same modus operandi as the one in Kensington, how they hadn't been able to get to the hotel via Duck Lane and had thus sought alternative methods. 'If you'd just let me in on things, Tone, I wouldn't have to go snooping around like this,' she finished rather lamely.

'Who says I wasn't going to bring you in on this one? And who are these two nice young ladies accompanying you on your sleuthing mission? D.S. Palmer,' he said, introducing himself to them.'

'Er, this is Zoe, my best friend, and, er, Kay, a friend of ours.'

'Kay... you're the little troublemaker getting everyone panicking about a serial killer...' Tony frowned at Kay.

'True though, innit?' Kay grinned cheekily at Tony. 'This is the third prostitute to be murdered, that we know of...'

'I think we'd know. There's not exactly a whole load of undiscovered dead bodies lying around in hotel rooms and alleyways all over London, you know.'

'Well, yeah, but if you read my blog you'll see that in May there were a total of–'

'Pushy little thing, isn't she?' Tony winked at Sasha as the grumpy waitress appeared.

'We're closing now.'

'Right, come with me.' Tony stood up and they followed him.

'I'm not officially on this one, it's not my jurisdiction, but I got a call because of the similarities, and,' he sighed, 'because of the fuss in the media, so we're sharing information.'

'And? Surely there are enough similarities for you to drop the case against Eric? He couldn't have done this while you've got him locked up in a custody suite, could he? Are you going to let him go?'

Tony stopped suddenly and looked Sasha directly in the face. 'If I didn't know you better, I'd wonder if you hadn't done this to clear his name and get him out. He's your boyfriend and there you are standing outside the bleedin' window of the room the woman was murdered in. And then you tried to get away from the scene of the crime. I'm pulling your leg, you daft bag.' He laughed at Sasha's expression of disbelief.

'He's not my boyfriend,' she said mutinously.

They headed into Duck Lane and Tony nodded to the officer manning the police tape barrier to let him and Sasha through. 'Your friends will have to stay here.'

~

'I can't believe Sasha gets to go with him and not me,' Kay said indignantly, standing on tiptoes to watch them as they walked towards the hotel.

Smiling, Zoe placated her. 'I'm sure she'll tell us all about it, and she is a private investigator you know, so she's worked with D.S. Palmer before.'

'But I'm the one who called her about this, and found a way to see into the room.' Kay was still feeling mutinous.

'She's very impressed with you.'

'She is?' Kay smiled happily. 'We might end up working together. I feel like everything's coming together for me and my life is finally going to take off.'

They stood quietly, watching the movements of officials further along the lane, occasionally being jostled by an eager bystander, and moved aside for a news crew to film their live report.

A loud braying laugh sounded out from behind them and they looked round to see what was so funny.

'I'll be back in a sec.' Kay slipped away into the small crowd, reappearing a minute or two later.

'What was it?' Zoe was intrigued.

'One of those blokes back there looked familiar, there's something creepy about him. I dunno, maybe I'm seeing things, but I'm sure I've seen him–' She was interrupted by a microphone being shoved in her face, and turned to the reporter, squinting in the sudden bright light.

'Matt Savage, Universal News. What can you tell us about this evening's tragedy?'

Kay beamed into the camera. 'Kay Saunders, owner of Kay's Killer Blog.'

'*The* Kay Saunders? You're the one linking the murders of prostitutes together. Ladies and gentlemen, we're live in Duck Lane, Soho, with Kay Saunders, who warned the public of a serial killer on the prowl, but the police didn't listen.'

Kay nodded, her face reddening unbecomingly with excitement. 'That's right, this is the third murder of a prostitute by The Street Cleaner, and it won't be the last, I'm sure of it. Tonight's vicious murder was almost identical to Tuesday night's stabbing of an escort in Kensington. You can read all about it on my blog, which can be found at–'

'Yes, yes,' the reporter interrupted, not liking the impromptu hijacking of his report. 'So, you've seen the crime scene? What can you tell us about the victim?'

'I'll be posting an exclusive story on my blog tomorrow, but I can tell you that she was–'

Zoe nudged her sharply in the ribs, trying to stay off-camera, and shook her head frantically at Kay. *The girl was a liability.*

The camera swung away from Kay as police officers moved everyone aside to allow a van to move down the lane to the hotel.

'It looks like they're about to move the body,' Matt Savage announced to his viewers, forgetting about Kay in his excitement.

'Why did you stop me?' Kay huffed.

~

Tony led the way through the somewhat unprepossessing entrance. 'Welcome to the Duck Palace Hotel, known fondly by its regulars as the– well, I'll leave that to your imagination, but it's nothing more than a knocking shop, and not a glorified one. One of the last of the old kind in this area – as far as I know, there's only a couple of others, one in Glasshouse Street, and one in

Archer. The night receptionist, and I'm using the term loosely, is the lovely Shirley.'

Sasha looked around at the tiny space, noting the doors leading off to the left and right, and the narrow, enclosed staircase leading up to the right of the poky reception desk. Behind the desk was a small room with glass windows, through which she could see the back of a woman's head, her hair a vivid shade of orange. A television fixed high on the wall at the back of the small room blared, clearly the object of the woman's attention, irrespective of the murder that had been committed on her watch.

'You could walk in and out of here and she wouldn't have a clue. Does she even remember the victim coming in and getting a room?'

Tony turned the book on the counter to face them, pointing at the columns. 'They just sign in the time under their name and settle up at the end of each month. Officially, and I'm using the term loosely again, they're renting the rooms as private flats so what they do in there is their own business. Here's our victim's column – Pippa Robbins – went by the name Roberta. When we asked our Shirley here if they ever had tourists coming in for a room for the night she just cackled like a witch and shook her head. She did the same when we asked her if she'd seen who was accompanying Roberta. Not sure if she's all there, to be honest. If it hadn't been for one of the other girls who went to Roberta's room to pinch a couple of condoms, I doubt we'd have even known about the murder for a few days. It seems the rooms only get cleaned once a week if that.'

He raised his voice. 'Shirley, we're just going back upstairs to 2C, alright?' He turned back to Sasha, shrugging. 'If she didn't hear that, I doubt she'd have heard someone walking in and out quietly.'

They walked up the staircase, the dirty carpet tacky underfoot, and along to room 2C, where the murmur of voices could be heard.

'You can stick your head in the door, that's all. There's nothing to see, it's a tiny room with a bed and a table, and a loo and washbasin behind a thin partition wall.'

Sasha took in the scene from the doorway, noting the similarities to the scene of the escort's murder in Kensington.

'Seen enough?'

She nodded at Tony and they returned downstairs.

'So, she was stabbed through the bedding again? But the blood on the floor – it looks like she put up a bit of a fight. Same number of stab wounds? Which was–?'

'Looks like seven, but we'll wait for the official report. And yes, there appears to have been a bit of a struggle, which is the opposite of the girl in Eric's case. Hard to say whether there was any sexual activity with the killer, at first glance anyway. According to the book in reception, she had two other clients earlier in the evening. There were about fifteen condom wrappers in the bin, but seeing as the room's only cleaned once a week they could have been there for a few days.'

'She walked up the stairs with her killer, was attacked, forced into the bed, and was stabbed to death. Not quite the same as Eric's night of fun and games with his high-class escort...' Sasha mused.

'You sound like you don't want it to be the same.' Tony raised a quizzical eyebrow at her. 'Having second thoughts about him? Tell you what, come and see me tomorrow, I've got a copy of the crime scene photos being sent over to compare to the Freedom Hotel murder. Technically it's got nothing to do with your bloke's case, so you could have a crafty little butcher's, I suppose. I can't help it if I happen to have the other photos up on the board, can I? How does that sound?'

'Sounds good, thanks, Tone. I'd better get back to my friends.'

~

'We should go.' Sasha re-joined Zoe and Kay. 'Has she behaved herself?'

'Of course I have.' Kay chirped petulantly. 'I was just on telly until Zoe mucked it up.'

'Zoe did you a favour. I told you, this isn't a game. The last thing you want is to be shooting your mouth off on the news and attracting the attention of whoever's doing this, otherwise, you might be next.'

'Let's go.' Zoe yawned. 'We'll have to get a taxi, my station's probably closed by now.'

'What about you, where do you live, Kay?' Sasha asked her, concerned about the girl being alone at such a late hour.

'Earl's Court, but I can catch the tube, don't worry about me. I might hang around here a bit longer.'

No, we'll drop you home on the way. There's nothing more to see and I need to know you're home safely. Do that for me?'

'Alright.' Kay begrudgingly accepted. 'Thanks.'

They walked back along Duck Lane and turned towards Wardour Street, flagging down a passing cab, and mulled over the latest murder until Kay had been dropped off, gratefully arriving at Zoe's flat a little while later.

'A nightcap is called for, I think,' Zoe announced. 'Whisky?'

'Sounds good to me.' Sasha sank onto the settee. 'What a day.'

They switched the TV on, hopping from one news channel to another, settling on Universal News as Matt Savage's earlier report was replayed, and Kay's face appeared on the screen.

Sasha watched, concerned. 'She worries me, she's so determined to draw attention to herself. I keep telling her it's not a game.' She leaned forward suddenly.

'What is it, babes?'

Sasha shook her head. 'Probably nothing. I thought I saw a face I recognised in the crowd for a moment.'

'That's what Kay said. Same person, d'you think?'

'Doubt it, I'm pretty sure we don't know any of the same people.' Yawning, Sasha downed the last of her whisky. 'I'm ready for my bed. Your spare bed has never seemed more appealing than at this moment.'

~

Despite her tiredness, Sasha was awake early the next morning. Scrolling through the news on her phone, she read account after account of London's latest serial killer – The Street Cleaner – with articles urging women not to be out alone after dark. There were interviews with street prostitutes, their identities protected, as well as some with anonymous high-class call girls, but although they all allegedly expressed concern for their safety, they all insisted that they would continue their lives as usual.

She laid back on her pillow for a moment, wondering how Tony would react to the media reports, and how it would impact Eric's situation. She had to admit, the stabbing of both women appeared almost identical, even if they were from different walks of life. Well, she'd know more once she'd been to see him and found out everything that she could about both murders.

The sound of the shower switching off and the bathroom door opening and closing meant that Zoe was finished in the bathroom and, ignoring the email from her insurance broker containing an attached form for her to complete, she forced herself out of bed and into the shower, before getting the kettle on and putting some bread in the toaster, which she pushed down once she heard Zoe's hairdryer turn off.

'You're an angel.' Zoe blew her a kiss as she picked up the mug of tea and sipped it thankfully. 'How did you sleep, babes?'

'Like a log, I'm hardly awake now, even after a shower. How about you?'

'Same.' Zoe picked up a slice of buttered toast, took a large bite and munched happily. 'My favourite, hot, buttered toast. So, what are your plans? After last night's excitement I wish I didn't have to go to work, I'd rather go sleuthing with you and your new friend Kay.'

Sasha grinned. 'I wish you could. But I'm not sleuthing with my new friend Kay, as you so sweetly put it, I'm sleuthing all on my own, and it's going to be a boring one, so you're not missing out on anything, I promise. I'm meeting Tony and will hopefully get to see both sets of crime scene photos, I'm meeting Shuggy, Eric's friend – real name Harry – to see if he can shed any light on what happened on Tuesday evening, and then I'm going to Freedom Kensington to try to chat to the staff. So, if you can bear the suspense, I'll update you tonight over a bottle of wine, unless you're seeing James?'

'No, I'm letting him have a break from me, besides, you need looking after at the moment.'

'I'm fine, Zo, don't neglect James because of me.' Sasha finished her slice of toast and bent over to brush the crumbs into the bin, holding the counter as a sudden feeling of nausea hit her.

Zoe watched her, frowning. 'Something's not right, what is it?'

'Nothing, honestly, I just bent over too quickly.' She straightened, smiling. 'I suppose I should check what horrors Kay's exposed the world to this morning.'

A moment later she sat back, shaking her head. This girl was cheek personified. 'Listen to this. *Following my exclusive interview with suspect Eric Latimer's ex-fiancée, I can confirm that he did indeed spend the night at Freedom Kensington with a high-class escort, who was murdered that same night, and that the police continue to hold him pending further investigation. Sasha Blue, the suspect's ex, and a well-respected private investigator confided in me that she and the suspect are still friends and that she would work tirelessly to clear his name.*

'She makes it sound like I told her everything, but I hardly said a flippin' word. She goes on to say, *Sasha and I collaborated yesterday evening, as we checked out the crime scene of the serial killer's latest victim at The Duck Palace, Soho. We are both firmly convinced that the same hand wielded the knife that stabbed the prostitute multiple times, resulting in her death.*'

Sasha looked at Zoe in despair. 'This girl isn't doing me any favours with Tony. I'm going to have some major explaining to do when I see him now. She's promising further details of last night's murder in her next post and says she also has something shocking to reveal that her readers will see nowhere else, concerning the Kensington murder. What the hell's she on about?'

'Nothing, babes, and don't worry about Tony, I'm pretty sure he's got her number now. You said it yourself, she's got one hell of an imagination on her, which is probably why she's so good at writing her murder blog.'

'You're right, she's good at stringing her readers along.'

~

Well, this Sasha Blue should be grateful. So keen to clear her ex's name, meanwhile it had been done for her with last night's grubby little murder. Not that it mattered one jot what happened to him, that wasn't the point of the exercise. But why was she collaborating with the girl who wrote this blog? And what was this shocking revelation to come?

Tiredly, the hand clicked on various news articles as the media frenzy and scare-mongering blithely thrown about to cause panic among women on the streets was noted. Good, let them panic, they deserved it anyway.

Sitting back, the situation was assessed. No evidence had been left behind last night, it was all safely disposed of with little chance of recovery, and by now it had to be safely assumed that the chef's jacket had not been found from Tuesday's killing.

It was time to get a few hours' sleep, everything was in place for the next one, and murder did rather take it out of one. Last night had not been enjoyable in the least, purely a necessary evil for the greater good, but the next killing would bring immense pleasure...

~

Sasha walked into Kensington police station and handed her card to the officer manning the reception desk, saying, 'D.S. Palmer's expecting me.' A few minutes later she was standing with Tony as they both gazed at the two sets of crime scene photos.

'Have a good look, Sash, because I doubt I'll be able to wangle getting you in here again.'

She assessed the scenes rapidly. 'Both victims stabbed through the hotel bedding multiple times. Why through the bedding? Because their killer didn't want to look at them when he killed them? Both women fully dressed, which is odd, and with the duvets pulled up it's almost like they're sleeping.' Her eyes moved from the short blonde hair of the first victim, visible above the duvet, to the long, messy, and badly-dyed hair of the second victim, as it lay spread out on the pillow.

Tony nodded. 'Both stabbed seven times, not sure if there's any significance in that, and the first two stabs to

Roberta were made while she was standing. First victim, Lisa Pennington, appears to be a high-class prostitute, possibly an escort who took bookings through an agency, second victim, Pippa Robbins, definitely a low-class street prostitute. We can find no link to the murder of the prostitute earlier in the year, Sonia Clark, which also occurred in Soho.'

'But you can't rule it out.'

'No.'

'If Lisa Pennington was an escort wouldn't Eric have made a booking through her agency?'

'If he did, we're none the wiser. With no cards on her, and with his apparent lack of memory concerning how they both ended up together in the hotel room, we're no closer to finding out. We've got an address for her and I'll be going along with a couple of the lads to have a look a bit later. And no, you're not coming with me. This is as far as you go, you're lucky enough to have seen these–'

She put her hand on his arm. 'There's no whisky bottle. In the photos – there's no sign of the whisky bottle that Eric said was there.'

'Yeah, well, when it comes to that night, he doesn't seem to know his arse from his elbow regarding what went on in there. He was probably drinking whisky in the pub earlier. He got it wrong about the bottles of champagne as well.'

'But he does know, he's remembering bits and pieces. He was pretty sure about drinking the whisky, and he said that she would only drink the champagne, d'you remember? Like she'd been given instructions beforehand, which would make sense if she'd been booked.'

'But if she'd been booked it would usually be in advance, not at the last minute.'

'Eric said something about a last-minute call. What if she'd been booked at the last minute? Someone could have booked her for Eric, to set him up, why else would she say all that about only drinking champagne and having to leave straight away? He said he felt like he was on a high – could he have been drugged? In the whisky, maybe?'

'We'll only know about drugs once we get the results of his blood and urine tests, but you're not telling me that Eric never liked to indulge in a little something extra? It won't prove anything. So, unless he's got an enemy who disliked him so much they set him up for murder, then there's nothing here that lets him off the hook.' Tony checked his watch.

'Apart from the almost identical murder last night.' Sasha stared desperately at the photos – she was missing something, it was staring her in the face...

'Apart from that.' Tony conceded. 'But he's still suspect numero uno for this one. All we can say categorically is that he didn't kill Pippa Robbins last night. I'm afraid we're looking at two different killers who just so happened to use the same method – multiple stabbings aren't that uncommon, I'm afraid, sweetheart. Ask your little murder blogger friend.' Tony steered her from the room.

'So, you won't be releasing him?'

Tony shook his head. 'We've been granted an extension while we continue to examine the evidence.'

Sasha left the police station and pulled out her notebook, flicking through the notes she'd made after she'd last talked to Eric, to find a clean page, and scribbled down everything that she could remember from the photos, no matter how insignificant it seemed. Something would stand out to her in time.

She put the notebook in her bag and checked her watch. She was meeting Harry Reddingham, aka Shuggy, in the women's handbag section of Harvey Nichols. A strange place for a meeting but she'd gathered from his hurried call the previous day that he planned to buy his wife a birthday present and thought they could talk while he shopped. She had plenty of time and a walk would be nice, she decided, setting off.

~

After a pleasant, meandering walk, she finally wandered into Harvey Nichols about an hour later, breathing in the mingled scents of designer perfumes as she made her way to the handbags.

She'd been wondering how she would recognise Harry, but glancing around at the almost entirely female, designer-clad, and heavily laden with expensive-looking shopping bags, clientele browsing the bags, she grinned – the rather huge, messy-haired and helpless-looking man holding a small, bright pink bag and looking at it as if it might come alive and bite his hand, had to be him.

'Harry?'

'Ah, you must be Sasha.' Relief washed over his face. 'Please, call me Shuggy, everyone does.' He clasped her hand in a bear-like grip. 'I desperately need your help, I'm useless at this kind of thing. Would you mind? My secretary usually sorts these things out for me but she's on leave, hence my rather poor attempt at roping you in to help me. I hope I can repay the favour by helping our Erica out.'

'Not at all, there's nothing I like better than spending other people's money. Any clues as to what we're looking for?'

Shuggy looked around doubtfully. 'Lydia loves pink.' He indicated the bag in his hand, replacing it on its stand. 'She mentioned something called a tote. Does that mean anything to you?'

'It does, but this is a clutch. Over there.' She led the way to the tote bags, appraising them as she tried not to wince at the price tags.

'You called Eric, Erica… is that some kind of joke thing with you all? I know you all have these nicknames…'

Shuggy grinned boyishly. 'He looked like a girl when we were at school, all that blonde hair falling over his eyes.'

Nodding in amusement, Sasha turned over the price tag of the tote held out hopefully by Shuggy, turning it to show him.

'Good God. For a bag?' He dropped the bag onto the display and stepped back in shock.

'It's a top designer so it's top price. Here, this one's half the price, and this one…' She selected a bag from a lesser-known designer. 'Look, they're practically giving this one away…' she joked.

Shuggy glanced at the price tag through his spread fingers, laughing. 'I'll take it, at least we'll still be able to eat. Do people really pay those prices? For those bags?'

'Apparently. Funny old world, isn't it? All about priorities, I suppose, and how much you value material things. And talking of funny old worlds…' she said, as the assistant smiled, taking Shuggy's credit card.

Shuggy nodded. 'How the hell did Erica end up in bed with a dead escort beside him?'

'How do we prove he's not a murderer? I think he was set up somehow, but his memories of the night are too vague. He's relying on you to remember things.'

Shuggy took his purchase, thanking the bewildered-looking assistant, and he and Sasha made their way towards the exit, still talking.

'Where do I start? We'd arranged to have dinner on Tuesday night, and Eric was in good spirits, they were celebrating some acquisition or another, a property they had development plans for, so he was definitely in the drinking mood, taking ample advantage of the *Press for Champagne* button on the table at Bob's, as we affectionately refer to it.'

'Yes, he mentioned that to me. Sounds right up his street.'

Shuggy laughed. 'Indeed, and we both took full advantage of the wait time for the Beef Wellington, I'm afraid to say, which means we were well-watered by the time we ate our main course. Anyway, we sat around for a while after our meal, had a few more glasses of the red stuff, and then Eric suggested we join up with Red and the lads to continue the evening. Red is Rowan,' he added helpfully.

'Red and Dealer – that's Drew Merton, the chap they'd just done the deal with – had gone for early drinks when Eric joined me for dinner, and somewhere along the way they'd accumulated a few of the other fellows. By the time we met up with them at Bar Simone, it was quite a party, let me see, there was Red and Dealer, Ham, Franco, his friend Rain Man, and a business associate of Rain Man's who went by the name Max, if I'm not mistaken. Strange sort of chap, although Red seemed to get on with him. Matter of fact, he turned up at The Ship last night, while I was having a couple of pints with Red and Franco.'

They were standing outside on the pavement by now, and Sasha scribbled awkwardly in her notebook as they were jostled by passers-by.

'Shame about the murder last night. Franco and I walked along to see what all the fuss was about. Quite a crowd gathered there, reporters, the lot. Seems Red and Max had the same idea. Where was I?'

'Wait, what murder? The one in Duck Lane?'

'If Duck Lane's in Soho, then yes, we'd been drinking just around the corner. But I digress, back to the fateful Tuesday evening, and Bar Simone, although I'm not sure how reliable my testimony is going to be.'

Sasha sighed inwardly. *It was the same story every time with these guys...*

'We were a pretty loud bunch, I'm afraid, the result of far too many beverages, and somewhere along the line we appeared to attract several extremely attractive members of the opposite sex – but don't tell my wife that. We probably bought a few of them drinks, some unfortunate soul must have ended up with a large bar tab, and there was some flirting and phone numbers being shared, or rather, business cards being handed out. Somehow, we ended up with some escort agency cards on the table, at least one of the women had been handing them out, to much cheering and hooting. It was all in good fun, you understand.' He looked embarrassed.

'I should say here that I'm dreadfully sorry about you and Eric, we all are, but he assured us it was only temporary, hence our jokes about his being married, or as good as, when one of the girls enquired. In fact, and I'm rather proud of myself here, I moved the card away that Eric had been given and someone else must have picked it up because I noticed it had disappeared. Maybe one of the chaps fancied a bit of excitement, there were discount codes or something scribbled on the reverse of them. Anyway, long story short, various of us departed home to our respective spouses, and by the time I stumbled off I'm pretty sure there was just Erica, Red, and that chap Max left, and by the state of them all I find it hard to believe that Erica somehow managed to get himself to a hotel in Kensington and an assignation with an escort.'

'Shuggy, I can't thank you enough, you've been so helpful and given me plenty to think about. Maybe somewhere in your recollections of the night is a clue to what really happened.'

'Least I could do.' Shuggy hugged her suddenly. 'Thanks for helping me with this.' He held up the Harvey Nichols bag. 'But surely they'll let him go now, after last night's murder? The papers are full of it, women beware, prostitutes in danger, serial sex killer, the street sweeper they've called him, or something?'

Sasha nodded her head. 'You'd think so, yes, both were very similar, well, identical in some ways, but the trouble is, whichever way we look at it, Eric was in that room, in that bed, covered with her blood. What I have to figure out is if someone set him up, maybe because they had a grudge against him, or they just needed to provide the police with a suspect, or if he was simply in the wrong place at the wrong time. Hell, I don't know, maybe the killer didn't even know he was there, he'd definitely been out on the balcony smoking at some point.'

'The whole thing's awful.' Shuggy's face was creased in distaste at the thought of it all. 'That would just about be the worst luck ever, to go out for a smoke while someone pops in and murders the escort lying in your bed, and then, to crown it all, to be so drunk that you crawl into bed beside her dead body, and pass out.'

'Something like that could only ever happen to Eric.' Sasha smiled. 'Maybe it did.'

'Maybe it did, and if so, we'll all be relying on you to prove it.' He took her hands in his, squeezing them. 'Good luck. And call me if you need anything.'

'I will, thanks, Shuggy.' She walked off, feeling warmed by Shuggy's comments. He believed in Eric's innocence and had given her so much information, some of which, she was sure, would prove to be important. She hoped she'd got all the names right from his account of their Tuesday night drinking binge, they sounded like the weirdest bunch of friends ever. Turning to begin her walk back to Kensington for her plan to try and interview the staff at the Freedom Hotel, she slowed to a halt. *Friends...*

Was she missing something? Eric had been drinking with a group of men on the night of the call girl's murder, for which he was now the suspect, and last night four of the same men from that group had been drinking in Soho while Pippa Robbins was being murdered just around the corner from them. It could just be a coincidence, or it could mean something more, she just couldn't figure out what...

THE LAST OF THE GREAT STREET GIRLS

Walking into the entrance foyer of Freedom, Kensington, she paused, looking around. It was a strange set-up, having no reception desk, just the tablets for self-check-in. There was, she noted, a call button if help was needed. The lifts were inaccessible without a key card, and the only doorway led as per its sign to the bar and restaurant, where she now headed – she might as well have a spot of lunch while she was here.

Thanking the waitress for the bar menu, she glanced down the list of options, selecting the quiche and resisting the urge to add a portion of chips, but ordering a Coke for a much-needed sugar rush.

Her drink arrived, the ice cubes clinking invitingly in the glass, and she took a large swig before bringing up the hotel's website on her phone and studying it. The Freedom Hotels numbered five and were scattered around London in convenient locations, all within about half an hour or so from each other – namely, Camden, Chelsea, City of London, Kensington, and Soho. They all boasted small restaurants and bars, the restaurants being open twenty-four hours and the bars offering room service during the night.

Sasha leaned back thoughtfully, wondering how to make enquiries about Tuesday night's murder without directly asking about it, and then she had an idea – Tony might have told her to keep her nose out of Eric's escort murder, as she tended to think of it, but he was quite happy for her to look into last night's murder in Soho, where the Freedom brand happened to have a hotel... She put her phone aside as the waitress brought her lunch.

'Thanks, this looks delicious,' she said, smiling. 'I can't believe your restaurants are open twenty-four hours. Do you ever have to work nights?'

'We work on a rota, so yeah, sometimes, but I don't mind, it's normally quiet so we get to put our feet up a bit.'

'Yes, I can imagine that nights are quieter, well, not for the staff at that other place last night in Soho though, when that poor woman was murdered. Different hotel, of course. I was there working on the case,' she explained helpfully to the girl's quizzical expression.

'You're police then?'

'Well, a private investigator, but I often get called in as a consultant.'

'So, you know about our murder here on Tuesday night then? We're not supposed to talk about it, of course, bad for business.' The waitress shrugged. 'But that murder last night wasn't at our hotel, scary though, all these women getting stabbed to death.' She shuddered. 'Makes you wonder if you'll be next, my boyfriend won't have me coming home on my own when I work late anymore. Course, it's prostitutes it said on the news, but how does the killer know, that's what I want to know?'

The girl was clearly up for a chat. 'Good point, I suppose we've just got to be careful, but they *were* both killed in hotel rooms. Er, were you working that night? Tuesday, I mean?'

'No, I was off, but Henry was on bar duty.' She nodded her head towards the man behind the bar. 'My mate, Samantha, she was on last night in Soho, said some bloke stayed there and gave Fran a right old time of it. Said she was quite shaken up – I bet she's glad she's taken up boxing classes, maybe I should sign up as well – Samantha reckoned he was well dodgy.'

'Er, Fran is?'

'Oh, sorry, Fran's our night floater, she's on-call for check-in problems. Me and Samantha were saying, how do you know who anyone is? It could have been him, couldn't it? He could have killed that girl then booked himself into our hotel as an alibi. He even made Fran go up to his room with him to check it and tried to make her have a drink with him in his room, no wonder she was shaken up, Samantha said he was a creepy bastard. Listen to me, I sound like a detective, don't I? You'd better eat your quiche, it'll be going cold.'

'Yes, thanks, er, Donna. Listen, I'll need to chat with a few other staff workers if that's okay.'

'Well, I could call Mrs Carter, she's in charge?'

'Oh no, that won't be necessary, I don't want to cause a big fuss. Perhaps you can just show me where to find them after I've had my lunch? If you don't mind? You've been so helpful, and offered some real insights into the case.'

'I have?' Donna beamed. 'Well, alright then, I'll see you later.'

Well, that worked like a dream, Sasha thought, tucking into her quiche ravenously and making short work of it.

She settled her bill with Donna, tipping her generously, and suggested that she have a few words with Henry.

'Yes, I was on duty Tuesday night, but nothing happened out of the ordinary down here, as I told the cops.' Henry leaned on the bar counter, happy to chat. 'All the action was going on upstairs and none of us knew, terrible to think about.' He shook his head sadly. 'I probably sent drinks up to their room, imagine, sending up a tray of drinks to a murderer.'

'Did anyone order any champagne at all?'

'A few, it's popular with the late-nighters, we sell it by the glass so it's a bit more affordable. Oh, and room thirty-three ordered a bottle sent up, but I already told your people that.'

'Yes, we have a note of that, thanks. What about whisky? Anyone order a bottle?'

'No, that would be a bit out of the ordinary, bottles of wine maybe, but not generally whisky.'

'Hmm, so, er, do guests ever come down to the bar to get their drinks for their room?'

'No, wouldn't make any sense, that's why we've got room service. We're open to the public though, so we get people here all the time 'til last orders, that's one in the morning.'

'Right, and you didn't have any customers who were acting strangely or anything?'

'Nope. We had a bunch of drunk blokes, three, I think it was, making a bit of noise, that was quite late, seemed like they were waiting for someone. One of them had red hair, ginger, like, you know, kept laughing too loud, and the blonde bloke looked like he didn't know what planet he was on. He kept drinking though, credit to him for that. Thought I might have trouble with them, to be honest, but they moved on. Oh, and a woman who looked a bit worse for wear, you know, she'd had a few too many, she bought a bottle of champagne to take away – paid cash as well, best part of two hundred quid for the bottle.' Henry whistled admiringly. 'She gave me twenty quid as a tip, so I was a happy boy.'

'Well, thanks, Henry, you've added some important information to our enquiries, you both have. Donna, if there's any chance that I could have a quick word with the kitchen staff...'

She followed a nervous-looking Donna down to the kitchen, the reason for the girl's nervousness making herself clear immediately.

'Can I help you?' The woman, who had to be Mrs Carter, appeared in front of her.

'This lady's with the police, Mrs Carter, she needs to speak to Alfredo.'

'Do you have identification?' Mrs Carter eyed Sasha suspiciously. 'Only we've had some news reporters finding their way in here under false pretences. The other day it was a girl impersonating a representative from Laundry King, I only found out after I called them to follow up on our meeting.'

Suppressing a smile, Sasha handed Mrs Carter one of her cards. 'Sasha Blue, I'm a private investigator and police consultant.' She paused while Mrs Carter frowned and studied her card meticulously. 'You'll be aware of the murders lately, one in this hotel, and one last night in Soho?'

'Oh yes.' Mrs Carter tutted. 'Thank God it wasn't in another of ours, no one would want to stay with us.'

'Of course, but something's cropped up concerning a guest who checked in at Freedom Soho last night, so I'll also need to speak to, er, Fran, I believe it is? She works as some kind of stand-in receptionist or something?'

'Oh, poor dear, there weren't any problems were there? The poor girl's such a brave soul, working nights, travelling from one hotel to another. It's such lonely work, I said to her, are you sure you wouldn't rather work a day job now that you're on your own? But she said, no, it suits her. She lost her husband in March, poor thing, Adrian, seven years they'd been married, a real charmer he was too, very handsome,' Mrs Carter added. 'But you'll find no receptionists at our hotels, the guests generally check themselves in, and between you and me I'm still not sure if that's such a good idea. Small issues are dealt with by a member of staff from the restaurant, no matter whether it's day or night, but if it's something tricky then Fran's on call at night. Head of housekeeping generally deals with issues during the day, which would be yours truly, for Kensington, and on that note, I should get on. You can't miss Alfredo, he's the one shouting and waving a large knife about.' Mrs Carter waved her arm towards the chef as she turned to leave.

'Thank you, er, so how would I get in touch with Fran to find out about last night's Soho guest who had a problem? Does she base herself at one of the hotels, or...?

'Well, you're in luck there, there's a large booking at our Chelsea hotel tomorrow night, about two busloads of foreign businessmen attending a conference, I believe, so Fran mentioned that she'd probably stick around there as it was the most likely to have problems. I'm sure she won't mind you popping in for a quick chat. Fran Baxter, that's her name.'

Sasha thanked Mrs Carter and turned to brave the knife-wielding lunatic known as Alfredo.

'I suppose you want to take the rest of my knives away?' He screeched at Sasha before she opened her mouth. 'I tell them, how am I supposed to make the best food in London when they take all my knives away? What, they think I go and murder the guests in their beds in the middle of the night after I've cooked for them the Chateaubriand?'

So, Tony's guys had been back then... 'Alfredo? It's nice to meet you, I'm Sasha, and I promise you I don't want your knives.'

'Stefan.' Alfredo yelled at the man sidling out of the kitchen. 'Come and talk to the lady. You tell her about the knife.'

'Nothing to tell.' Stefan sounded bored. 'I tell them everything I know already. I wash up the knives as usual, by hand, because Alfredo is very fussy.' A snort sounded from behind Sasha. 'Is a good thing.' He added hurriedly. 'I put them back in their place and I go home, that is all.'

'And you didn't notice anything about any of the knives the next day? Or anything else that struck you as strange?'

Stefan beckoned Sasha to follow him, turning to her and speaking in a low voice. 'Is Alfredo who acts strange. First, he says his knife is missing, then he finds it, then he says is dirty, then he says I lose his chef's jacket.' He rolled his eye. 'Everyone says they lose things, knives, uniforms, glasses, they all come poking around here yesterday, then they look at me like I am to blame, but I do nothing.'

'He does nothing.' Alfredo sneered as he came up beside them. 'Then why we pay you, eh?'

'Now he think *he* pays me.'

'Okay, I'm sure no one's accusing anyone else of doing anything they shouldn't.' The smells from the kitchen were beginning to make her feel queasy.

'You go now, lady, we don't have knife and we don't have jacket, and we don't have jobs if we stand around talking all day.' Alfredo waved a raw leg of lamb in the air, wiping his bloody hand on his apron.

She left the kitchen hurriedly, relieved to escape the heat and the sights and smells of uncooked meat and blood. Something Alfredo had said had struck a chord with her, she realised, as she retraced her steps and left the hotel... she also needed to work and get paid, and trying to help Eric wasn't putting money in her bank account...

~

'What are you busy with?'

Sasha jumped. 'Zo, I didn't hear you come in. How was your day?'

'Boring compared to yours, probably. We might have sold a painting, but she was one of those floaty interior decorator types, you know the ones, spending other people's money and wasting a lot of our time while they drink the complimentary glass of wine and waltz around holding up fabric swatches to see if the colours in the artwork match the curtains. Flavia goes crazy.' Zoe struck a pose, imitating her boss at the art gallery. 'They need to see the art, Zoe, not the colours. The artist pours their soul into their painting and these imposters are concerned with whether it matches the colour of their stupid stair carpets. Pah! Who has carpet on the stairs anyway? Then they must go to the department store and buy a set of prints.'

'Poor Flavia.' Sasha grinned. 'Good impression though.'

'Thanks. Glass of wine? Then you can tell me what you've been up to.'

Sasha caught Zoe up with her news, which didn't seem like much, she decided, and they moved on to dinner deliberations, debating the merits of the contents of Zoe's freezer rather unenthusiastically. Neither of them felt like fish in breadcrumbs, or steak and ale pie, and certainly not the rather sad-looking container of vegetable soup languishing in the bottom drawer which appeared to have been in there for over two years.

'Let's go out,' said Zoe. 'We can walk down to the little bistro, they do pastas and things.'

'Sounds good, but tomorrow I'll get some bits in and do some home cooking. The thing is, I've got to watch the pennies a bit, I'm not earning anything. That's actually what I was busy with, catching up on my e-mails and seeing if there was a case I could take on.'

'Then tonight's on me. We can discuss which case you should take, and tomorrow you can cook us one of your delicious meals. Deal?'

'Deal.' Sasha nodded, smiling.

'Perfect. We'll have another drink and then head out.'

A couple of hours later they were halfway through their second bottle of wine, having shared a huge creamy salmon carbonara, and were sitting out at their pavement table, pondering Sasha's options.

'I'm not sure, Zo, I've never really been keen on the suspicious wife thing, the whole following the husband around, taking photos, trying to catch him cheating on her.'

'But she'll pay well, babes, check out her feed on Graffic, looks like she's loaded.' Zoe held her phone out to

Sasha, and they stared at the photos of the woman in exotic locations, of her shopping trips to Harrods, and of her new car given to her by her husband for her fortieth birthday. 'Looks like she enjoys spending his money, she definitely doesn't work, she's too busy shopping and going on holiday.'

'So, she wants me to find her the proof so that she can get a nice fat divorce settlement, I suppose. What about this one? She lives in Belgravia and thinks her nanny is stealing from her. But she wants me to work there as a cook while I investigate.'

'Well, you can certainly cook, but do you want to be stuck in someone's house? You're still going to be investigating Eric's case, aren't you?'

'Yes, I have to, even if it sounds stupid. Half of me wants to let him rot, but the other half says I have to find out the truth, whatever it turns out to be.'

'But you don't think he did it, do you?'

Sasha shook her head. 'No, not in a million years, and I don't think Tony does either, but unless we find something, he's likely to go down for it, the circumstantial evidence is just too strong. Listen to this one, she said, giving Zoe a brief synopsis of the enquiry. 'I need your assistance with a difficult situation. I need you to deal with my gardener before he causes a problem. My husband must be kept out of it. I was never convicted of anything, the case against me was dropped, and we thought we'd heard the end of it, and now this. I require you to handle this with the utmost discretion and look forward to your earliest response.'

'Curiouser and curiouser,' Zoe leaned forward, lighting a cigarette and offering the packet to Sasha.

'Thanks.' Sasha took a cigarette, smiling. 'Her name's Brenda Mosham, let's profile her before we look her up.'

Clapping her hands, Zoe fired a question at Sasha. 'Where does she live?'

'Somewhere well to do obviously, she does have a gardener, after all, maybe Kensington, yeah, I'm going with Kensington, because of the husband's job.'

'What's his job?'

'Politician.'

'How old is she?'

'Er, she'll be in her early sixties, I'd say.'

'Does she work?'

'She used to, perhaps a secretary, yes, her style of writing sounds secretarial, and that's where she met her husband, then she gave up work, so she's a housewife. I'm guessing he still works, hence the concern about discretion.'

Zoe leaned back, whistling, as she tapped on her phone. 'Not bad, Sasha Blue, private investigator extraordinaire.'

'Tell me then.' Sasha laughed, what did I get wrong?'

'She lives in Chelsea, not Kensington, but close enough. She's sixty-two, she met her husband, Sir David Mosham, who received his knighthood for contributions to British retail, when she worked as his personal assistant, before leaving work to become a housewife.'

'So... I got it all wrong then.'

'You were close on her age and her job, and about her being a housewife.'

'You're too kind. I suppose I could go and see her although, if I didn't know better, it sounds like she wants me to off her gardener. Is there anything about the case against her that they dropped?'

'No, don't think so, now you'll have to go, to find out what she's supposed to have done, and to find out why she wants you to take out her gardener. Sasha Blue, hitwoman for hire. I kind of like the sound of that. Here, let's finish this last drop of wine.'

'Compliments of the owner.' The waiter smiled, placing two shot glasses down on their table.'

'Oh, my word, Limoncello, delicious, thank you.' Sasha held up the ice-cold glass. 'Here's to a promising side case and me earning some dosh – as long as it doesn't involve my having to take anyone out, as you so nicely put it. You've been watching too many films.' Laughing, she downed her drink.

'I think we were supposed to sip it,' said Zoe, as they slammed their empty glasses down on the table.

'Oops, let's get another one and try again.'

'Let's get drunk,' said Zoe, 'we deserve it.'

'We do deserve it,' Sasha agreed, laughing and ordering more drinks, thinking how nice it was to forget all her troubles and just spend time with her best friend.

~

Kay groaned, running to the bathroom again and leaning over the toilet. Why did she have to get sick now, right in the middle of the most exciting time of her blogging career? She was letting her readers down, they'd been promised her exclusive report on the Duck Palace stabbing and she hadn't even been able to face switching her laptop on all day.

She flushed the toilet, washing her face and staring despondently at her wan reflection. It was so unfair, Sasha was probably out there investigating, and she could barely make it between her bed and the bathroom. She crawled back to bed miserably, thinking longingly about her big reveal of the blood-stained chef's jacket. Maybe she'd feel up to it tomorrow.

~

Nothing. The girl had nothing. All this talk of the big reveal, hints of something shocking about the Kensington killing that no one else knew, it was all talk. She hadn't even had anything to say about last night's murder, which was a pity as it had been her insistence that a serial killer was doing the rounds and murdering prostitutes, that had got everyone going. Still, the media had taken up the cudgels on her behalf, convinced now, as was the general public, that women on the streets were in danger.

It was time to relax completely about the chef's jacket. If nothing was posted tomorrow then it could be considered safely gone. Maybe a small, celebratory drink was in order, the night stretched ahead and sleep wasn't an option.

'I'll have a vodka and lemonade, please.'

~

'Here, have a smoke.' Sorbet held out her packet to Crystal. 'We're missing a few of the girls tonight.'

'No surprise there,' said Crystal, her blond hair falling forward as she lit her cigarette. 'Cops are going round moving the girls on, telling them it's not safe.'

Sorbet watched the cars moving along Charing Cross road. 'Maybe we should walk through to the square, find ourselves a few drinkers leaving the pubs on foot.' She smoothed her hand over her lilac-coloured wig and adjusted her hotpants.

'Giving up already?' A voice called from a doorway as they walked along.

'You shouldn't be on your own at the moment, with what's been happening.' Crystal peered into the darkness.

'I'm doing just fine.' Gretel stepped forward, looking down at the two shorter women, her height exaggerated by her stiletto boots. 'Three customers tonight and no problems.'

'Be too late if there was a problem, look what happened to Roberta last night. Although I'd like to see any of them try that with me.' Felicia strode up to them, her Amazonian figure and striking looks attracting a hoot and a wolf whistle from a passing car. Her dark skin gleamed in the glow from the streetlights, and she grinned, red lips baring around white teeth, as she waved at the man slowing down and pulling into the kerb.

The three women watched as Felicia leaned in provocatively, speaking to the man, before walking round and getting into the passenger seat, giving them a wave over the roof of the car as it drove off.

'Roberta wasn't the only one who had trouble last night,' said Sorbet, as she and Crystal made their way to Soho Square. 'Lacey had a cutter. He sliced her up nicely while he had her up against the wall in Livonia Street, bloody bastard. She got one in herself though, twisted his hand round and got his arm. – and got a punch in the head for her troubles. She won't be able to work for a couple of days, poor thing.'

'D'you think it was the same person? The one who's killing the girls?' asked Crystal worriedly.

'No, if they hurt, they don't kill, they just get their kicks out of hurting us. Like the one who gave me this beauty.' She lifted her top, exposing the angry bruise spreading from one side of her stomach to the other. 'She said she's seen him before lurking around the area, said you can't forget him, not once you've seen his dead eyes. Wonder if it was the same bloke? My one had weird empty eyes. They were empty while I gave him what he wanted, and they were still empty when he punched me in the stomach, not even a glimmer of excitement in them. Roberta's room will be going begging now, wonder who'll take it?'

'No one at the moment, there's a copper hanging around the Duck Palace.'

'Bummer,' said Sorbet. 'Alright, darling? See anything you like?' She moved away from Crystal, sauntering up to the man who had just exited the massage parlour ahead of them.

'He's already had something he likes,' sniggered Crystal, as the man scurried off.

'Hard to imagine what it was like here back in the day, innit? Too many punters to keep up with, so they say.' Sorbet looked around. 'Now we skulk around, fighting over the odd few customers. The last of the great street girls. We'll have to sign up with an agency eventually, maybe it would be safer...' She sighed, as Crystal nodded.

'And give up half our earnings. Didn't help that escort on Tuesday night did it though? Felicia said there's good business near Paddington Station, we could try there one night?'

'Too much competition,' said Sorbet, knowingly. 'Here we go, couple of young 'uns coming up.' They stopped, sticking their hips out and smiling at the pair of men approaching.

'Don't think we were the right sex. Fancy something to eat?'

'Go on then. I could murder a Maccy D's.'

WHERE DID OUR LOVE GO?

The sound of her phone sounded excruciatingly loud, and Sasha pushed back the duvet, reaching for her phone to check the time. Exclaiming, she jumped out of bed and ran through to Zoe's room to find it empty.

'Zo?' she called as she walked into the living room, finding it equally empty. A piece of paper propped up on the kitchen counter caught her eye and she read it, smiling. Well, at least one of them had woken up. Poor Zoe, she thought, running a hand through her hair and feeling bad. They'd overdone it last night but Zoe had managed to head off to work, although if her note was anything to go by, she blamed Sasha for leading her astray and was begging for a quiet night. Well, it wouldn't do either of them any harm, she decided, heading for the bathroom. She'd shower and then go to the supermarket for groceries, maybe she'd do them a roast, something mumsy and comforting, and they wouldn't drink. And, she added to her thoughts, it had been Zo doing all the leading astray last night, not her, cheeky cow. Hadn't it?

Fortified by some tea and toast, she went to the supermarket, throwing in a chicken and a pile of vegetables to her basket, virtuously avoiding the wine aisle, before doubling back at the last minute to pick up a three for the price of two deal. *Just in case...*

~

There was nothing left inside her body, it felt hollow like she'd wrung it out to get the last drops of anything out. Like an old dishcloth, Kay thought, which is probably what she looked like. She hadn't had to traipse to the bathroom for the last four hours, had managed to fall asleep, finally, at about six o'clock this morning and was, hallelujah, feeling hungry. Gently easing her fragile body from the bed, she reached for her dressing gown, wrapping herself up in its softness as she slipped her feet into her pink, fluffy slippers. She slowly made her way to her kitchenette, where she filled the kettle, switched it on, and slid a slice of bread into the toaster. She'd try one piece of toast, no marg, just a dab of marmite, and see how she got on. If that stayed down, she could move onto the big stuff a bit later, maybe beans on toast.

With her tea and toast on the coffee table, Kay wriggled her bottom to get comfortable on the settee, before savouring each small bite of the dry toast as she flicked through the news stations on the television. All appeared to have been quiet on London's streets last night then. She switched to Universal News just as they played a re-run of Matt Savage's interviews at The Duck Palace in Soho from Thursday night, and she couldn't help grinning proudly when she saw her face on camera. She re-played her thirty-second interview a few times, frowning at a sound in the background. That laugh – like a donkey – that's what had made her look round, and then she'd thought she'd seen someone she recognised. Picking up her phone, she clicked on her voice note from that night to listen to her observations. Her stomach suddenly turned horribly, and she reluctantly unfolded herself from the settee and headed for the bathroom, after which she tearfully climbed back into her bed, feeling desperately sorry for herself, to only resurface in another four hours' time.

~

Blasting a music radio channel playing eighties hits, Sasha sang along tunelessly to the Human League as Phil Oakey repeatedly questioned whether the girl did, in fact, want him or not. She'd peeled the potatoes and par-boiled them, and they now sat in their dish, sprinkled with olive oil, sea salt, and rosemary, ready to pop in the oven tonight. Her chicken was marinating in a red wine and garlic sauce, so she was just left with the veggies.

She encouraged Eileen to come on, together with Kevin Rowland, as Dexys Midnight Runners pounded out, while she chopped and steamed cauliflower and broccoli, whipping up a white sauce and pouring it over them in their dish, before sprinkling some cheese on top. All the time, her mind wandered over everything she'd learned so far, and as her hands made order of her vegetables in the kitchen, so her mind made order of all the questions flying around in her head.

There was already a bottle of champagne in the room according to Eric, but they'd ordered another one. So where did the third one come from? The one hidden by the overhanging duvet? Why had a champagne glass disappeared, together with Eric's alleged bottle of whisky? Of course, Eric could always have thrown everything from the balcony, nothing was out of the realm of consideration when he was drunk, but surely that would have been noted somewhere? The indisputable fact about the whole dreaded night was that Eric and his friends had been well and truly drunk. She thought about his friend and colleague, Rowan Penrose, what an unpleasant bloke and that laugh of his... her hand stilled as she mashed the soft carrot and butternut... *that laugh of his...* hadn't Donna, the waitress at Freedom Kensington, mentioned someone laughing loudly in the bar? No, it had been the barman, Henry, and he'd said something about red or ginger hair but, deflated, she remembered that he'd told her they'd moved on. But one of them had been blonde, and Eric was blonde... was it possible that Eric, Rowan, and one of the other blokes, had gone to the bar together? But if so, why had Rowan kept quiet about it, especially when his friend and business partner was in police custody as a suspect for murder?

Lisa Pennington had told Eric that she was leaving, that she *had* to go, but what if she'd been the woman Henry had told her about, the one looking a bit worse for wear? What if she'd bought a third bottle of champagne and taken it back up to the room? Yes, and paid cash, cash Eric reckoned had been pinched by the police, idiot that he was, although his wallet did appear to be missing... But so what at the end of the day? What did any of it prove?

Her thoughts returned to Eric, sadly, as she asked the same question as Marc Almond – where did our love go? Was it ever love? Yeah, tainted love, more like, she snorted at her wit as she spooned the carrot and butternut into a dish and dropped a blob of butter on the top.

The radio station had moved onto a new show featuring hits with a friendship theme and was playing the theme song from Friends. Well, The Rembrandts had got that right, she was soon going to be broke, and it definitely hadn't been her day, her week, her month, and certainly not her year. Which reminded her – she should reply to Mrs Brenda Mosham, and arrange a time to go and see her about her gardener, she thought, as she mixed sauteed leeks with the peas and liberally seasoned the dish.

Standing back, she admired her handiwork. Yes, a delicious and filling roast chicken dinner was just what she and Zoe needed, and if they managed to resist the lure of the three bottles of red wine lined up on the counter then perhaps they'd get themselves off to bed at a decent hour, even if she did still have to shoot through to Chelsea a bit later. Zoe was the best friend she could ever have, always there for her, and never more so than at the moment. I'll always be there for you too, Zo,' she said, as the song drew to a close.

But what about Eric, she pondered, as she listened to the sweetly sad ballad by Carole King, reminded of all her precious records that she'd lost in the fire. Would his friends come running, or would they desert him, for surely this was his darkest night? One of them must know something that could help him? She still had Franco, Max, and Rain Man to chat to, so maybe one of them would give her something helpful.

Her phone rang and she answered the call from Shuggy, wondering what he wanted.

'Sasha, sorry to disturb on a Saturday, but I've just had an intriguing call from old Franco, something that Rain Man said to him. He seems to think that some of the chaps might have, er, indulged, to put it delicately, on the night that Erica got himself into so much trouble. I just thought you should know, maybe one of them used one of the cards the woman was handing out from the escort agency. Look, I don't know the first thing about investigating and all that, but you'll know what to do. You've got their phone numbers and all that stuff, I suppose?'

'I have, and thank you, Shuggy, I'll try to give Franco a call, and see if we can meet up.'

'You'll be able to chat to both of them this evening, if you're out and about, seems they're hitting the bars in Soho again. Between you and me, I rather gather Franco fancies himself as a bit of super sleuth, something about Cherchez la femme and whatnot. Oh, and Lydia loved her bag, it seems I've fully redeemed myself, and thanks to you in no small measure.'

She smiled into her phone, Shuggy was really very sweet. 'It was a pleasure, Shuggy, I'm pleased she liked it, and thanks for the call.'

'Well, goodbye then, and, er, be careful if you're out on your own in the evening, can't be too careful by the sounds of it.'

She thanked Shuggy and turned her attention to Brenda Mosham, sending out an email and receiving a reply within minutes. Mrs Mosham could receive her at her home at five o'clock, while her husband was at the club.

Next, she called Franco, introducing herself and agreeing, after a brief chat, to meet him and Rain Man in

Bar Soho at around nine-thirty that evening. Frantically doing mental calculations in her head, she called Zoe. If she put the chicken in the oven on low, when she went to see Mrs Mosham, Zoe could throw the potatoes in when she got home from the gallery. By the time she got back, they'd be able to have an early dinner and then she could go to meet the guys in Soho, and after that, she could head to Freedom Chelsea to have a quick chat with the woman called Fran Baxter. It was a bit of a long shot, but worth following up on an allegedly threatening male guest who had checked in on the night a prostitute was murdered just around the corner from the hotel in Soho.

'No, you're not going on your own, not at night, babes. I'll come with you, James can come too and protect us from any knife-wielding serial killers we come across.' Zoe's voice was firm.

'Tell him to come for dinner first then, payment in advance for his protection services.'

Feeling a little grotty after all her cooking, Sasha took a quick shower and headed off to see her potential client.

~

Kay towel-dried her hair after her shower, feeling marginally better after her second sleep, and made herself a cup of tea. She had to post something on her blog, that was how it worked. If you snooze you lose, she muttered to herself, as she switched on her laptop. She'd write something about the Duck Palace killing, maybe pop on a couple of exclusive crime scene photos – heavily censored, of course. She had to be careful, that Tony bloke from the cops would love any opportunity to haul her in and give her a hard time, she was sure of it.

She added a link to the clip of her short interview with Matt Savage, *after all, it was the first time that she'd ever been on telly*, inserted three photos, and went heavy on the serial killer angle throughout her article, sitting back and reading it through as she pondered a title, finally deciding on *Deadly Date at The Duck Palace*. It hadn't been a date, of course, but it tripped nicely off the tongue. She finished with the one-liner: *London's serial killer isn't a dead duck yet*. Not bad, Kay conceded, considering her weakened state. She pressed post, before sending the link to Sasha and asking her what she was up to – best to try to stay in the loop.

~

Poor Kay, thought Sasha, reading the girl's message as she sat on the tube to Sloane Square, still, at least if she was feeling poorly then she wasn't out getting herself into trouble. She read her latest blog post, wondering how Tony would feel about the photos – Kay might have censored them but it was still a crime scene under investigation.

She sent Kay a reply, telling her that she'd give her a call tomorrow, that she was following up a few leads that evening, and that she hoped no one would be murdered that night, adding a get well soon message and smiley face, before alighting and heading along the King's Road, looking in at the window displays of the clothing boutiques and trying not to cringe at the prices.

These houses must cost a bomb, she thought, as she walked along the row of properties bordering Wellington Square, before turning in at the last house in the row, number thirty-six. Sir David Mosham had certainly done alright for himself. The door was answered by a maid. *A maid*. And Sasha informed the woman that Mrs Mosham was expecting her.

'Take a seat in the drawing room, please, miss, I'll inform Lady Mosham.'

Sasha followed her through to the rather austere room overlooking the small front garden, and took a seat, looking around at the unenchanting paintings on the walls. The room felt cold, and she shivered, wishing she'd brought a cardigan with her.

'Lady Mosham,' announced the maid, disappearing silently, as Brenda Mosham made a scurried entrance.

Sasha studied her with interest once they'd completed introductions and she'd declined the offer of tea. Brenda Mosham looked every bit of her sixty-two years, something she fought against, judging by her liberal application of make-up and her style of dress. Her foundation had sunk into the creases of her face and her dark lipstick bled into the wrinkles around her mouth. She sat down opposite Sasha, pulling at her short skirt as she crossed one leg over the other, her platform shoes looking slightly ridiculous.

'Cigarette?' She lit a cigarette, before holding the packet out to Sasha, who declined politely.

'Did you see him? Was he out there?' Brenda Mosham suddenly jumped up, rushing to one of the front windows and peering around the lace curtain. 'He might be in the back garden, come with me. He watches me all the time.'

Raising her eyebrows, Sasha followed the woman along the hallway and into a large living room at the rear of the house, where Brenda Mosham now stood at the French doors, looking out.

'D'you think he's gone? He looks so like Thomas. David said that's why I hired him, which is absurd.'

'Er, Thomas?' The woman was batty, surely.

'Yes, Thomas, that's when it all started. He was infatuated with me, you see. He wouldn't leave me alone, he wanted me to leave David to be with him.'

'Er, where did you meet him?' *She had to start somewhere if only to get to the finish line as soon as possible.*

'He was Petra's son, a dear boy, he couldn't help his feelings for me. We were just trying to help him after our previous gardener left, that was Rick. He was a problem so David got rid of him. His girlfriend even came round here shouting at me and demanding money. She accused me of trying to seduce him. The nerve of the woman, cheap bit of low class if ever I saw one. David had to give them money to shut them up. But the worst thing was that I saw them one day when I was shopping, and they laughed at me. Do you know what she said? She said, did I want Rick to take his shirt off so I could ogle him? And then they laughed.'

Right... things were becoming clearer... 'So, what went wrong with Thomas? How old was he exactly?'

'The dear boy was nineteen, such a sweet thing, terribly handsome, and nothing was too much trouble. I used to let him bring his friends here to sit in the garden, all of them laughing and having fun. He'd even come in and help me with small problems around the house during the day, you know, a stiff drawer, or a difficult tap, that sort of thing. I couldn't stop him from developing feelings for me. I tried to resist, of course, said all the right things, but I was the one in the wrong when David came home early and caught him trying to kiss me. He had to leave, David said it was for the best, and then there were the wretched accusations against me. They got the police involved, but David sorted it all out. Come upstairs.'

Sasha followed as the woman rushed up the stairs and into a room overlooking the rear garden and an outhouse.

'That's where Steven showers after work and gets changed. Look, there he is.'

Sasha gazed down at the outhouse, its large window giving a clear view into a room with an open shower and a bench seat below a row of towel hooks. The naked figure of a young man appeared, pausing to stare up at the window with a grin, before stepping into the shower, and she looked away, noticing Brenda Mosham's hungry expression as she stared down at the man.

'Let's go back downstairs, Mrs Mosham, and you can tell me a little more.'

'Call me Brenda. Did you see the way he looked up at me? He's taunting me. I went in there last week, purely to ask him something, that's all. I didn't realise he'd be in the shower, of course, but he was unkind to me, and he said some terrible things. He'd made me think he liked me, you see.' Her eyes welled with tears as she looked mournfully at Sasha. 'I had to give him a thousand pounds,' she whispered, 'or he said he'd tell David. That's why I need you to deal with him, David can't hear about it. He must be dismissed immediately, you'll know how to go about it. Otherwise,' she said quietly, 'he said I must give him five hundred pounds as a tip each week. I'll get a new gardener and everything will be alright.' She looked at Sasha with desperate eyes. 'It gets so lonely here, that's all. David plays golf all the time or goes to his club, and it just gets so lonely.'

She found herself feeling repulsed by, and sorry for the woman, in equal measures. 'Mrs Mosham, you shouldn't be watching him when he's in the shower, you do see that, don't you? Look, let me go and have a word with him alright?'

She waited until the gardener had left the outhouse before stepping forward.

'Steven?

'Yeah? What's it to you?'

'I'm a private investigator and I'm here to tell you that you're fired. Mrs Mosham won't be paying you any more money.'

'You're kidding? The old bat's a sex maniac, got her eye on me every chance she gets, even tried to get in the shower with me the other day.'

'She's not well and she's going to get help, but using her weakness against her and blackmailing her isn't the answer.'

He laughed. 'I deserve some backpay at least, then I'll go, can't stand gardening anyway.'

'Alright, give me ten minutes, okay?' She went back inside to a hovering Brenda Mosham.

'Steven's leaving, and he won't be back. I think we can sort this out if I can use a computer to type up something for him to sign, and if you can arrange to pay him backpay of, let's say five hundred pounds. How does that sound?'

With everything sorted, and the blackmailing gardener dispatched, Sasha sat in the drawing room with a tearful Mrs Mosham, wondering how to broach the subject delicately. 'Er, Mrs Mosham, it won't do to just employ another young man, you do realise that, don't you? Perhaps you're giving the young men the er wrong idea? How about a woman gardener?' *This had to be one of the most absurd situations she'd ever found herself in.* A sixty-something sex maniac having fantasies about young male gardeners falling in love with her. But worse than that, the woman had tried it on with them, yes, possibly with the cruel encouragement of those seeing a way to get themselves some easy cash from a desperate woman, but she was in the wrong, and she also, without a doubt, had a screw loose. She somehow needed to ensure that it wouldn't happen again, but how? As if in answer to her question, the front door slammed and a man appeared in the drawing room doorway.

'Who are you?' boomed Sir David Mosham.

'Could you excuse us for a minute, Brenda? Perhaps I can explain things to your husband.'

'She came to help me, David, it was a problem with the gardener, but it's all sorted out now.' Brenda Mosham fluttered around, looking at Sasha pleadingly.

'Oh, for God's sake, not again.' He sank into an armchair.

Sasha nodded at Brenda to leave, before addressing him. 'I'm a private investigator, Sir David. Your wife got herself into a bit of a muddle, she, er, became confused about your gardener and tried to speak to him in the outhouse–'

He groaned, dropping his head into his hands, his voice muffled. 'She did it again, didn't she? We'll never live it down, I can't keep paying them off, the woman's a menace, she could go to jail.'

'It's alright, he's gone, and he signed this.' She held out the signed statement silently, feeling unclean somehow.

'Sasha, I can't thank you enough. His expression turned serious. 'But the damned rotter was trying to blackmail her, and that's just not cricket. But that's not the point, is it?'

'No.' Sasha shook her head. 'Your wife will end up in trouble, Sir David if she does this kind of thing again. I also think there are unscrupulous young men out there who can spot a wealthy older woman going through a difficult time. I think she's... lonely... and vulnerable, and she's got problems, so perhaps some kind of help?'

'Yes, you're absolutely right. I've tended to turn a blind eye, putting it down to some kind of mid to late-life crisis with no harm done, but if it was the other way round...'

They nodded understandingly at each other.

'I'll get her away, take her abroad for an extended trip, see if we can't find a good doctor...'

'And perhaps your next gardener could be a woman? I believe there are such types, it's not uncommon...'

With everything finalised satisfactorily enough, Sasha took her leave.

'You're sure you won't accept payment of any kind?'

'No, thank you, it was an hour of my time, nothing more. I hope your wife gets the help she needs.'

'I won't forget it, Sasha, thank you, and if you ever need anything, please give me a call.'

She departed the Moshams feeling a little like she'd temporarily stepped into a parallel universe, and not altogether sure whether she'd done the right thing or not. The woman had behaved in a predatory manner towards young men on more than one occasion, even if they had all possibly seen a way to fatten their wallets – was there any difference between her and the person killing female sex workers? Both were predators in their own right, after all. Except one *was* committing murder, she reminded herself...

~

'Wow. Just, wow,' Zoe said after Sasha had finished telling them the sorry tale, having sworn them both to secrecy. 'It's kind of sad in a way...'

'Part of me felt sorry for her, that these blokes had possibly spotted her weakness and had encouraged her, like maybe it was all a joke to them and a way to make some money out of it. But then I kept thinking, if it had been a man behaving that way with a young woman, I would have been disgusted. So, I don't know if I did the right thing or not, I feel like my hands are dirty.'

'It's always such a grey area,' said James, helping himself to another roast potato and some more vegetables. 'We tend to think only men can be predators, but we never know the whole story, and this woman sounds like a terribly sad case. This meal's delicious, Sash.'

'She's a brilliant cook, I think I should keep her,' said Zoe, smiling at Sasha. 'Shall I open another bottle of wine?'

'I thought you said you weren't drinking tonight?' James grinned at their sheepish expressions. 'I thought that sounded a little farfetched for you two.'

'I'm kind of disappointed that Brenda Mosham didn't want to take a hit out on her gardener, after all. It would have been quite exciting. What would you have done, babes?'

'Zo, seriously? Your imagination's getting as bad as Kay's.'

'Have you heard from her today? Has she caused any more shit?'

Smiling, Sasha nodded her head. 'She's not well, but she posted on her blog, and I don't think Tony's going to be too chuffed about it. I'll be honest, I had a feeling that she was keeping something back from me, that she'd somehow got hold of this chef's jacket that the killer wore and that she was going to display photos of it on her blog. At least I was wrong about that.' She checked the time. 'We're going to have to think about heading off to Bar Soho, guys, although I can go on my own, I'll be fine.'

'Are you kidding? Zoe's got me feeling all manly and like the big protector of women, I'm not missing out on my chance to shine.'

'Alright, but the only thing you'll need to do tonight is to buy us a drink, I promise you.'

~

Rick Turner cursed as he dried himself hurriedly and dropped the towel on the bathroom floor, he was going to be late for the lads at this rate, they were probably all down in the bar waiting for him. Checking his phone for any last messages, he switched it off and threw it into his flight bag – he wouldn't need that tonight. Knowing that he would be hungover the following morning, he grabbed his remaining clean clothes from the wardrobe, dropping them into his suitcase, followed by his suit bag folded in half, added his bag of dirty washing, splashed some aftershave on and threw the bottle in. Just his toiletry bag to go in the next morning, and then he could look forward to a good sleep on his flight back to The States – he'd need it, this was going to be one hell of a night. He grinned, drained his glass of brandy and Coke, and left the room.

'Awright, me old muckers?' He sauntered into the bar as cheers went up.

'Oi, oi, oi, Ricky boy, you old bugger, long time, mate.'

Hugs and back-slapping were accompanied by much laughter as the group of old friends reacquainted themselves. Someone put a pint of lager into Rick's hand and passed him a shot of vodka. He dropped the shot glass into his pint and downed it to much cheering. Slamming the glass down, he threw his head back. 'Let's get the party started.'

The other customers in the bar looked on, amused, as the men threw their heads back and howled.

'Dillon's in charge, it's a pint per pub and by the sounds of it, we're going to every bloody pub between here and the Thames. Hope you haven't got soft in your old age.' Mike slapped him on the back.

'He'd better not have.' Felix chimed in. 'We'll chuck him in the river if he can't handle himself.'

'It's not him I'm worried about,' said Will, grinning. 'The last time I had a night like this was before me and Viv ended up with a houseful of kids.'

'I can't believe you've got three kids, Will. And you, Jimmy? Maggie let you out then?'

'I've got a late-night pass.' Jimmy grinned.

A tray of shooters appeared. 'Down the hatch, guys, our chariot awaits.' Dillon handed out the shots. 'This is going to be a night to remember.'

'If any of us can,' laughed Mike. 'Let's go.'

'Hold on.' Rick slapped his hands to his pockets outside the hotel. 'I've left my wallet in my room.'

'Yeah, sure. Tightwad. Typical Rick.'

Dillon interrupted the friendly jeers. 'Tonight's on us, mate, you don't need your wallet. Let's go.'

They left the hotel and climbed into the waiting minibus, heading off to their next pub in high spirits.

PORNSTAR MARTINIS AT BAR SOHO

Bar Soho was crowded, the music competing with the chatter and laughter of customers. Sasha turned to Zoe and James. 'I don't know how we're going to find Franco and Rain Man.'

'What are their real names? I'll ask the barman, might get lucky,' said James.

'Warren and Quentin, and I've no idea what they look like, which doesn't help.'

'I do,' said Zoe, mysteriously, grinning. 'Look over there, I bet you anything you like that's Franco.'

They turned and looked through the crowds.

'That's James Franco.' James's jaw dropped in surprise. 'I don't believe it.'

'No, that's Warren Porterhouse. Zoe's right though, he's the dead spit. Not sure about the other bloke though.'

'He certainly doesn't look like Dustin Hoffman.'

'Maybe he's really brainy and can memorise a telephone directory.'

'Do they even exist anymore?'

'You go and confirm it's them and I'll get some drinks,' said James.

'I'll go with Sash,' said Zoe.

'She just wants to see James Franco's lookalike,' grinned Sasha, winking at James.

'No, I'm protecting you, missy.' Zoe squeezed James's hand and kissed him on the cheek. 'We should have cocktails, babe.'

'And you behave yourself,' he kissed her back, smiling at her. 'I'm the only James in your life, don't forget it.'

'And you're the only James I want.'

'You two need to get a room.' Sasha grinned at them. 'Zo, stay here with James, I'll just check if it's them.'

She pushed her way through and approached the two men, who looked up, smiling.

'Er, you're not by any chance Warren, are you? Franco, I think they call you?'

'I am, and you must be Sasha. Nice to meet you. This is Quentin, but you know we call him Rain Man. That's because he's got a brain the size of a house.'

'Pornstar Martinis. Sorry, blame Zoe.' James grinned apologetically, handing Sasha a glass of orange-coloured liquid with a slice of fruit floating in it. 'I'm James, and this is my girlfriend, Zoe.' They all shook hands and James and Zoe excused themselves, telling Sasha they'd be close by.

'Sorry about poor old Eric,' Franco shouted above the music. 'He's got himself into trouble in the past but nothing on this scale. He's innocent, of course, and lucky to have you in his corner.'

'Not that he sounds like he deserves it,' Rain Man chimed in. 'I wasn't at school with him like Franco, but I've known him for enough years to know he's his own worst enemy. We want to help in any way we can.'

Franco nodded. 'We've been trying a bit of investigating, but so far we've come up empty-handed.'

'It's good of you both to try and help. So, this was one of the bars you all came to last Tuesday night? Someone has to remember something about how Eric came to end up in the hotel with the escort. And please, don't worry about protecting my sensibilities.' She sipped her drink and smiled at the two men. 'Eric and I are history, so I'm involved as a friend and because I'm a private investigator, nothing more. Tell me what you can.'

'Ham, that's Vernon, and I, met Red, that's Rowan, and Dealer, that's Drew, here on Tuesday evening. Before they met us, they'd been to two other bars, the Golden Lion was one of them. They were both pretty hammered, and we weren't exactly sober, one of those nights.' Franco shrugged his shoulders. 'Rain Man here joined us and brought along his business associate, a guy called Max.'

'Max Canning, we'd had a meeting and I asked him if he fancied joining me and the guys for a drink,' Rain Man added.

We polished off a few and then moved on to Bar Simone, which is where Erica and Shuggy joined us. Shuggy is–'

'Harry, yes, I met him yesterday, and he called me earlier to say you might have remembered something.'

'Right, so it just turned into one of those nights. We all drank way too much and at some point, we went home, but when I left, Eric and Red were still there. And I think,' Franco turned to Rain Man, 'I think your chap Max was still with them. He didn't leave with you, did he?'

'Nope, I went home before you. He seemed to be enjoying himself, seemed to get on with the guys, and then there were the women, of course...' Rain Man looked awkward.

'Yes, I've heard about the women chatting with you all, about the flirting and the business cards going around.'

'Right, well, there was a woman handing out escort agency cards, she had a bit of a laugh with our table, some sort of joking about whether we were married or not, it was all in good fun. Anyway, we were all given a card, even though most of us have other halves, something we were quite honest about as we weren't interested, not seriously. Oh, and then another girl moved in after she'd left, and she also gave us cards. As far as I can remember, we left the lot of them lying on the table.'

Rain Man picked up the story. 'The bar was quite full for a Tuesday night, and we'd been having a bit of a back and forth with the table of women next to ours. Stupid bunch that we are, we thought they were just a bunch of girls out for a night of fun. We felt a bit embarrassed when the escort cards came out, our show of male bravado was in danger of getting us into trouble. We've been trying to remember if anyone pocketed one but it's hard to remember clearly. Like Franco says, there was a pile of cards left on the table. Look, if you want me to be totally honest, Red tried to make out that he was unattached, as did Eric, but we cleared that up. The only single one is Max, he's divorced, so no harm done if he did take a card.'

Franco took over. 'We've been to Bar Simone tonight and looked for the girls, but if any of them were the ones who were there Tuesday night then they're keeping quiet. Sounds awful but I'm afraid we can't remember what they looked like, other than to say they were all attractive, nicely dressed, or rather, provocatively dressed, but in a subtle way. We were hoping to speak to the barman who was there that night but we got unlucky, it's his night off.'

'Well, you've done what you can. I don't suppose you know what the barman's name is? Maybe I can try to speak to him.'

'Dillon, as far as we know,' said Rain Man. 'It might be worth going there on Tuesday evening, being the same night? You might find some of the girls there. It's just an idea.'

'And a good one, thanks.' She looked at Rain Man, wondering why he looked hesitant. 'Quentin, is there anything you've not mentioned? Shuggy mentioned something...'

'You should probably speak to Max in case I'm wrong, but, well, he was holding a couple of the cards. One was pink, they were the ones the woman on her own was handing out.'

'Hold on, you've reminded me, saying it was pink,' said Franco. 'Red put something pink in his pocket when I said goodbye. I wonder if he and Max do know something, they were huddled in conversation at The Ship the other night. Have you spoken to Max? No?'

'Here's his number.' Rain Man handed her a hurriedly scrawled number on a paper serviette.

'Thanks, I'll call him. The Ship, you said, was that in Wardour Street? Round the corner from the prostitute murder? Shuggy mentioned that you were there on Thursday night.'

'Yep, bit close for comfort, good job we've all got alibis,' joked Franco.

Yes, but their alibis all supported each other's, had he realised that? 'Thanks, guys, you've been a great help.'

'Any joy? asked Zoe hopefully, when Sasha re-joined them.

'I'm not sure... these guys do seem to crop up in the wrong places at the wrong time, and all their stories are similar...' She shook her head to clear it. 'Maybe I'm just buying into Kay's theory of the prostitute serial killer too much, and focusing all my attention on them because I've got no one else.'

'Maybe you don't need anyone else,' suggested James. 'What does your intuition tell you?'

'Not much, I'm afraid. I like them, they're a decent bunch, well, most of them. Okay, I can't stand Rowan, Eric's business partner, but all the rest seem really nice, so, yes, I trust them, I do.'

'And you've spoken to all of them now?'

'One left, a guy called Max Canning, I need to get hold of him. There's a chance that he and/or Rowan both picked up escort cards. If so, Rowan didn't mention a word about it to me, but maybe Max will be more forthcoming. If I could just find out how the escort came to be there with Eric, it would be a starting point. So now for my final long shot of the night, a quick visit to Freedom Chelsea to talk to a woman called Fran who had an unpleasant male guest check in at their Soho hotel just after the murder was committed on Thursday night.'

'The mystery man... let's go, who knew sleuthing could be such fun?' Zoe grinned, hooking her arms through James's and Sasha's.

'I'll second that,' said James, hailing a passing cab. 'Any time you need a backup team, Zoe and I are your guys.' They climbed into the taxi, arriving at Freedom Chelsea a short while later, and following the sounds of laughter coming from the bar.

'Red wine?' James asked the two women, waving to a waitress, who nodded.

'So much for not drinking tonight,' said Sasha, rolling her eyes at Zoe.

'It's your fault again, you bought wine for our roast dinner and then took us out on the town.' Zoe squeezed Sasha's arm, grinning.

'Hey, I can't help it if all my investigations take me to bars, can I? I'll go in search of Fran and find you back here in a few minutes.' She walked up to the barman, smiling, pleased to have company, it did make it more enjoyable.

'Same again please, good sir.' A hand slammed down on the bar counter beside her as a shout went up from the group of men in the corner.

'Shots, shots, shots, Mikey', they called loudly.

'And a round of tequilas for good measure,' said the man, laughing.

The barman served their drinks before turning to Sasha, smiling apologetically. 'Sorry about that, I'm surprised any of them are still standing, looks like they've had quite a night. What can I get you?'

'Is Fran around? Fran Baxter? I just need a quick word with her, please.'

'Sure, I'll buzz her, hold on a sec.' He spoke into a phone and called over to a passing waiter. 'Can you take this lady through to see Fran in the office, Neil?'

'Certainly, come with me.' The waiter led her through behind the bar then, after passing through a couple of storerooms and the kitchen, down some stairs and along a corridor. 'Frannie, darling,' he called, poking his head around a door. 'Someone to see you.'

'Thanks, Neil, could you wait outside?' A slight-looking woman stood up from behind a desk, tiredly running a hand through her blonde hair before smiling at Sasha. 'How can I help you?'

'I'm sorry to bother you, my name's Sasha, and I'm an investigator helping the police with the recent prostitute murder which occurred in Soho.'

Worry creased Fran's face. 'But that wasn't at our hotel, I'm not sure what it's got to do with me?' Her eyes darted to a bank of computer screens showing entrance foyers of, presumably, the various Freedom hotels.

'Probably nothing,' Sasha hastily reassured her. 'It was just that we had a report of a difficult customer checking in just after the murder, and as it was just around the corner, well...'

'Oh yes, I see.' Fran glanced at her watch. 'Who told you about him? It was nothing, really, I didn't think anything of it. I wasn't supposed to speak to the police, was I?'

She looked so worried that Sasha felt sorry for her. 'No, not at all, if you could just tell me what you can remember about him?'

'He was just rather rude, that's all, there'd been a problem with his check-in, and I'd had to come through to sort it out, which meant he'd had to wait for a few minutes. He was in London for an early meeting the next morning. He insisted that I go with him to his room to make sure the room card worked and that everything was alright, and then he asked me to stay and have a drink with him. Which I didn't. I suppose it was Samantha who told you or told someone, she's a bit of a gossip. I just mentioned it to her in passing. Honestly, I wasn't bothered by him at all. They're all the same, these married men, using business meetings and trips as an excuse to cheat on their wives. I suppose I did find him a bit intimidating, but that's all. I need to toughen up,' she said, laughing.

'So he was married?'

'He was wearing a wedding ring. Sorry, I'm just tired, I don't mean to moan about things.'

'I understand. Night work must be tiring. Do you always work nights?'

'Yes, I don't mind, keeps me busy, and it's better than sitting at home on my own.' She gave Sasha a small smile before glancing anxiously at the computer screens again.

With a flash, Sasha remembered Mrs Carter, from the hotel in Kensington, telling her that Fran had lost her husband earlier in the year. 'Look, I don't want to take up your time... if you could just give me his details so that we can exclude him from our enquiries?'

'Yes, of course.' She tapped on a keyboard and printed out a sheet of paper. 'Here we are, a Mr Anderson. All his details are on here.'

'Thank you, that's very helpful. Er, one last question, if you don't mind? Last Tuesday night there was a murder at your Kensington hotel, you'll know all about it, of course?' *This was dodgy, Tony would be furious with her.*

'Well, yes, we all heard about it, a dreadful thing to happen. They're saying women aren't safe at night. But I can't tell you anything about it, I wasn't there, and our receptions are unmanned, it's all self-check-in, so whoever it was must have checked themselves in and there must have been some kind of disagreement or something, I suppose?'

'Yes, possibly, and you wouldn't have seen anything on your screens?' Sasha indicated the bank of computer screens.

'Nothing that caught my attention. I'm sorry I can't help you any further.'

'Not at all, it was kind of you to see me, and thanks for this.' She waved the piece of paper at Fran.

'Neil will take you back up. Well, goodbye then.'

'Bye, and thanks.'

'I hope you catch him soon,' Fran added.

'Me too, stay safe.' Sasha walked out of the office. Fran looked anxious, and no surprise, a small, defenceless woman on her own, working nights.

'Poor Frannie, we all worry about her.' Neil interrupted her thoughts, twittering on as they retraced their steps to the bar. 'She lost her husband in March and she's worked all hours God sends ever since. I expect it keeps her mind off things, poor love, but between you and me I expect the Valium helps, and you can't blame her. Here we are. That your boyfriend? He's handsome.'

'Not mine, my friend's.' Sasha smiled.

'Pity.' Neil winked at her.

'Find out anything useful?' Zoe asked eagerly, as Sasha sat down and picked up her glass of wine.

'Not really, I'll try to get Tony to follow it up but it's probably nothing. Oh, and I think Neil, the waiter over there, fancies James.'

''Drink up, we're leaving.' James downed his wine as Sasha and Zoe sniggered at his discomfort.

They finished their wine just as the group of men who'd been making all the noise left the bar and, deciding that it was time to go home, walked out to the hotel foyer.

'This isn't my hotel. I'm not staying here,' slurred one of the men from the same group.

Sasha grinned. How hammered must he be to not even remember that he was staying here? She watched one of the men fumble with a card as he tried to negotiate the self-check-in. No doubt Fran had her eye on things from her office, she thought, noticing the camera in the corner of the foyer, and would be ready when the call came for assistance. Poor thing, she'd seemed a little frazzled. Still, at least this bunch looked harmless enough, they were just in high spirits, although she doubted that they would be the next morning, judging by the state of them.

'Wait here while I look for a cab,' said James.

The foyer cleared as the men moved out through the entrance door, one of them having staggered into the lift to go to his room, and Sasha and Zoe headed for the door as James waved at them to come, stepping aside as a glamourous woman entered, trailing a whiff of expensive perfume in her wake.

They both turned and watched her for a moment, before locking eyes with each other and grinning as they joined James.

'What is it now?' he asked, smiling as they sniggered.

'Did you see her?' Zoe looked back through the glass. 'Gotta be an escort.'

'No way,' said James, staring as the woman entered one of the lifts.

'Heels the height of Nelson's Column, sheer black stockings, freshly applied make-up, expensive scent, and a belted summer coat,' explained Sasha. 'Look around you, see anyone else dressed like that?'

James's eyes took in the few women walking past in their short sleeves, with bare legs and sandals. 'I see what you mean. Well, it wouldn't harm you two to dress up like her occasionally, I wouldn't complain. Ow.' He stepped back, laughing as Zoe whacked him, and they climbed into the waiting cab.

'What is it, Sash?' Zoe was looking at her friend.

'I'm wondering how she just walked into the lift. You can't use them unless you're a guest with a room key card, so maybe we're wrong, maybe she's staying there.'

'So, she's not an escort? Pity, thought I had something exciting to tell the lads at work about tomorrow.' James ducked as Zoe took another swing at him.

~

Rick stumbled into the room, blinking at the lights as he slid his room card into the slot on the wall. Where was he? Not his room. What had Dillon said? You've got two hours of heaven on us, mate. He headed for the bathroom to relieve himself, before noticing the bottle of Rum and the glass beside it sitting on the table in the bedroom. Not his drink anymore, but why not? He poured himself a large measure, grabbing some ice from the bucket containing a bottle of champagne. He grinned, guessing what the lads had organised for him, and threw back the Rum, pouring himself another as there was a knock at the door.

'Well, hi there, darlin', what's your name?' He leaned against the wall, feeling suddenly dizzy.

'I'm Monique, and I'm yours for the next two hours.'

'Well, come on in, Monique. Fancy a drink? I've got Rum or champagne.'

'I'm only supposed to drink the champagne.'

'Then champagne it is.' He popped the cork, shaking his head to dispel the dizziness. Sober up Ricky boy, you're going to enjoy this, he said to himself, downing his drink.

Monique smiled into his eyes as she removed her coat and let it drop to the floor.

~

Kay awoke on Sunday morning and knew immediately that she was better. It felt wonderful. No rushing to the bathroom, no aches and pains and feeling sick. She'd slept well and she stretched in her bed luxuriously as she planned her day – she had lots to catch up on.

She took a shower and made herself some scrambled eggs on toast, swallowing the food appreciatively, before making herself a mug of tea and switching her laptop on. This was it. This post was going to blow up the internet – actual photos of the chef's jacket worn by the escort killer, complete with blood spatters. She'd definitely get invited for a TV interview after this. Maybe that Matt Savage would contact her, he owed her something better than those few words the other night.

Oh, this was good, she smiled to herself a while later, admiring her title – *Murder on the menu*. Taking a deep breath, she pressed *publish* and sent her words and photographs out to the world.

~

She felt like crap. Groaning, Sasha turned over in bed, wincing as her boobs pressed against the mattress. She rolled onto her back and lay looking at the ceiling as she tentatively pressed her belly, annoyed by the stabbing pain. Her stomach suddenly turned and she climbed out of bed, making her way to the bathroom, feeling a little dizzy. Maybe Zoe had been right and her endometriosis had returned, it was probably about time, it never gave her long between its vicious attacks on what was left of her insides.

Oh great, she was spotting. She groaned, hunting in Zoe's bathroom cupboard for a tampon as Zoe knocked on the door.

'Sash? Are you okay?'

'Give me a sec,' she called out, splashing some cold water on her face.

'Did you just puke?' Zoe stood with her hands on her hips, glaring at Sasha. Her eyes swept over Sasha's huddled form.

'A tiny bit,' she said. 'I'm probably coming down with something, maybe it's what Kay had.'

'Right, come and sit down, I've made some tea. It's time we had a chat.'

'They nursed mugs of tea as Zoe studied her friend. 'Do you think it's your endometriosis?'

'I'm not sure, it feels different, like I said, I'm probably–'

'Have you looked at yourself in the mirror lately? I mean properly? Sash, your boobs are bigger, you've been tired, you've been feeling pukey. Does any of that sound like anything to you?'

'What? Don't be stupid. What are you saying?'

'I'm saying, I want you to do something for me. Do you think you can pee?'

'Zo, what is this? Yes, I can probably pee, but–'

'Come with me.' Zoe pulled her to the bathroom, where she took a box from the cupboard beneath the basin. 'I had a scare a couple of months ago, don't ask,' she said, at Sasha's enquiring look.

Five minutes later the two friends sat in silence back in the lounge, staring at each other.

'I'm pregnant,' whispered Sasha.

'You're pregnant,' Zoe confirmed.

'Oh, crap.'

PRETTY WOMAN

D.S. Tony Palmer was called out early to a suspicious death at an all-night café in Earl's Court, leaving at home an unhappy girlfriend who had planned to make them a leisurely Sunday brunch consisting of eggs, bacon, croissants, freshly-squeezed orange juice and some bubbles. It was supposed to be his day off and their exchange of words had left him in a sour mood, which wasn't helped when he arrived to find reporters already hovering in the vicinity.

'Get these bleedin' reporters out of my way and hurry up with that tape,' he yelled at the officer busy cordoning off the area around the café.

'Has The Street Cleaner struck again?' someone called out.

'Is the victim another prostitute?' called out another.

'No, it bleedin' well isn't,' he shouted over his shoulder.

Donned in his white suit and shoe covers, he marched into Brenda's, scowling at the officer closest to him. 'What have we got?'

'Female victim stabbed with a knife and fork, sarge. Looks like she was eating a plate of sausage and chips.'

'I don't care what she was flamin' well eating, do I?'

'She could be a prostitute, hard to tell sometimes, looks like she was dressed a bit, you know, risqué. D'you think it was him?'

D. S. Palmer glared at the eager officer at his shoulder. 'Do I think it was who?'

'Well, this bloke they're calling The Street Cleaner...' The young officer's voice trailed off fearfully as he took in Tony's darkening face.

'Let's get something straight, everyone. There's no such person as The Street Cleaner. That's our beloved press for you. Since when does a supposed serial killer go from strangling a woman on the street in Soho, to stabbing an escort to death in her bed in a hotel in Kensington, to stabbing a street walker at the damn Duck Palace in Soho, to attacking a woman with a knife and fork in an all-night bleedin' café in Earl's Court?'

One brave officer piped up about the fact that two of the deaths had been stabbings of prostitutes in hotel room beds, followed by an even braver officer querying whether they'd got the wrong guy in custody. Had it not been for the arrival of their Detective Chief Inspector, they both privately agreed later, it had looked, for a moment, as if the sarge had been about to go for the cutlery.

~

Kay was bursting with energy and tempted though she was to just sit and watch her numbers go up on her blog, she decided that she'd walk down to her local supermarket and buy herself something nice for dinner. She deserved a treat, she thought, suddenly craving a Sunday roast like her mum used to make.

She walked around the supermarket, picking up a pack of chicken breasts, a couple of potatoes, a small bag of ready-prepared cauliflower and broccoli, and threw in a couple of loose carrots, before grabbing a small tub of ready-made gravy. Life was good, she thought, as she grabbed the Sunday paper and paid for her groceries, strolling out into the sunshine and deciding to walk along to the bakery for a giant sausage roll for her lunch.

Soon she'd be eating like this all the time, once the paid sponsorships started pouring in, she thought happily. No more living on beans on toast and watching the pennies. Resisting the urge to have a bite of the warm sausage roll, she popped it into her shopping bag and looked up as a police car drove past, its lights flashing lazily. Her curiosity piqued, she looked up and down the road, noticing the small cluster of people standing around Brenda's, the all-night café. Well, what do you know?

Something was happening, maybe a murder, it could be her lucky day. Her even luckier day, she sniggered to herself, heading towards the group.

~

No, no, no. The jacket was gone, thrown away with the food waste. This couldn't be real, the girl had made it up, surely?

White knuckles gripped the mouse as the article was scrolled up the screen and paused on another photograph with red arrows pointing to bloodstains. This would be the end of it. If the police got hold of it, they'd find direct evidence, they'd have DNA. Everything would be over and all the hard work and planning would have been for nothing.

Despairingly, eyes scanned the article, and then the entire blog, looking for something that would give a clue to where the girl lived. Nothing. But this girl was hungry, and a little fearless, and an idea took root – maybe there was a way of getting hold of the jacket after all...

~

'It's got to be false,' declared Sasha, finishing her third mug of tea. 'I can't even get pregnant, you know that. Malcolm Bailey, my specialist, made it quite clear to me when he removed half of my insides last time. It was only a matter of time before the whole lot had to come out, he said. Besides, I've been spotting, so that settles it.'

'You don't know that, babes, maybe you got lucky...'

'Lucky? Zo, there's nothing lucky about this. Look at me. I'm thirty-six, single, homeless, and soon to be penniless at this rate, and if I was, by some crazed act of sick humour by the Gods above, pregnant, the bloke who would have to be the father is my serial-cheating ex who just so happens to be in custody for murdering an escort.' She laughed hysterically. 'It would actually be just my luck, wouldn't it? What the hell am I going to do?' she whispered.

Zoe came and sat beside her, hugging her. 'You're not alone, you've got me, you've always got me. We'll sort this out. Tomorrow you can go and see your specialist and then we'll know, alright?' She eyed the packet of cigarettes lying on the coffee table, picking them up and putting them in a drawer. 'Won't do any harm,' she said, shrugging. 'Let's have a rest day, let me spoil you. I'll make us some breakfast, how about an egg and bacon roll?'

Sasha cupped her hand to her mouth, jumping up and running to the bathroom, reappearing a few moments later.

'Sorry, false alarm. But maybe just some toast? And, Zo? Can we not talk about it? Can we forget about it until I've seen Malcolm?'

~

D.S. Palmer turned to leave the crime scene, satisfied, along with his D.C.I. that they had all the facts. The woman had been identified, witnesses had all corroborated the story related to him by Brenda, the owner, and officers had been dispatched to arrest her boyfriend for murder. It was a sorry old world, he thought bitterly, when a young couple went out clubbing, overdid things, and ended up having a fatal, *for one of them*, row in an all-night flamin' caf. He recognised a face among the group gathered outside and stormed out. 'Oi, you.'

Kay beat a hasty retreat, slipping her phone into her pocket and clutching her bag of groceries. She'd got a nice little story to keep her blog interesting. If D.S. Palmer didn't want her and Uncle Tom Cobley and all knowing all the details then maybe he shouldn't shout his mouth off so much.

But Tony Palmer wasn't done with her. 'Oi, bane of my life. You need to watch it, if I catch you near one more of my crime scenes, I'm going to lock you up, you hear me? You're too nosy for your own good.' Sighing, he jabbed at his phone, sending his girlfriend a message to tell her he was on his way home. If he wasn't careful Sandra would be having a go at *him* with a knife and fork.

~

Sasha showered and stood in front of the mirror towel-drying her body as she assessed it through the steam. Turning sideways she looked at her stomach, before holding her boobs, her heart sinking at their increased size and weight. Could she be? No, it was impossible, it had to be some kind of weird hormone crap going on. Home tests were unreliable, weren't they?

As she dressed, she allowed herself to imagine an alternative world where she was pregnant, where she told Eric, and where he told her she'd got it all wrong, that he'd never cheated on her. She pictured their little house, the two of them decorating the nursery, her body blooming and, skipping over the thought of actually giving birth, she pictured her and Eric cradling their son or daughter as they gazed lovingly at each other. And then she put the whole thing out of her mind, despising herself for even going there.

Reminding herself of the reason that Eric was currently in custody, she dressed and typed out a message to the last man on her list, Max Canning, asking him if he could possibly meet her at Bar Simone that evening to talk about Eric.

His reply came back almost immediately. No, he couldn't meet her there, but she was welcome to come to his house that afternoon. She thanked him and turned her attention to Kay's blog, her jaw dropping.

Kay had lied to her, she'd got hold of the chef's jacket, after all, had taken crucial evidence from the hotel – evidence which may well have exonerated Eric – had now contaminated it, and had plastered photos of it all over her blog to boot. Tony wasn't the only person who was going to be furious with her, there was a ruthless killer out there who would go to any lengths to get hold of the jacket. If they found out where Kay lived, she could be in grave danger. Picking up her phone, she called Kay, willing the girl to answer. She hoped she wasn't too late.

~

Listening to her voice note from the scene of the cutlery killer, as she'd dubbed him, one last time, Kay finished off her post about the Brenda's café murder and, feeling chuffed with herself, published it, eating the last mouthful of her sausage roll and wiping her mouth, wishing she'd treated herself to two. It was obvious that the woman's death by cutlery was nothing to do with the serial killer, *her serial killer*, as she found herself fondly thinking of him, but it didn't hurt to suggest that it might be, it kept her readers coming back for more, and it kept everyone in a state of anxiety so that they constantly checked for updates online – which meant, she smiled smugly, that at some point they inevitably ended up on Kay's Killer Blog. More visitors to her blog meant more chance of her getting sponsorships, which meant more money, she thought happily. 'Ka-ching,' she shouted at her laptop. 'Ka-bloody-ching, baby,' she yelled jubilantly at her settee, getting up and doing a jig around her lounge. *Maybe she'd buy a small car, she'd need one when she teamed up with Sasha...*

Her laptop pinged with a notification, and she sat back down to see what it was. Clicking on the message sent via her blog, her eyes almost popped out of their sockets.

Her phone rang and she dismissed the call without looking to see who it was, reading the message again in mounting excitement.

~

No answer. But she could just be out somewhere, Sasha reasoned, still, she'd feel better knowing that this irritatingly likeable girl was alright. Grabbing her bag, she went in search of Zoe. 'I'm popping round to Kay's to make sure she's alright.'

'Why shouldn't she be? What's happened?'

'She's plastered photos all over her blog of the blood-stained chef's jacket, which she retrieved from the laundry, which was more than likely worn by the killer of Eric's escort.'

'Well, that's good, right? The police can test it and find out who the killer was, can't they? What do they call it, forensics? CSI?'

'Forensic scientists, I think, and yes, hopefully, they can, if she hasn't contaminated it too much, who knows? But she's removed crucial evidence from the scene of a crime, which is going to get her in a whole load of trouble. But I'm more concerned about what the killer will do when they see this. They'll be wanting to get hold of it to destroy it, and the only thing standing between them and their goal is Kay.'

'She could just be making it all up,' said Zoe, 'I wouldn't put it past her to cut her own finger and drip it over the jacket, would you?'

'True... but what if she isn't?'

'Shall I come with you?'

'Sure, as long as you're not babysitting me.' Sasha winced. 'Poor choice of words.'

'Come on, it'll be nice to be out for a while.'

Half an hour later they stood at the door to Kay's flat, pressing the bell and banging on the door.

'She's not here,' said Zoe.

'Or she is and she can't answer. I'll try her phone again.'

'Sasha.' Kay answered on the third ring, sounding breathless.

Relief flooded through Sasha. 'Kay, where are you?'

'Wouldn't you like to know?' Kay gave an excited laugh, before changing her tone. 'You're going to tell me off about the chef's jacket, aren't you? I couldn't tell you,' she whined, 'you'd have made me give it to the cops and then I wouldn't have the most exclusive story in the whole world attracting thousands of readers to my blog. Sasha, my blog's blowing up, it's incredible.'

'Alright, I can see why you're excited, but you need to hand it over to the cops now. If it's what you say it is then they need to do some tests as soon as possible. It could lead them to the killer and get Eric released, but more than that, it could stop anyone else from getting killed. You've had your fun, Kay, but there's someone who will do whatever it takes to make sure that jacket doesn't make it into the hands of the police. Why don't you let me take it to them? I'm at your flat right now.'

'I promise you I'll hand it in tomorrow, there's just one more thing I need to do. I'm busy preparing for it now. You'll never believe it when I tell you. Wait, you're at my flat?' Kay laughed. 'You can't seriously think our serial killer's going to smash my door down and stab me to death? He only kills hookers.' She giggled. 'You have no idea how funny that is at this moment. If you could see what I'm buying you'd get the joke. You'll thank me once you find out what I'm going to do, and so will your ex. I have to go, sorry, but I'll post a clue on my blog later, how's that? And Sasha, don't worry about me, I'm fine, I'm on a lucky streak.'

'Kay, wait.' She looked at Zoe. 'She's gone. What the hell is she up to?'

'No idea, her last post on her blog is about a murder at Brenda's all-night café, look.'

'Perfect, something else to piss Tony off about. I swear, Zo if the serial killer doesn't get her then it'll probably be Tony who does. Shit, look at the time, I have to be at Max

Canning's place, he's agreed to talk to me about last Tuesday night.'

~

The room attendant at The London Henrietta Hotel, Marble Arch, slid her card into the slot and opened the door, calling out, 'Housekeeping.' It was two hours past check-out and her supervisor had advised her to enter the room, having called the room and received no answer.

The room had an unoccupied feel, and she walked to the window, pulling back the curtains before looking around. The bed was unslept in, but a still-damp towel lay on the bathroom floor, so someone had used the shower although, she decided, that had probably been the day before. A toiletry bag sat beside the basin, and a suitcase sat on the luggage rack in the bedroom, packed but unzipped, accompanied by a small travel bag sitting on the floor beside it. The only other evidence of use was the glass on the coffee table. Noticing something black sticking out from beneath the bed, she bent down to retrieve it, finding a wallet.

She flicked through the wallet, finding bank cards for an American bank, a few twenty-pound notes, and various dollar bills totalling seven hundred and fifty dollars. Her heart racing, she paused, considering the risk. The guest must have dropped his wallet without realising, so wouldn't be sure where he'd lost it. The money would come in handy, and her boyfriend would know what to do with the cards and the foreign notes. Taking out her mobile phone, she called him, before hurrying down and out of the staff entrance, hiding the wallet, as agreed, wedged behind the recycling bins. Smoothing her hair nervously, she went in search of her supervisor to inform her of the guest's absence.

~

The room attendant's experience at The Freedom Hotel, Chelsea, was an altogether different experience.

Screaming at the sight of all the blood seeping through the duvet, and the open, lifeless eyes staring at her from the pillow, she fled the room, as doors opened and enquiring faces appeared.

Mrs Mason, the housekeeping supervisor, sat the hysterical woman down, calling for some sweet tea. 'Now, tell me what's the matter, I can't make any sense of what you're saying. What's all this about blood and eyes?'

'Dead. Murdered in the bed. I'll never forget it, seeing those eyes staring right at me. Oh, Mrs Mason, the eyes are still open.'

'A dead body? In one of our beds? Nonsense. And what's all this talk of murder?'

'Blood,' moaned Giulianna, rocking back and forth. 'There's blood everywhere, I think they've been stabbed.'

'Drink this.' Mrs Mason forced the cup of tea into the girl's hand. 'What's the room number, I'll go and have a look.'

'No, no, please, he might still be there.' Giulianna burst into fresh fits of hysteria, spilling the tea into the saucer.

'Who? Who might still be there? You're not making any sense.'

'The murderer,' wailed Giulianna.

'Alright, I'll take someone with me. Now, calm down and tell me the room number.'

Five minutes later, Mrs Mason, to a lesser degree, experienced some of what Giulianna had been feeling, as she backed out of the room. 'Stay outside the room,' she instructed Peterson, the dishwasher, and the first person on hand she'd found to accompany her. 'I'm calling the manager.'

~

The front door opened and a large man appeared wearing a dressing gown, his gaze sweeping over Sasha uncomfortably.

'Max? I'm Sasha.' She smiled, receiving a blank look in response. 'Er, you said it would be okay to pop round to chat about the events of Tuesday evening? The night you were drinking with Eric Latimer?'

'Oh, right, you sent me a message earlier.'

He still made no move to welcome her in and she hovered awkwardly, picking up the distinct smell of booze on his breath. His eyes had a slightly glazed look to them and she wondered if she was making a mistake in coming here alone. But that was ridiculous, she decided, he was a colleague of Quentin, Rain Man, whatever, who was, in turn, a friend of Franco. Still, for added insurance, she threw in a casual aside. 'I met Franco, last night at Bar Soho, and said I'd be coming to see you today. Oh, you probably know him as Warren, he's a friend of your colleague Quentin Thomas.' *You're gabbling, rein it in, he'll sense you're nervous.*

'Except you couldn't have done, could you?' His grey, rather flat-looking eyes stared down at her as his mouth curled into a smile. *This guy was creepy as fuck.*

'What?'

'You couldn't have mentioned it to Warren, or anyone else, last night, because you only knew you were coming to see me this morning after you sent me a message. Come in, Sasha.' His hand reached around her back, gently pushing her into the hallway, as his other hand closed the front door behind her.

Shit.

~

Kay excitedly assessed her purchases, feeling a thrill. She'd never dressed up like a hooker before, she'd have to take a photo of herself later for her blog. So far, she'd found herself the perfect pair of pole dancer's shoes and a scarlet halter-neck top. Her denim mini would do for a skirt, no need to buy another one, and now she hovered at the market stall displaying wigs, wondering if she was getting carried away. But they were kind of gorgeous, she thought, eyeing the bright purple bob-styled wig mounted on the polystyrene head.

'Wanna try one on, love?' The stallholder asked her, sensing her interest. 'How about this one?' She lifted a platinum blonde wig from one of the heads, positioning it expertly on Kay's head and turning her to face the mirror. 'Who does that remind you of? You're the spitting image of Julia Roberts.'

'Pretty Woman,' breathed Kay, gently pushing the fringe to one side as she gazed at her transformation. 'Wow. Er, how much is it?'

'Fifty quid, love. Suits you, you should get it.'

'I'll give you forty,' tried Kay, hopefully.

The woman grinned, whisking the wig from Kay's head and shoving it into a plastic bag. 'Lucky for you I'm about to pack up. Forty quid it is.'

~

'Is this the best you've got?' Tony Palmer glared at the young lad standing behind the counter of his local corner shop as he held up the dusty, cellophane-encased bouquet of carnations.

The lad shrugged. 'You're lucky, it's the last one.'

'I'll have to take it then, and a box of those chocolates. Tell your boss I should arrest him for daylight robbery,' he grumbled, taking his meagre change from the twenty-pound note he'd handed over.

'My Tony Wony's feeling guilty,' teased Sandra when he walked in through the front door a couple of minutes later.

'Sorry, sweetheart, we're short-staffed today. But I'm all yours now.' He swooped her into his arms, kissing her neck as she laughed.

'Go and freshen up, I'll get the bacon on. Your Sandy Wandy forgives you.'

He grinned and headed up the stairs, thinking guiltily that he hoped she never used that insane baby talk in front of his colleagues, he'd never live it down.

The aroma of frying bacon reached his nostrils as he came back downstairs and walked into the kitchen. 'That smells good, I'm starving.' He froze as his phone rang.

Sandra turned off the gas and shovelled the bacon onto a plate, her expression resigned as she listened to his side of the call.

'Go,' she said, buttering a couple of slices of white bread. 'I'll make you a bacon sandwich to take with you.'

'It's another stabbing.' His face was grim.

'Is it him?'

'Who?'

'The serial killer, you know, The Street Cleaner, they're calling him.'

'Not you as well,' he sighed, as doubts filled his head. *Had he got the wrong bloke in custody then? Either that or there was a copycat out there.* 'Thanks, babes.' He dropped a kiss on her cheek as he took the bacon sandwich wrapped in a sheet of kitchen towel, and headed back out of his front door.

~

'Drink?' Max Canning picked up the bottle of whisky and waved it at Sasha as she hovered awkwardly in his sitting room.

'Er, no, thanks. Maybe just a glass of water?'

Moving to the kitchen doorway, she watched him as he reached up into the cupboard for a glass. The sleeve of his dressing gown fell back from his wrist and she glanced at the large plaster affixed to his forearm.

Max caught her glance and she looked away quickly. 'You've got a nice house, do you live on your own?'

'Since I kicked out my whore of a wife. Come and sit down.'

He sat on the settee, letting his legs fall open, and leaned back, taking a large swig of his drink. 'Fire away,' he said, smiling at her.

He totally gave her the creeps. He was one of those blokes who liked to intimidate women, and he was doing a good job. 'Right, er, could you just try to tell me everything that you can remember from Tuesday evening?' She took out her notebook, rifling through it. 'I understand that you and your business associate, Quentin Thomas, joined Eric Latimer's business partner, Rowan Penrose, who was with Drew Merton, Warren Porterhouse, and Vernon Abaoke, at Bar Soho?'

'Correct so far.'

'Okay... and that you all then moved on to Bar Simone, where Eric Latimer and Harry Reddingham joined you?'

'Correct.' He smiled at her.

'And that while you were all drinking at Bar Simone, your group was approached by various women who offered their services?'

'Right again. You're good at this,' he said, looking at her beneath hooded eyelids. 'Want me to describe them? The whores?'

He was enjoying this. 'You can if you want to.' *Two could play that game.*

He leaned forward, cradling his glass. 'They were all pretty hot, I suppose, in the way that cheap street whores are hot.'

'I thought they were high-class escorts?' she interrupted.

'They're all cheap whores, like all women, offering to lie on their backs for money, some just cost less. Present company excepted, I'm sure.'

He was a misogynist. 'Can you tell me what transpired between your group and the women?'

'Not much.' He yawned. 'They fawned around us a bit, giving out their cards, trying to drum up some business. The guys got a bit excited, probably pocketed the odd card which they'll never have the guts to use.'

'And you? Did you get excited? Maybe pocket a card or two?'

Max smiled, saying nothing.

'Do you recall if any of the cards were pink? Or what any of the names of the agencies were on the cards?'

'Nope.'

'And you didn't go to The Freedom Hotel in Kensington, with Eric, or anyone else, after leaving Bar Simone? Or book any of the escorts to meet you there?' *This was a waste of time and he was beginning to get to her.*

'Nope. I'm afraid it sounds like your boyfriend had all the fun on his own. He really went all out, by the sounds of it.'

He was disgusting, but she wasn't going to let him have the satisfaction of getting a reaction out of her. 'Okay, well, thanks for your time.' She stood up, dropping her notebook into her bag.

Max made no move to follow her as she headed towards the door.

'Can you tell me why your wife left you?'

His eyes flashed with something, anger maybe, for a second. 'Nope.' His tone was clipped.

'And what happened to your arm?'

'I kicked her out, remember?'

'What?'

'My wife, she didn't leave me, I kicked her out.' He stood up and she walked the last few steps to the front door, pulling it open and stepping out onto the front step as the door closed firmly behind her.

Taking a deep breath, she walked off along the pavement, excitement thudding in her chest. Was she onto something? She had an idea and pulled out her phone.

'Quentin? Sorry to bother you today. Do you happen to know why Max Canning kicked his wife out? His words, not mine.'

'Yes, but he didn't kick her out, she left him after he found her in bed with his best friend. I don't think he ever got over it, to be honest.'

Thanking Quentin, she dropped her phone back in her bag.

His wife had cheated on him with his best friend; he hated women; he thought all women were whores; he had a cut or something on his arm. Had she just found her killer?

GOOD GIRLS DON'T DRESS LIKE THAT

Tony Palmer's heart sank when he entered the hotel room at The Freedom Hotel Chelsea and looked at the crime scene. It was like a repeat of the Kensington killing – a half-drunk bottle of champagne bobbed in its bucket of water, the one lipstick-smeared glass sat on the bedside table, and the victim's head was the only part of the body visible above the crimson-stained duvet. He turned as his D.C.I walked in behind him.

'No rest for the wicked today, D.S. Palmer. What have we got, people?'

'Multiple stab wounds,' he was informed by the SOCO peering at the duvet. 'Looks like seven, all made through the duvet.'

'Identical to your Kensington escort murder, and the Duck Palace murder, D.S. Palmer. We need to find something fast if we're going to charge Latimer, something that separates his case from these others.'

'Will this do, sir?' The SOCO had pulled back the duvet and was looking at the detectives enquiringly.

'Well, I'll be bleedin' buggered,' Tony exclaimed, grinning. 'That'll do very nicely, very nicely indeed.'

~

'Come on, Tony, answer the phone,' she muttered, on her third attempt to call him as she made her way back to Zoe's. She let herself in, ignoring the cramps in her abdomen as she smiled at Zoe's barrage of questions.

'All alright, babes? How are you feeling? Any joy with your Max bloke? Are you going to take it easy now and have a quiet evening? And you'd better say yes to my last question.'

'I'm feeling fine, cross my heart. As for my Max bloke, what a gross creep. And I'll tell you something else, Zo,' she said, her eyes sparkling, 'I might have found my killer.'

'You're kidding. Right, hold it while I make us a cuppa. I picked up some chocolate digestives for a treat.'

Sasha finished recounting her visit to Max, grabbing a second chocolate digestive without thinking.

'He sounds revolting.' Zoe pulled a face. 'You shouldn't have gone on your own, anything could have happened.'

'What? He was going to murder me in his sitting room? No, he was enjoying it, the questions, making me feel uncomfortable...'

'And sitting there with his legs splayed open, urgh.' Zoe imitated gagging as they both laughed. 'Tell me he was wearing something underneath, please?'

'I didn't give him the satisfaction of looking. But he hates women and thinks they're all whores, plus his wife cheated on him. He could easily have picked up an escort card or two and organised it all. I've got this hunch that maybe he, Rowan, and Eric were in the bar at Freedom Kensington that night. Zo, what if they all had escorts up in the rooms?'

'But why murder Eric's escort?'

Sasha sat back, thinking. 'I don't know... Eric was so out of it, he was a sitting duck, anyone could have gone into his room and killed her and he would have been none the wiser... Max could have got a thrill from doing it and letting Eric go down for it, after all, they barely knew each other so it's not like he cared what happened to Eric.' She reached down and pulled her notebook from her bag, flicking through the pages. 'I've just thought, yes, here it is. How's this for a coincidence? Max was round the corner from The Duck Palace the night the prostitute was stabbed in her room – he was at The Ship in Wardour Street, which is just round the corner. I've got two witnesses – Shuggy and Franco.'

'He's your murderer,' whispered Zoe. 'You've got to tell your friend, Tony.'

'He's ignoring my calls, but I'll give him another try.'

'Tone, finally,' she said when he answered. 'You've been ignoring me.'

'Hello to you too. I've had a hell of a day, Sash, two crime scenes and the day's not over. I'm cream-crackered, Sandra's about to leave me, it's supposed to be my day off, and all I've eaten all day is a bacon sarnie on the run. Whatever it is, can't it wait until tomorrow, babes?'

'Give me one minute of your time? Please?' She spoke rapidly, telling Tony of her suspicions and how Max had been on the scene for both murders.

'It's not a crime to drink in a pub in Soho, plenty of people were out drinking that night, and as for the bar at Freedom Kensington, all you've got is your barman saying there was a bunch of drunks making a bit of a noise. And why him? He wasn't on his own, was he? One of the others was with him, you said. Did he say that any of them looked like your prime suspect?'

'Well, no, but–'

'And what the bleedin' hell am I doing even discussing this with you? I told you to keep out of this and not to go sneaking around trying to clear Latimer's name.' He sighed into the phone. 'Listen, Sash, give it up, okay? My D.C.I. has decided to go ahead and charge Eric for the Kensington murder, so that's the end of it. I'm sorry, babes, it's not what you want to hear, but today's events have changed how we were looking at his case, and that's the last I'm going to say on the matter.'

'Today's events? Why? What's happened?'

'I can't discuss it, but all this talk doing the rounds of a serial killer is absolute bleedin' nonsense. That's it, I'm going home.'

Her phone went silent and Sasha realised he'd ended the call. She looked at Zoe. 'They're charging Eric.'

~

Kay studied her appearance in the mirror, turning sideways and sticking a leg out as she admired her shoes. All that remained was to put on her make-up, and she rummaged in her cosmetic bag for suitable eyeshadow and lipstick, applying both heavily, before adding another coat of mascara. Her stomach was full of butterflies as she thought of her evening ahead. She was going to find out who her serial killer was and she was going to solve the whole flippin' case before the police. And she was going to clear Sasha's ex-boyfriend's name into the bargain. Sasha would owe her big time after this.

And when she got back tonight, she thought happily, she'd cook her Sunday roast and enjoy her slap-up meal as her blog exploded. It would have to be a midnight feast, kind of like a party for one and all that. She hummed cheerfully as she pictured herself raising a glass later to celebrate the imminent rise of Kay's Killer blog from mediocrity to flippin' amazeballs.

Picking up her phone, she took a photo of her feet in the pole dancer's shoes, grinning as she uploaded it to her blog. This would be her first clue to what she was doing. It would be like a live undercover assignment, she thought excitedly, with her posting photos of her evening until she exposed the killer to the world. She allowed a fleeting thought about her witness – wondering who they were – they were obviously scared, hence all the secrecy. Well, she wasn't scared.

A few minutes later she grinned as her phone pinged repeatedly. Her increased readership numbers meant that she was attracting rather more of the mouthy types with lots to say and plenty of critical opinions. She skimmed down the comments...

Dressing like a hooker to hunt down a hooker serial killer is not the brightest move, Kay.

Women who dress like whores deserve what they get.

Good girls don't dress like that.

Two-faced lot, she thought to herself. Like none of them ever wore a pair of sexy heels or, if they were men, never looked at a girl wearing a pair. And that was nothing, they hadn't seen her full outfit yet. 'Oh, just wait, my lovely readers, you ain't seen nothin' yet,' she said out loud, grateful that she'd developed a thick skin over her years of writing her blog.

What was that saying, she racked her brain, about glass houses? *People who live in glass houses, blah, blah...* She typed it in and found the full saying, smiling to herself. It was too good to be true and would make the perfect cryptic clue for her next post, which she'd publish in a few minutes. Would Sasha work it out? Possibly, but she'd be too late to stop her. Looking at the time, she paced her small living room impatiently, eager to get going. Maybe she'd just go along a bit earlier and get a feel for it...

~

'I wasn't going to answer your call, but I couldn't resist. I bet you've seen my blog posts. What d'you think?' Kay laughed excitedly.

'Nice shoes.' Sasha smiled into her phone. 'But, Kay, if you're doing what I think you're doing, then you need to tell me where you're going.'

'Sasha, come on, this is half the fun of it. I'm doing a live undercover assignment and posting clues as I go. If anyone can work it out, you can.'

'Well, save me some time, and just tell me this – who is it you're meeting?'

'Wouldn't you like to know?' Kay asked her in a singsong voice. 'Oh, go on then, my mum always said I was a blabbermouth. I've got a mystery witness. A witness to the whole thing, Sasha. Can you believe it? They know who the escort killer is and they're going to tell me. I told you that you and your ex would be thanking me.'

'Okay...' Sasha's mind was racing as she formulated a plan. Kay was going undercover so she had to be headed for one of the few places where street prostitutes still operated. 'Kay, how will they know what you look like?'

'They don't need to, we've arranged the meeting place already, for ten o'clock. Don't try and talk me out of it, it's too late.'

'Let me come and hang around close by, to keep an eye on things. Just tell me where you'll be.'

'The clue's on my blog, let's just say, we've got into trouble near there before.' Kay giggled as she ended the call.

'Kay? Grr.' She threw her phone down angrily on the settee and turned to Zoe.

'Zo, can I borrow some clothes, babes?'

'Course you can, hun, I told you, whatever you need, help yourself. 'What's going on? More trouble with Kay?'

'More than you know. The stupid girl is off somewhere dressed as a street hooker to meet a so-called mystery witness who's going to supposedly tell her who the escort murderer is.'

'And you want to borrow clothes because...?'

'I'm going to look for her and I'm going to take her place. Whoever it is doesn't know what she looks like. It's either a genuine witness who, for some reason or another, doesn't want to go to the police, or it's the actual killer – and my money's on the killer,' said Sasha, her mouth set in a grim line. 'I told you, Kay's treated this like a game from the beginning, but she went too far when she posted photos of the chef's jacket on her blog. The killer will go to any lengths to retrieve it.' She marched into Zoe's bedroom and began rifling through her wardrobe, pulling out shoe boxes.

'And just what exactly do you plan to do when you take Kay's place?' Zoe stood in the doorway, her hands on her hips. 'Single-handedly take down a killer? March him to the police station and hand him over?'

Sasha paused in her rummaging of Zoe's clothes. 'I don't know, I hadn't got that far.'

'I won't allow it, absolutely not, no way. You're not putting yourself in that position, babes, and that's final. What makes you think you owe Eric so much that you must put your own life at risk? Or Kay, for that matter? And it's not just your life now, is it?' Zoe's expression was stony as she glared at Sasha.

Sasha suddenly doubled over, holding her stomach.

'What is it?' asked Zoe.

'I have to go to the loo. Find me your most tasteless top and skirt, and a pair of heels.'

'Charming,' said Zoe, laughing despite herself. 'Are you sure you're alright?'

'I'll tell you in a minute.'

Blood. So much blood. The words sprang into her mind as she perched on the toilet. Eric had used the same words when he'd called her at the start of this nightmare. Well, she wasn't pregnant anyway, she thought with mixed feelings which she refused to analyse right now.

'Tell me.' Zoe narrowed her eyes as she quickly dropped something on her bed.

'That's my phone? What did you do, Zo?'

Zoe looked sheepish. 'I tried to call Tony, alright? But he cancelled the call without answering.'

'He won't answer, I told you, he doesn't want to discuss it with me at all, not now they're charging Eric. That's why I have to do this, you do see that, don't you?'

'What happened in the bathroom just now?'

'I'm not pregnant, end of.' Sasha picked up a couple of skirts, holding them up against herself in the mirror. 'What d'you think? This one, or this one?'

'So, you've come on then? But the test... it was positive. No, you could still be pregnant, maybe you're just spotting?'

'Trust me, it's a lot more than just spotting. Zo,' she sighed, 'I know my body and I know how damaged it is. Now, I need to get dressed and I need to down some painkillers, there's time enough tomorrow to worry about all this other stuff, right now I have to get to Kay.'

Zoe sighed huffily. 'Then I'm coming with you. Where are we going?'

'That's what I'll have to work out on the way, but it's somewhere in Soho.'

They turned their attention to the clothes, dressing silently and quickly.

'Reminds me of when we used to go clubbing.' Zoe grinned as she finished making up Sasha's face and looked in the mirror over Sasha's shoulder.

'Me too, except we'd have been downing the voddies and blasting our music as we sang along completely out of tune. Not bad.' She pursed her lips and struck a pose, tilting her head to one side as she studied their reflections. 'We make a pretty good couple of hookers, babes.' She blew Zoe a kiss in the mirror, winking. 'You look kind of cute, you should send James a photo.'

'If James saw me dressed like this, he'd have a nervous breakdown.'

'We need to go. Tube or taxi?'

'Taxi. No way am I going on the tube like this.'

~

Kay sauntered down Charing Cross Road, feeling a thrill as she saw a couple of working girls standing in a doorway. Word was that it didn't go on anymore around here, but she knew differently, of course. She smiled at them, wondering why they didn't return the smile. Maybe they see me as competition, she thought, heading into Soho's network of small streets.

She was way too early, even though she'd told Sasha a tiny white lie about what time she was meeting her witness. *I wasn't born yesterday, Sasha, if I'd told you I was meeting them at nine o'clock instead of ten, you'd have rushed to get here to try and stop me, that's if you managed to work it out from my clues.*

There was something thrilling about being out dressed like she was, although she wished it was a little darker. Still, the sun would start to go down soon. She stopped in front of an arcade on Wardour Street and pulled out her phone. It was time for a full-length selfie and another post on her blog.

She carried on along the pavement, admiring the outfit of one the girls in front of her, complete with lilac wig and hotpants. *Should she? Why not?* Quietly taking a photo, she leaned against a shuttered shop window and uploaded it, adding the caption: *I'm in good company.*

She glanced at the business cards tucked into the shutter. *Hot Busty Blonde*, said one, while another offered *Big and Black Bondage*, and another still, *Plastic Fetishes My Speciality.* She shook her head in amusement, slipping the cards out of the shutter and putting them in her bag – *they might make a good photo for her blog.*

Picking up her pace, she headed along Brewer Street, arriving in Glasshouse Street a short while later, and walked along, looking for the coffee shop she'd been told to wait in front of.

This part of the street was quite deserted, most of the businesses being daytime operations, and consequently now closed up for the day. Her heels sounded loud on the pavement, and she looked behind her, suddenly feeling vulnerable. *Come on Kay, get a grip*, she admonished herself. *No time for nerves, this is your biggest break ever.*

With relief, she saw the coffee shop ahead and walked quickly past the shabby entrance of something called The Ballroom, glancing into the lighted foyer and glimpsing a door and a small window above a counter beside it. The door swung open and a man crossed the small foyer, exiting the building and walking quickly off.

She stopped outside the coffee shop, realised it was closed and tried to calm her butterflies, looking up as a tall woman in stiletto-heeled boots strode out of the same building. Noticing her, the woman sauntered up to her.

'New here, aren't you? Did you clear your pitch?'

'Clear my–? Oh, my pitch. Er, no, I'm not–'

'Sure.' Her eyes swept over Kay, her mouth smirking. 'You dress like a hooker in a television show. But this is not your spot, you can't stand around here. I need a smoke.'

She held out the packet to Kay, who refused.

'I'm Gretel. You should go home, there's nothing for you here.'

'I'm Kay. I'm just meeting someone,' Kay squeaked, willing her contact to appear.

'Kay is not good sex name. Is not so safe here nowadays, not with this lunatic on the prowl. Some of the girls have had problems, one of them did not live to tell the tale. Go home, baby girl.' Gretel strode off, glancing back as she turned the corner at the end of the street.

Kay was alone again in the quiet, empty street.

~

'I know she's in Soho somewhere,' Sasha muttered, as she stared at her phone. 'What does she mean by this? People who live in glass houses shouldn't throw stones?'

'I think you should try D.S. Palmer again, Sash. At least let him know what we're doing.'

'Tony made it quite clear to me earlier that he's pissed off with me and doesn't want to talk to me, Zo. He's made his mind up about Eric and that's that. This could be the best opportunity we'll ever have to clear Eric's name. Either the person meeting Kay is genuinely a witness, in which case we'll hear what they have to say, or it's the killer, in which case, well, I'll be prepared.'

'Prepared? When, Sash? When he's stabbing you to death? This is crazy.'

'She's put more photos on her blog.' Sasha held her phone out to Zoe and they peered at the photo of Kay in her blonde wig. *Pretty Woman meets Las Vegas, in London.* Where's she standing? She's in front of an arcade.'

'Wardour Street.' Zoe punched some words into her phone. 'There's a Las Vegas arcade in Wardour street.'

'That's it, it has to be,' Sasha confirmed, looking at the photo of the arcade.

'Made your mind up yet, ladies?' The cabbie asked over his shoulder.

'Wardour street, please, the arcade.'

They tumbled out of the taxi a minute later and Sasha looked at the recent photos on Kay's blog again, grabbing Zoe's arm. 'This girl in the lilac wig and hotpants, I think I know who she is. Some of the girls helped me when I was on a case around here a couple of years ago, and this was Sorbet's signature look.' They stood looking up and down the street helplessly.

'What do we do now?'

'We check inside the arcade, maybe they're meeting inside. What's the time?'

'It's twenty past nine.'

'Kay wasn't meeting the person until ten o'clock so we've still got some time but I need to find her well before then. Zo, you take the left side, I'll take the right.'

They met back at the entrance, shaking their heads.

'This way.' Sasha took off at a pace and turned down a narrow street as Zoe rushed after her. Stopping suddenly, she turned around quickly and stared back up the street.

'What is it, Sash?'

'I don't know, it felt like someone was following us.' She shook her head.

'What are we going to do when we find her?'

'She's going to tell me where she's meeting her contact and then you're going to restrain her and I don't care how you do it, but you're going to march her off and buy her a coffee somewhere.' She stopped suddenly and Zoe smashed into her.

'Have either of you seen Sorbet tonight? With the lilac wig and hotpants? She's a friend of mine.' She held up her phone. 'Her. Or maybe you've seen this girl?'

The two women glanced up disinterestedly and peered at the photos as one of them waved a hand towards the end of the street.

'Which one? Who did you see?'

'Sorbet was down there with Crystal maybe ten minutes ago.'

'This way? Thanks.'

They carried on to the end of the street, stopping and looking in either direction.

'This is hopeless, we'll never find Sorbet, and we'll never find Kay.' Zoe sighed.

'Never say never, Zo, we're going this way, we can cut through to Brewer Street.' She stopped suddenly again. 'What did that quote say again? Something about glass houses?' Sasha typed into her phone and turned to Zoe. 'Forget Sorbet, there's a Glasshouse Street in Soho, this way.' She hurried off with Zoe doing her best to keep up.

'But that doesn't mean that's where she was going.'

'It's all we've got right now, and she did say the clue was on her blog.'

'Sasha!' A voice called out of the darkening night as they neared their destination. 'What are you doing dressed up like a tart? Business that bad?'

'Sorbet, it is you.' The two women hugged briefly, as Sorbet introduced her companion, Crystal.

'This is Zoe, my best friend. Sorbet, I need your help, I'm looking for this girl.' She held her phone out and showed them the photo of Kay in front of the arcade. 'Have you seen her?'

The two women peered at the photo before shaking their heads. 'Sorry, never seen her before.

'Is it about the cutter?'

Sasha's head jerked round. 'What cutter, Sorbet?'

'Sorbet reckons we've got a cutter doing the rounds, Lacey got carved up badly the same night Roberta got in trouble,' added Crystal. 'She managed to cut him back – got his arm with his own knife – bastard can't say he don't deserve it.'

'Yeah, probably the same bloke I had a run-in with, left me his calling card, look.' Sorbet lifted her top to expose a huge purple bruise. 'Least it matches my outfit.' She laughed, lowering her top. 'Creepy bastard, I knew it when I looked into his eyes, but what can a girl do? Gotta earn a living, ain't we?'

'D'you think he's our killer?' Zoe nudged Sasha, wide-eyed at the conversation.

'What, The Street Cleaner, you mean?' Sorbet sniffed disdainfully. 'Nah, he ain't got it in him, he just likes to hurt girls.'

'You can't be sure, can you? Promise me something? Stay together until this killer's caught, yeah? And even if your creepy guy's not the killer, maybe you should give him a wide berth anyway. Listen, we've got an emergency on our hands about this girl. Kay's in trouble and we need to find her urgently. Is there anywhere in Glasshouse Street where someone might suggest meeting?'

Sorbet and Crystal looked at each other, shaking their heads.

'There's not much open there at night.' Crystal pursed her lips. 'Not unless you mean The Ballroom?'

'What's that?'

'Working rooms,' explained Crystal. 'Not exactly somewhere you'd meet someone, not unless you're one of us.'

'Kay, you said her name was?' Sorbet piped up. 'Gretel passed us on her way to Charing Cross road. She mentioned a girl called Kay, said she was dressed up like something from a seventies show. A bit like you two.' She grinned.

~

Kay looked up at the sound of footsteps approaching. *This was it. She was about to get her story of a lifetime.* Smiling, she turned towards the person approaching her through the gloom. 'Oh, it's you.'

SHE'D BEEN QUITE A SWEET GIRL…

'Where did Gretel see her, do you know?' Sasha looked at Sorbet anxiously.

'She didn't say, sorry, darlin'.'

Where will we find Gretel? What does she look like?' Sasha looked at her watch. 'Have you got her number? Can you call her for me?'

'Sure, hold on.' Sorbet took her phone out, tapping the screen with long purple nails.

'Ask her if it was in Glasshouse Street.' Sasha turned to Zoe, while Sorbet spoke into her phone, murmuring, 'Have you got some cash, babes? Twenty?' She tensed at the sound of a police siren nearby, trying to stay calm.

'Next door to The Ballroom, but it was almost an hour ago. When she looked back at the end of the street, the girl was gone,' Sorbet informed Sasha, glancing at Zoe's open purse as a twenty-pound note was extracted. 'I'll have that tenner as well, phone calls are expensive these days.'

Zoe handed over the cash as Sasha mouthed *sorry* at her.

'Cut down there and turn left.' Sorbet tucked the cash into her bag as Sasha enveloped her in a quick hug.

'You're a lifesaver, Sorbet, literally, I hope.'

'We should go.' Crystal nudged Sorbet, nodding her head towards the sound of police sirens as blue lights flashed past at the end of the street.

Sorbet stared intently at Sasha. 'It's him, isn't it? The Street Cleaner. That's why your friend's in danger. You catch the sick freak, Sasha, and when you do, you make sure he hurts real bad, yeah? What he did to Roberta? Poor girl never harmed no one, she was just trying to survive, like we all are. She was one of us. What gives him the right to treat us like that? You ever need our help, you call me, yeah?'

The two women took off, with Sorbet calling out, 'Take care of yourself, Sasha. Don't be a stranger.'

'You too, stay safe. And thanks.' She grabbed Zoe's arm. 'Let's go.'

'Thirty quid, Sash.' Zoe hobbled as fast as she could, wishing she wasn't wearing such high heels.

'I'll pay you back, I promise. Down here. Oh no.' She pulled Zoe along faster, her eyes on the police cars parked in front of The Ballroom.

They rushed through the front door and into the foyer in time to see police officers racing through a door and up the stairs.

'What's happened?' Sasha grabbed the arm of one of the girls hurrying out of the door in the opposite direction.

'Someone's been attacked.'

'Which room?' Her voice was high-pitched with anxiety.

'Top floor, room twenty.' The girl was gone.

They clattered up the four flights of stairs, passing other girls heading down at speed, their breath ragged, banging the door to the passageway against the wall as they flew along looking for room twenty.

'Hold it, miss. Oi.' The police officer at the door fell back against the doorframe as Sasha pushed past him, dragging Zoe with her. 'Come here,' he yelled, grabbing Zoe's arm as Sasha stopped dead, gazing at the scene in front of her, deafened by the sounds of a woman's screaming.

Another officer pulled her roughly back.

'Take 'em downstairs, line 'em up with the other ones,' instructed the officer holding Zoe.

'You don't know what he try to do to me.' The naked woman in the corner of the room screeched and sobbed as an officer tried to approach her.

'Keep back.' She jabbed a broken bottle at him, grabbing a water glass and hurling it at the wall above his head as he ducked.

'Get her out of here.' An overweight man in white vest and pants cowered on the floor, cornered by the woman. 'She tried to kill me,' he shouted, holding his arms up as they dripped with blood.'

'I try to kill you? Look what he did to me.' She turned to face the officers, her body's wounds on full show. 'He attack me with this bottle. He attack me everywhere.' She collapsed, sobbing, as an officer wrapped a blanket around her.

'Let's get her to a hospital. Arrest that thing in the corner.' The officer who appeared to be in charge, turned, frowning as he saw Sasha and Zoe still hovering, their arms loosely held by an officer. 'What are these two still doing here? Downstairs, now.'

'I don't understand.' Sasha stumbled against Zoe as they were frogmarched down the stairs.

'At least it wasn't Kay. Did you see that poor woman?'

'I did, what a bastard.' She struggled against the officer's grip as they reached the foyer. 'We can take it from here, thanks. I'm a private investigator and this is my associate. We're on a case.'

The officer looked them both up and down, smirking. 'Yeah, right, and I'm George bloody Clooney and I'm on a film shoot. Get your skinny arses out with the others. Two more coming!' he yelled to the officer stationed at the entrance door.

'Great,' Sasha muttered to Zoe, as they were pushed into line together with about a dozen other women from The Ballroom. 'We fit right in, look at us.'

They looked at the other women and then at each other and began to splutter with laughter.

'Oh my God, if anyone saw us now.' Doubling over with laughter, Zoe howled.

'Stand up and shut it.' A baton was tapped on her shoulder by the growling officer.

Sasha blinked. 'I think they'll all see us, Zo.' Camera lights flashed again as reporters took photos of the line of sex workers outside the Ballroom.

'Right, names and addresses please, ladies, let's be quick about it, some of us have got work to do.'

'I got work to do too, Mr Policeman, any time you want.' A girl further down the line grinned, pushing her hips out and winking at the officer.

'Me too, any time, baby,' crooned another.

I do a good job on you right now, officer.' A woman next to Zoe made an obscene gesture which brought forth much laughter from the girls, and catcalls and hooting accompanied the women's further teasing comments as names and addresses were taken down.

A blast of sound from a police radio preceded two ambulance staff carrying the injured woman on a stretcher out to the waiting ambulance, and a few seconds later a man was led out in handcuffs and put inside a police vehicle.

A police officer was speaking into his mobile phone. 'It's okay, sarge, all sorted – one female off to hospital with lacerations, mostly superficial but a few nasty looking ones, and one chappie off to the nick. Oh, you're just round the corner? I'll wander up and have a word with you. What d'you want us to do with the rest of the girls? Should we bring 'em in or let 'em loose? Yeah, all low-class sex workers, unofficially of course, and a bit of a grotty-looking bunch, between you and me.'

Charming, Sasha fumed. *They didn't look that bad, bloody nerve.*

'Off you go, ladies, behave yourselves.' The officer walked off up the street and the women scattered in an instant, some sidling back inside while others sashayed off in search of business, and Sasha and Zoe looked up and down the suddenly deserted street as the police vehicles moved off. A camera click and flash made them jump in the sudden silence.

'One more picture, ladies. Give me your best working girl pose. Have we got names?'

'Yes, we've got bloody names. How's–?' Luckily for Sasha, the sudden burst of music from the open window above them drowned out her outpouring of expletives as she hurled one of her shoes at him, thus saving her from further mortification when the reporter's video went viral on youtube later that night.

'Brilliant, you ever thought about acting, love?' The reporter winked, laughing, as he tossed her shoe back to her and walked off.

~

Leaning on Zoe's shoulder, Sasha bent down and replaced her shoe, straightening her clothes as she stood up. 'So, where the hell is Kay?'

'Back to square one, we must have got it wrong. Maybe you should try calling her again?' Zoe shrugged. 'She'll have met her witness by now so maybe she'll answer your call.'

A bloodcurdling scream came from somewhere within The Ballroom, followed by shouting and the clatter of footsteps. A door banged open and someone thumped on the small reception window in the foyer, as a girl wrapped only in a towel ran out, looking up and down the street.

'Where have the police gone?' she asked, her eyes wild.

'What's happened?' Sasha grabbed her arm. 'What is it?'

The girl pointed back inside with a trembling finger, and Sasha dropped her arm, running back inside, with Zoe in hot pursuit.

'Call the police,' a woman was screaming at the person out of view behind the small window to reception.

'This way, follow the screams.' They charged along the ground floor passage towards the cluster of hysterical women gathered around a doorway at the end of the corridor, pushing them aside and running into the small room.

'Kay!' Sasha leaned over the blood-soaked bedcover, lifting the dislodged wig to expose the girl's face. 'Kay, can you hear me?' She threw the cover back, not caring about evidence, her heart sinking at the deep wounds still oozing blood. She turned to Zoe with horrified eyes, before holding her fingers to Kay's neck. 'I think I can feel a pulse. Kay,' she pleaded, 'speak to me.' And then, raising her voice, 'Call the police and get an ambulance here somebody. And get some towels on these wounds. Zo, help me press on them.'

A tiny moan escaped Kay's mouth and her head moved slightly on the pillow as her eyes opened a small crack.

'Quiet, everyone,' Sasha barked. 'Kay, hang on for me, you're going to be alright.' She pressed down on the instantly crimson-soaked towel on Kay's chest as her other hand stroked the girl's face, looking desperately at Zoe, who was kneeling on the bed, pushing towels down firmly on Kay's wounds with both hands.

Sirens sounded outside and blue lights flashed across the room through the window of the room across the passage, its door standing open. The sound of running footsteps approached the room and Sasha peered at Kay's face as a man's voice was heard shouting, 'Move out the bleedin' way.'

'Kay,' she whispered, 'it's alright, help's coming.'

Kay's eyes opened wide and she stared at Sasha in confusion as she murmured, 'It was the same person... from the hotel... it doesn't make sense... I don't understand... I was going to cook a roast dinner like my mum used to make...' Her head rolled to the side as she emitted a small sigh, her eyes staring sightlessly at the dirty ceiling.

'Get these women out of here. What are you doing? Someone get her off.' D.S. Palmer's voice was harsh in the room. Someone spoke urgently into a police radio as uniformed bodies filled the small area.

'No, Kay, come back.' Sasha pleaded as tears rolled down her face, and she looked at a weeping Zoe as hands pulled her away from the bed.

'Oh, Sash, no.' Zoe's bloodied hands gripped Sasha's equally bloody hands as the two women looked at each other in horror.

'Sasha?' Tony Palmer turned her chin to face him, looking at her, and then at Zoe, in astonishment. 'Don't move, either of you. Stand over there,' he said angrily.

They held each other as police officers and ambulance staff clustered around the bed. The bedcover was pulled back up a short while later to hide Kay's face and body, and the room thinned out.

'Who is she?' Tony stood in front of Sasha. 'You knew her. What's her name?'

'Kay Saunders. We were too late,' whispered Sasha. 'She was lying right here while we were upstairs. If we'd got here quicker...'

The curtain moved gently in the breeze and Sasha let go of Zoe, moving towards the window.

'I told you not to move,' snarled Tony, his face like thunder.

'The window's open, he could have got out that way.' Her voice was barely a whisper. 'He can't have got far.'

'Who's she talking about, sarge?'

'The bleedin' Street Cleaner.' He glared at Sasha, directing all his anger at her. 'Happy now? This is all your fault, you stupid bitch, you encouraged her and look where she ended up. Take them in,' he ordered his officer. 'I'll want to speak to them both later. Right, everybody out, let's clear the room and get the SOCOs in. I want all the rooms along this passage emptied and any occupants put together for questioning; get the passage cordoned off and get someone round the back of this building; get eyes on the streets and find this bastard, he can't have got far and he'll be covered in blood.'

Sasha took her last look at Kay's covered body as she and Zoe were removed from the room, her eyes frantically sweeping the scene and memorising it.

~

How convenient, she hadn't even tried to hide it somewhere. Best to hurry, although it was unlikely her body would be discovered until the morning in that place.

The chef's jacket was bundled into the black bag, joining the bloodied raincoat and trousers wrapped around the knife, the shower cap, plastic food hygiene gloves, the plastic bags worn as shoe protection, and the girl's handbag. The knife used was a concern, having been taken from home, there having been no other option, but once it was disposed of it should be damaged enough to destroy any possible evidence remaining on it.

The door to Kay's flat closed gently and the second pair of gloves were dropped into the bag, together with the keys, as footsteps took off along the road. All that remained was to dispose permanently of the last of the incriminating evidence.

The girl had been easier than expected – so eager, so compliant, so... greedy for the details that she hadn't even thought it weird when it had been suggested that they act out the scenario as allegedly witnessed through a crack in the adjoining door. Oh, Kay, how gullible could you be? You thought this killer, who planned their murders down to the last detail, would overlook something as simple as a crack between the door to the adjoining room and the doorframe?

She'd gulped down the cheap fizzy wine and accepted generous refills, seemingly unaware that her notes in her notebook were becoming almost illegible as the drugs kicked in.

Of course, she'd realised what was happening too late, as the person she'd thought was her witness had emerged from the bathroom fully garbed in protective plastic clothing, while she lay accommodatingly acting out the part of the escort.

Her body had refused to cooperate with her brain and the knife had plunged into her with ease as her eyes had widened with alarm and confusion.

Had she understood the words that had been spoken to her as she lay dying – the reason for it all and the reason that she'd had to die? For some reason, it had seemed important to tell her. Maybe, maybe not, only she would know, and she'd taken the truth with her when she'd taken her last breath.

It was a shame really, she'd been quite a sweet girl...

The area around the disused underground car park was littered with rubbish, the odd person scrabbling through it searching for who knew what. Flickering lights from down below indicated fires around which the homeless and the drug addicts gathered for either warmth or to cook something to eat. Heading down into the basement, surprise registered at the sheer number of people sleeping rough. Eyes took in the prone bodies lying around on the pitted concrete floor, some in small groups, some using large cardboard boxes they'd attempted to turn into some kind of temporary home, while others lay isolated in dark corners – huddled bundles of filthy clothing covering filthy bodies, which slept as soundly as if they were tucked up under a goose down duvet with thousand thread count sheets on a memory foam mattress. All alone... unconscious and unobserved... the idea came out of nowhere. It was so... tidy... so perfect...

The blood on the knife was still wet, its plastic shroud having kept it moist, and it smeared easily across the hands, face, and clothing of the unconscious man. The keys to Kay's flat were slipped into a pocket of the stinking jacket, and a quick sort through the contents of her handbag produced her purse and, how perfect, a few sex workers' cards from Soho. This would tie up not only Kay's death, but the other girl as well, and put an end to all the talk of women not being safe at night. The police would close their cases and, as for the man they'd arrested for the first murder, well, too bad, no doubt he deserved it. Everything would settle down and life could go back to normal...

Kay's handbag, smeared with a touch of blood, was placed beside the hapless homeless person, and her purse containing her bank cards was positioned invitingly on the floor next to it. The cards offering their disgusting services were tucked into the torn pocket of the man's shirt and underneath his dirty, foam mattress. There was nothing more to do. It was over.

No one paid any attention to the person shambling past them in the near darkness with their hood pulled up, they were just one of many similar-looking types wandering around. And not one of the spaced-out bodies lying in semi-conscious states from their over-indulgence in drugs or alcohol so much as twitched when the black bag was dropped into the fire around which they lay. The hooded figure waited just long enough to watch the flames dance ravenously, as they began to devour the bag and its contents, before shambling off.

~

'I'm cold.' Zoe shivered, rubbing her bare shoulders and huddling up against Sasha in the custody suite.

'Me too. I'm sorry, babes, I should never have roped you into all this.'

'I roped myself in, you've got nothing to apologise for. How are you feeling? Your belly, I mean?'

'I'm fine, a bit sore that's all. I wish Tony would hurry up.'

'They're not going to make us wait here all night, are they? I can't believe he called you a bitch.'

'He's angry with me and he's probably right, I should have tried harder to discourage Kay. I keep wondering if, on some unconscious level, I wanted her to do the things she did, like finding the chef's jacket and meeting her so-called witness.'

'Don't you ever go blaming yourself, Sash.' Zoe stood up, hands on hips, and faced Sasha. 'You told her to do the right thing every step of the way, it's not your fault if she didn't listen. Bloody hell, you were even going to take her place tonight so that you could keep her safe. Sash, you were prepared to risk your life for her – you knew it could be the killer, but you were going to go ahead anyway.'

'But I failed. I was too late.' Sasha slammed her fists down repeatedly on the hard bench, making an angry drumming sound. 'Tony!' she yelled angrily. 'When are you going to come and talk to us, you bastard?'

'Yeah, let us out.' Zoe joined in, shouting and banging on the door as it suddenly swung open.

'Nice.' D.S. Tony Palmer walked in grinning. 'Right couple of wild cats we've got here. You two not only dress the part to perfection but you act it too. Come on, let's move to an interview room and you can explain to me what the bleedin' hell you were both doing dressed up like a couple of tarts and hanging around in a flamin' knocking shop on a Sunday night.'

They cradled the cups of tea gratefully as Tony spoke.

'I'm sorry I called you a bitch earlier. I've had a hell of a day.' He yawned, stretching his arms over his head. 'I was supposed to be off relaxing, having a lie-in, a lazy Sunday brunch, and reading the papers – the sort of thing normal people do – instead of which, I've been up to my eyes in stabbings all day. Some poor bastard and a young girl both got themselves stabbed to death last night or the early hours of this morning, one of 'em by a bleedin' knife and fork if you can believe it. Anyway, your turn, start talking.'

Sasha gave a garbled account of events as they'd transpired, with Zoe loyally adding the odd comment in support of her actions. She finished with them finding Kay, and expressing her confusion. 'I still don't understand it, she told me she was meeting the person at ten o'clock, but we must have got to The Ballroom by about a quarter to, and she was nowhere to be seen.'

'That was when the police arrived for the first attack,' added Zoe, helpfully.

'Gretel told Sorbet she'd seen her waiting next door round about half past eight or quarter to nine, so why was she so early? She lied to me.' Realisation hit and she leaned back. 'She didn't want me spoiling things so she told me an hour later, just in case I worked out where she was going.'

'See, babes? There was nothing you could have done.'

'Zoe's right, Sasha. No good blaming yourself. Look, technically you haven't done anything wrong, either of you and by the sounds of it, you tried to help the girl and keep her out of trouble. Now, you said she tried to speak to you when you found her?'

Nodding, Sasha recounted Kay's fragmented words, 'She said something about it being the same person from the hotel, that it didn't make sense, and then something about cooking a roast dinner, and her mum.' Her eyes filled with tears. 'And then she died. We were both trying to stop the bleeding, but she just died in front of us.' Unable to stop the tears, she covered her face as Zoe cradled her. 'She was lying there dying while we were running around three floors up with the police watching a woman waving a broken bottle about at a man who'd attacked her. We were right there...' Her voice was muffled as she wept in frustration. Finally, she wiped her eyes with the back of her hand and, sniffing, asked, 'Have you got a tissue?'

Tony pulled a tissue from his pocket.

'Thanks.' Blowing her nose loudly, she cleared her throat. 'Sorry, I don't know what's wrong with me.'

'Not been your finest hour, has it, love?' Tony's eyes were sympathetic.

'Try year,' she said bitterly, before pulling herself together.

'Come on, babes, it'll be alright.' Zoe looked worriedly at her friend, catching Sasha wince and hold her stomach.

'But it won't, not until we catch the bastard who did this.' Her eyes flashed. 'Tone, whoever killed Kay did it to shut her up and to get hold of evidence that she had which would incriminate them. Did you see her blog today?'

'Like I've had time to look at blogs. Why, what was on it?'

'She posted photos of the chef's jacket.'

Tony stared at her blankly.

'The chef's jacket, Tone, worn by the person who killed Chardonnay, the escort in Eric's hotel room. The same person who probably killed Roberta at The Duck Palace, and who killed Kay. We need to get to her flat before the killer gets there.'

Tony had taken out his phone and was tapping at it frantically. He stared at Kay's blog, frowning as he reached the photos Sasha had referred to. 'This can't be true, no way. No way she found this after we'd searched everywhere.'

'She was resourceful, she had a way of finding things out.'

'But we don't know her address yet.'

'We do,' said Zoe.

'Then perhaps you'd be so good as write it down for me.' Tony pushed a pen and pad of paper towards Zoe.

'Her bag was missing.' Sasha's eyes were screwed up as she tried to picture the room in which they'd found Kay. 'Her killer took it, didn't he? He's got her keys, he's got everything. We need to go there right now, we're wasting precious time.'

'The only place you're going is home.' Tony stood up, opening the door and calling to someone. He issued instructions regarding Kay's address and turned back to Sasha and Zoe.

'He's right, babes. She's not well,' Zoe explained to Tony, 'she needs to rest.'

'Zo, please, I'm fine. There was a glass in the room with liquid in it. Did you bag it?'

'Sasha darlin', you're white as a sheet, you look like crap, you both do, to be honest, and you're both covered in blood, it's one o'clock in the bleedin' morning and your friend was just murdered. Why don't you listen to Zoe, here, and go home? Yes, we did bag the glass and its contents, and we'll get it analysed. Contrary to what you seem to think, we do know how to do our job. She was probably drugged with something, and yes again, her bag was missing. Now, you two are going home and the rest of us unlucky bastards are going to carry on working.' He held the door open. 'Now, scarper.'

'And what about Eric? You can't charge him? Not now?'

'That's up to my D.C.I. But I'll be bringing him up to speed with everything a bit later today.' Tony cocked his head to one side, thinking. 'Sit down, you two, there's something I want to say.' He waited for them to resume their seats.

'All this, will we charge Eric, won't we charge Eric, for the murder of Chardonnay, is irrelevant to anything else that's been happening. Simply put, if the evidence in the room is deemed sufficient to incriminate him then he'll be charged — a decision my D.C.I.'s already made.

'Someone stabbed Roberta at the Duck Palace in the same manner as Chardonnay, and Kay Saunders decided it was a serial killer – in effect, she *created* a serial killer. Maybe there never was one. But once she'd got everyone panicking about it, it became fact, and she gave him a name, The Street Cleaner, the killer of female escorts or sex workers. The scenario was similar to Eric's, inasmuch as a woman was stabbed in the bed, but we were missing any drinks or glasses, and most importantly, a suspect still in the room, plus, unlike Chardonnay, Roberta had put up a bit of a struggle. There's every chance that whoever killed Roberta was a sick punter who got too violent, nothing more. Sometimes coincidences happen. We'll catch him, we're not sitting on our hands here, we've got officers speaking to all the girls who frequent The Duck Palace, as well as around the Soho area, and someone will remember something, in time.

'And that's really all we had when you narrow it down, ignoring, of course, her ridiculous attempt to link the prostitute Sonia Clark's death, by strangulation, to her serial killer. Quite simply, we had a couple of women stabbed to death in hotel rooms in London, which, in my experience over the years is, sadly, not completely out of the ordinary.'

'Until Kay's murder last night.'

'Alright, I'll give you that, but then I'll take it back, and here's why. Kay wasn't a sex worker. Kay brought it on herself. But let's go back a bit earlier in the day yesterday to when I got called out to another death by multiple stab wounds. A bloke had been murdered in his hotel room bed sometime Saturday night – not a female, not a sex worker, just a bloke minding his own business. Nothing found in the room, no identification, no wallet, no cash or cards, so

– a robbery plain and simple maybe? What I'm trying to say is that it happens.'

Sasha's expression was militant as she leaned forward, placing her elbows on the table. 'What, a bloke just lay in his bed and let someone stab him to death?'

Tony hesitated and she picked up on it.

'There's something else, isn't there?'

'Alright, I'll tell you then, but it won't get you anywhere close to getting Eric off the hook. There was a champagne bottle in a bucket, and a dirty glass. Now, if it had been another female escort lying there dead, we might have wondered a bit about whether the ladies of the night were in danger from a knife-wielding madman, but it wasn't so that's that.' He shrugged his shoulders. 'Can I get back to Kay, now, is that alright with you, boss lady?'

'Cut it out, Tone. Go on then, what were you going to say about her?'

'Kay's murder looks like the other two female victims', but she was killed for different reasons, you said so yourself. But, and hear me out here, if you take out all this talk of evidence, for which all we've got is some photos of some kind of kitchen worker's uniform on a blog until my men search her place, then what we're left with is a girl who drew attention to herself in all the wrong ways. There's millions of nutters out there, they're bleedin' everywhere, and here's this girl going on and on about serial killers and sexy girls, and stabbings in hotel bedrooms. How long did you think it would take before some nutjob lost it and decided to do to her what she was describing so enthusiastically on her blog? She practically begged someone to do it, that's the way they'd see it.

'So, what did he do? He fulfilled his wildest fantasies, which he might not have even known he had, not until Kay started putting ideas in his head. He arranged to meet her, fed her some cock and bull story about being a witness, who knows? He told her to dress up nice and sexy for him, like a hooker, and then he got himself all nicely excited, took his big old chopping knife from his kitchen, met her in a room at The Ballroom where he knew no one would pay the slightest bit of attention to them, and did to her what she'd kept telling him she wanted him to do to her on her blog – according to his mad, crazy, lunatic bleedin' sick twisted head. A sick nut job like that won't stay off our radar for long, you can trust me on that.'

'Zo, I don't feel so...' Sasha slumped down in her seat, holding her stomach, her face white.

'She's bleeding. Babes?' Zoe looked at the blood pooling on the floor, back at Sasha's face, and then at Tony. 'Get an ambulance. NOW.'

LIKE PEAS IN A POD

Malcolm Bailey walked quietly into the room and nodded at Zoe as she awoke and stretched.

She rubbed her eyes, aware that early morning light was beginning to filter in through the window. 'Sorry, I must have fallen asleep. Is she alright? Did she lose the baby?' She looked anxiously at Sasha's sleeping form, and then at Sasha's specialist.

'There was no baby,' he said softly. 'It was ectopic. She's going to be fine, she just needs to rest.'

A hand reached out and weakly took hold of Zoe's. 'I told you there was no baby.'

'You're awake. How are you feeling, love?'

'Pretty shitty.' Sasha managed a smile, turning her head on the pillow. 'Sorry about causing you all this trouble, Malcolm.'

'Nothing to apologise for, that's what I'm here for. It was in what remained of your left tube, and it dissolved on its own. It happens, albeit rarely. You're going to be fine, but we'll need to talk about what we're going to do with you, moving forward. You don't need me to tell you what a bugger endometriosis is, Sasha, and it's taken its toll on your body. I've recommended it before, but now I think we'll have to face the fact that you'll be better off if we do a hysterectomy with salpingo-oophorectomy. Maybe it's time.' He looked sympathetically at his patient.

'Can it wait? The timing's kind of bad.' She struggled to sit up.

Zoe jumped up, plumping the pillows. 'You need to rest.'

'It can wait, for now, but the sooner we get it done the sooner you can get on with the rest of your life. You'll feel much better, trust me.'

'I know.' She smiled at him weakly. 'Thanks, Malcolm. I'll schedule an appointment, I promise. I want it all gone, it's like an alien life form in my body trying to destroy it and I'm so sick of it. But I feel fine now, much better. Can I go home?'

'In a few hours. I want you to rest. You'll be feeling pretty spaced out from the Diazepam, I expect, so you should try and sleep. I've given you some to help you through the next few days and I recommend that you take them, plus I've written you a prescription in case you feel the need for more. You're likely to experience some anxiety and depression, it's quite natural. There'll be some blood loss over the next few days and probably mild cramping, but things will settle down.'

He turned to Zoe. 'She'll need someone to keep an eye on her, to make sure she rests for a few days. No running around, just bed rest, some healthy food to build her strength up, that sort of thing.'

'She's staying with me, I'll look after her and I'll make sure she rests. I won't let her move from her bed.'

'Right, good.' Malcolm Bailey patted Sasha's hand. 'Look after yourself. The nurse will be along a bit later to check on you and to tell you when you can leave. Then it's straight home to bed. And whatever the two of you were doing last night, out clubbing in a nightclub or whatever, there's to be none of that, d'you hear me?' He gave them both a fatherly frown, followed by a smile and turned to leave the room.

Embarrassed, Zoe turned bright red, tucking her feet under her chair and tugging at her skirt.

'We were undercover, on a case.' Sasha flushed, not wanting her specialist to think the wrong thing. 'I'm in the middle of an investigation.'

'Not now, you're not. You're lying in a hospital bed. Whatever it is it can wait. Doctor's orders. You hear me?'

They both nodded obediently as he left, giving them a wave.

'Zo, I need to get home and take a shower.'

You heard your specialist, you've got to wait for the nurse.' Zoe looked at her friend suspiciously.

'Little Miss Goody Two-Shoes.' Sasha smiled, her eyelids heavy as she fought sleepiness.

'Yeah? Well, Miss Goody Two-Shoes is in charge by order of Mr Bailey. Get some sleep and I'll go home and bring you in some clean clothes a bit later, alright?'

'There was a man in my room, standing by the bed...' Sasha's voice was drowsy.

'That was Malcolm, babes.'

She shook her head. 'No, not him, someone else, not nice...'

Zoe smiled at her friend, realising that she'd fallen asleep. Standing up quietly, she tip-toed out of the room and took a taxi home.

~

Disorientated, Sasha looked around, trying to get her bearings, before remembering what had happened. Sadness engulfed her and she indulged for a moment, thinking about Kay and thinking about her body's betrayal. Then she gave herself a stern talking-to and climbed out of bed.

Returning from the bathroom, she noticed the banana and yoghurt sitting on the table beside her bed and, realising that she was hungry, took a bite of the banana while she checked the drawer beside her bed, found her phone, and called Zoe.

'It's me. Are you at home? I feel fine, Zo, honest. I'm on my way. What? No, you don't need to fetch me, I'll be fine, I'll just take a taxi. Yes, the nurse said I can leave,' she lied.

Taking a couple of mouthfuls of yoghurt, she gathered the rest of her belongings, slipped on her shoes, and left the room, walking along the corridor, pausing to look through the window of the baby unit.

'Like peas in a pod, aren't they? They all look the same when they're tucked up like that with only their little heads showing.' The nurse smiled brightly as she stood beside Sasha. 'Can I help you at all?' Her eyes glanced surreptitiously at Sasha's outfit.

'What? Oh, no, I'm just on my way out.'

'Just along there and turn right at the end.' The nurse stood guard over her charges until Sasha had clip-clopped her way down the corridor and turned the corner. *You could never be too careful, and she hadn't looked particularly savoury. Maybe, to be on the safe side, she'd let the nurses' stations know to look out for a... well, a woman of ill repute was what they'd called them in the old days...*

About to walk out, Sasha had a feeling of guilt and headed along to the nurse's station. 'I'd like to check myself out,' she said, wondering why the nurses were giggling and nudging each other as they gave her sidelong glances.

~

'You're what? You're charging me?' Eric's face turned white. 'What was that?' He shook his head to dispel the buzzing sensation.

'I said, you'll be moved to Wormwood Scrubs until your court date.'

'Wormwood Scrubs? The prison?' He began to laugh, sinking onto the chair, his body shaking uncontrollably as his words came out in juddering snatches. 'I'm living in a nightmare; this can't be happening to me; it's a sick joke; I didn't kill anyone; I was robbed, I'm the damned victim here; you should be looking for whoever took my wallet; where's Brian, does he know? I need a bloody drink.' Groaning, he buried his face in his hands.

'Do you want us to call Mr Trefoyle in to see you?'

'Yes, I bloody do. What am I paying him for? And where's Sasha? She was supposed to be helping me by doing your job for you. You're a bunch of bloody incompetents, that's what you are, there's a killer out there. D'you hear me? There's a bloke out there who stabbed a woman to death in a hotel room I somehow ended up in, and instead of looking for him, you're sending me to Wormwood Scrubs to be crammed in a cell with murderers and rapists. I'm a property developer, I live in a nice flat, I wear expensive suits, and I drink fine champagne. What I don't do is go round killing people. This shouldn't be happening to me.' His voice had risen angrily as he lashed out.

'Alright, calm it, Mr Latimer, shouting won't get you anywhere.' Tony wondered whether he should say anything about Sasha, and made a mental note to check on how she was.

'Sasha was taken to hospital last night.' *Well, he'd said it now.*

'What? Is she alright? What happened? Was it an accident?'

'No, not an accident, she, er, had something wrong with her insides.' *Now he'd dug himself a hole.* 'I'll find out how she is and let you know, and I'll give your solicitor a call.' He stood up abruptly, leaving Eric to compute everything as best he could.

~

'Sash, you're home, let's get you out of those clothes and into the bath. Would you like that? Or a nice shower? And then you can rest in bed while I make you something to eat. How does that sound?' Zoe fussed around, behaving like a mother hen, much to Sasha's amusement.

'Zo, I'm fine, babes, you don't need to do the Florence Nightingale thing on me. You've been the best friend in the world, especially these last few days, but it's not fair on you that all my problems are affecting your life so much. And what about you? You must be exhausted. What about the gallery?'

'I phoned Flavia and explained that I won't be in today, that I had to look after you.'

'You shouldn't have done that, Flavia's a bit of a drama queen, I don't want you to lose your job because of me.'

'You let me handle Flavia, and you let me worry about whether I want to be affected by your problems or not. Right, bath or shower?'

'Bath, I think, that sounds good. But then, and don't shout at me, I have to go out...'

She waited until Zoe had finished her apoplectic tirade.

'You're absolutely right, of course.' She continued quickly, as Zoe opened her mouth to say something else. 'But I was thinking on the way back here from the hospital, about everything that Tony said last night, or this morning, about the murders. You see, they've tidied it all up in their heads and made sense of it. They've decided that Eric killed Chardonnay in some kind of drunken or drugged stupor, they've decided that Roberta was killed by a violent customer, and they've pretty much decided that Kay brought her murder on herself by writing about the serial killer on her blog and attracting the attention of a madman.

'So, they're done. They're not looking for connections between the murders, they've got Eric, and they're looking for two other blokes with no connection to each other. Don't you see, Zo? If I don't keep working on this, someone else is going to get killed. It's not only about clearing Eric's name anymore, it's about making sure no more girls get murdered.

'The clues are all there, I'm sure of it. There's something about the night that Eric was drinking with the guys, all the escort connections, the moving from bar to bar. I've spoken to them all and their stories are all pretty similar, but one or more of them knows more than they're saying, I'm sure of it. Do they know something that could help Eric? And if they do, why aren't they helping him? Or were they all genuinely so hammered they haven't got a clue what happened that night? If I'm to believe Franco, then both Rowan and Max were seen holding at least one of the cards that were being handed out. What happened to the cards? Did they use them? And another thing, they're all the alibi for each other, I mean, Zo, some of them were round the corner from The Duck Palace the very night that Roberta was murdered. What are the odds? I'm not saying one of them is going round killing escorts, or prostitutes, or women in general but, well, I've got questions... And then there's the barman from Bar Simone, I haven't spoken to him yet, or the escorts who handed out their cards. I've got to speak to them as soon as possible. So, that's why I can't just lie in bed all day. I can rest when this is all over, and I do feel fine,' she concluded, flashing Zoe a firm smile.

Huffing, Zoe nodded. 'Alright, I suppose. So, you're just going to go to this bar and speak to the barman and the girls?'

'That's all, just to see if any of them are there, otherwise, I'll go tomorrow night, like Quentin, who they call Rain Man, suggested. The girls might not be there during the day, after all. But I have to try today, I have to do something otherwise we lose more precious time. I'll do that and then I'll come home and be the perfect patient for the rest of the day, how's that? So, you can go to work and not worry about me.'

'Hmm, except I won't be here to check on you if I go to work, will I?'

'Since when did friends become so untrusting of each other?'

'Since their best friend is Sasha.' Laughing, Zoe hugged her friend. 'Alright, I trust you, and I'll go to work, but I'd better find you home when I get back tonight.'

~

Dillon Brown put the phone down, wondering what that had all been about. He wiped a cloth along the bar counter, nodding at a waiting customer and serving them their drinks before returning to his ruminations.

Why was a cop phoning him to confirm his name and address? And more than that, his date of birth? No, he'd told them, he wasn't married but yes, he was divorced. Sure, he'd told them, they were welcome to pop in to confirm his identity any time, he had nothing to hide.

Mystified, he considered their final question. Was he in the habit of staying in hotels in London? Why would he, he'd countered, when he lived in London? The uncomfortable thought had flashed through his mind that although he hadn't stayed in a hotel in London, his card had been used to book a room for his mate. That wasn't a crime though, was it? But he was a little unclear about the laws around booking escort services, even if he hadn't used them himself, so he certainly wasn't going to mention it to the cop and bring a whole load of legal troubles down on his head.

Oh well, no point in worrying about something when he didn't even know what it was he was supposed to be worrying about. He turned his attention to the group of foreign tourists who had just walked in and wanted to try all the cocktails on the menu and was kept busy by them, as well as a regular stream of customers until Sasha arrived a couple of hours later and announced that she was looking for someone called Dillon.

'That's me, Dillon Brown at your service,' he said, deciding that she didn't look like a cop, although you couldn't be sure, maybe she was undercover. 'What can I do you for?'

'My name's Sasha Blue, and I wondered if I could ask you a couple of questions? I'm a private investigator,' she clarified.

What was it with everyone asking him questions today? 'Come and take a load off,' he said, wiping his hands on the cloth, before walking round the bar and leading her to a quiet table.

'It's about last Tuesday night, I know it's a bit of a long shot but I'm hoping you might be able to tell me about some of the customers who were here.'

'I'll try, but we get pretty busy most nights.'

She explained about Eric and Shuggy joining up with the others, about how they'd all been drinking heavily and had quite likely made a bit of a scene. She showed him a photo of Eric from her phone, described the others as best she could, and finished up with the fact that they'd been receiving a lot of attention from some of the female customers who had been giving out their business cards.

'Hookers, you mean?' *Careful, Dillon boy, this could be a trap.*

'Well, escorts maybe. They would have looked classy but hot, I suppose?'

Dillon laughed. 'You're describing the majority of our evening female customers, that's when everyone gets dressed up like a dog's dinner. We don't condone prostitution, of course, and we can't help it if we get groups of chicks out on the pull, blokes too, obviously.'

'I understand, well, can I leave you my card in case you think of anything? It's just, well, a friend of mine's in trouble and I'm trying to help him.' She stood up to leave, smiling her thanks.

Dillon took her card. *It looked legit, so she wasn't a cop then.* She looked pale and drawn and he felt a moment of sympathy. 'You're definitely not a cop?'

'No, definitely not, nothing to do with the police, this is personal.' Sasha looked at him hopefully, sensing he wanted to tell her something. 'Was there something...?'

'They were sitting over there if I'm thinking of the right bunch.' He pointed to another table. 'And there was a group of girls at that table next to them. That bloke you showed me in the photo, with the blonde hair, he was off his trolley, ordering bottles of champagne, and the girls kind of moved in on them. They were a right noisy lot, but the bar tab was running up nicely so I wasn't going to ask them to keep it down. You mentioned a red-haired bloke? I think I remember him, a loud laugh like a donkey or something. Bit of a tosser, if you ask me. Sorry, he's not your friend you're trying to help, is he?'

'No.' Sasha grinned. 'You've kind of nailed it, I thought the same thing. His name's Rowan.'

'Right. Well, I can't tell you if anyone specific was an escort or whatever, but when they all left and I was cleaning up, I did find a few cards on the table.'

'Escort cards? I don't suppose you remember the name of the agency?'

Dillon shook his head. 'I chucked them in the bin. Some of them were pink, with writing on the back.'

'Writing on the back? Like what?'

'Sorry, promo codes maybe?'

'Dillon, thank you, you've been a massive help.'

~

Excitement gave her renewed energy, and she left Bar Simone with thoughts buzzing through her head.

Franco and Rain Man had both told her they'd seen Max and Rowan holding pink cards, but neither of them had admitted it to her. Her stomach turned at the thought of speaking to Max again, which left Rowan – the tosser, she thought to herself, liking Dillon's simple but descriptive term.

Why hadn't Rowan mentioned it to her? Was he lying because he was guilty of more than just possibly spending time with an escort? He was Eric's friend and business partner, he'd picked up an escort card the same night his friend had ended up in a hotel room in which an escort was murdered later that night, and yet he'd said nothing. Well, we'd see about that, she decided grimly, calling his number. There'd be no more pussy-footing around, time was running out – for Eric and for the next victim of whoever was doing this.

Rowan's phone went to voicemail and she reined in her impatience with difficulty.

'Rowan, it's Sasha here, we spoke the other day at your office, about Eric? I've just left Bar Simone where the barman was telling me about the escort cards that were given to you all on Tuesday night. I know that you and Max both took cards when you left and that they were pink. Can you give me a call back as soon as possible? I've got some questions for you and it's pretty urgent. Thanks.'

Her phone rang immediately and she answered it without looking. 'Rowan, thanks for calling back, I–'

'Sash, it's Tone. How you doing, sweetheart? You gave us a bit of a scare last night. You don't sound like you're in hospital?'

'No, I checked out this morning. It's sweet of you to call, Tone. I'm fine, it was nothing, just my endometriosis giving me trouble. But I'm back on track and feeling strong. Thanks for looking after me last night, I'm sorry I caused you a problem. So, what's new? Any updates on Eric?'

'He's being charged, darlin', it's not up to me, you know that, but even if it was, I don't see who else could have done it. I'm sorry, I know it's not what you want to hear, especially with your health troubles. Look, it's over now, you did what you could, now you can put your feet up and have a bit of a rest. You've got nothing to feel bad about, he's lucky he even had you in his corner after the way he treated you.'

She'd been resigned to hearing it but it was still a jolt. 'Are you letting him out on bail, at least?'

'No, he's being transferred to The Scrubs until his hearing, but he's still with us at the moment. Oh, and we've had Kay Saunders' flat checked out – no chef's jacket to be found.'

'Someone's been there, her killer's been there, Tone.' Her heart thudded in her chest as someone in the sudden passing crowd brushed against her, giving her a chilled feeling.

'Nope, she probably faked it and then got rid of it once she'd done her blog post. No signs of forced entry, no signs of any disturbance in there. I've solved one little mystery for you though.'

'What?'

'You mentioned something that she said about a roast dinner and her mum? There was a packet of chicken pieces, some vegetables, and a tub of gravy in her fridge, plus a couple of potatoes sitting on the kitchen counter. Looks like she was planning on cooking herself a little Sunday Roast.'

'Like her mum used to make,' Sasha whispered.

'Yeah, exactly. Kind of sad when you think about it. Oh, we found a relative in her phonebook, her sister, so she's going to clear out Kay's flat and take care of things. Well, I'll be off then, criminals to catch and all that. You take care now, you hear me?'

She put her phone back in her bag and walked along the pavement slowly, her earlier excitement gone, replaced with sadness. Life really was a bloody bitch at times.

~

Alex walked into Rowan's office and looked at his phone as it stopped ringing. Picking it up, she walked back out and went through to the small bathroom cubicle past their kitchenette, listening at the door. Wrinkling her nose in disgust, she backed away. He was a total gross-out sometimes, she thought, wondering why she'd ever fancied him.

'Alex?' Her boss's urgent cry made her smile.

'What's the matter?' she shouted back at the door.

'There's no loo roll.'

Smiling wickedly, she looked down at the carrier bag with the toilet paper and teabags she'd picked up on her way in that morning. 'I'll just pop out to the shop and get some, won't be long.'

'What? I don't believe this. I should fire you. Who runs out of toilet paper? Hurry up, I'm stuck here. Flippin' waste of space, can't even remember to buy toilet paper.'

His shouted rant continued unheeded as she sat on her desk, swinging her crossed leg, and thinking about what she'd heard him saying on the phone earlier.

He'd obviously got a new bird, and had been with her last night. *After he'd taken her for a drink and tried to get into her.* He was a disgusting rat, she decided, and she was done with all his stupid flirting. Her flatmate was right, she could do better than some bloke who cheated on his wife and who always stunk of body odour. She tapped his security pin into his phone and read his text messages back and forth with his latest conquest, grimacing, before listening to the voice message left by the caller just moments earlier. Writing down the caller's phone number, she replaced his phone on his desk, removed something from her bottom drawer, picked up her handbag, and walked to the bathroom door, dropping the packet of toilet paper outside it.

'Here's your toilet paper, I'm going to lunch.' She walked out, smiling to herself as she heard the door crash open, accompanied by further invectives. Fingering the pink card, she tapped in the phone number.

'Is that Sasha? It's Alex, Rowan and Eric's secretary. I listened to your message to Rowan. Yeah, he left his phone. I've got something for you, it's an escort card. I think it's what you were talking about. D'you wanna meet up? I'll be in Oxford Circus in about half an hour, I'm going shopping.'

She walked along to the tube station, swinging her bag. It was all tied up with the murder of that escort, she just knew it. Maybe Rowan was a murderer. Shuddering with horrified excitement, she imagined telling Jen about it over drinks later. She'd probably get interviewed and be on telly and in magazines – she should probably get her hair done just in case. Of course, if he was the murderer then that meant he was that serial killer – the one they'd given the name to in the papers. She shivered again, picturing her photo, with the story title above it, in her favourite magazine: *I almost slept with The Street Cleaner*. Frowning, she shook her head slightly. No, that was no good, it made it sound like she'd nearly ended up in bed with some bloke who cleaned the rubbish out of the streets.

~

'Alex.' Sasha waved to catch the attention of the younger woman hovering outside H&M.

'Hi, Sasha.' Smiling, Alex walked over to her. 'I haven't got long, I've got shopping to do and I've got to get back to the office.'

'No problem, thanks for calling me and meeting me. You said you've got an escort card. Can I see it?'

'You can have it. Dunno why I kept it really, I found it in his rubbish bin and put it in my drawer.' She laughed as she handed Sasha the card. 'Maybe I thought it would come in useful someday if his wife ever gave me any gyp about me and him. Oh–' she looked at Sasha. 'There's not really a me and him, he's a total pig, dunno why I liked him before. He cheats on his wife all the time, did you know that? Even last night, he tried it on with me and then went off somewhere with some other woman, then home to his wife. So, is this tied up with the murders? Is Ro tied up in it? Is this what this is all about? What does the card prove?'

Blinking, Sasha laughed. 'Hold on, I can hardly keep up. Right, let's have a look. Discreetly Elite... Hmm, it's thin card, not very good quality, and the pink's pretty garish... Somehow, I was expecting something a bit more upmarket...' She turned the card over, looking at the handwritten capital letters and numbers. 'SPROMO54. Okay, so that's a promotional code giving them some kind of discount, I suppose. You say you found it in his rubbish bin? I don't suppose you can remember when, by any chance?'

'I can, as it goes, it was Thursday morning when I found it. I'd opened up and the place needed a bit of a clean-through – part of my glamourous job description those tight fists didn't tell me about until they'd got me working there. More fool me, I suppose.' She pulled a wry face. 'Anyway, yeah, so I emptied the bins Thursday morning and saw it in Rowan's, and fished it out. And before you ask, I'd emptied the bins on Tuesday night when I left work, so he could only have put it in there on Wednesday. And that escort was murdered Tuesday night, wasn't she? Was she from this place?' Alex tapped the card in Sasha's hand. 'So, d'you think Ro had something to do with it? What about Eric? How's he doing? He's a nice bloke, I feel kind of sorry for him.'

'I honestly don't know anything at the moment, but I do think this card is important in some way. It all revolves around the evening leading up to the night of the murder and how they ended up with escort cards, and then one, or more, escorts, I'm sure of it. Anyway.' She shook her head, smiling. 'You don't want to listen to me going on when you've got shopping to do. Would you say that Eric and Rowan were, apart from being business partners, genuinely close friends?'

Nodding, Alex replied. 'Yeah, I think so. Like, they're always egging each other on, always laughing about the old days, and always encouraging each other to go out and get smashed.' She looked at Sasha. 'That's not the kind of close friends you meant, is it?'

'Not really, but it sums them both up pretty well. My grandma used to call people like that fair-weather friends – there for the good times but gone in a flash when things turned bad. And things have definitely turned bad for Eric...'

'And Rowan's not there for him... Yeah, I get it, makes sense that...' Alex looked at her watch. 'Well, I should get going. Are you alright? You look pale.'

'Just a rough night. Thanks, Alex, you may have helped Eric immensely with this. And, er, maybe don't mention it to Rowan?'

'He won't know anything about it, I deleted your message.' She grinned mischievously. 'Together with a few from his latest bit on the side. You're nice, I wasn't sure about you the other day, but I like you. Eric's a real plank, a cute one, but a total and utter plank. You deserve better.'

'Thanks.' Warmed by the girl's kind words, Sasha smiled. 'You're nice too. I suppose I didn't form the right impression of you the other day, either. Just goes to show how we can have completely the wrong idea about someone. You deserve better than to work with Rowan and Eric – if Eric ever gets back there.'

'Maybe I should look for a new job... Maybe I should come and work for you, I like the sound of this detective work.' Alex gave her a hopeful look.

'Much as I like the sound of that – you remind me of someone I knew recently who wanted to come and work with me – I'm afraid I don't have an office.' She pulled a wry face. 'I don't even have anywhere to live since my flat burned down five days ago – I'm living at my friend's.'

'Oh, poor you.' Alex's mouth turned down at the corners. 'Then the first thing we need to do is to find you an office and a new flat.' She gave Sasha a cheeky grin. 'What happened to her? The girl who wanted to work with you? You said *knew*, not *know*?'

She was sharp. 'She was murdered by the same person who killed the escort in Eric's hotel room, and at least one other woman so far.'

Wide-eyed, Alex considered Sasha's words. 'Then you owe it to her to catch this bastard.'

'I do. And I will.' Sasha hugged Alex. 'Thanks, it was nice to see you again.'

'You too and, I meant it, about coming to work for you. Once you get sorted out, give me a call, you've got my number now. I reckon we could be a great team.'

'That's exactly what Kay said to me.'

'Was that her name? The girl who was murdered?'

Sasha nodded, and they set off in different directions. She stopped once, turning round and studying the faces in the crowd. Why couldn't she shake this feeling that someone was following her?

WILD CAT WOMEN OF THE NIGHT

By the time Zoe arrived home from the art gallery, Sasha was sitting on the settee with her feet up, looking every inch the model patient. Zoe stood in the doorway and looked around suspiciously. 'This looks too good to be true.'

'Well, you know what they say, when it looks too good to be true…'

'It probably is,' they finished together.

'How was the lovely Flavia?'

'Oh, her usual self, drifting around drinking wine and scaring the customers with her mumbo jumbo.'

'How does it go? Art is food for the soul, are you hungry, or something like that?'

Grinning, Zoe continued her boss's favourite line. 'Tell me that you're famished and I'll feed you. Anyone who stays to be fed finds themselves a few hundred pounds lighter and the owner of an original artwork by a yet unknown, but on the brink of discovery, artist. She's got a good eye though, I'll give her that.' She tossed her bag on the coffee table and sank into an armchair.

'Right, how did your search for the barman go? Did you find him?'

'I did, and he described Eric's partner, Rowan, as a bit of a tosser, which I thought summed him up nicely. He also told me that a blonde bloke in the group was off his head and ordering bottles of champagne for them and the girls at the table next to them.'

'Eric,' breathed Zoe. 'And the girls were escorts, I bet you. What else?'

'Well, when they left and he was clearing the table, he found some escort cards, some of which were pink, but he threw them away.' She leaned forward. 'Rowan and Max both took the pink cards, so all I need to know is whether they used them to book escorts that night.'

'And if they did, what does it mean?'

'Yeah, well, that's where I get stuck. Maybe it means that all three of them booked escorts from the same agency? Did they all book rooms at the same hotel? If so, why have they both kept quiet while Eric is sitting in custody charged with murder? Is one of them the killer? What about the girls they were with?'

'So many questions.' Zoe sighed. 'If only we had one of the cards.'

'Tada.' Sasha slapped the pink card down on the coffee table, grinning at her friend.

'Where did you get it? Wait, you said the barman threw them away, then how–?' Zoe picked it up, turning it over in her hand as she examined it. 'It feels kind of cheap, thin card, not very good quality.'

'And the colour's too gaudy, not classy like you'd expect. There's something off about it. If it was the personal card of an escort, I'd say maybe they printed them on their home printer, but it's an agency card.'

Zoe snorted in derision. 'Must be one tacky escort agency if they give out cards like this.'

'Which is weird, because Lisa Pennington, aka Chardonnay, was a high-class escort, so why would she be associated with a low-class agency? I've got too many questions and no flippin' answers.'

'I've got a question.' Zoe gave Sasha one of her looks. 'Where did you get this card when all you did was go and see the barman at Bar Simone and then come back here?'

'It's not what you think.' Sasha gave her best innocent look. 'All I did was stop off at Oxford Circus and meet Alex.'

'Oh, Sash, you promised me, babes. Alright, so who is Alex?'

'She's Eric and Rowan's secretary.' Sasha explained about leaving a message on Rowan's phone and about Alex calling her to meet her with the card. 'So,' she finished off, 'I think she had a bit of a thing for Rowan, but not anymore. Bottom line, Rowan's hiding something, I just don't know how bad it is.'

'And the other bloke.'

'Yes, him too, Max. Shall we have some wine?'

'What? You came out of hospital this morning, you can't have wine.'

'I feel fine, Malcolm didn't say I couldn't have a glass of wine, did he? Zo, what was in my body never had a chance of staying in there, so it came out, end of story. It was no worse than some other months I've had.' Sasha gave Zoe a firm smile.

Zoe's eyes were soft with sympathy. 'Oh, Sash, I know you're sad. Don't you want to talk about it, love?'

'I... no, I can't talk about it. I'm not going to think about it, it's over.' She took a deep breath. 'There was one fleeting moment, I'd got out of the shower after you made me do the test, when I allowed myself to think that I could be a mum... it felt nice... I pictured it for a second...' She shook her head, dispelling the memory. 'Then I came back to reality. I knew my body would betray me, it was just a matter of when.' She gave a bitter laugh. 'It didn't take long, did it? Christ, I can't believe that was only yesterday.'

Zoe moved to sit beside her, pulling her into a hug. 'You've been through so much, I wish I could make it better for you.

Sasha blew her nose and smiled. 'Maybe a glass of wine would help?'

'Well, I can't say no now, can I?'

'I suppose my boobs will shrink. Pity, I quite liked them a bit bigger.'

Zoe fetched a bottle of wine and two glasses, knowing her friend was putting on a brave face, and deciding to play along. 'Now, we both know I'm the one with the big boobs, stop trying to step on my turf.'

~

'We should eat something, I suppose.' Zoe held the second empty wine bottle upside down a while later, pulling a surprised face at Sasha.

'I could make us a toasted sandwich?' Sasha opened the fridge, examining its contents. 'Cheese and tomato?'

'I'll make them, you pour us some more wine. What about those tablets Malcolm gave you? Are you taking them? You should.'

'I'll take one after I've eaten, but I don't think I need them, I don't feel anxious or depressed.'

'That's the wine.'

'Then that's the medicine I need.'

The sound of something falling on the doormat distracted them and Sasha walked through to see what it was. Picking up the envelope, she read the note written on it and tore the envelope open.

'Zo, listen to this, it's from my insurers. It got delivered next door by mistake. They've approved my claim and are depositing the money into my account.'

'That's fantastic, it's the first step.' Dropping the toasted sandwiches onto plates, Zoe clapped her hands.

'Now I just need to find a flat to rent, once I get some work...'

'There's no rush, you're here with me, you're taking some much-needed personal time, and you're all over the place with this Eric business. Put this to bed and then you can worry about your next case and a new flat. I'll help you look when the time's right, it'll be fun. Let's eat.'

They took their plates and sat down, munching on their sandwiches.

'Toasted sarnies are the best, aren't they?' Sasha finished her last mouthful. 'You know, Alex said she wanted to come and work for me. She reminded me of Kay, the same kind of pushy, cheeky, mix. Maybe it's time I fulfilled my dream of having my own proper private investigation agency, instead of working from my flat.'

'I love that idea. But you'll have to toughen up a bit, babes. No more getting involved in personal cases to help out people you know. I mean, look at you at the moment, you're spending every minute investigating Eric's murder case and no one's going to pay you a penny, are they?'

'I know, I can hardly present Eric with a bill, can I?'

'You should, he bloody well owes you big time. We should celebrate you feeling better and getting your insurance money. And we should drink to you having your private investigator agency, with an office and an actual assistant. Oh, and we should toast your new flat, which you'll find when the time's right, and which will be perfect. I've got a bottle of bubbles in the fridge, I'll grab it.' Zoe jumped up. 'I do declare I'm feeling a bit tipsy.'

Feeling much better about everything, Sasha looked at the strip of pills on the table beside her. She might as well take one, she didn't want this happy feeling to go, she hadn't wanted to tell Zoe earlier how flat she'd been feeling. She also wanted to drown out her feelings of guilt over Kay's death, she acknowledged.

'Cheers,' they toasted each other, throwing back their glasses of fizz and refilling them.

Sasha glanced at the escort agency card sitting on the coffee table. 'Maybe I should call it?'

'Yeah, call it. But what are you going to say?'

'I don't know, nothing.'

Zoe spluttered with laughter. 'You'll have to say something.'

'I'll ask them if they've got two male escorts available for tonight.'

They both dissolved into fits of laughter as the doorbell rang.

Zoe stood up, holding her finger to her lips. 'Shh,' she said, as she tripped over the coffee table.

Sasha jumped up to steady her, losing her balance, and with a loud crash, they landed on the settee, screeching with laughter.

'I needed a laugh so badly. This is the best evening ever.' She wiped her tears as the doorbell rang again, repeatedly.

They looked at each other with exaggeratedly wide eyes.

'I'm going to go and answer the door now.' Zoe stood up. 'I'm coming,' she shouted, walking to the door and yanking it open. 'Jamesh!' She blinked in surprise.

Sasha frantically picked up the books and magazines that Zoe had knocked from the coffee table, straightening the piles and sitting back as James walked in, an innocent smile on her face.

'Hello, Shames.'

Realising how drunk they both sounded, they caught each other's eyes, trying not to laugh.

'Well, well, well, you two look like you're having fun.' James kissed Zoe, before smiling oddly at them both.

He threw some newspapers down on the coffee table. 'Perhaps you'd like to explain to me what this is all about?'

They each picked up a paper, staring at the photo on the page that James had folded the papers open at.

'*The Street Cleaner claims his next victim as prostitutes are arrested.*' James recounted the title of one of them as he sat down in an armchair. 'How about this one? *Lucky to be alive – the sad scraps of a once booming sex industry.* This one's perfect, *Soho sex workers lined up outside The Ballroom in police raid.* And you've got to love the first line, listen to this, *Haggard and burnt out, these old relics should be put out to pasture.*'

Don't do it, Zo, don't laugh. Sasha gave her friend a sidelong look, catching her eye as they began to shake with laughter, erupting with spluttering giggles.

'That's so rude, though.' Sasha was indignant.

'Thass you.' Zoe slurred, pointing helpfully at the photo, indicating Sasha in the line of women. 'You look terrible.'

'You don't look so hot yourself, look. James–' Sasha tried to look serious. 'It's my fault, don't blame Zoe. And I don't know why we're laughing after what happened. It was awful.'

'We were working,' added Zoe, realising as she said it how it sounded, and collapsing into fresh peals of laughter, nudging Sasha, who let out a loud, drunken shriek, despite her attempts at seriousness.

'Zo, we need to be serious. James isn't amused.'

'And this?' James held up his phone, playing them a video from youtube.

They watched, aghast, as Sasha shouted obscenities, the worst of them obscured by beeps, and hurled her shoe at the camera, accompanied by a delighted Zoe clapping her hands in glee. *Wild Cat Women of the Night*, the title helpfully explained.

Sasha tried to sober up. 'I shouldn't have taken that Diazepam,' she groaned.

'Drugs as well? What the hell is going on with you two?' James's face was bewildered.

'Sasha's not well.' Zoe turned to her. 'We have to tell him.'

'I'll do it.' Sasha explained the previous evening's events to James as best she could, telling him about Kay, and about her failed attempt to keep her safe. She praised Zoe, telling him that she'd insisted on accompanying her when they went to Soho undercover, to keep her safe, finishing off with a brief mention of their visit to the police station and of her time spent in hospital.

'You must blame me, James, not Zo, she was just being a good friend.'

'I don't blame you, Sash, or Zoe for going with you, although I think you've both behaved in a completely reckless manner. No, I blame Eric for getting you involved in this in the first place. Whatever he did, or didn't do, there's no reason for the two of you to go putting yourselves in harm's way when there's a bloody psycho on the loose killing women left right and centre. I don't know whether to be mad or amused at what the pair of you got up to. Is there any wine left in that bottle?'

'I'll grab another one.' Zoe crossed to the sideboard, opened the door and took out another bottle of red wine, handing it to James silently, together with a glass.

They sat, shame-faced, like naughty schoolgirls as James continued to reproach them.

Zoe opened her mouth to speak.

'I'm not done yet.' He raised his eyebrows at her and she closed her mouth.

'I'm sorry about your health problems, Sash, you've been through a rough time lately with everything. Don't you think it's time you took some proper time out? Ex-boyfriend, or rather fiancé, arrested for murder, your flat burning down, losing all of your possessions, trying to investigate a serial killer of prostitutes, losing a friend to that serial killer, and going through an ectopic pregnancy. Listen to that list of woes – most people would have ended up in a padded cell after all that, but here you are, still going at everything hammer and tongs. You're not going to be able to keep it up, something's going to break and, Zoe, that's where I blame you.'

'Me?'

'Instead of making Sasha rest so that she heals, mentally and physically, you've encouraged her to sit and booze away which, on top of her medication, might explain why she's pretty hammered. I'm not sure what your excuse is though.'

'The Valium. Diazepam and alcohol. That could be it!'

'What, babes? What is it?' Zoe was a step behind.

James's ticking-off was pushed aside as Sasha voiced her sudden idea about the drug used on Eric and probably Kay. 'I was feeling pretty woozy a bit earlier, and I only took one. Imagine taking three or four dissolved in booze?' she expounded, excitedly. 'You'd be out of it before you knew it. Eric said he was feeling spaced out and couldn't remember anything about his night with Chardonnay. If Kay's killer gave her a drink packed with Valium, she'd have been out of it in no time. She'd have been powerless to stop him as he plunged the knife in. You can't get Diazepam without a prescription so it's another possible way of linking our killer to the crimes.'

'Once you identify him,' James contributed, interested despite himself.

'Yes, but we have a few suspects that we can start with.'

'What about Roberta?' Zoe had moved to snuggle with James, his earlier reprimands forgotten.

'I don't think she was drugged, there was a bit of a struggle, but it seems like she was overpowered by someone stronger than her, or it could have just been that she was taken by surprise. And no wonder...'

'Why was Eric drugged?'

'What?' Sasha stared at James. 'Why was Eric...'

'And not the escort, Chardonnay?' he clarified.

'Dammit.' She punched the arm of the settee. 'No, wait, she could have been, maybe Tony hasn't had the results back or something. She must have been either drugged or completely drunk to not have put up the slightest struggle.' She looked confused as she tried to think. 'I don't know if I ever questioned this before... why drug both Eric and the escort, then kill her and leave him lying there?'

'So that he takes the blame? The killer takes pleasure in stabbing women and setting up other blokes to be arrested.' Zoe nodded enthusiastically from James's lap.

'Except there was no bloke left sleeping in Roberta's room as a convenient suspect, or Kay's, although she was killed for other reasons, we know that. No, something about Eric's escort's death was different...'

'Personal vendetta?' suggested James.

Zoe snorted. 'Can't say I'd blame anyone. If you think about it, Sash would be your most obvious suspect. Payback for the way he treated her.'

'Kind of fitting, I must admit.' Sasha grinned. 'The cheating fiancé set up to take the fall for the murder of the escort found in his hotel room. Talk about karma.' She paused, staring blankly at the wall. 'Eric has upset a lot of people over the years, I'm sure, probably most of them women...'

'Which brings us back to you.' James winked at Sasha before checking his watch. Draining his wine glass, he gently turfed Zoe from his lap. 'I've got to go. I've done what I came to do, I've had my fun and ticked you both off, but now I have to get home and hit the sack.'

Zoe accompanied James to the front door and said goodnight, assuring him that she and Sasha wouldn't take any further risks, and returned to the living room, looking at Sasha, her mouth beginning to twitch.

'Don't you dare,' Sasha started to grin. 'Don't you dare start us off again. But his face when he threw those newspapers down.'

Zoe held her mouth as laughter threatened to erupt. 'And that video. Oh, Sash, it's got to be one of the best things I've ever seen.'

Their shrieks of hysterical laughter could be heard the length of the street, and James paused as he walked to his car, looking back and shaking his head in amusement.

'Easy for you to say, you're not the one screeching like a banshee. You should get to bed, Zo, you've been at work all day and you have to get up in the morning.'

'What are you going to do?'

'I think I'll just sit for a while and think about everything, see if I can make any better sense of it all.'

'What about your main suspects? Who's your money on now? D'you still think it could have been one of Eric's friends, or do you think it could have been an ex-girlfriend now? Let's just finish this wine while we run through the suspects, then we'll go to bed.'

'Go on then, but this is my last glass. Right, main suspects... not an ex-girlfriend, too much like the plot of a bad film that went straight to DVD. Not Shuggy, not Franco, even though they were out drinking with Eric the night of the Freedom Hotel murder, as well as having drinks just round the corner from The Duck Palace the night of that murder. Rowan and Max, on the other hand, are both extremely tempting as murder suspects – they tick all the right boxes, they were the last ones seen drinking with Eric that night by Shuggy, they were seen taking the escort cards, they were both near Duck Lane Thursday night, they're both repulsive... yeah, I know...' She grinned at Zoe. 'Not relevant... okay, but Rowan actually had a card from that night so that puts him at the top of the list, and the barman at Freedom Kensington referred to someone laughing loudly in the bar... Rowan has the most grating laugh ever... and the barman mentioned someone with red hair, or ginger hair, who was with a man with blonde hair...'

Taking a sip of wine, she asked Zoe a question. 'You said that Kay recognised someone in the crowd in Duck Lane? Did she give you any idea of who? Could it have been Rowan?'

'It could, it really could. Sash, listen to this–' She leaned forward. 'We both looked round because there was this really loud laugh and then Kay went off for a minute or two. I'd forgotten about the laugh until you said about Rowan. When she came back, she said she'd seen a bloke who'd seemed familiar, said he was a real creep or something.'

'He's definitely a creep. And I remember putting the news on later that night and thinking I saw a familiar face in the crowd on the television, but I can't remember anything more than that. Maybe it was him?'

'It's Rowan, Sash. He's your main suspect. Everything you've just said points to him.'

'We're forgetting one thing though.'

Zoe looked questioningly at Sasha.

'Why? Why would Rowan Penrose murder an escort in Eric's hotel room and leave Eric to go down for it? They're friends, they've known each other since school days, and they're business partners. I mean, they'd just signed a new deal with Drew Merton which they were extremely happy about. I think that's how the heavy drinking started, as some kind of celebration. So, Rowan fits as my main suspect in every way except he has no earthly reason to wish Eric harm.'

'Then you have to find the reason, babes. But first, you need to find out if he also had an escort that night, and whether he was at the same hotel. Then you can find out what happened – if he won't tell you, maybe she will, you just need to find out who she was.'

'The escort agency card – where's it gone?' Sasha began lifting the piles of magazines and books. 'It was right here on the coffee table.'

Zoe knelt down and peered under the settee. 'I see it, mind out the way. It must have got knocked off when I fell over the table.' She retrieved the card, blew the dust off and set it back on the coffee table. 'What are you going to do?'

'I'm going to call it.' Sasha tapped the number in, put her phone on speaker, and placed it on the table as they listened to the ringing sound.

'Discreetly Elite,' a soft, husky, female's voice answered.

Sasha and Zoe looked at each other.

'Er, hi, I've got one of your cards and I–'

'Who is this?' There was a click and then silence.

'What happened?' asked Zoe.

'Did I get cut off?' Sasha pressed redial and they listened to the ringing sound again.

'No one's answering,' whispered Sasha. 'Why?'

CASES CLOSED, BABY, CASES CLOSED

Each time that she awoke in the night, Sasha asked herself the same question – why wouldn't the person from Discreetly Elite speak to her? She could come up with only two possible explanations: one, the woman was scared for some reason, or two, it was something about Sasha herself that was the problem. Yawning, and giving up on sleep, she pulled on Zoe's spare dressing gown, shivering at the unexpected chill in the air and, having used the bathroom, crept through to the kitchen and put the kettle on.

She was nursing her second mug of tea when Zoe appeared, padding through in her slippers and yawning noisily. 'Tea?' She waggled her mug at Zoe, already reaching for the teapot as Zoe nodded.

'Zo, women call escort agencies, right?'

'I spose so. Thanks.' Zoe gulped a mouthful of tea and put her mug down on the counter, pulling her dressing gown around her. 'Is it just me or is it colder today? They could be secretaries maybe, or personal assistants?'

'It's definitely colder. Or they could just be into women? So, it wasn't because I was a woman that she wouldn't speak to me, which means she was scared...'

Zoe grinned. 'You can be a bit scary sometimes.'

Throwing the tea towel at her, Sasha tried to think. 'But why was she scared? What's she hiding? Maybe it's the same agency that Lisa Pennington worked for and they don't want to be connected to her murder... maybe it's been shut down...'

'Or they only take male clients?' Looking at the clock on the wall, Zoe jumped up. 'I need to shower and get ready for work.'

Sasha finished scribbling notes in her notebook. She'd speak to Tony a bit later on and ask him about the agency that Lisa Pennington had worked for. Her eyes fell on the newspapers that James had brought round the night before, and she picked up the top one, grimacing at the photo of the line-up of prostitutes in which she and Zoe appeared. That had to be the worst highlight of her career, she thought, leafing through the paper distractedly.

A small headline caught her eye and she flicked back a page to see what it was about.

The identity of the man found stabbed to death at The Freedom Hotel, Chelsea is still not known, the report informed her, but since no wallet or personal effects were found in the room it looked like it was simply a case of a robbery gone wrong. The small paragraph went on to lament the increase in violent crime in London, and Sasha's mind wandered as she carried on paging through the news stories, pausing at an advert for package holidays to exotic climes as she considered extravagantly blowing her insurance money on a luxury holiday. The sound of the bathroom door opening brought her back to real life and she got up to take a shower and get on with her day.

~

Tugging a comb through her wet, tangled hair, Sasha considered her limited clothing options. All she had were the clothes she'd taken with her to Parva Crossing for her investigation into Dorothy Newton's murder at Meadowvale Retirement Home, which wasn't much. At least she had her favourite boots, she thought with a smile, thanking Zoe silently for bringing them with her when she'd visited. She also had her gorgeous new cardigan from Madam Couture in the village, the unlikeliest of places, which would be useful today seeing as it was quite a chilly one.

'Well, Sasha, you're going to have to buy some new clothes with part of your insurance money,' she said to herself, checking her bank balance on her banking app to confirm that the money had been deposited.

With her plan made to return to Bar Simone that evening, in the hope of finding some of the same girls that were there the previous Tuesday night, her next few hours did not require any pressing action, and Sasha took the tube through to Oxford Street for a shopping trip.

First up was Marks and Spencer, where she stocked up on basics, underwear and tee shirts, before throwing in a couple of pairs of flip-flops from the footwear department. Wandering up Oxford Street, she went into H&M and browsed the clothing racks, picking up a couple of tops and a long, tiered, summer dress to try on. The tops were good but she discarded the dress in favour of a skirt in the same style and, having paid for her purchases, moved on to John Lewis.

The delicious scents of expensive perfumes assailed her nostrils as she entered the store, and she inhaled deeply, smiling at the saleswoman holding out a bottle, and lifted her wrist for the obligatory squirt of pricey temptation. She began to make her way to women's fashions as an elegant woman walked towards her, her hair and makeup immaculate, her clothing of high quality, and Sasha moved aside as she passed her, leaving in her wake a strong whiff of expensive perfume.

Looking back at the woman, Sasha admired her ability to walk so effortlessly in her high heels, looking down at her biker-style boots ruefully. *Face it, Sash, you're not cut out to walk around looking like a model... or a high-class escort.* The thought came into her head from nowhere and she stopped suddenly as a memory flashed into her head of Saturday night.

They'd been leaving the hotel in Chelsea, she, Zoe, and James, and a woman had entered the foyer, a woman who she and Zoe had been convinced was an escort, due to the way she was dressed and her expensive perfume. She'd probably just got escorts on the brain, but it had been The Freedom Hotel in Chelsea which was, she suddenly realised as her brain connected the dots, coincidentally the same hotel a man had been found murdered at on Sunday – and not just murdered – *stabbed* to death. Did it mean anything or was it just a coincidence?

She forced herself to think back to the night in question. There'd been a bunch of high-spirited blokes in the bar, she recalled – the same bunch who'd been in the foyer when she'd left. One of them had gone up in the lift to his room, and just after that the woman had entered the hotel and also entered the lift. No, she shook her head, it didn't mean anything, although... taking out her phone, she punched in a few words and read the results, clicking on various reports. He hadn't just been stabbed in his room, he'd been stabbed in his bed, according to one online news site. She could ask Tony about it later if she dared to incur his wrath any further, which was all she seemed to do lately.

Losing interest in clothes shopping, Sasha exited John Lewis and wandered along Oxford Street, window shopping as her mind drifted. She'd got nowhere, she'd failed, Eric was being transferred to The Scrubs, and Kay was dead. Well, she thought mutinously, if she'd failed then so had the police because whoever did the killings was still walking free. She answered her phone disinterestedly.

'Sasha, babes? It's Tone. Alright?' His tone was animated. 'Thought you should be the first to know before it gets on the news. We've got him. It's over, sweetheart, we've only gone and bleedin' well got the bastard who killed your little friend. He was stupid enough to use her bank card to buy some cider.'

She stopped in the middle of the pavement, oblivious to the tutting from people behind as they almost bumped into her and had to skirt around her. 'You've got him? What did he say? Did he confess?'

'Nah, no confession, bloke doesn't know what planet he's on. But we've got him good, Sash, for both girls' murders, Kay Saunders' and Pippa Robbins', we've found the knife – he'd tried to destroy it – and he had blood on him which I'm telling you right now will be a match. Oh, and the best part? Stupid chump had Kay's keys in his pocket. 'It wasn't me, I didn't kill no girls,' he says, all wide-eyed, as we fish the keys out of his jacket. He'd kept her handbag as well, back at his squat in Earl's Court, down in some disused underground car park – that's where he'd tried to burn the knife.

'And as if that's not enough? We found a stash of sex workers' cards in his possession, all from Soho, obviously his hunting ground. Bloke's got an obsession with prostitutes – killing 'em mainly. It's almost like he wanted to get caught. Course, some of 'em do that, want us to stop them so they make it easy for us. And you won't hear me complaining, no siree,' Tony cackled with jubilation. 'So that's it, cases closed, all three of 'em, and your Tone's going to be getting nicely lubricated with the lads down The Churchill Arms tonight.'

She tried to process Tony's words, her brain failing to keep up with the speed of his exultant jabbering. 'So, what about Eric's case? Will you have another look at it and see if this bloke could have killed Lisa Pennington as well?'

'Move out the way,' a male voice complained behind her and, looking round, she scowled at the man and moved to the side, standing to stare unseeingly at the window display in one of Selfridges' windows.

'Sweetheart.' His tone was heavy with amused sympathy. 'Think about it. Like some stinking, filthy, homeless druggie would be able to walk into some posh London hotel, go up in the lift, walk into a guest room, and stab a woman to death, all without being noticed? And I'll tell you something else,' he said, beginning to laugh. 'If that had happened, your Eric would have remembered, the stench would have woken him up and had him puking his guts up all over the room.' He reined in his laughter. 'No, Mr Latimer's case is a separate matter, no last-minute reprieve for him, I'm afraid, darlin', and after the way he treated you, you should be the first to cheer, so you're going to put it all out of that pretty little head of yours and come and join me for a bevvy tonight, alright? Don't forget, Churchill Arms. Cases closed, baby, cases closed.'

'Bugger,' she said to the mannequin staring back at her blankly, oblivious to the strange look from the woman standing beside her. 'Bugger, bugger, bugger.' The woman looked at her again and moved away cautiously.

She should be relieved, she thought, turning to retrace her steps. She should be pleased that they'd caught Kay's and Pippa's killer. So why wasn't she?

~

Sitting on the tube on her way back to Zoe's, Sasha analysed her feelings.

She felt cheated, that's what it was, cheated out of solving the case, of clearing Eric's name, and of finding some kind of connection between all three murders. It was all too clean-cut, too simple... all the loose ends tied up... what was it Tony had said? *It's like he wanted to get caught.* She sat up straighter, her mind buzzing as the train pulled into Earl's Court. Alighting, she waited for a train for Ravenscourt Park, running through points in her head.

She believed that Eric was innocent, even if she didn't have a satisfactory explanation for what had happened that night in his hotel room. That meant that she believed there was a killer out there, and because of that, she believed that the same killer had lured Kay to her death to stop her from drawing attention to Eric's escort's murder and to gain access to her flat and remove the incriminating evidence of the blood-spattered chef's jacket. Admittedly, she had no explanation for Pippa's murder, although Kay had been convinced that it was her serial killer, and if she added in the convenient appearance of a suspect for both women's murders, then... A train stopping at Ravenscourt Park pulled in but she ignored it, remaining on the platform deep in thought. Then... if she believed that the killer of all three women was the same person, it meant that they had just got away with three murders, one for which Eric was charged, the other two for which an arbitrary homeless person was being charged with. *Cases closed, baby*, her mind echoed Tony's words.

What if... what if Pippa's murder had been a decoy... to give the media and the public something to get excited about – a serial killer of escorts... something to which Kay had amply contributed, or even led the way, in feeding the media frenzy? What if whoever had killed Lisa Pennington had simply wanted to draw attention away from the real reason for her death? Which was? She thought of Rowan, her main suspect... Had he wanted Eric arrested and charged with murder? If he had, then somewhere in their history was a reason why he would set up his friend and business partner... she just had to find it...

And what of Kay's words to her as she'd lain dying? What had she said? Something about it being the same person? From the hotel? And that it hadn't made sense... When, Kay? When did you see him? It must have been when she'd retrieved the chef's jacket. Had Rowan gone back? Could they have crossed paths somehow? How could she find out?

She could still go to the bar tonight to see if any of the same girls were there from the previous Tuesday night, maybe one of them would remember something helpful about Rowan. Apart from that, there was nothing more she could think of doing right at this moment.

But... snapping her fingers, she exclaimed aloud in frustration. She knew what Rowan looked like and he was not someone that Tony or his fellow officers would have been looking for in connection with Eric's escort murder. They hadn't been looking for *anyone* else in connection with the murder, they'd had Eric, covered in his alleged victim's blood, in the hotel room with her dead body, with no signs of anyone else having been there. They'd had no reason to review video footage of the hotel's foyer to see who had come and gone because they simply hadn't needed to look for anyone else.

She made a snap decision. She'd head through to the Chelsea hotel and see if she could watch the footage of that night – she knew that the woman she'd spoken to the other day, Fran, had a bank of computer screens in her office on which she could observe the foyers of all the Freedom hotels. Surely they had tapes? She could review the footage and look for Rowan – not only on the night of Lisa Pennington's murder but on Thursday morning, sometime before she'd met Kay for lunch. The police would not have paid any attention to a girl dressed as a Laundry King employee, or to a red-haired man entering the hotel that Thursday morning. Crossing the platform, she jumped into the train about to depart for Embankment station and sat impatiently tapping her fingers on her leg until she arrived at Sloane Square, where she alighted and made her way to Freedom Hotel Chelsea.

~

As usual, the foyer was deserted, and Sasha walked through to the bar, looking for the waiter she'd spoken to on Saturday night.

'Neil, isn't it? Not sure if you'll remember me? You took me through to see Fran on Saturday night?'

Neil pursed his lips, studying Sasha for a moment. 'Yes, I remember. Ooh, what a terrible night it was.' He placed his hand on his chest dramatically. 'A guest was murdered here. I still get the shivers just thinking about it. Poor Giulianna found him the next morning and nearly died on the spot. To think I was right here, talking and laughing with the guests while someone was creeping around with a knife, looking for someone to rob. You're just not safe anywhere, are you, not even in your hotel room? He was just lying there, sleeping peacefully, and the next minute, bam, he's been stabbed to death.' His eyes sparkled with excitement as he went on, sotto voce, 'I couldn't help overhearing the other night, you're a private investigator. Are you here investigating? Have you got any leads?'

Not disavowing him of his assumption, Sasha smiled knowingly. 'I can't talk about it, of course...'

'No, no, of course not,' he agreed hurriedly as he looked at her expectantly.

'What I need,' she said, as Neil leaned in towards her, 'is to see Fran or someone who can let me have a look at video footage of the foyers at your various hotels.'

'Our various hotels... right...' He gasped, clapping his hand over his mouth. 'You're investigating that other murder as well. We've been banned from talking about either of them with the public or reporters, and no surprise when you think about it, no one would want to stay in our hotels would they, when we've got guests getting stabbed to death left, right, and centre?' He frowned. 'I thought they'd arrested the man who killed the poor escort? No?' Realising that he wasn't going to get anything out of Sasha, he turned his attention to her request. 'Now, the thing is, and Fran will correct me if I'm wrong, but I don't think they record anything on those videos. Real-time, I think they call it. She's not in, Fran, she's had a couple of nights off and she never really comes in during the day anyway, not unless there's a computer problem.'

'Perhaps there's someone else who can help me? Someone who can show me how it works?'

Neil looked thoughtful. 'We could ask Mrs Mason, she's our head of housekeeping here, she might know, but between you and me, she's hardly a computer expert. No, you need to speak to Fran...'

'Perhaps I could give her a call? If you've got her number? It's quite urgent,' she added, as Neil looked doubtful.

'I'm not sure, that is, I ought to ask Mrs Mason...'

'I tell you what, let me have a word with Mrs Mason, how's that?' *This was getting complicated, and if Mrs Mason was anything like Mrs Carter at their Kensington hotel, it would explain his hesitation.*

Relief flooded Neil's face. 'That'll be the best thing. I can take you to her office?'

'Perfect.' Sasha smiled encouragingly and followed him through behind the bar and along the same route she'd followed when she'd visited Fran on Saturday night, arriving at an office door where she was asked to wait.

'I'll go and look for her,' Neil informed her.

Minutes passed with no sign of Mrs Mason and Sasha began to wonder if Neil had forgotten about her, just as a flustered-looking woman hurried along the corridor towards her.

'Mrs Mason? Did Neil tell you that I was here?'

The woman looked at her above the pile of files in her arms. 'What a day. Do they even know what housekeeping is supposed to encompass anymore? Let me just put these down before my arms fall off.'

'My name's Sasha, I'm here to see Fran about the computers...'

'Ah, we were expecting you earlier. Not one screen working, it's a disaster and I haven't a clue about all this computer technology stuff. Yes, here's the printout. It doesn't mean anything to me, but Fran will know all about it of course. She's at home but she has something called remote access which I expect you'll know all about, so you'll have to pop round and speak to her there, she's already okayed it – you've got her address?'

She hadn't, of course, but two minutes later Sasha left, armed with a mysterious printout in a brown envelope, and Fran Baxter's address who, she was informed, would be expecting her. *She hadn't lied about anything, not exactly, perhaps by omission... no, she'd just been economical with the truth...*

~

Ringing the doorbell, Sasha was aware of the sound of a vacuum cleaner roaring somewhere in the house, and she pressed the bell a couple more times, giving the door a knock for good measure. The vacuum cleaner fell silent and a moment later the door opened.

'Oh good, you're here, sorry to make you come to my house but I've been trying to catch up with the housework as well as getting my shopping done, and somewhere in between all that, catching up on some sleep.' Fran smiled at Sasha, her eyes registering puzzlement and then recognition, followed by puzzlement again.

'I'm not who you were expecting,' Sasha pre-empted. 'Sasha? Sasha Blue, we met on Saturday in your office, I'm involved with the investigation?'

'Oh, oh yes, I do remember you. Which investigation was it? I thought you'd closed the case, wasn't someone arrested? There was something on the news about it.'

Thankful that Tony had given her the heads-up earlier, Sasha smiled, nodding. 'Yes, we do have someone in custody, well, er, two people actually, so we can all sleep a little easier now, I'm sure you'll be as relieved as I am.'

'So, it really is all over?' Relief showed on the woman's face and Sasha felt sympathy for her, it must have been additionally nerve-wracking for a woman on her own, working nights at the hotels in which two murders had been committed.

'It is, so all I'm doing is tying up loose ends and,' she held up the envelope, 'bringing you this. It's some kind of computer printout that you were expecting.'

'Pop it down here, I'll go through it later.' Fran moved a pile of envelopes aside, flushing as she picked up a plastic-wrapped brochure. 'I wish they'd stop doing that.'

Sasha placed the envelope onto the server, glancing at the name on the address sticker. 'Harking? Isn't your name Baxter?'

'It is.' Fran's hand trembled slightly. 'Even after all this time, I still get things arriving using my married name. It's upsetting, you know? I'll just throw it away.'

Hovering in the hallway, Sasha waited for Fran to reappear from the kitchen, feeling guilty with imposter syndrome at her blatant misrepresentation of the truth. Well, she was here now so there was no going back.

'Sorry about that.' Fran returned, smiling. 'Now, how can I help you exactly?'

'It's just about the video footage of your hotels' foyers. I know you have cameras in each one and Mrs Mason said that you have remote access.' *It didn't harm to name-drop for a little extra authenticity.* 'I'd just like to review the footage from Kensington for last Tuesday night and Thursday morning. Like I said, it's just to tie up the loose ends.' She smiled encouragingly.

'Someone's sent you on a wild goose chase, I'm afraid.' Fran's smile was apologetic. 'Our cameras don't record anything, they're just in real-time, in case any guests are having problems with the self-check-in. I'm sorry that you had a wasted journey.'

Her hopes of catching sight of Rowan at the Kensington hotel dashed, Sasha gave Fran a rueful smile.

'Thursday morning as well, you said? I don't understand?'

'We were just hoping to verify if our man returned to the hotel on Thursday, but I suppose we'll never know

now. Look, I'm sorry to have bothered you, I'll let you get on, I can see that you're busy.'

'But you have got him? The man who killed those women?'

'We have,' Sasha hastened to reassure the anxious woman. 'You can relax, it's all over.'

'Thank you, it is a huge relief. And thanks for bringing me the computer printout.'

She left Fran, feeling sorry for her and a little uncomfortable that she had so blithely assured her that the police had got their man when she was unconvinced. Well, it's not like Fran's at risk, is it, she reassured herself as she headed back to the underground station, stopping to buy a bunch of cellophane-wrapped pink carnations for Zoe from the flower seller outside the station. If Rowan was her man then he certainly couldn't have any beef with a hotel employee who worked nights and who had no connection to Eric whatsoever, in fact, Rowan shouldn't have beef with anyone at all now, if what Sasha thought might be the truth – that Eric had been the target and the deaths of the women purely a decoy – for he'd achieved his aim and got his friend and business partner charged with murder and on his way to Wormwood Scrubs...

Someone sneezed further down the train carriage and she looked up, catching sight of a flash of red hair. A small chill crept through her as she craned her neck to get a better look at the person, but he stepped from the train as the doors opened, and was swallowed up in the crowd. Was it Rowan? Was he behind the sensation that she'd had, more than once, that someone was following her?

A BOOKING FOR MURDER

'Is it true, Sash, that they've caught the serial killer? Ooh, pink carnations, my favourite.' Zoe smiled at the flowers now gracing a vase on the counter as she dumped her grocery shopping beside it and kicked her shoes off. 'It was all over the news. But what about Eric? Are they letting him go? I can't believe that after he'd got away with it, the idiot used poor Kay's bank card and that's what got him caught. They said he had her handbag as well, they found it at some squat in Earl's Court? So, you're done, babes, you can relax and forget all about the mysteries of the escort agencies. It must be a relief?' Her face fell as she looked at Sasha. 'Oh, you're not going out? I've bought goodies to cook you a nice dinner, and look–' She wiggled the two bottles of wine. 'I've got wine... delicious wine...'

'Ooh, yum.' Sasha grinned, picking through the shopping bags. 'Steaks, creamy pepper sauce, potato wedges and.... cheesecake for pudding.' She held up the cheesecake slices. 'My favourite.' She gave Zoe a woeful look. 'But I do have to pop out, just for a little while.'

'But why? The case is closed, they said so, and you're still my patient, I promised Malcolm I'd look after you and make you rest. Where are you going?' Zoe's hands had moved to her hips.

'You do know you're acting like my mother, don't you?'

'Well, someone's got to. And you still haven't answered my questions.'

'Alright. Yes, Tony called me earlier to tell me they'd caught some guy red-handed, using Kay's bank card, and yes, they did find some of her belongings back at his squat. But like you said, what idiot goes to all the trouble of trying not to get caught and then does something so stupid as to use the card of one of his victims? I'm not buying it...'

'You think the real killer's still out there? D'you still think it could be Rowan?'

'It's definitely a possibility, I just don't have a motive for him at the moment, but he's hiding something, he has to be, otherwise why would he have acted so surprised about Eric and the whole escort thing? Think about it, he acts like they were just chatting some girls up in the bar, meanwhile, he knew damn well that they were escorts, at least some of them, and he took one of their cards – this one.' She slapped the pink card down on the counter, frowning at it, before picking up her phone and dialling the number again.

'No reply.' She shook her head. 'That's about the tenth time I've tried calling Discreetly Elite today. What are they hiding? Have they shut down? Anyway, that's where I'm headed off to, Bar Simone, I want to see if, by any fluke, some of the same girls are there from last week, and if they are, maybe one of them will remember something about Rowan.'

'D'you want me to come with you?'

'No, you've been working all day, Zo, and anyway, you've got my dinner to cook.' Laughing, she ducked as Zoe threw the tea cosy at her.

~

'Back again?' Dillon acknowledged Sasha with a nod. 'Get you anything?'

Yeah, find me an escort who serviced Rowan at Freedom, Kensington, last Tuesday night, and who saw him dressed in a blood-covered chef's jacket, wielding a large carving knife. 'Er, just a mineral water, please.'

'Still looking for your escorts?' He expertly twisted the top off the bottle, pouring the water into the glass. 'Ice and lemon?'

'Thanks.' She took the glass. 'I don't suppose any of the same girls are here this evening?'

He nodded towards the far corner and Sasha followed his gaze, taking in the group of glamourous-looking women. 'Some of those look familiar, you could start there.'

Moving to the table next to the women, Sasha studied them covertly for a minute or two, listening shamelessly to their conversation.

One of the women moved away and wandered over to a table where a couple of male customers were sitting drinking shooters. Accepting a seat, the woman sat down, smiling and nodding as she accepted their offer of a drink.

Deciding it was time to make her move before her escorts disappeared, she stood and walked over to the group, who looked at her enquiringly. Sometimes honesty was the best policy, she told herself.

'My name's Sasha and my ex-boyfriend is in prison for last week's murder of Lisa Pennington.' Ignoring their surprised gasps, she continued. 'Maybe some of you knew her? She went by the professional name of Chardonnay?' One or two of the girls nodded slowly. 'His name's Eric and he's a cheating bastard, which is why he's my ex.' Sympathetic smiles followed.

Encouraged by her reception so far, Sasha elaborated further. 'He was here drinking last Tuesday night with a group of male friends and I'm hoping that some of you might remember him or one of his friends.' Taking out her phone, she pulled up a photo of Eric, placing her phone on the table as the girls leaned in to take a look. 'He was buying bottles of champagne for everyone, that's the kind of thing he does, and he was probably horribly drunk and pretty loud. But I believe he's innocent which is why I need your help.'

One of the girls picked up Sasha's phone, studying the photo. 'I think I remember him,' she said slowly. 'He was with a really noisy crowd, it was quite late.'

'Let me see?' Another of the girls took the phone, nodding. 'Yes, he was definitely here. He was with a bloke with ginger hair and there was another huge bloke, like a giant teddy bear. He was sweet.' She smiled. 'But not interested, if you know what I mean.'

'That's his friend, Shuggy,' Sasha confirmed.

'We called him huggy bear,' another girl added.

'But didn't they just catch the escort killer today?' another girl enquired. 'Why's your ex still in prison?'

'It's complicated. I think they've got the wrong person. Look, cards on the table, I'm a private investigator and I've been trying to get to the bottom of this. Two other women have been murdered by someone now known as The Street Cleaner – one of them was my friend, Kay.'

'Oh, you poor thing.' Clucks of sympathy went round the table as the women clustered closer around Sasha in solidarity. 'Was she an escort too?'

'No, she was a blogger and she met with someone in Soho who convinced her that they had information on the killer. They drugged her and stabbed her to death at The Ballroom.'

More gasps sounded and looks of distaste appeared on some of the girls' faces.

'That's where the burnt-out ones end up, so sad. But what can we do to help?'

'I need to know whether any of you or anyone that you know, went to the Freedom Hotel, Kensington, on Tuesday night, with any of the men that were with Eric. The ginger-haired man's name is Rowan, and he had this card from Discreetly Elite. Do any of you know it?'

Immaculately coiffed heads leaned in over the table as the pink card was studied.

'It looks cheap,' said one girl.

'What a terrible colour,' said another.

'Not a high-class agency. Here's mine, you can see the difference.' One of the girls dropped an ivory card on the table.

Sasha picked up the card, noticing its thickness as the girl carried on talking.

'We usually write our names on the back so that they can request us, but our agencies will send someone else if we're already booked.'

'I've not heard of this agency, is it new?' The girl who had accepted a drink from the male customers had returned to the table. Picking up the card, she grimaced. 'What a shoddy job.' She sighed. 'How many times can they use the words discreet and elite, so unoriginal.' She looked at Sasha enquiringly.

'I'm Sasha.'

'Her boyfriend was arrested for Chardonnay's murder last week.'

'Her ex-boyfriend, and he's innocent. The real killer killed her friend at The Ballroom.'

'But didn't they just catch that person?'

Sasha explained again as one of the girls held up Sasha's phone with Eric's photo on it.

'I remember him, he bought us champagne, he was so funny. There was a whole bunch of them drinking, some kind of celebration.' She pulled a face. 'There was a red-haired bloke, horrible laugh, remember? He was a bit on the sweaty side and we said pity the girl who ended up with him?'

Nods of assent went around the table.

'So, none of you took bookings with any of them for that night?'

'They took our cards, the three that stayed behind. They were interested if you know what I'm saying. But I don't know where this card came from.'

'But some of the girls aren't here tonight. Marbella could have had a booking with one of them, could have been the sweaty one, now that I think about it. She changed agencies recently.'

'Could she have worked for this agency?'

'Not if they're as cheap-looking as their cards, no, she's high-class.'

'What about Lilly?' A hush fell on the group.

'What? What about Lilly?' Sasha looked around at their concerned faces.

'Lilly works for the same agency as Marbella, Private Company, it's called, but she wasn't here last Tuesday so we don't know when it happened or who she was with.'

'When what happened?'

'She had a bad experience a few nights ago. It happens, you get the odd weirdo, hazards of the job.' The girl speaking shrugged her shoulders. 'But it freaked her out. Poor thing's quite new and she hasn't worked since.'

'Do you know where? Was it at a hotel?' *She was onto something, she had to be.*

'It's nearly always a hotel. Most of them are married.' Nods of assent did the rounds.

'You could call her? Who's got her number? I'll send her a message and tell her she can speak to you.'

Thanking the girls, Sasha took her leave, armed with Lilly's mobile phone number and, heart thudding with excitement, called the girl.

'Hello?' A timid voice answered.

'Hi, is that Lilly? It's Sasha, I was just talking to some of the girls at Bar Simone and they said it would be alright to speak to you?'

'You want to ask me about *him*.' It was a statement, not a question.

'I do, but first, can you tell me what night it happened?'

'It was Tuesday night, you don't forget something like this.'

'I'm so sorry that you had a bad experience and I hate asking you to relive it, but could you tell me a little about what happened and try to describe the man? You see, I believe that someone's getting away with murder, literally, and I think that this man is connected in some way.'

'You don't think he's The Street Cleaner, do you?' She began to cry. 'Did he go and kill Chardonnay after he did this to me? She was in the room next door. Oh my God, I can't bear to think about it.'

'The room next door? Where, Lilly? Listen, take a moment, and then tell me what happened from the beginning.' *She'd bloody well got him.*

Sasha listened in rapt horror and sympathy as Lilly began to haltingly recount the events of the previous Tuesday night, ending her account in noisy sobbing.

'He was a butcher, Sasha. I'll be stuck with the scars forever. The bruises will go, but I feel like they're imprinted on my body, I can't even bear to look at myself. Every time I lie in bed it all comes rushing back to me, every awful minute of it. He made me lie on a plastic sheet on the bed – I knew then that he was going to do bad things to me, that he'd done it before. I should have left right then, I'm so stupid. He took pictures of me and he threatened me. He said if I ever told anyone about it, he'd put them on the internet for everyone to see. He went through my bag and he knows my real name and where I live, every time someone rings the bell, I think it's him. I'm terrified. I was so grateful that he let me go, I just ran from the room and I don't think I stopped running until I got home. He must have gone to the room next door and done worst things to Chardonnay, and then killed her... and it's my fault, I left her to be murdered...'

Fury raged through Sasha's veins. 'I'm going to make sure he goes away for a long time, Lilly, I promise you. I'll make sure he can't hurt you or anyone else ever again. And it's not your fault, don't let anyone ever tell you that, alright? Listen, I have a friend, he's a policeman, and he's a good bloke. If he promises to keep your name out of it, would you be willing to tell him what you've told me?'

'I suppose so,' Lilly agreed nervously. 'But people talk, what if he finds out somehow? He knows where I live.'

'Is there somewhere you could go, just for a few days, to feel safe?'

'I could go to my mum's...'

'Do that, pack a few bits and go to visit your mum.' *How dangerous was he?* 'Lilly, go tonight, okay?'

'Alright, I'll go and pack a bag and call my mum.'

'And this bastard, he had red hair, right?'

'What? Red hair? No, that was Marbella's client.'

What?

'He... he had these kind of dead eyes... like, he looked at me as he was hurting me and there was nothing there, it was like they were empty. They had no colour, they were just... grey, dead, creepy eyes...'

Max. She was describing Max Canning...

~

Jumping in a cab, deciding that her newly flush bank account could handle it, she gave the driver Zoe's address as her mind did a rapid recalibration of the facts.

She'd been right about Rowan inasmuch as he had been there that night, but wrong that he was her man. No, her man was Max, that creepy, dead-eyed bastard who'd made her feel dirty just by being in his house.

There was only one way it could all have happened... Eric, Rowan, and Max had all booked themselves escorts and had taken rooms at Freedom Kensington. Max had viciously assaulted his escort, Lilly, for there was no other way of describing what he'd done to the poor girl, and he'd carried out his disgusting acts in the room next door to Eric's.

When he'd finished with Lilly, he must have moved next door and found Eric passed out drunk – no surprises there – maybe Eric wasn't drugged at all, she'd got that wrong – *something else to add to her list of failures* – and he'd murdered Chardonnay. Had she also been passed out? Eric had implied they were both out of it. Had Max seen an opportunity to take his depraved desires to a new level? He'd been able to take a woman's life by violently stabbing her to death, and walk away, leaving Eric to take the blame.

How had he got hold of the chef's jacket? That was something she was going to have to think about. And Rowan? He knew something, he had to, for why else had he kept quiet about the fact that he'd been right there? Was he in on it somehow? She had so many questions and her mind felt like it was spinning out of control.

She walked into Zoe's flat in a daze. She needed to tell Tony, but she needed to get it all straight in her head first.

'You're back, babes. How did it go? Shall I start the dinner?'

'I need a drink, Zo, a big one.'

Sash? What is it? What's happened?'

She took the glass of wine from Zoe and dropped onto one of the stools at the kitchen counter.

'I know who the murderer is. It's Max, the bloke I went to see on Sunday.'

'Tell me everything, the dinner can wait.'

Zoe listened, open-mouthed, as Sasha recounted her conversation with Lilly.

'He's got away with it, Zo. And when Kay started having too much to say on her blog, he shut her down and he went to her flat and retrieved the chef's jacket so that he could destroy the only evidence against him. He killed Chardonnay, he killed Roberta – why? Because he'd acquired a new taste for killing women? Because he'd done it once and liked it? Because he'd got away with it? And then he killed Kay.'

Another thought occurred to her. 'Remember Sorbet telling us about one of the girls who'd been cut up badly? She called him a cutter?' She gulped down her wine as all the pieces fell into place.

'He must have been the cutter. And Sorbet said she'd had a client who'd beaten her and left her bruised, remember? It sounded like the same man? Listen to this, Roberta was killed on Thursday night, and Sorbet's friend was cut up the same night. And who was drinking in a pub in Soho the same night? Max. Shuggy said he saw him speaking to Rowan outside The Ship in Wardour Street. Sorbet said something about him being creepy, something about his eyes. I'm telling you, Zo, he's our man. He's our bloody murderer. He killed them all, and Tony's down at The Churchill Arms celebrating closing both his cases because Eric's a useless drunk who made it easy for Max to set him up; because he passed out with an escort in his hotel room who was then stabbed to death; and because some poor homeless bloke had drunk his bottle of meths, or whatever it is they drink these days, and was passed out at some squat just waiting to be set up by Max for the other two.'

'You've got to tell Tony.'

'I've got to tell Tony.'

They spoke in unison as Zoe refilled her glass and passed the bottle to Sasha to do the same.

For a moment they both sat there in silence and then Sasha took out her phone.

'I've got to tell him right now, there's no time to waste, for all we know Max is hunting for another victim as we speak.'

'He doesn't even need to hunt,' said Zoe bitterly, 'all he has to do is pick up his phone and call one of the agencies.'

'A booking for murder. Am I missing something, Zo? Have I got it wrong? I thought Eric had been drugged but now I'm wondering if he was just blind drunk,

Chardonnay too – that they were both victims of circumstance, rather than planning – but what about Roberta and Kay? Roberta did put up a fight so maybe he just tried to take her by surprise, but Kay? No way she would have just laid down and let him stab her in the bed – she had to have been drugged… and it would have needed to work pretty quickly… so Max still had to have got hold of drugs from somewhere.'

'Malcolm wrote you a prescription for Diazepam without any trouble.'

'For anxiety and depression – that's all Max would have needed to do, tell his doctor he was suffering with anxiety or was depressed about something…'

'And we know what the effect of taking just one with alcohol is, it made you pretty woozy…'

'So, two or three tablets dissolved in alcohol would have knocked Kay out pretty quickly. Maybe I can get Tony to get hold of Max's medical records and find out if he's been prescribed anything, it might help convince him.' She clicked on Tony's name on her phone.

'Sasha, baby, where are you? You're missing all the fun,' Tony shouted above the noise of music and laughter. 'What's that? I can't hear you?'

'I said I need to speak to you urgently, Tone.' She listened impatiently as someone's voice shouted about getting another round in. 'Tone, are you there?'

'You'll have to carry me out at this rate.' Tony's laugh cackled down the phone and she held it away from her ear for a moment.

'Tony, it's really important that you hear this. You've got the wrong person. I know who it is, listen– argh.' Exasperated, she forced herself to remain calm as more laughter drowned out Tony's reply.

'Hold on a sec.'

The noise slowly receded and she guessed that he was moving outside.

'That's better. Right, what's up? Make it snappy, babes, I've got pints lined up on the bar with my name on. And why aren't you here?' His tone changed to concern. 'You're feeling alright?'

'I'm fine, thanks. Listen, I don't want to spoil your party but give me one minute, yeah? Just listen and don't say anything.' She spoke rapidly, telling him everything, and waited for him to respond.

A loud groan sounded down the phone, followed by one word. 'No.'

'What d'you mean, no?'

'No to everything. No to your ex-boyfriend being set up, no to putting all the blame on his mates, no to his friend creeping into the room and stabbing the poor bird to death while he was passed out beside her, no to there being something suspicious about Discreet and Elite, or Elitely Discreet, or whatever the hell you called it, escort agency, not taking your calls, no to your theory of Eric's mate hunting down hookers and enticing them to hotels so that he can beat them up and murder them or, if he's in a lenient mood, just leave them cut to ribbons, no to us having the wrong bloke after we caught him with our victim's flamin' bank card and all her personal possessions, not to mention the fact that he was covered in her blood, and no to whatever the hell it is you're gonna say the minute I stop talking.'

Her heart sinking, she tried to protest.

'Not another word, babes, you hear me? Now, you've got two choices, you either get yourself down here, paste a smile on your face, give me a big kiss and congratulate us all on a job well done – and for that, I'll buy you a lovely big drink of whatever your poison is, or else you get yourself off to bed and wake up tomorrow to find that your normal intelligent brain is back in that pretty little head of yours from whatever flight of bleedin' fancy it's been on. Got it?'

The line went dead and she dropped her phone on the counter, shaking her head at Zoe.

'He's shut me down. It's hopeless, Zo, what am I going to do?'

'Maybe try to talk to him tomorrow? He's probably just a bit fired up, that's all. He'll listen to you tomorrow when he's sober, won't he?'

'What if tomorrow's too late?' She picked up her phone again, scrolling through her contacts.

'What are you doing? Who are you going to call?'

'I'm calling Rowan, maybe I can get him to talk.' She held her phone to her ear, her face grim.

'Hello? Who is this?' A woman's voice answered, sounding suspicious.

'Oh, er, hi, could I speak to Rowan, please? I'm a friend of his business partner, Eric.'

'Of course you are.' The woman's tone was sneering. 'Well, he's not here so don't call him again, okay?'

'No, wait, please.'

There was the sound of scuffling and then a man's voice. 'I told you not to answer my phone. Who is it? Give it here. Hello?'

'Rowan? It's Sasha, Eric's ex-girlfriend, I came to your office the other day?'

'Sasha, how are you? I'm sorry about Eric, I heard they've charged him. Sorry there wasn't more I could do to help.'

'There is something you can do now actually, Rowan.' *Like you've done anything to help so far.*

'Maria, give me some privacy, will you? This is about Eric, the poor bloke's in prison. She's his girlfriend, for crying out loud. No, I'm not lying.'

Sasha waited, listening to Rowan and his wife as they argued.

'Sorry about that, my wife's suffering from some kind of paranoia.' He gave a forced laugh. 'Thinks that every woman who calls me is some kind of secret lover.'

Biting back a sarcastic response, she held the phone away as his loud, braying laugh resounded in her ear.

'Are you still there? What did you mean, there's something I can do? I've told you all I know.' He sighed. 'Poor old Erica, he really got himself in a jam this time.'

'You can start by telling me the truth this time, Rowan.' Ignoring his expostulations, she continued firmly. 'I now know, having spoken to several witnesses, that you, Max, and Eric took rooms at the Freedom Hotel in Kensington last Tuesday night and that you all used escort services. I know all about your friend Max's little disgusting peccadilloes – which aren't little at all, seeing as he's a cruel, evil, and violent monster who enjoys hurting women and who has recently taken it up a notch or two. I know what he did, Rowan, and if you don't tell me the truth then you're party to it.'

'That's ridiculous, I don't know what you're talking about. I wasn't anywhere near Freedom Kensington last Tuesday. I hardly know Max, I'd never even met him before that night.'

'I've got witnesses who saw you there, I can trace the escort you hired, and I know that Max murdered Eric's escort – that's after he enjoyed the services of an escort himself. And he didn't stop there, Rowan, he's murdered two women since then, one of them was a prostitute and the other one was my friend. I know he was with you in Soho last Thursday night, at the Ship – that's the night the other prostitute was murdered. I know everything, Rowan.'

There was a momentary silence.

'If you know all this then why aren't the police calling me? It's all in your head. Eric always said you had an overactive imagination – now I know why.' Again, he gave his braying laugh, but this time there was an air of uncertainty to it. 'I'm going to go now. Don't call me again.'

'He hung up on me. He bloody well denied everything and hung up on me.'

'Well, we can prove it,' said Zoe desperately. 'You can put evidence together, can't you?'

'It's all just a theory, Zo, I was hoping to unnerve him, get him to own up to having been there that night, at least. It's hopeless.'

'So, what now? What's your next move? What about that Max bloke? Could you call him?'

'Call the killer? I don't know, he's dangerous, I'm not sure it's the wisest thing at this moment. No, we need to think things through. You know what?' She looked at Zoe, smiling. 'Let's forget it all for a moment, have some more wine and enjoy our dinner. What temperature do we need the oven on for the chips?'

They worked together companionably, preparing their meal, finally sitting down to eat their steak and chips at the kitchen counter, although neither had a huge appetite, their minds being preoccupied with the frustrations of the situation.

'This was nice, Zo, thanks for making the effort to provide us with a nice meal.'

'You're welcome, babes. I'll open another bottle of wine, yeah?'

'Why not?'

Sasha's phone rang as they sat outside on Zoe's small patio, enjoying a cigarette.

'It's Max,' she whispered to Zoe, looking at her screen.

'Are you going to answer it?' Zoe's eyes were wide.

'I think I'll have to.'

'Hello, Max.'

His voice was soft. 'Hello, Sasha. I understand from our mutual friend that you've been having rather a lot to say to him.' He gave a mocking laugh. 'Don't you think you've allowed yourself to get a little carried away?'

Swallowing, her mouth suddenly dry despite the wine, she replied. 'Not really, no. Did Rowan tell you that I've got witnesses?'

He laughed softly. 'Come, come, Sasha, if you had witnesses it would have been the police calling Rowan, not you. You were just sounding him out, hoping he'd give you something. Now, be a good girl and let it drop, alright?'

Anger made her brave. 'No, I won't let it drop. I know what you did, Max. I know you killed Chardonnay, and Roberta, and my friend, Kay.'

'And I know where you live.'

A chill crept along her spine as she put her phone on speaker, holding her finger to her lips as she looked at Zoe.

'I don't think so, Max.' She looked triumphantly at Zoe. 'Seeing as my flat burnt down last week, I don't think you have a clue where I live, and I don't take kindly to threats.'

'Nice try. So, tell me, how was your little shopping trip today? I liked the skirt you bought in H&M.'

She and Zoe looked at each other in panic.

'You've been following me?' Her mind ran through the times she'd had a feeling that someone was following her.

He laughed again. 'Are you and your friend enjoying your cigarettes and wine? You know, it isn't advisable for two women to sit outside at night, you never know who might be out there.'

Sasha looked at Zoe in horror as they both glanced towards the end of Zoe's garden where the back gate opened onto the small lane running behind the row of terraced houses.

A mocking laugh echoed from the phone before it fell silent.

'We need to get inside. NOW.'

They scrambled to grab their wine glasses and cigarettes, struggling to hold them and their phones, as they hurried through the back door, slamming it behind them and turning the key.

Zoe slid the bolt across for good measure and they stood looking at each other in silence, the only sound being their panicked heavy breathing.

'He's here? He's watching us?' Zoe's hand trembled as she placed her glass on the kitchen counter.

Sasha's phone gave a soft ping and they stared at it for a moment.

'It's a message from him.' She clicked on it and a photo appeared on her screen. Gasping, as she looked at the blurry image of her and Zoe sitting on the patio, she with a glass of wine lifted to her lips, Zoe in the act of lighting a cigarette, her eyes darted to the lounge window which overlooked the front street. 'The window's open.'

Dropping her phone, she ran across the room, slamming down the sash window and pulling the latch across firmly, before closing the curtains.

'My bedroom window's open a bit.' Zoe ran out of the lounge and along the passage, the sound of her feet thumping on the floor followed by the sound of a window slamming shut.

'Close all the curtains,' Sasha yelled, running to check her own bedroom window before racing into the bathroom and closing the window.

They reconvened in the kitchen, hearts racing as they stared at each other.

'Did you lock the front door when you came in?' Zoe's voice was croaky.

'I think so, yes, I'm sure I did.' Running to check, she breathed a sigh of relief.

'What do we do?'

'Could you call James, d'you think? Ask him to come round?'

Shaking her head, Zoe gave a small groan. 'He's out of town on a business trip, he went this morning. He's not back until tomorrow night.'

Sasha looked at Zoe across the kitchen counter, her friend's face as white as her own.

'So, we're on our own.'

THE OLDEST ESCORT IN THE BUSINESS

'I'm sorry, Zo, this is all my fault, I've put you at risk and all because I had to go shouting my mouth off and throwing accusations around.'

'Babes, look at me. It's not your fault, alright? Don't forget how you got dragged into this in the first place, you didn't ask to be involved, did you? Eric pretty much demanded that you help him, and that's all you've tried to do. And, Sash, you've done it, you've almost there, all you've got to do is work out how to prove he's the killer.'

'You're the best friend I could ask for, Zo.' She gave her a quick hug. 'But first, we've got to get through tonight.' She gasped. 'Lilly, what if he's worked out that I spoke to Lilly? I promised her I wouldn't let him get to her. I need to call her.'

They waited anxiously as Sasha held her phone to her ear.

'Sasha, is that you? I was just about to send you a message.'

'Hi, Lilly, I thought I'd just check that you were on your way.' She forced herself to sound calm.

'I'm in a cab on my way to the station.'

'Oh, that's good, well, have a nice time with your mum, yeah?'

'Thanks, I will.'

'She's safe.'

'That's good. So, what now? What about calling Tony?'

'What, apart from the fact that he's probably unconscious under a pub table with his face in the carpet by now? He wouldn't listen to me even if he could, babes, he made that quite clear earlier.' She glanced towards the curtained front window. 'D'you think he's still out there?'

'He might be, I could take a quick peek...'

'No, if he is there and he sees you, he'll know he's got us freaked out. We could try reporting an anonymous intruder...'

'I'll do it.' Zoe dialled the emergency services number and spoke to the operator, who put her through to the police.

'There's someone outside my flat, a man, and it's just me and my friend here alone. He looked in my front window at us and a bit later we saw him at my back gate. We're really worried, it's only a small gate, he could climb over it and...'

She put her phone down, having given her address. 'They're sending someone and we're to stay indoors with the doors locked until they've checked. That should do it, shouldn't it?'

Sasha nodded. 'Once he sees the cops looking around, he'll go, he won't want to answer any awkward questions.'

'Are you crossing your fingers?'

Grinning, despite the situation, Sasha nodded sheepishly. 'It's something I saw Kay doing while she blatantly lied to my face.'

'So, you're lying, you don't think he'll go?'

'No, I'm sure he'll go, it was more for good luck.'

Zoe eyed her hands suspiciously as Sasha splayed her fingers out, giving her an innocent look.

They both laughed, releasing some of the tension from the last hour, as they heard a car pulling up outside, followed by a knock at the door.

'Zoe Pullman? Police responding to your call.'

'Thanks for coming.' Zoe stood at the open door, indicating the side passage to her back garden and explaining about the lane which ran the length of the houses at the end of the gardens. Told to wait inside while the area was checked out, she closed the door and walked back to Sasha.

Finally, the officer knocked on the door again. 'No sign of anyone or any meddling to your back door or windows.' He held up a bunch of flowers wrapped in cellophane. 'This was lying outside your back door.' He looked quizzically from Zoe to Sasha as they glanced at each other. 'Mean anything?'

'No.' Zoe shook her head slowly as Sasha did the same.

He handed over the flowers, turning to leave. 'Nothing you're not telling me? You didn't know the man? Problems with a boyfriend or something?'

'No, we didn't see his face.'

'Alright, well, keep your doors and windows locked. I'll drive past later when I'm in the area, just to keep an eye on things.'

Thanking him profusely, they closed and locked the door, looking at the flowers in Zoe's hand.

'Pink carnations.' Zoe glanced towards the vase on the kitchen counter.

'The same as the bunch I picked up at the tube station earlier today. I think he was following me. Is that a card?' She read the words out loud, '*You're wrong, now leave it alone.* What does he mean, I'm wrong? It's clearly a threat though.'

'Should we keep it as evidence?'

'I suppose so, but not the flowers.'

With the flowers dumped unceremoniously in the bin, they picked up their wine glasses as Sasha looked at Zoe. 'You should get to bed in a minute, babes.'

'What are you going to do?'

'I'll stay up for a bit, go through my notes and stuff. Something about Kay's bothering me.'

'I'm staying up too, two heads are better than one and I couldn't sleep if I wanted to.

'Alright, we'd better open another bottle then.'

They sat at the kitchen counter with their drinks as Sasha elaborated. 'It's about what she said about it being the same person from the hotel. I thought she meant Rowan but I haven't followed up on it. I spoke to the woman who deals with their computer stuff but they don't record, they only watch the foyers in real-time. If Max was seen at the hotel by Kay, then it must have been when she went in search of the chef's jacket, but I've no way of finding out about it.'

'What if she made notes about it? Of her investigations, I mean?'

'Maybe on her laptop… but I'd have to gain access to it…' Sasha opened her laptop and scrolled through Kay's blog mindlessly. 'If only Kay could speak to us from beyond the grave…'

Zoe shuddered. 'That sounds so sinister.'

'Sorry, you know what I mean though.'

'But what about context? Or maybe she got her words wrong? After all, the poor girl was dying, she could have been muddled.'

'It's possible… Zo, you've just reminded me. When Tony was listing all his negatives at me earlier, he got muddled and said a couple of permutations of Discreetly Elite – Discreet and Elite was one of them. I'm going to try something.' She tapped into the search engine, sitting back as the results loaded.

'Look.'

They stared at the results.

'One of the escorts I spoke to at the bar said there were loads of agencies with similar sounding names using these kinds of words. I didn't pay any attention.' She clicked on the first two results, scanning the websites and shaking her head. 'Nothing jumps out at me, not that I know what I'm looking for.' Clicking on the third result – for Elitely Discreet – a website loaded, complete with a pale pink background. 'This is interesting, Zo, look.'

Taking the card from her notebook, she laid it on the counter as they compared the two.

'Someone's made this to make it look like it's from this agency. Look, look at the colours and the typeface, they're similar but not the same. And look at the logo. At first glance, it could be mistaken as the same agency.'

'But why?' Zoe stared at the screen and then at the card.

'That,' said Sasha grimly, 'is a very good question.'

~

It wasn't too soon to go ahead with the next one, was it? After all, the cases were closed, the killers behind bars, and the media were already moving on to other more newsworthy stories.

No, it would be fine, and besides, there was no time to waste – they were a never-ending scourge causing pain and distress to the innocent parties, ruining people's marriages as well as their lives. Someone had to do it, didn't they?

With the details planned out, the call was made.

'I'd like to book an escort for tomorrow night, please.'

Specific instructions were given with regard to the location, as well as to what the escort was required to do, both on arrival as well as during and after the act and, satisfied that the receptionist had noted everything down correctly, the card details were given for payment.

Doubt surfaced for a moment. Maybe it was too soon. Perhaps it would be wise to stop for a few weeks, after all that recent mistake had made life complicated, necessitating some unpleasant actions to be taken. It certainly wasn't good for the nerves.

Smiling at the irony of that thought, fingers played with the small blister pack of white tablets, popping one out, and swallowing it with some water. A good sleep wouldn't do any harm.

No, tomorrow night's cleansing would go ahead, well, technically tonight's, seeing as it was already Wednesday morning, and the situation would be assessed after that depending on the news coverage. But it was hard to imagine stopping, even for a few, short weeks... it was no longer easy to wait for a month or two in between each one, it had become like a hunger that had to be fed...

~

Pouring them some more wine, Sasha stared at the escort agency's website. 'Maybe I should call them?'

'It's the middle of the night, will they be open?'

'They're probably open all the time, at least for bookings. It's probably their busiest time.'

'But what are you going to say?'

'Hmm, good question, I've got no idea.'

They laughed sleepily as Sasha tapped in the number on her phone.

'Elitely Discreet. How may I help you?' a husky voice enquired after a couple of rings.

'Er, hi, er, I'm calling about the escort services?' She rolled her eyes at Zoe, shrugging her shoulders.

'Did you want to make a booking? We have three ladies still available for tonight.'

'Okay, er, no, it's alright, I was just making an enquiry. I don't want to book an escort, I, that is–'

'Oh, I see, sorry, I misunderstood. Do you have any experience?'

'Not– no, no actual experience, I'd just like to have a chat with someone, would that be okay?'

Sasha shoved Zoe's arm as her friend spluttered with laughter.

'Certainly, perhaps you can e-mail us a couple of photos and call tomorrow morning to arrange a time? Could I just take your name?'

'It's Sasha, Sasha Blue.'

'Right. Age?'

'Er, thirty-six.'

There was a momentary pause. 'Okay, Sasha, call after nine and ask for Meredith.'

'Thanks, I'll do that.'

She put her phone down and looked at Zoe, her mouth trembling with laughter. 'I think I've just applied for an escort job.'

'Oh God, don't tell James, he'll have a conniption.' Zoe howled, wiping her eyes. 'Thanks for giving us a good laugh, babes, we needed it after all the stress. Thirty-six, the oldest escort in the business.'

'Hey, it's not that old. They want me to send photos.'

Zoe held her stomach as she screeched with laughter. 'Oh, this is classic, Sash.'

'I don't have to send any, do I?'

'If you want to get in to talk to them you might as well make sure they'll see you. Give me your phone.'

Sasha handed her phone over mutely.

Zoe's fingers whizzed through her Graffic account, critically appraising her photos, before selecting two. 'This one of you on our holiday on Paxos, and this one when you'd just had your hair done.'

Looking doubtfully at Zoe, Sasha e-mailed the two photos with a short message. 'They'll take one look and tell me they can't see me.'

'Don't put yourself down, you look gorgeous in those pics, and besides, I bet they get loads of blokes wanting a more mature woman...'

'Yeah, sure.' Sasha grinned, wondering what she was getting herself into and how she was going to extricate herself the following day.

The sound of a car moving slowly along the road distracted them and Zoe jumped up to peer out of the curtain. 'It's a police car.' She yawned as she sat back down at the counter.

'That's good of them. No way Max will have hung around. He did what he wanted to do – unnerve us. You should go and try to get some sleep.'

'And you? Are you going to bed as well?'

'I am. We're fine and tomorrow's another day. You've got work and I've got an interview for an escort position.' Grinning, she shooed Zoe off to bed and, once satisfied that her friend was tucked up in bed, collected her duvet and pillow, settling herself on the settee, checking out of the windows every hour, just in case.

~

'I don't believe you.'

'What?' Sasha squinted as Zoe pulled the curtains back. 'What time is it?'

'Eight-thirty. You said you were going to bed, you promised me. I would have stayed up with you.'

'That was my job, not yours, babes. Besides, I couldn't sleep, not really.'

'Well, anyway, the shower's free. You should go and get ready. You've got to look your best if you're going to convince Elitely Discreet that thirty-six isn't too old for an escort.'

'Very funny,' said Sasha, pulling a face.

'I'll put the kettle on.'

Once Zoe had left for work, Sasha anxiously scoured the online news, looking for any mentions of attacks or murders on females and, finding nothing, allowed herself to relax a little. That meant she had the day to find a way to talk to Tony and get him to take her seriously about her concerns regarding Max.

First off, she decided, she needed to confront Rowan in person, which meant she had to go to his office. Calling Alex, she confirmed that he would be in the office all morning, and told her that she would be coming through to talk to him.

'He's in a really bad mood, thought I'd better warn you.'

'That's probably partly my fault, I called him late last night and kind of confronted him about a few things.'

Alex gasped. 'Have you found something out? You better tell me, Sasha, I'm here with him all on my lonesome, if he's some kind of axe murderer then I need to know. A girl's gotta protect herself, know what I'm saying?'

'I think you're safe, I was just trying to scare him into talking. Listen, I've got to go but I'll see you in a bit.'

'Have you found anywhere to live yet? There's a couple of nice flats to rent in today's paper.'

'I haven't looked. I will, soon.'

'Well, you've got to sort things out. I told you I'll help you, you can make it my first job. I can't stay here working for this plonker, not with Eric in prison, and him stinking the place out with his sweaty body odour.' She cackled down the phone. 'He's rank in every way, he is. See you soon.'

Picking up a paper from the kiosk as she entered the station, Sasha sat on the tube paging through it. Sometimes it was nice to hold a real newspaper in your hands and take a break from screens, she thought, pausing to flip back a page and re-read the small paragraph she'd skimmed over sub-consciously. *Especially when you found things you might never come across online...*

She stared at the words, trying to make sense of them. How the hell could the man who was stabbed to death in a *robbery gone wrong* have checked into The Freedom Hotel in Chelsea as Dillon Brown? Dillon Brown was alive and well and working as a barman at Bar Simone. Either she was going mad or there was something strange going on...

Leaving the tube station, she walked along to Latimer and Penrose Property Development, climbing the stairs and trying to ignore the smell of onions coming from the kebab shop. Surely they could have found a better office? They were in property development for crying out loud.

'Hi, Sasha. Fancy a cuppa?' Alex jumped up, grinning, as Sasha entered.

'You'd better not be running up my phone bill yakking to your mates or I'll start docking your wages, you stupid tart,' Rowan yelled from his office.

'Yeah? We'll see what Eric has to say about that, shall we?' Alex yelled back, winking at Sasha.

'Well, Eric's not here, is he? He's rotting in prison for a very long time – should've learned to keep it in his trousers, shouldn't he?' Rowan's braying laugh faded as he appeared in the doorway and noticed Sasha.

'Hello, Rowan. Nice to know you're bearing such kind and supportive thoughts towards your friend and business partner, as well as treating your staff so well.' Sasha gave him a tight smile.

'What are you doing here?'

'You told me not to call you again, remember? Last night? So, if I can't call you, I'm left with no other choice but to speak to you in person.'

'But I don't know anything. Look, I don't know this Max person, I saw him at the bar that night, that's all.'

'Cut the crap, Rowan.'

Alex grinned behind her computer, her head moving back and forth between Sasha and Rowan as if she was watching a game of tennis.

'Haven't you got work to do?' Rowan scowled at her.

'I'm doing it, aren't I?'

'Max called me last night after I spoke to you, and after you called him, so stop telling me you don't know him. And he didn't just call, he made threats against me, he tried to intimidate my friend and me by coming to her flat and taking pictures of us through the window.'

Alex gasped. 'He what? That's bad, that is. Did you call the cops?'

'Oh yes. They found a bunch of flowers at the back door – turns out it was from Max, complete with a card from him telling me to leave things alone – it also turns out that he'd been following me. So, I'll say it again, Rowan, cut the crap.'

'Alright, come in, we can talk in here.' His shoulders sagged slightly as he disappeared back into his office.

Sasha leaned over Alex's desk, whispering hurriedly. 'I'm going to have to tell him about the escort agency card. Is that going to cause you a problem?'

'Go for it.' Alex shrugged her shoulders. 'I won't be here much longer, remember?' She gave Sasha one of her cheeky grins and Sasha smiled her thanks, whispering a few more words to her before following Rowan into his office.

She dropped the pink card on his desk and awaited his response.

'Where did you get that?' He stared at it as if it might bite him.

'You threw it in your waste paper bin on Wednesday morning, the day after your night at Freedom Kensington with Eric, Max, and three escorts.'

An air of defeat surrounded him as he sighed, picking up the card and fingering it. 'The escorts were Max's idea. The girls had been all over us all evening, and this hot bird had been giving out these cards with promotion codes on the back. Maybe single blokes got a better discount than married ones, I don't know, that's what the big laugh had been about, but she wrote different codes on different cards and gave us each one.

'There was just me, Max, and Eric left, when Max suggested it. His treat, he said. He picked up the card Eric had been given and made him a booking but when he tried to book two more escorts, they wanted more promotional codes, so he picked up his card and gave them the code, but they told him they had no more escorts available for that night. This was his card, I pocketed it for future use.' He had the grace to look uncomfortable. 'He picked another card from the pile on the table, Private something or other it was called, and he booked two more girls from there.

'The first agency, this one, booked the room as well, at Freedom Kensington, so when he booked the other two, he booked us in at the same hotel. We went to the bar there, had a few more drinks, and then we went to our rooms. That's all I know.' He shrugged his shoulders.

'What happened then?'

'You want me to tell you what I did with my escort? What d'you think I did? Use your imagination. I sent her off afterwards and I went home. That's it.'

'Did you see Max or Eric again? Did you hear any noises from their rooms or anything?'

Shaking his head, Rowan gave her a twisted smile. 'A few moans, I suppose, from Max's room. Sounded like she was enjoying herself.'

Sasha glared at him. 'What you heard was a girl being tortured by your mate Max. She's terrified of him. He beat her, cut her up, and went through her bag so that he could threaten her by telling her that he knew where she lived, thereby guaranteeing her silence. But she's brave, she told me everything, and she's safely out of his reach now. Shame the same couldn't be said about Lisa Pennington, his first murder victim, or Pippa Robbins, the girl he murdered on Thursday, or Kay Saunders, my friend that he murdered on Sunday. He's dangerous, Rowan, and he has to be stopped.'

Rowan groaned, his head in his hands as he leaned over his desk. 'He's not my mate, alright? Stop calling him that. I did see him at The Ship in Wardour Street on Thursday night, but only for a few minutes. He'd called me and said he wanted a word about last Tuesday night. He wanted to make sure we were on the same page – that no one knew we'd been there that night, and that I wasn't going to change my story. He made a point of saying to me that all we did was enjoy a couple of hours with a couple of escorts. I didn't know what he was doing in there, did I? But none of this helps Eric, does it?'

'It does if you speak to the police and tell them everything you've just told me. I believe that after Max had indulged his depraved taste for violence, he went into Eric's room where he found the girl passed out in the bed. I believe that he saw an opportunity to take things to the next level and walk away blameless. In short, I believe that he murdered Lisa Pennington and left Eric to take the fall. If you come forward the police will have to take the suggestion seriously, otherwise, Eric will stay in prison because nobody's looking for another killer.

'No way.' Rowan shook his head. 'I didn't do anything wrong and you can't rope me into it. So what if I was with an escort? It's not a crime, is it? I didn't hurt anyone and I'm not about to ruin my marriage over it.'

There was a snigger from the doorway. Alex sneered at him. 'Ruin your marriage? What marriage? It's about time your poor wife learned the truth about you. It'd be doing the poor woman a favour anyway.' She waved her phone at him as she grinned at Sasha.

'Did you get it all?'

'Every lovely word of it. I've sent it to your phone.'

'Thanks, Alex.'

'You can't do that.' Rowan's face was white. 'That's illegal.'

'We'll worry about that when and if we need to. I think the police will be more concerned about catching a murderer, don't you? I'll be in touch.'

Sasha swooped out of his office, pulling Alex with her. 'Good work, Alex, thanks. But I've put you in a difficult situation.'

'Don't worry about me, I can handle myself. I can handle him too. You go and get that bastard off the street and give me a call, yeah?'

'I will.' She gave Alex a quick hug, holding her at arm's length and smiling at her. 'You'd be an asset for any business, they'd be lucky to have you, you know that?'

'That's what I've been telling you.' Beaming, Alex walked with her to the door. 'Good luck. Speak to you soon.'

'You will, I promise.'

Exhilarated, Sasha walked back to the tube station, playing Alex's recording of Rowan's admission. No way could Tony turn his back on this – at the very least he'd have to speak to Rowan and Max, and once he did that, he'd have cause to look for evidence that Max had also been in Eric's hotel room that night. He'd find it, Max had been there committing murder, and once he acknowledged that, he'd look further into the two other murder cases and would quickly realise that Max was responsible, not some poor drunk, homeless patsy.

Her exhilaration fading, she sighed. The only problem she had was that Tony outright refused to listen to anything that she said, had practically banned her from talking to him about any of the murders. But maybe if she went to his office, after all, the worst he could do was throw her out...

~

As it turned out, Tony didn't throw her out of his office because Tony had never made it to work that morning. A stomach bug, she was informed. *Yeah, likely story, Tone.*

She stopped dead outside the police station. She'd forgotten all about phoning Elitely Discreet to confirm a time to go in and talk to them. Bringing up the number on her phone, she called and, allowing the charade of her interest in working as an escort to continue, for the time being, was informed by Meredith that she could come in at three o'clock that afternoon.

Feeling a little nonplussed as to what to do next, Sasha wandered along Kensington High Street, eventually finding herself in Kensington Gardens, where she continued to meander along the pathways, stopping to take a couple of photos of a squirrel as it scampered across her path, before pausing on the Serpentine Bridge to smile at the swans gliding gracefully across the surface of the Serpentine Lake, their tiny cygnets gathered closely behind them. Taking some more photos, the sound of a baby's cry distracted her, and she looked round, smiling, as a young mother stooped to soothe her infant as it lay in its pram, its head of fair hair just visible above its blanket.

Feeling suddenly emotional, she wiped her eyes, hunting in her bag for a tissue on which she blew her nose noisily. Leaning on the parapet of the bridge, she gave herself a talking-to. *So what if the whole world around you looks picture-perfect? It never is, not underneath. Everyone's got their problems, yours are no worse than anyone else's. That squirrel probably couldn't remember where he hid his stash of nuts, those cute little cygnets were probably squabbling and driving the mother swan crazy, and that young mother with her baby was probably exhausted and craving just a few hours of uninterrupted sleep. You've got plenty to be grateful for, Sasha Blue, so stop feeling sorry for yourself.*

As if to prove her point, a group of waterfowl had a disagreement beneath her, resulting in much flapping of wings, splashing of water, and angry hooting sounds. Crossing into Hyde Park, she found a park bench and sat down, deliberating what to do next. At a bit of a loss, and feeling as though she were losing her grip on the case –

what would she do if Tony wouldn't listen to her, she wondered – she scrolled through her photos, popping a couple of pictures of the squirrel and the swans onto her Graffic feed. Hitting her profile, and almost as if she was trying to remind herself of all the good things in her life, her finger flicked upwards, causing memories to fly past in front of her eyes as the screen whizzed up through the graphics before slowing down and grinding to a halt. Great, it would have to stop on a photo of Eric, wouldn't it?

She'd taken it on their holiday on Paxos quite recently, but now it felt like it was a hundred years ago, so much had happened since then. She looked at the photo of Eric, taken of him while he was asleep, not that you'd know it was him, she smiled to herself, you could only see his blonde hair flopped messily on the pillow above the bedcovers – she'd posted it because it represented a moment of sheer happiness, she'd felt so in love with him right then, she recalled. For a moment she was reminded of the mother on the bridge bending over her baby's pram. Into her head popped an image of the baby unit at the hospital, during her recent visit, and of the nurse commenting on how they all looked like little peas in a pod. Another memory hovered in her periphery, just out of reach, but try as she might, she couldn't reach it. More than one memory... what was it? What did the photo remind her of? *You've got babies on the brain, girl, and we both know that's a pointless exercise. Focus, you've still got work to do.* Obeying her inner voice, she left the park bench and continued through Hyde Park, walking past a deserted Speakers' Corner before heading out of the park.

A little under half an hour later she was in Soho and she walked along to Bar Simone. Apropos of nothing, the oddity of the barman's name appearing in the newspaper, as the person who had checked into the hotel and been robbed and murdered, was intriguing. And, she justified her interest, there was a slight connection since the escort cards had originated here.

~

'I'm starting to wonder about you.' Dillon looked up from the bar, grinning at Sasha. 'You sure you're not angling to get a job here? Or maybe it's the escort work you're interested in?' He winked, to show that he was joking.

Laughing, Sasha informed him that he wouldn't believe it if she told him, to which he demanded she explain.

'I always like a good story.'

'Well, you'll like this one.' She told him about her late-night call to Elitely Discreet as part of her investigation and about how she'd somehow ended up with an interview for escort work. 'Talk about the oldest escort in the business,' she finished, laughing.

'Oh, I dunno.' Dillon stood back, mock-appraising her. 'You'd do alright, might even give the young'uns a run for their money.'

'Yeah, and pigs might fly. But thanks for the vote of confidence. I'm actually just here about something that's kind of weird. It's probably some kind of mix-up, but there was a man who was robbed and killed in his hotel room on Saturday night.'

Dillon tutted. 'Shocking the increase in crime these days.' He shook his head sadly. 'And all for his mobile phone and his wallet, I'll bet.'

'That's what they're saying. But the thing is, they've said he checked in under the name Dillon Brown.'

'You what?' He whistled. 'Well, would you Adam and Eve it, that's the same name as me.'

Sasha nodded, about to continue, when she realised that Dillon was standing motionless.

'What was the name of the hotel?' he asked.

'The Freedom Hotel in Chelsea. Why, does that–?'
She didn't get to finish. Dillon's face had drained of all colour as he reached out to steady himself against the bar counter.

THE WRONG WAY ROUND

'Dillon, what is it? What do you know?'

Swallowing, Dillon walked around the bar, pulling Sasha towards a table away from other customers.

'Cards on the table,' he said, his pallor an unhealthy greenish-grey, 'and please, God, tell me this is a mistake.'

'Take your time, start from the beginning.'

'The beginning, right.' He nodded and began to speak.

'That night, the night you were asking about, last Tuesday, it was when the girls were handing out their cards and your friends were here. Well, I took one of the cards when I was cleaning up and I thought it would be a bit of a laugh for an old mate of mine. Ricky moved to the States more years ago than I care to remember, lot of water under the bridge since then, and anyway, he was back here on a short business trip and we were all having a get together on Saturday for his last night.

'So, me and the lads all chipped in and I booked him an escort. The agency did the whole booking, even the hotel, kind of all-inclusive like, all I had to do was give them a time and tell them what his bevvy of choice was – I suppose they chucked in a complimentary drink in the room or something. We picked him up at his hotel, The Henrietta Hotel in Marble Arch, had a couple of drinks in the bar, then we went on a bit of a pub crawl, got off our heads, and ended up in the bar at Freedom Chelsea. A couple more down the hatch there and then we saw him off into the lift after I'd checked him in on their self-check-in system. He didn't have a clue, probably thought he was at his own hotel, he was totally out of it, and to be honest, I was worried he'd forget the room number before he got there.'

'And did you speak to him the next day?'

'Nope, but he was flying back to the States the next morning so I wasn't too surprised. I must admit, I thought it was a bit weird that he hasn't called since he got back, I thought he'd have something to say about it, but you know what blokes are like. Matter of fact, I was thinking of giving him a call this evening, he's about eight hours behind us if I recall. But this is all crazy. He wasn't staying there, it was just for a couple of hours. He'd have sobered up a bit and gone back to his hotel, wouldn't he?'

'Did you book it under your name or his?'

'Well, mine, I used my card to pay.'

'And the escort agency that you used, can you remember the name of it?'

'It was one of the pink cards, Discreetly Elite, I think it was.'

A tingling ran along Sasha's spine. *What the hell?*

'You're sure? Was it like this?' She took out the, now rather crumpled-looking, pink card and showed it to Dillon.

'Yeah, exactly like this. Are you going to tell me what's going on? Is Rick alright?'

'I'm trying to figure it all out, I'm not sure what this all means. Did it have anything written on the back of it?'

Dillon flipped the card over and studied the letters and numbers on the back. 'Yeah, I was asked if I had a promotional code and I gave her the code off the back of the card, something about promo, and there was the letter M, if I remember right, then maybe some numbers. Sorry, that's all I've got – I threw it away after that.'

Sasha studied the code on the back of the card that had originally been handed to Max, according to Rowan. *SPROMO54.* It was similar to the code that Dillon recalled. Did that mean anything? Probably not, but it was weird that they weren't all just the same with consecutive numbers.

'I think we should check with The Henrietta Hotel, we could make sure that your friend checked out Sunday morning as planned.'

'I'll call them.' Dillon took his phone from his back pocket and, after looking up the number, sat back as he waited for someone to answer, his fingers tapping anxiously on the table.

Sasha listened to the one-sided conversation, deducing correctly that Rick had not returned to his hotel in Marble Arch and that his belongings had been placed in storage pending contact from him and settlement of his bill. With a sinking heart, she acknowledged to herself that the man found murdered at Freedom Chelsea must be Dillon's friend, and she placed her hand over his in sympathy as he put his phone down.

'I don't understand it.' Dillon looked at her, shaking his head, his eyes wide in puzzlement. 'Are you telling me Ricky got himself murdered? Why? What for? He didn't even have his wallet on him, he forgot it, I remember him saying. The lads were giving him a hard time, teasing him, like, but I told him to leave it, the night was on us. But who killed him? Was it the escort? Are they running some kind of murder scam? Book an escort and get yourself killed into the bargain?'

Were they? A connection to Discreetly Elite was the last thing she'd been expecting when she'd decided to follow up on what had sounded like a simple case of mistaken identity, and all it had served to do was to confuse her. And if they *were* murdering their clients – which sounded absurd – it was hardly the best way to go about drumming up repeat business, not to mention the mess they were making of things, seeing as the escort Lisa Pennington had been murdered and not the client Eric Latimer.

'Dillon, do you have a photo of your friend, Rick that you can send to my phone?' She gave him her number. 'And what's his last name?'

'Turner, Rick Turner. Rick's dead? I can't get my head around it. It could be a mistake though?'

'It could be, let's not jump to conclusions. Look, I feel bad, this was the last thing I expected when I saw your name in the paper. Didn't anyone contact you about it?'

'I had a call from a copper and he did ask me a few questions, but I'll be honest with you, I was a little concerned in case it was about me booking the escort. He didn't ask and I didn't tell if you get my drift. I gave him my address but my bank's still got my old one, I keep forgetting to tell them I moved. I suppose I'll be in all sorts of trouble now. Wish I'd never gone and done it. I'll never forgive myself and that's the truth.'

'Wait until we know more, okay? I'll get onto my police contact and ask him about it. He'll want to come and speak to you, his name's Tony Palmer, he's a detective sergeant.'

~

Tony would at least have to speak to her now, she thought grimly as she left the bar.

Sending Tony the photo of Rick Turner, she added a question: *Is this your male victim from Freedom Chelsea? His name's not Dillon Brown. Call me.*

Her phone rang in less than a minute.

'Moved onto missing persons now, have we? At least you've seen sense and stopped sniffing around the escort murders.'

That's what you think. 'Nice to speak to you too.'

'Alright, let's try again. Hello, Sasha, how are you, babes?'

'Fine thanks, Tone, and you?'

'Fine thanks. Right, what's this all about? His name *is* Dillon Brown, we just haven't found the right one yet, for the record.'

'Dillon Brown's card was used to make the booking, but it was for his friend who was over from the States. If you got his address from the bank, you got the wrong one because he forgot to let them know he moved.'

'And you know all this how?'

This was the tricky bit. 'Okay, it came about from my investigations into the escort murders, alright? Everything that's happened to Eric, Lisa Pennington, Pippa Robbins, and Kay Saunders, stems back to Bar Simone, where Dillon works as a barman, and where Eric was drinking with a group of friends last Tuesday night, one of whom is Max Canning, who–'

'Sasha, I'm warning you, not the escorts again.'

'Alright, I'll shut up about it.' *He wasn't going to listen to her, not until she had absolute proof.* 'Your murder victim's name is probably Rick Turner.' She gave him all the details of where he'd been staying, as well as Dillon's phone number. 'He's in a terrible state, Tone. I told him you'd be in touch.'

'We'll check it out.' Tony paused. 'Er, Sash, thanks for this, if it turns out to be correct then I'll owe you one, yeah? And, look, sorry if I came on a bit strong last night on the phone, but we were having some bevvies, you know how it is... tell you the truth, I can't remember much about last night at all...' His tone was sheepish.

'Don't worry about it, okay? Let me know about this?'

She checked the time after they rang off and realised that she was cutting it fine for her appointment at Elitely Discreet. Hailing a cab, she gave the driver the address and ran through in her mind what she wanted to ask – *once she'd dispelled them of the assumption that she was there for escort work, that is...*

~

Elitely Discreet's office in Mayfair lived up to its name, thought Sasha, having walked up and down the small Mews twice before realising it was the glossy black door between two apartments.

Ringing the buzzer, she opened the door as it clicked, and climbed the thickly carpeted stairs to the first floor.

A heavily made-up woman in her forties looked up, frowning over her spectacles, as Sasha walked into the small reception. 'Can I help you?'

'Er, yes, Sasha Blue, I've got an appointment with Meredith?'

'Fill this in.' The woman handed Sasha a clipboard, her eyes sweeping over her dubiously. 'I see you called and spoke to our night receptionist. Did you send us your photos?'

'I did, I e-mailed them last night, well, early this morning.' *But you won't be needing them.*

'Ah, yes, here we are.' The woman's nails clicked on her laptop's keyboard as she looked from her screen to Sasha, her eyebrows raised.

'I'm not looking my best today, it wasn't the best night. It's not been my best week, to be honest. Well, not even my best year – probably my worst, if I'm honest. *What was this, a confessional?* I expect you think I look nothing like my photos.' She gave a nervous laugh. *Why was she feeling nervous? She wasn't actually applying to work as an escort, for crying out loud.*

'Yes, well...'

This was stupid, she should just tell the woman why she was there so that she could get on with asking her questions. 'Look, I'm not actually–'

'Excuse me.' The woman rolled her chair back silently and disappeared through a door to her right.

Murmurings could be heard from behind the door, followed by a click as the door opened slightly. A much older woman peered out, frowning.

Standing up quickly, Sasha walked towards her. 'Are you Meredith? Look, I haven't been completely–'

'Yes, I am Meredith. I understand that you've been having a hard time of things lately, but our books are full at the moment.'

'No, I, look, I'm not here about escort work. There was a bit of a miscommunication over the phone and somehow it seemed easier to let it go rather than explain my real reason for being here.'

'Which is?' The older woman arched her eyebrows as she remained within her inner sanctum.

'I'm a private investigator. I should have been honest from the start but I thought you might refuse to see me.'

'Is it about Lisa? Or Saskia?' The door opened wider as the receptionist reappeared.

Saskia?

Meredith put her hand on the woman's arm, her eyes narrowing with suspicion. 'Are you a reporter? We've got nothing to discuss with you. Gill will show you out.'

'I'm not a reporter, look, here's my card. It's concerning Lisa Pennington's death last week.'

Meredith gave a heavy sigh, releasing her grip on Gill's arm. 'Alright, you'd better come in and take a seat. Gill, you can stay.'

'Thank you.' Once seated, Sasha began to explain her connection to the case and Eric's arrest.

'Let me get this straight, you're trying to clear your boyfriend's name after he's been charged with the murder of Lisa? I don't see how we can help you. Lisa was a lovely girl, very professional, and popular with her clients. What happened to her is an absolute travesty, but we can't undo the past.'

'But why are you trying to help your boyfriend after all this?' Gill added a question of her own. 'It seems awfully generous-hearted of you.'

'He's not my boyfriend anymore. I firmly believe that he is innocent and I believe that I know who the real murderer is, but I need to figure out what the connection is between your agency and him. If you could confirm the name of the man who booked Lisa Pennington last Tuesday night then I'll have my connection.' A thought occurred to her. 'Didn't the police contact you about Lisa?'

'Firstly, we never give out details about our escorts or their clients, that's part of our professional service, and secondly, no, we've had no enquiries from the police.' Meredith's expression revealed her distaste at anything so unsavoury as a police enquiry. 'Our escorts never give out any information about themselves or the agency when they visit a hotel, for obvious reasons. It's strictly between our client and the agency. You'll understand that we can't have our name involved in a police investigation – the damage to our reputation would be unfathomable.'

Never mind that it might help the police trace and arrest a murderer. 'Even if it would help the police to find the real murderer?'

'But they have found him, we saw it on the news. I'm sorry about your boyfriend, my dear, but sometimes we have to face the truth no matter how hard it is. Living in denial isn't going to help you.'

'If I'm right, then the murderer is still out there and is going to do it again. How will you feel if another of your escorts is found stabbed to death in a hotel room? How long can you remain quiet for?'

'It won't happen to another of our escorts, we've already blacklisted him.' Gill spoke before Meredith had a chance to hush her.

'So, you do know who booked her?'

Meredith frowned at Gill. 'Gill spoke out of turn. But yes, we know and we've blocked him from using our services again, so our girls are safe.'

'But girls from other agencies aren't. Doesn't that bother you? Other women have been attacked and or killed by this man. He's not going to stop. And didn't you think it was odd that the man who booked your escort was a different man to the one the police arrested?'

'My dear, we do watch the news, you know. We are aware of the other unfortunate deaths of two women in Soho, but again, we are also aware that the police have arrested a man for those murders. And, of course, those women were from a vastly different situation to our escorts – not professional or upmarket – although they have our utmost sympathy, that goes without saying. As for the different names, well, we're not the police, are we? We can't do their job for them.'

'So, an escort from your agency was murdered and you're going to do nothing.' Sasha could feel her blood boiling. 'Would it interest you to know that I believe Lisa's murderer is the same man who killed the two women in Soho, and most definitely not the man that the police have arrested?'

'Well, whatever you believe, the police obviously have very different feelings about it all, so surely you'd be better off speaking to them about your ideas.' Meredith was clearly not to be swayed. 'In twelve years of running this agency, Lisa Pennington is the only escort who has been murdered. I think that's a pretty good track record.'

Gasping in disbelief, Sasha almost missed Gill's comment and Meredith's stern look.

'What was that?' she asked Gill.

'I– nothing.' Gill looked at her boss awkwardly.

'You said *the only escort*. What did you mean?' *These two were hiding something.* 'Who else was murdered?'

'We should tell her, it's no reflection on us as an agency.' Gill was flustered.

Sighing, Meredith informed her, 'One of our escort's clients was murdered. But it was a long time ago and had absolutely nothing to do with our girl. It happened later that night after she left him – probably a robbery or something.'

'What was the name you mentioned earlier? Saskia? Was she the girl?' Sasha directed her question at Gill. 'You might as well tell me about it, we've come this far.'

Meredith took over. 'It was back in the early part of the year, possibly February or March. Saskia had a booking for a client at The Luxe Hotel in Camden.'

'That was before it was called Freedom,' added Gill, 'they were in the process of taking it over.'

'Yes, quite.' Meredith nodded. 'That's all I can tell you. Saskia left her client and we later found out that he'd been killed.'

'And his name?' *It was really like pulling teeth with these two.*

'I'd have to check the system,' said Gill, glancing at Meredith for permission, who nodded imperiously.

Sasha followed Gill back to her desk, as Meredith hovered nearby, and Gill's nails tapped on the keyboard as she brought up the information.

'Here we are. His name was Adrian Harking. He'd used us quite a few times previously. Such a shame, he'd been a good client.'

Striking while the iron was hot, Sasha proffered her thanks and quickly pushed for the information she was there for. 'While you've got the bookings up, can you tell me if the name of the man who booked Lisa Pennington last Tuesday was Max Canning?'

Gill's eyes scanned her screen as she tapped in some details. 'Yes, it was, that's correct, it was a third-party booking.'

'What does that mean exactly?'

It means that it wasn't the client himself who made the booking. Sometimes we have bookings made by secretaries, personal assistants, that kind of thing.'

'Isn't that a bit strange?'

'Not really. They might be in London for business or something and want company. Their assistant will make all the arrangements for them.'

'But you still take payment on their card? Was his card used?'

'Yes, let me check, yes.' Gill nodded. 'Payment was for Max Canning's card. Hotel details given, special requests – champagne, no conversation, escort to leave directly afterwards.'

'Which is quite usual,' interjected Meredith. 'Many of our clients don't want the girls to hang around. And, of course, sometimes an escort is booked for someone else, maybe as part of business entertainment for a client, which is obviously what happened in this instance. Now, if that's everything?' She moved to usher Sasha to the door.

'One last thing.' Sasha retrieved the battered-looking pink escort agency card from her notebook. 'Have either of you ever seen a card like this before?'

'Let me see that.' Meredith virtually snatched the card from Sasha's hand. 'Imposters,' she hissed. 'Where did you get this?'

'This card, or one just like it, was used to make the booking for Lisa Pennington. I understand that three escorts were requested but that you only had one available?'

'That's not correct, we had a few girls available according to the system.' Gill tapped away, frowning.

'Someone's made cheap cards to look like our agency. How dare they.' Meredith's face was creased with anger. 'Look. Look at the quality of our cards.' She thrust a card at Sasha, who took it, noticing immediately the thickness of the card and its stylish design.

'This is insufferable,' fumed Meredith, pacing the floor. 'Does Saskia still work for you?'

'What? No, the poor girl was upset about the whole incident, no idea why, it's not as if she was in the room when it happened. She left us and went to work as a doctor's receptionist, I believe. Such a waste of a pretty face.'

The sympathy and compassion here were just too much... 'I'd like to have a word with her, perhaps you could give me a few details?'

'Gill, see what we have on Saskia, will you?' Meredith was still examining the pink card from Discreetly Elite. 'This card – they can't do this, it's a blatant impersonation of our agency. The names could so easily be confused with each other. They've tried to sound like us and look like us – of course, they've failed miserably with these terrible cards.' Her tone was scathing. 'You have to stop them.'

'Me?' Sasha looked at her in surprise.

'Yes, of course, you. You're the one who brought the card to our attention. They must be stopped because we have no idea what kind of girls they employ, and if one of their clients is dissatisfied with them – which is highly likely, if their services are anything like the cheap quality of their cards – and has a lot to say online, well, one can only imagine the damage that could be done should wires get crossed and our agency gets caught in the crossfire. No, we can't have that at all.'

'Is that for me? Thanks, Gill.' Sasha smiled as she was handed a printed sheet of paper with Saskia's details on it. *It was time to extricate herself from the situation.* 'Perhaps you should speak to the police about these impersonators? I'm sure they'd be happy to open an investigation into the whole thing.' She smiled sweetly at Meredith, who gaped, clearly unsure whether Sasha was being helpful or sarcastic.

'Well, er, I, we wouldn't want a police investigation...'

'No, I quite understand, just like with the murders of those poor innocent girls, including Lisa, it really wouldn't do to have the police poking around – God forbid your agency's name should feature in the news, or they should catch the real killer. Well, thanks for your time, ladies, and for this.' She waved the piece of paper, smiled again at the sight of Meredith's befuddled face, and turned to leave the office.

'Actually, we've got another booking for The Luxe for tonight.' Gill was still looking at her computer. 'Unusual name, too...'

'You mean Freedom,' said Meredith distractedly, still trying to compute the meaning of Sasha's last comment.

'Sorry, old habits.' Gill tsked at herself.

Stopping suddenly, Sasha turned back. *Why was an alarm bell ringing in her head?* 'Did you say you had another booking for tonight for The Luxe Hotel? That's Freedom Camden, right? The same hotel that Saskia's client was killed at?'

Gill nodded. 'It's a third-party booking again with the same requests...'

'Can you give me the details?'

Meredith pursed her lips, caving under Sasha's determined stare. 'Very well, give her the details, Gill.'

~

'Saskia?' Sasha smiled at the young woman behind the desk in the doctor's surgery.

'Yes?' The woman looked at her quizzically, trying to place her.

'You don't know me, my name's Sasha Blue and I'm a private investigator. I wondered if I could have a quick word in private?'

'I can take two minutes, that's all. What's it about?' Saskia walked around her desk and guided Sasha to two chairs in the corner of the empty waiting room.

'I've just been talking with Meredith and Gill, from–'

'I know where they're from,' Saskia interrupted, looking uncomfortable. 'Is this about the murdered client? Meredith didn't want the agency connection to come out.'

'Kind of, although it's part of a larger investigation. I'm just trying to connect a few dots, there's nothing to worry about.'

'It's not that I'm worried, more that I've left that part of my life behind me. Don't get me wrong, it paid well but it was more that I kept thinking it could have been me. What if I'd stayed a bit longer? Would I have been murdered as well?'

'I can understand that.' Sasha nodded sympathetically. 'Can you remember when it was? It was at The Luxe in Camden, is that correct?'

'Yes, but it's not called that anymore, it was taken over. It must have been about mid-March. And before you ask, there was nothing strange about it, everything was fine. Afterwards, I left and we found out the next day that the client had been attacked and killed. I couldn't do it anymore after that.'

'Could you just run me through what happened, not the sexual side, just from when you were given the booking?'

'Alright. I was told to go to the hotel, I can't remember the room number, but I keyed it in and was buzzed up to the room by the client who, it turns out, had been my client a couple of weeks before, and he offered me a drink. He seemed like he'd been drinking quite heavily, but lots of clients do. My instructions were to only drink the champagne and not to engage in conversation with him. So, that's what I did, and afterwards, I left, as I was instructed.'

'Was there anything, even the smallest thing, that seemed odd to you?' *Why was she pushing the girl? There was nothing unusual about the encounter – only about what happened afterwards.*

'I do remember thinking it was a little bit strange that he seemed so drunk, I mean, he had a whole bottle of something on the table, and he was, like, a bit clumsy? The last time he'd seemed more with it...' Saskia shook her head, smiling. 'I don't know, I'm not sure what you want me to tell you.'

'You're doing great.' *Might as well give it one last push.* Encouraged, Saskia looked upwards as if searching for inspiration. 'Ok, I did wonder why he gave all the instructions that time, about not talking, and leaving straightaway afterwards. I suppose I was a little bit hurt, sounds stupid – feeling hurt by a client – but I thought we got on quite well the last time I'd been with him and I wondered why he didn't want me to talk to him. But the clients get what they want, they're paying after all.' She shrugged. 'He probably had an escort who had too much to say and made a nuisance of herself, and didn't want it to happen again.'

'And I don't suppose he knew which escort he would get?' Sasha took a guess.

'Oh, I never thought of that.' Saskia's face brightened.

Sasha thanked Saskia for her time and left the surgery. She'd not learned anything helpful from Saskia. *So why did she feel as though she'd just missed something important?*

~

She walked slowly as what seemed like a million thoughts and images collided with each other inside her head.

Crime scene images, the number of stab wounds on each victim, the nurse's comment about the babies, a fake escort agency, a hotel's change in ownership, posts on Kay's Killer Blog, the photo of Eric, mistaken identity, a pile of post, missing wallets, Kay's last words, the woman in the foyer of Freedom Chelsea, clean water glasses,

James's predator comment he'd made during their roast dinner on Saturday evening at Zoe's, Eric's missing cash, the tablets Malcolm Bailey had given her after her ectopic pregnancy, the mother soothing her infant in its pram...

She stopped dead as her jumbled thoughts positioned themselves cohesively to form an outrageous scenario in her head, her heart thudding alarmingly in her chest.

It couldn't be. Had she been looking at this the wrong way round?

MURDER AT MIDNIGHT

Taking a chance that Kay's sister was still at her flat clearing it out, Sasha took a cab and walked up to her front door, ringing the bell.

A woman with Kay's eyes opened the door, looking at Sasha enquiringly. 'Can I help you?'

'I was a friend of Kay's, just for a short time, but I was fond of her. You must be her sister? I'm so sorry for your loss. My name's Sasha, by the way.'

'Thanks, Sasha, it's nice of you to stop by. I'm her sister, yes, Miriam.' The woman still hovered at the half-open door, her eyes wary.

'Here's my card, I'm a private investigator and Kay and I were kind of working together on the recent escort murders. I'm also a friend of D.S. Tony Palmer from Kensington police.'

'Okay, but I'm not sure what...'

'I was with Kay when she died.' Sasha's eyes were soft with sympathy as she looked at Miriam.

Opening the door wide, Miriam gestured for Sasha to enter. 'I was about to make some tea, would you like a cup?'

'That would be nice, thanks.'

While Miriam busied herself with the kettle and teapot, Sasha explained a little more about what had happened with Eric, and how she and Kay had become involved, so that, by the time they sat down with mugs of tea, Miriam had a better grasp on the situation.

Smiling sadly, Miriam nursed her mug. 'She was always a pushy little thing, Kay was. Ten years younger than me and such an imagination on her, always so determined to achieve something in her life. This blog of hers was her latest project and, much against my better judgement, I must admit that I was impressed by her writing skills.' She gave a cracked laugh. 'If anyone could make murder entertaining, Kay could. Except then she went and got herself murdered.' Her voice dropped to a whisper as she looked across at Sasha through tear-filled eyes. 'Who would do that to her? They said it was a homeless man but it just doesn't make sense.'

'No, it doesn't. I think it's what the real killer wanted the police to think. I believe the real killer is still out there and has killed at least five people, if not more.'

'Five people? Miriam's jaw dropped open. 'So, all her writing about a serial killer – was that him? The man who killed her?'

'It was and it wasn't...' *She had to tread carefully, at least until she was sure.* 'Kay was correct about there being a serial killer, but she had a few of her wires crossed. It was thanks to her persistence that she convinced me we were looking for a serial killer, otherwise, I might have given up and eventually believed that my ex-boyfriend killed a woman.'

Shifting in her chair, Sasha told Miriam about Kay's last words, explaining why it would help if she could take a look at Kay's laptop in the hope that Kay had written notes somewhere.

'There's no phone, I suppose the police have it, but I did have a look on her laptop. There are some photos on there, one of them looks like a selfie of her in some kind of uniform with a Laundry King badge, but she never worked there, I'm sure of it. Nothing makes much sense to me, and some of them are unpleasant, are they– did she take photos of a murdered woman?'

'She did, at a place called The Duck Palace in Soho. I was with her. She almost got me into real trouble with my policeman friend.' Sasha smiled at the memory. 'Would you mind if I took a look?'

Indicating the dining room table, Miriam stood and flipped the top open, stooping to switch on the socket. 'You're welcome to go through it if it will help.'

The laptop was old and took a while to power up, finally asking for a password.

Sasha turned to Miriam, helplessly. 'It wants her password, I should have thought of that. I've got absolutely no idea.'

'It's our dog, Sylvester.' Miriam stepped forward. 'She always used his name for everything.'

Opening up the photos first, Sasha scrolled through them, nodding as she recognised some of the images including the chef's jacket, before pausing on a photo of familiar handwriting – her own.

'Well, Kay was certainly cheeky, I'll say that. See this? This is from my notebook.' She couldn't help smiling at Kay's resourcefulness. 'We met for lunch and it seems she snapped a photo of my notes where I'd listed some names. And this photo of her with the Laundry King badge on – she was dressed like this when we met, she'd been undercover doing a little investigating of her own.' She quickly checked the rest of the photos before turning to the documents. 'I'll just be a few minutes, I know you're busy...'

'Go ahead, I'll carry on with some packing up.'

Feeling intrusive, Sasha waded through Kay's many files, dismissing them until she opened a document and found herself staring at images of Eric's friends, their names typed beneath them. *Why had Kay researched Eric's friends? For the same reasons you did, Sasha, because she thought one of them might be the killer – namely Rowan or Max.* But with nothing else contained within the document, it was of no help to her. A fruitless half an hour later, she closed the laptop. *Kay must have kept notes somewhere, but where?*

'You didn't come across a notebook by any chance, Miriam? It's just that I'm banking on Kay having recorded her notes somewhere, from which she would have written her blog posts.'

'She was always recording herself as a young girl.' Miriam smiled fondly at the memories. 'She used to pretend she was being interviewed. She used to play the part of the reporter and herself.'

Voice notes. Could she have recorded all her notes on her phone? If so, they were lost forever... Unless...

Opening the laptop again, Sasha looked for Kay's e-mail, clicking on it and scanning the subject lines. A number of e-mails contained only a date in their subject line and, upon closer inspection, had been sent by Kay to herself, all having been subsequently opened except the one sent on Sunday, the day Kay had been killed.

This had to be what she'd been looking for. Clicking on the attachment from the earliest e-mail, she opened it and found herself looking at five voice note files. She looked over at Miriam as the woman rubbed her back after cleaning inside the fridge. 'You might find this upsetting, it's recordings Kay made of her notes.'

'You go ahead. It might be nice to hear her voice.'

Sasha listened to recording after recording, beginning with the day she'd arrived back in London barely a week earlier, leaning forward as she listened to Kay's notes from her visit to Freedom Kensington, disguised as a Laundry King employee. She replayed the recording, listening intently as Kay rattled off details about Soreena, the chef's jacket, Mrs Carter, Fran, Alfredo, missing glasses, Mr Penrose, and dead, grey eyes...

Continuing through the voice files, Sasha listened to Kay's observations from The Duck Palace murder night, noting her comments about the loud laugh like a donkey, and about the creepy bloke who'd seemed familiar, before reaching Kay's last day, and her excited babblings about her preparations for her meeting in Soho with her supposed witness. Her final voice note was short but filled with anticipation. *I'm waiting outside the coffee shop, a few minutes early, and have just been chatting to a sex worker called Gretel, who came out from The Ballroom, which is just along the street. She told me I look like a hooker from a TV show and that Kay is not a good sex name.* At this point, Kay dissolved into giggles, before finishing her recording. *It's almost dark now, and I'm all alone, starting to feel a bit nervous. Hope I'm not gonna regret this.*

Sasha's eyes were filled with dismay as she turned to look at Kay's sister. 'I'm so sorry,' she whispered, 'I didn't know…'

Selecting the relevant files, she e-mailed them to herself and, having thanked Miriam and expressed her condolences again, she left Kay's flat, making her way to the nearest coffee shop where she ordered a cup of tea and brought up Kay's Killer Blog on her phone.

Starting at the beginning of the year, she read through Kay's posts again, but this time she knew what she was looking for.

Putting her teacup down, Sasha sat back experiencing a mixture of shock and relief. Her wish made to Zoe had come true – Kay had spoken to her from beyond the grave.

She knew without a doubt who the murderer was. She also, unless she was losing her mind completely, knew that another murder was planned for that very night…

~

'I have to speak to D.S. Palmer, it's a matter of life or death. No, I'm not being dramatic, I assure you. Please, just call him for me.' Sasha pushed her hair back, tapping her fingers on the counter as she listened to the officer speaking on the phone all the while giving her sidelong glances.

'Take a seat over there please.'

She sat, crossing her legs, her foot bouncing impatiently as she watched the minutes tick by on the clock. *In less than five hours the killer's next victim would be dead.* About to stand up and return to the counter, she stopped as the officer approached her.

'D.S. Palmer's just going on surveillance and his phone is switched off, but I'm to tell you that he said you were right about Rick Turner, good work, and he's grateful. Now, if you'd like to leave your number, I'll make sure he gives you a call later.'

'But– no, I have to speak to him, you don't understand. There's going to be another murder.'

Taking in Sasha's wild eyes and unkempt hair, the officer looked at her warily. 'Are you trying to tell me you're thinking of harming someone, miss? I have to warn you that–'

'What? No, of course I'm not. I'm trying to– oh, it doesn't matter.' *She didn't have time for this.* Out of the corner of her eye, she saw him motion discreetly to another officer, who circled her at a distance.

'I'm going to give you my card, alright? D.S. Tony Palmer knows me well, I've consulted on cases with him. Can you please get one message to him? Tell him–'

A disturbance distracted the officer and he frowned at the man struggling with the two officers as they marched him in through the entrance.

'Tell him he needs to be at Freedom Camden tonight–'

'Picked him up in Kensington High Street pinching wallets, tried to tell us– oi, watch it.'

Sasha was knocked sideways as the officers grabbed the writhing man.

'You alright, love?'

'Kensington, you say?' The officer looked around for a pen.

'I'm fine. No, Camden, listen, please just tell him it's happening at midnight. It used to be The Luxe, and it's–'

'I wasn't anywhere near Kensington High Street, you're fitting me up. Alright, darlin', fancy sharing a cell?' The man leered at Sasha.

'You, quiet.' The officer glared at the man before turning back to Sasha. 'Right, got it, anything else?'

'Yes, there's going to be another murder. An escort is booked for ten o'clock, and–'

'Bit old for an escort, ain't you? Alright if you like that kind of thing, I spose...'

'Take him through to the desk sergeant, will you?' The phone rang and the officer sighed, looking from Sasha to the man, who'd started singing loudly. 'What's that? Yeah, you can say that again, can't hear myself think down here. Hold on.'

Sasha tried again. 'Tony has to meet me there, if I could just speak to him, I could explain everything.'

'I'll tell him. Everything will be alright, you go on home now, and D.S. Palmer will contact you later. I'll give him your message as soon as I'm done here, and then–'

'I demand to speak to the officer in charge.' A woman's shrill voice drowned out the officer's words. 'A man just exposed himself to me on the–'

'He must've been desperate,' the wallet thief cackled. 'What d'you want the cops to do, find out where he lives so you can go round there and get another look?'

Sasha looked around at the disparate group in desperation.

'This is disgraceful, I shouldn't be spoken to like this, and in a police station of all places.'

'No, you shouldn't, madam, and I'm sorry about that. Take him to the desk sergeant *now*,' he hissed at the officers holding the man.

But the man was enjoying himself and, renewing his struggles, managed to move closer to the woman, wiggling his tongue at her as she shrieked in horror.

'We've got him, we've got him.' Breathlessly, one of the officers forced the man to move, and they steered him from the reception area as he continued to shout out obscenities.

'Yes, I'm still here. Where's that, in Chelsea? Right... hold up.' Waving a piece of paper at Sasha, he spoke to her, his hand covering the receiver. 'I've got your message, I'll pass it on, now you have to leave. Blimey, Casey's Court round here, it is,' he said to his caller. 'Hold on again. Now then, madam...' He looked wearily at the indignant woman drumming her fingers on the counter.

'Thanks for your help.' Sasha turned and walked out, filled with angry frustration. *It was no good relying on Tony getting the message, and even if he did, it told him nothing to make him believe her. No, she had to come up with her own plan.*

Taking out her phone, she opened the voice recorder and began to speak as fast as she could.

'Tone, if it's the last thing you ever do for me, please listen to this message. We don't have a lot of time – if I'm right then the next victim is going to be murdered in less than five hours.'

She began in January with the first victim, quoting from memory, from Kay's Killer Blog to back up her story, and moved on to the March victim, rapidly giving her reasons for how and why she believed that she'd identified the killer, as well as the killer's reasons for selecting their victims. Moving onto June, she described what she believed had happened the night of Lisa Pennington's murder, when Eric had accepted the supposed generosity of a violent monster, and how she believed it had been the killer's first mistake, adding in Lilly's account of her assault on the same night, before taking him through her theory about the murder of Pippa Robbins as a means of misdirection, as well as Sorbet's account of fellow prostitute Lacey's experience at the hands of the sick individual that Sorbet called *the cutter* on the same night – someone whose violence Sorbet had also experienced first-hand.

The next victim, she informed Tony, had never been written about by Kay because, once she'd revealed photos of the chef's jacket worn by Lisa Pennington's killer, she'd sealed her own death warrant. She explained how the killer had lured Kay to her death before letting themselves into her flat to retrieve the incriminating chef's jacket which they had then destroyed before setting up the homeless man with Kay's belongings.

Stopping to draw a breath, she spoke with urgency. 'Don't you see, Tone? Everything's been covered up – you've got Eric and a homeless man for three of the murders, and the other three murders *that we know of* have been put down to robberies gone wrong, unrelated in any way to the other three. Sure, eventually a pattern would have arisen, of that, I have no doubt, but until then the killer's free to continue their murderous spree thanks, in part, to their mistake with Lisa Pennington which threw everyone way off any scent of the real reason behind the murders. I think they've made it their mission to kill as many as they can before they get caught.' Concerned that her message was becoming too long, she saved it and began a new one.

'The real reason is revenge. Revenge, Tone. The number of stab wounds – they're the same every time – that's the clue. You can verify this right now – look up the details for the March murder and you'll see that I'm right. But hurry.

'I know I was wrong about Rowan, and then Max, I saw it from the wrong angle, so I know you probably think I'm wrong again, but I'm not, Tone, I'm sure I'm not. You can't let Eric and a homeless bloke go to jail to save face because you won't admit that you might have got it wrong, and we can't let this person take one more life, no matter how justified they believe their actions to be. This killer's taken enough innocent lives and tonight we can stop another one from being taken.' She drew another ragged breath, about to move onto the subject of the cutter to say that he had to be taken off the streets before he brutalized any more women but, looking at her watch, she stopped herself. *She needed to wrap this up.* 'Tone, I've told you everything I know, I've given you everything you need to arrest the killer. This is what I'm going to do –

'I'm assembling a team and I'm going to stop this murder. The client and the escort are due to arrive at Freedom Camden, which used to be called The Luxe, at ten o'clock tonight, that's just over two and a half hours from now. The escort is booked for two hours and the client's name is Christian Hamilton-Hughes. I don't have a room number yet. That's it, that's everything.' Pausing, she wondered if she'd said enough to convince him. 'My phone will be on silent from ten o'clock, but I'll be switching it off at some point. And, Tone, we need to catch the killer about to carry out the act – I think I know how. Call me.'

Was that enough? Would he believe her? Would he come?

~

She sent the recorded messages to Tony's mobile phone, hoping that he'd listen to them in time. But in case he didn't, she had to make her plan and call in reinforcements. Running through her options in her mind, she called Zoe first.

'Sash, where are you, babes? Are you in this evening? You're still supposed to be taking it easy, you know. Listen, James is here and he wants to take us both out for dinner.'

'Zo, listen, I could do with your help. Do you and James want to help catch a murderer tonight?'

'Hell yeah, damn right we do. What d'you need us to do?' She listened to Sasha's rapid explanation, repeating back when and where they were to meet and turned to James.

'Put that glass of wine down, baby. Sasha needs us to help her stop a murder.'

'Fantastic,' said James, grinning.

~

Sasha considered the next person on her mental list. Smart, brazen, and quick-thinking – exactly what she needed and what's more, had never been seen before by the killer so would raise no suspicion. She made the call.

'I'm your person. Anything you need. Let's nail this sick weirdo. Yep, uh huh, got it, you'll have to get me my money back though, ha ha. I'm going to enjoy this, I always liked the idea of doing a bit of acting. Right, I'll be in position and make contact shortly.'

Satisfied with how her plan was coming together, Sasha made her next call, hoping that she wasn't misplacing her trust.

~

Fran Baxter yawned as she put down her empty coffee cup on the bar counter.

'All quiet tonight then, Fran? No check-in problems?' Henry leaned on the bar, fancying a chat.

'No, it's nice and calm so far, but you never know. The night is young, as they say.'

'Don't say that, I'm knackered already.' Donna dropped onto the bar stool beside Fran. 'At least we don't have to worry about our safety now they've caught the bloke who murdered those two other women. My boyfriend's right relieved, don't think he was too chuffed about insisting he came and got me after my late shifts. Give us a shot of something, Henry, I need to wake myself up. Fran doesn't mind, do you, my lovely?' she said, slipping her phone from her pocket as it began to ring.

'Go ahead, it's none of my business.' Fran smiled, taking out her phone. 'Excuse me a sec.'

Henry filled three shot glasses while the two women nodded and spoke to their callers.

~

Sasha began her next call by briefly explaining the situation but giving no information away and, once she was sure that her instinct had been correct, gave her instructions. 'Now, it's crucial that you get the timing exactly right,' she finished. 'You can't tell another living soul about this, apart from the one name I'm going to give you, no matter how close a friend they might be. Trust no one except my contact and just do exactly as I've asked you, don't take no for an answer, and you will have helped save a life and catch a serial killer. Can I count on you?'

So far, so good, she thought, scrolling through her phone to make her next call.

~

'Trouble?' Henry pushed the two glasses forward as Donna and Fran reconvened at the bar.

'Not for me, thanks.' Fran shook her head, smiling. 'Problem with the system at Camden – looks like that's where I'm headed.'

'Be safe,' Donna called, picking up her shot glass and downing the vodka. 'My boyfriend.' She indicated her phone. 'Making sure I'm not drinking on the job, ha ha.'

~

'Sasha, alright, darlin', what's happening?'

'I need your help, Sorbet. Fancy getting payback for Roberta?'

'Yes please, sweetie. Just you let me and the girls get our hands on that bastard.'

'I need someone for tonight.' She explained her requirements and the reason for them. 'Have you got someone I can trust who can do this? You're sure? There is a risk involved, you understand that? Here's where we need to meet. Nine o'clock, not a minute later. You won't let me down?'

Anxiously running through everything in her head, Sasha turned her attention to the last two people on her list, sending silent thanks to whoever decided that only one man in London should be the bearer of his name. It took her a matter of minutes to find out where he worked and to bring up his photo on the company's website, a minute more to make a call confirming that he was still in the office, and twenty minutes to position herself outside his place of work.

~

Christian Hamilton-Hughes called his wife as he left the office, sounding appropriately rueful about the last-minute meeting which would likely run until late. 'I'll have to wine and dine the client as well, love, I'm sorry. Look, don't wait up, okay? Yes, I know it's the second time this week, but what can you do?' Slipping his phone into his pocket, he headed across the street to the pub. A couple of pints would go down nicely before he met the lovely Bonita.

Placing his pint on the mat on the table, he slid into the banquette seating running along the wall.

'Christian Hamilton-Hughes?'

'Yes?' Startled, Christian's head swivelled round as Sasha slipped onto the seat beside him.

Placing her card on the table, she spoke rapidly.

Two minutes later he left the pub with her, his pint untouched, and climbed into a taxi with her.

~

It was time to make her last call.

'Gill? It's Sasha Blue. I need you to do something for me. I need you to cancel tonight's escort for Freedom

Camden. It's imperative that she doesn't go. But – and this is important – if anyone calls you to confirm the booking, you need to tell them that it's still going ahead.'

'I'm not sure that Meredith will be too happy about this, Sasha, not without a good reason...' Gill demurred.

'Put me through to her, I'll give her a reason I think she'll agree is good enough.'

Two minutes later she finished the call and turned to her, still bewildered, companion. 'You can relax, your name need never come up in this. But right now, I need you on board.' She checked her watch anxiously, willing the taxi driver to drive faster.

~

Walking into The Horse's Head in Camden, with an unhappy Christian in tow, Sasha looked around, spying Zoe as she waved at her.

'This way.' She nudged him towards the table where Zoe and James were seated, their faces expectant, and introduced them all, before looking around. 'I'm expecting one more person.'

'Is this all entirely necessary?' Christian scowled as he thumped down into a seat. 'I don't see what use I'll be. And what is this? Amateurs anonymous?'

Sasha opened her mouth to retort, giving Zoe a kick underneath the table as she clocked her militant expression, stopping herself in time, it wouldn't do to antagonise him right now. 'We need your credit card to check in to your room, and your presence for authenticity.'

'Do you know those women, Sasha?' James was staring across the pub with interest and Sasha turned round.

'Don't stare,' hissed Zoe. 'Oh, I know her.'

'Sorbet, come and join us. I was only expecting one. Everyone, this is Sorbet, a friend of mine.'

'Alright, Sash? Zoe, isn't it? You've smartened up a bit since I last saw you.' Sorbet winked at Zoe, dressed in a business-like suit and shirt, as James looked confused.

'And, er, Crystal, yeah?' Sasha smiled at the blonde-haired girl who'd been with Sorbet the night they'd been looking for Kay.

'And this is Gretel.'

A tall woman in black stiletto boots stepped forward, staring down at them all imperiously as she nodded.

'And this is Felicia. She's going to be our escort.'

Felicia grinned, baring gleaming white teeth, her scarlet lips and dark skin in glorious contrast, her Amazonian figure towering above the small group as they looked up at her.

'Well, thanks for coming, ladies, take a seat everyone.' Sasha looked around at the motley crew assembled around the table – this was it – this was what she had to work with and she couldn't fail.

'We're all here for Roberta,' said Crystal.

'It's payback time, for her, and Chardonnay. She might have been high-class, but she was still one of us.' Sorbet's comment was met with murmurs of agreement from the other girls.

'Just give me one minute with him,' growled Gretel. 'I'll make him wish he'd never looked at a woman.'

'Only after I'm finished with the bastard,' spat Felicia. 'I've got just the thing to start with.' She pulled out a leather whip from her boot, flicking it expertly in the air.

James's eyes popped out on stalks and Zoe dug her elbow into his side.

'Did you bring the wig?'

Sorbet handed Sasha a crumpled carrier bag which Sasha passed to Zoe.

'What's this for? For me? Am I wearing this? I love it.'

Smiling, Sasha placed her elbows on the table. 'Right, first of all, thanks, everyone, for coming. We don't have any time to spare, so here's the plan. Listen carefully, we don't want any innocent people hurt, and we don't want another murder.'

They all leaned forward, listening intently to Sasha's instructions.

~

'It's time to go.' Sasha led her crew from the pub, stopping when they were a short distance from the hotel. 'Christian, you're up. Call me when you're in the room and give me the room number.'

They stood watching Christian as he approached the entrance to Freedom Camden and disappeared through the door.

Sasha's phone dinged two minutes later and she read the message, sending back a short reply.

'Are you sure he's not going to blow the whole thing, Sash? I could have gone in his place.'

'You could.' Sasha nodded at James. 'But we want this to appear as close to the real thing as possible. Zo–' She turned to Zoe. 'You're good to go? You know what to do?'

All eyes stared at Zoe in her voluminous black wig, as she nodded.

'Right, keep me posted, babes.'

~

Fran sat with her coffee, a short while after arriving at Camden, studying the monitors in front of her. A man walked into one of the foyers and fiddled with the tablet to check himself into his room, looking around nervously.

'Guilty conscience?' Fran murmured at the screen, looking up to note that it was the Camden foyer, and glancing at the check-in details as they came up on the system.

'Who's got a guilty conscience?'

Fran looked up, smiling at Ethan as he leaned on the doorframe. 'Helps pass the time, imagining what's going on with the guests. How's the bar tonight?'

'Oh, so so. I'm off to scrounge something to eat from the kitchen, want anything? Woah, check out the Grace Jones lookalike.' He walked in to peer at the screen. 'Where's she off to then? Which foyer is that?'

'It's here. Guest checking in, I expect.'

'Guest checking in, my arse. Did you see the way she was dressed? Someone's getting lucky tonight.' He whistled to show his appreciation, winking at Fran.

Laughing, Fran gave him a playful shove. 'Go and get your sandwich.'

'Hello. Trouble going on with someone. Where's that? Fiery little thing by the looks of it. Do you get sound on these things?'

'No, it's not entertainment, you little bugger. Probably entered the card details wrong or something.'

'Well, I'm off then. See you later.'

'Bye, enjoy your sandwich.' She watched the statuesque black woman enter the lift and turned her attention back to the drama playing out on the other screen. *What on earth was going on over there?*

A few seconds later her question was answered when she received the frantic call.

'Are you sure you can't sort it out? Did you try clearing it and entering the details again? Did you check the card? And it's the right hotel? Because sometimes they–' Sighing, she looked at her watch and grabbed her bag. 'Alright, I'm on my way.'

~

Felicia sneered at Christian as he sat nervously on the bed. 'What's the matter? Scared I'm going to use my whip on you? Maybe you'll like it, they all do, you know.'

'How long do we have to wait?' he whined. 'You know what, sod this, I'm out of here, I don't want any part of it, I've changed my mind. I've checked into the room, I've done my bit.'

A loud crack echoed around the room as Felicia loomed over him, holding her whip menacingly. 'Sit down. Stay right where you are, little boy.'

~

Yawning, Tony Palmer glanced at the time on his watch, rubbing his stiff neck as he peered out of the dirty window. 'Reckon we should wrap things up, doesn't look like we'll get lucky tonight. Either someone's playing us or we've got the wrong night. Let's go, you can drop me home and keep the car. Tell the others.'

Constable Simon Derry switched on his phone, frowning as it dinged impatiently in the silence.

'Turn the bleedin' volume down at least, why don't you? If they are there, we don't want them to hear us, do we, you berk?'

'Sorry, sarge.' Simon fumbled with his phone before listening to the messages.

'Anything important?' Tony sighed, wondering what the mood would be when he got home.

'Don't think so. Message from Dennis, some bird was in the station earlier insisting she spoke to you?'

'Yes, yes, I know about her. Anything else?'

'He says she wanted him to tell you there's going to be a murder tonight. Sounds like a crank.'

'Yeah, probably... wait a minute. Who told him that? The same woman?'

'Er, yeah, Sarah something, no, Sorcha maybe, hold up, I'll play it again.'

What the hell bee had she got in her bonnet now? He'd bet his life on it that it was Sasha with some new theory.

The woman was becoming a pain in his already aching neck.

'Sasha Blue, sarge. Murder at midnight at Freedom Kensington. Sounds like a book title dunnit? Something about an escort already booked. Er, says it was The Luxe? She wants to stop a murder...'

'An escort? Put that on speaker phone and play it again.' Tony listened to the somewhat garbled message from Dennis, picking up the salient points. Sasha was convinced there was going to be a murder at Freedom Kensington at midnight, was she? Well, it wouldn't harm to take a drive past there and make sure that all was in order...

'Let's go, we'll head over and check it out. Then, if all's well, we're going home.'

As the car moved through the late evening traffic, Tony switched on his phone and went through his messages, eventually coming to Sasha's voice messages and playing them, his phone clamped to his ear in an effort to hear clearly over the sound of his driver's tuneless singalong to the radio.

His hand reached out, turning off the radio, as his jaw dropped in shock.

NOCTURNAL LIES

Sasha answered her phone, nodding tensely. 'You're sure? Good work. I'll let you know when we're in position. I'll wait for your next message, don't call me, remember? Here's the room number – you know what to do after our next contact?'

Turning to her team, she drew a breath. 'Let's go, and remember, one at a time so we don't raise any alarms. Everyone remember the room number?'

'Three-oh-seven,' they collectively replied.

Sasha watched Sorbet saunter into the foyer and disappear into the lift a minute later. So far so good.

'I go next,' commanded Gretel, giving Sasha a swift nod and marching off confidently.

'James, you and Crystal go together, the sooner we're all in the better.'

'Let's go,' said James, touching Crystal's arm.

Sasha paced anxiously as she watched them disappear into the lift, giving it two minutes before making her own move. She entered the foyer, stopping at the row of tablets to key in the room number, before heading into the lift as it opened silently. Tapping on the door of the room, she walked in, and Sorbet closed it behind her.

'I just have to make another call.' She made the call, watched by six pairs of eyes.

'What do we do now?' asked Gretel. 'How long before I get my hands on him?'

'Now that we're all here, there's something I need to tell you.' She spoke clearly and calmly.

The six pairs of eyes widened in shock and six mouths gaped in the quiet room when she'd finished.

Sorbet was the first to speak. 'You've got to be bloody kidding me.' She stomped around the room angrily. 'I need a drink.' She reached for the bottle of whisky.

'Don't touch it.' Sasha moved quickly to stand beside her, holding her arm.

'You cannot be serious,' snarled Gretel.

'I'm deadly serious.' Sasha looked at her watch for what felt like the hundredth time and checked her phone for messages.

~

Fran pulled over to answer the call, sighing as she retraced her route to Freedom Camden – false alarm – the problem guest's issue had been dealt with and she was no longer needed.

The traffic was light and she was back at the hotel within fifteen minutes. Parking her car, she walked through the silent underground parking area, pausing as she thought she heard the sound of footsteps. A slight chill crept down her spine, and she shivered despite the warmth of the evening, looking around to peer into the shadowy corners. *Had that been a movement over there?* Taking a couple of steps closer, she stopped, shaking her head. This was silly, she was allowing her nerves to get out of hand. She turned back towards the basement entrance door, quickening her pace anxiously.

~

'We're here, sarge, what d'you want me to do?'

Holding his hand up, Tony listened to the end of Sasha's last message, his mind reeling. Checking the time, he pushed the car door open and jumped out. 'Come with me.'

Rushing into the foyer, he looked around, cursing the fact that the Freedom hotels had no reception. *Stupid flamin' idea if he ever heard one – how were you supposed to find out what room number a guest was in?* Heading through to the restaurant and bar, he looked around for someone to speak to, flashing his warrant card as he snapped at a passing waiter.

'I need to find out a guest's room number – pronto.'

He turned back to his accompanying officer. 'Wait in the foyer and stop anyone who looks like an escort.'

'How am I supposed to know?'

'I don't know, use your bleedin' imagination,' he retorted, exasperated.

'What's the guest's name, officer?' The barman looked at him expectantly.

'Christian Hamilton-Hughes.'

'Blimey, that's a bit of a mouthful. And how are we spelling that, exactly?'

Drumming his fingers on the bar, he waited while the barman tapped on a screen, tutting and shaking his head.

'Noo... nothing under Hamilton. Shall I try Hughes?'

'Why not?' Tony seethed. 'Take your time.'

Oblivious to the sarcasm, the barman typed and scrolled, shaking his head slowly. 'Nope, sorry, no one of that name here tonight.'

'Well, is there anyone else with a name that's similar? Here, let me have a look at that screen.'

'We're not supposed to give out–'

Distracted by a commotion, they looked over at the two women who'd walked into the bar.

'I want to speak to the manager, I've never been so insulted. We've just been asked if we're prostitutes. Do we look like prostitutes? What sort of hotel are you people running when two women are accosted by a random bloke in the foyer who's obviously looking for sex?'

He'd kill him.

The hapless waitress who'd been accosted by the woman looked around doubtfully. 'I'm really sorry about that, I can't think why that happened...'

His incompetent officer's brain the size of a pea, that's what happened, although the mutton dressed as lamb look probably hadn't helped...

'And what are you looking at?' The woman's voice was becoming shrill as she advanced towards Tony.

~

'Right, we're on, everyone, not long 'til it all kicks off,' said Sasha softly as she read her latest message.

'What's in the bottle then?' Sorbet asked. 'Is someone supposed to have drunk it?'

Shit. Grabbing the bottle with the napkin from the champagne bucket, Sasha unscrewed it and poured some into the glass beside it, before taking the bottle to the bathroom and pouring some of it into the sink. *She'd totally forgotten about setting the scene.*

She did the same with the champagne bottle and looked around – *what else?*

'Mess up the bed covers, quick.' Turning off the main light, the room dimmed, lit only by the small light on the desk in the corner. 'You need to get into the bed now, Christian, and pull the covers up so we can only see your head – and face the door to the balcony. Everyone else, take your positions. Let's be ready, in case our murderer becomes impatient.'

'When do I leave the room?' Felicia slipped her whip into the top of her boot.

'Soon. You've got the room key? Everyone's phones off?'

She switched off her own and watched James disappear out through the balcony doors, nodding as Sorbet and Crystal climbed into the, fortunately, large wardrobes.

'I can't do this.' Christian sat up, throwing the bed covers back.

~

What had he missed? Or had Sasha got it all completely wrong? Had she definitely said tonight?

'Your message definitely said Kensington, yeah?' he asked Simon Derry as they walked towards the car.

'It did, I can listen to it again if you want.'

But his message from Sasha had said something about The Luxe, and that was the old hotel in...

'You can tell Constable Hardy, I'll bleedin' well brain him when I see him. He's got his wires crossed and told us the wrong flamin' hotel. We're going to Camden, and put your foot down.'

Climbing into the car, he clicked on her messages again. 'And don't even think about turning that radio on,' he barked, as Simon's hand reached for the switch. 'And don't talk.'

They sped through the streets towards Camden as Tony listened to Sasha's messages again. *This was a right royal cock up if ever there was one.* If she was right – and it all made sense – then he was so wrong it made his toes curl. Not only that – she and whoever else she'd roped in for her hair-brained scheme to stop the murder were putting themselves in danger, and here he was, plodding around like an idiot going to the wrong hotel and missing the whole thing. 'Step on it,' he snarled, watching the minutes tick by on the clock. *They were going to be too late.*

~

Zoe hovered in front of the entrance to the hotel, her eyes fixed on the passing cars. *Where were the cops? Why weren't they here yet?*

She checked her watch, her stomach churning as she pictured the scene playing out in the hotel room.

A taxi pulled up and a young woman alighted, holding a small suitcase. 'Ta very much, mate, see ya later.' She looked around, smiling at Zoe as she passed her, and pushed through the entrance door.

'Wait up, you're Zoe, aren't you?'

'What?' Startled, Zoe stared at her. 'Do I know you?'

'Not yet.' She cackled delightedly. 'I've been practising my detective skills, reckon I've seen you on Sasha's Graffic profile. Nice wig. I'm Alex, by the way. What do we do now, then?'

'Sorry, I'm not sure that I–'

'Alex, I work for Eric and Rowan – but not for much longer – I'm going to work for Sasha once she sets up her agency. She didn't tell you?'

'Oh, wait, I remember now, you gave her the escort card.'

'That's right. So, is it all going to plan then?'

'Apart from the fact that the police aren't here and there's a knife-wielding maniac about to enter the hotel room where Sasha, my boyfriend, and crew, are waiting. I'm a nervous wreck, what if something goes wrong?'

~

'What d'you mean, you can't do this? You have to, you can't back out now, you'll ruin the whole operation.' Sasha looked at Christian's panicked expression, her heart sinking.

Felicia stepped towards him menacingly, pulling her whip from her boot, and he fell back on the bed, holding up his hands.

'I can't,' he cried, beginning to shake. 'Something's going to go wrong. Operation?' He gave a hysterical laugh. 'This is the most screwed-up, crazy, set-up I've ever seen. A bunch of women, most of them hookers, hiding in wardrobes, waiting to catch a killer in the act of stabbing their victim to death? And you want me to lie here in this bed? You've lost your minds. I'm a married man, I've got a wife at home, I've got–' his last words were lost as he dissolved into a paroxysm of sobbing laughter.

Felicia slapped his face hard. 'You call yourself a man? Then man up.'

Christian curled up into a ball, a quivering, sobbing, mess.

'No,' said Sasha. 'It's no good, he's done, he'll ruin everything.'

The balcony door opened at the same time as the wardrobe doors.

'What's going on?' asked James.

'I can do it,' said Crystal, quietly, as everyone turned to her. 'My blonde wig will look like him if I pull the covers right up.'

'I'll do it if I can borrow your wig.' Sasha looked around. 'We're out of time, Felicia's two hours are up in one minute. James, get him onto the balcony and keep him quiet.'

She pulled Crystal's wig on, making sure it was tight. 'Ok, this is it, I'll get into the bed, everyone else back in positions, and Felicia – it's time to go.' *If she'd got this all wrong, she was going to look pretty stupid in a little while...*

The room fell silent as the door closed behind Felicia, and they waited, hearts pounding as the minutes ticked by.

~

The door made a tiny click, as the key card was inserted, and swung open silently, the sound of footsteps soft on the carpet as they made their way into the room, pausing for a moment.

Sasha lay, motionless, beneath the bedcovers, trying to control her breathing, as the footsteps drew closer. She felt a gentle touch through the duvet, as a hand tentatively pressed on her shoulder. *This was it.*

'NOW!' she yelled, sitting up and reaching for the hand holding the knife, as the clatter of wardrobe doors opening, women's screams, and James's guttural yell, combined, and the killer was pinioned by firm hands.

Light flooded the room as the door burst open and more bodies rushed in.

'Bleedin' hell,' said Tony.

~

For a second, everything seemed to stop, and silence again filled the room, but then the figure in the midst of the confusion of arms and legs on the bed renewed its struggle, and everyone began shouting at once.

'Don't just flamin' well stand there, find the knife,' Tony barked at Simon Derry, who began to scramble around the room. 'And who are you exactly?' he yelled at the tall woman behind him, as he rushed towards the fray.

'I am Felicia, and now it's my turn.' She flicked her whip gently against her thigh.

'I'll tell you what it's your turn for, it's to stand in front of the door – no one in or out, got it?' *He'd like to see anyone mess with her.*

'James?' Zoe rushed to the bed as James sat up, his hand firmly clasped around an arm.

'Everybody off the bed. Sasha, I know you're under there somewhere, are you going to tell me who the bleedin' well who everyone is?'

'I'm not letting go until you've got the cuffs on.' Sorbet hung on resolutely to a leg.

'Nor me,' panted Gretel, her legs clamped around the other leg.

Tony took out his handcuffs, reaching for the remaining arm, held tight by someone's hand. 'Sash, is that you under there? You need to call off your dogs. No offence, ladies.'

'Sarge, I've found the knife, and–'

A man appeared from the balcony, his expression harrowed. 'Can I go now?'

'Another clown to join the circus. Care to tell me who you are and what you've been doing out there, mate?'

'There's blood on it, sarge.'

'There's what? Blood on what?'

'Sasha?' Alex ran to the bed, shoving bodies aside, helped by Zoe.

'There's blood. She's been stabbed. Sash? You alright, babes?'

'I can't...' her voice was barely a whisper.

'Do something,' Zoe pleaded, as Tony hoisted a body from the bed and snapped on his handcuffs.

'She can't breathe, that's what she's saying, and no wonder with you lot on top of her. Get off and give her some air, for God's sake.'

'Where's the blood coming from?' Alex pulled back the duvet as Sasha pulled off the blonde wig, which had twisted to partly cover her face.

'My ear.' Sasha sat up, red-faced from having been buried beneath a mass of bodies in the struggle. 'It's nothing, just a nick.'

She looked at the angry face staring back at her from beside Tony. 'Hello, Fran.'

~

Fran Baxter's shoulders slumped in defeat. 'You've ruined everything, you stupid bitch, don't you get it? I was doing it for women everywhere, I–'

A roar came from the doorway as Felicia advanced towards her, cracking her whip. 'Doing it for women? You killed women – you killed our sisters.'

'Oi, oi, leave it out, I think we've had enough violence for one night. Constable?' Tony nodded at his officer, who advanced tentatively towards Felicia.

'If you'd like to give me the whip, madam,' he said awkwardly.

'Oh, for crying out loud. Felicia, one more step in this direction and you'll find yourself in handcuffs as well.'

'Yes please, officer,' said Felicia, holding out her hands and winking at Tony, as some of the girls sniggered delightedly.

Exasperated, Tony yanked Fran's arm and pulled her away. 'Frances Harking, consider yourself under arrest.'

Whoops and laughter sounded around the room and the tension eased as the success of their operation began to hit home.

'We did it, guys.' Sasha grinned around at her motley crew, feeling exhilarated.

'Can we drink that champagne now?' Sorbet grinned at her. 'This was thirsty work.'

'No touching the evidence.' Tony glared at her, before relenting as he smiled at the group. 'Alright, you lot did a stupid, dangerous, unauthorised, but nonetheless brilliant bleedin' job, for which I hold Sasha completely responsible. Now, everybody stay here, I need names and addresses, there's going to be quite a lot of explaining to do. Constable Derry, I need a team here to check out the room, get onto that pronto, and I need another car to get Mrs Harking down to the station.'

'Can I leave now?' A timid voice piped up from the corner of the room.

'No, you can't. You stay here like everyone else.' Tony looked from Christian Hamilton-Hughes to Sasha. 'You and me need to have a very long chat, agreed?'

'Agreed. But first – are you going to drop the charges against Eric at last? And the poor homeless bloke she set up? And what about The Cutter? What are you going to do about him?'

'You don't give up, do you, not even for a flamin' minute? I'm sure your Mr Latimer and the other chap will be on their merry way soon enough, so you can relax about that, and can we just leave your cutter bloke until tomorrow? You can tell me all about him when you come down to the station for our long chat. Right, Constable

Derry, take down everyone's details so they can get the hell out of this room before the team arrives.'

'Drinks on me over at the Horse's Head, everyone,' announced Sasha, to much cheering, once they'd been permitted to leave.

~

'So, what put you onto her?' James asked once they were all seated with their drinks.

'We've got Kay to thank if I'm honest. If she hadn't written her blog about all the murders in London, I would have missed it. So–' She raised her glass. 'Here's to Kay.'

'To Kay,' they all said.

'And Roberta,' said Felicia.

'And Chardonnay,' added Sorbet.

'But why did she kill the girls if it was men she wanted to murder?' Alex wanted to know.

'And how did you know it was her?' asked Sorbet.

'What about Discreetly Elite – how did it fit in? Why wouldn't they answer your calls?' Zoe leaned her elbows on the table, eager for details.

'And how many blokes did she murder?' James leaned forward.

'How did you get her away from the hotel so we could all get into the room without her seeing us?' Gretel wanted to know.

Alex cackled. 'I can explain that one for you, that was my brilliant acting, that was. I was the angry guest kicking up a stink because I couldn't get the check-in to work. I gave poor Donna a major hard time, but we laughed about it afterwards. Course, there was nothing wrong with it really, we just needed it to look convincing so that when Donna phoned Fran, she didn't suspect anything.'

'Oh, poor Donna, she's probably wondering what's happened. I need to phone her.' Sasha switched her phone on and called Donna at Freedom Kensington, thanking her for her help and briefly explaining what had happened, as well as promising to drop in for a proper chat. Frowning as she saw that she had a voice message from Shuggy, she played it quickly.

Sasha, Shuggy here, sorry to bother. Don't suppose there's any news on old Eric? Ah yes, bit of an odd one, thought you should know. We've just left The Ship in Wardour Street, had a bit of a strange experience with that business colleague of Quentin's, Max something, I believe. Anyway, thought you should know. Oh, not explaining, am I? A lot of nasty talk, dangerous stuff really, your name came up rather a lot, quite got the impression that he er, well, that is to say, he sounded like he meant you harm. Fellow was pretty wasted, we got out of there, left him drowning his sorrows, most unpleasant, but, well, the thing is, I think you should be careful, he was mumbling a lot of old mumbo jumbo, of course, all sounded pretty gruesome, don't think the chap likes girls very much. Not sure if he might have– well, I'm no detective, of course, but I got the feeling he has a violent side, does that make sense? Just be careful, wouldn't want anything to happen to you. Alright then, cheerio.

Sasha put her phone down, processing Shuggy's message. It sounded like Max Canning, aka The Cutter, could be in danger of striking again, tonight. Tony wasn't interested, certainly not right now, but...

'What is it, babes?' Zoe noticed her friend's distracted mood.

'It's about The Cutter, I think he may be on the prowl again tonight...'

'Tell me when and where.' Felicia cracked her whip, her eyes flashing, much to the consternation of the drinkers at the next table.

'I think I'll just play this message again and I might accidentally put it on speakerphone...' Her eyes caught

Sorbet's, who nodded, catching her drift as Shuggy's voice rang out to the group.

'Drink up, girls, I reckon it's time we were leaving.' Sorbet drained her glass, standing up, as the other three followed suit.

'Oh, Crystal, I'm sorry about your wig, I'll replace it.' Sasha held out the blood-stained blonde wig sadly.

'That's alright, I've got loads, and it was worth it.'

'You gonna give me my wig back, honey?'

They all looked at Zoe, who looked at Sorbet in confusion for a second. 'I forgot I was wearing it,' she shrieked in amusement, the black curls bobbing around her face. Sorry.' She pulled off the wig and handed it to Sorbet. 'This was my disguise in case Fran recognised me while I reported her movements to Sash.'

'I'll get you another one, I kind of like it,' James said with a grin.

They watched the group of four women leave the pub a moment later after swift hugs had been shared all round, including with James.

Zoe grinned. 'That's something to tell the lads about, baby,' she teased him.

Laughing, James turned to Sasha. 'So, why did they rush off? What am I missing?'

'No idea,' said Sasha vaguely, 'back to their nocturnal lives, I suppose...'

'Street justice, innit?' Alex threw back her drink. 'Bloody good for them, if you ask me. Right, I'm getting another round in and you better tell us how you solved this whole thing. And don't forget the part I played.' She winked. 'Same again, everyone?'

With fresh drinks, Sasha gave a brief account of what she knew, prefacing it with, 'Course, it will all have to be confirmed by the police.'

'Fran Baxter's married name of seven years was Frances Harking, and her husband, Adrian Harking, who'd been cheating on her regularly with escorts, was her second victim. She murdered her first victim, Raymond Pinner, at Freedom City of London, as a trial run, having got her doctor to prescribe her diazepam or something similar – a detail which was mentioned to me by one of the hotel staff – maybe for anxiety, which is what my doctor did on my recent visit to hospital, and she then used it to drug her victims in a complimentary bottle of booze placed in the room, having taken up boxing classes to build up her strength to help with her murder method. I'm guessing that her original plan was just to kill her husband, Adrian, in March, and disguise it by muddying the waters with the similar death in January – she'd taken their wallets in both cases to make it look like a robbery gone wrong – but that she got a taste for revenge on married men and the nocturnal lies that they told as they enjoyed the services of escorts.'

'So, she moved around the Freedom hotels at night, to suit her agenda, and no one was suspicious because it was her job.' Alex nodded slowly. 'And by the time they found the bodies no one would remember if Fran had popped in for a while – talk about convenient.'

'But why did her husband go to a hotel that she worked at?' asked Zoe. 'Didn't he think there was a risk she'd see him?'

'That was the beauty of it.' Sasha smiled. 'Freedom Camden, where she murdered him, had only just been taken over by The Freedom group, and was still called The Luxe, so he had no idea. Fran must have seen the booking and known what he was doing. She could place the doctored bottle of booze in the room, and remove the evidence afterwards, without anyone being any the wiser. She always stabbed her victims seven times – one stab for each year of marriage – and always through the duvet. I don't know if that's because she didn't want to see them or whether it stopped the blood from spurting out, but in a way, that fact was her downfall.'

'And she wore a chef's jacket from the kitchen just in case any blood spattered on her. Like the one that Kay found and put on her blog.' Zoe's eyes were round as she connected the dots.

'She did, which, tragically for Kay, brought about her own murder.'

'But that was after the murder of the escort in Eric's hotel room,' said James. 'I don't get it, why did she kill the female escort and not Eric?'

'Kind of a twist of fate, if you think about it. I don't think she banked on Eric's ability to drink copious amounts of booze, or his charm, which worked wonders on poor Lisa Pennington who, instead of following instructions given to her by her agency – which actually came from Fran – I'll get to that – decided to take the cash from Eric's wallet and head down to the bar for another bottle of champagne. I suppose she was having a great time and wanted to carry on drinking. My guess is that Eric went out to the balcony for a smoke and passed out and that Lisa drank more champagne before passing out in the bed, pulling the duvet up because she was a bit chilly maybe so that only her hair was visible.'

'She was a blonde, like Eric?' Alex's eyes flashed. 'She thought Lisa was Eric, didn't she?'

'Yep, I reckon so. She thought she was stabbing Eric seven times, but it was Lisa. She must have seen Lisa enter the foyer from the lift and thought that she was leaving the hotel, not realising that she returned to the room a couple of minutes later. She then went to the room to murder Eric, removing the bottle of whisky and taking his wallet when she left to make it look like another robbery. She'd cleaned his whisky glass and put it back in the bathroom, as she did with all her victims, but this time Eric lived to remember pouring himself a large glass of whisky – which begged the question: where was the bottle and why was the glass clean and back in the bathroom? The answer of course, was that the murderer wanted it to look like her victims had been drinking champagne alone in their rooms.'

'Wow, Eric had a lucky escape when he passed out on the balcony, talk about his boozing saving his life' James whistled.

'So, what did she do with the knife? Why didn't the cops find it?'

'It was easy for her to visit the hotel kitchen each time, and to help herself to a knife, which she would use and then return to the kitchen where it joined the rest of the washing up. Gross, of course, but hiding in plain sight, just like the chef's jacket, hidden in amongst the rubbish where no one would go looking.'

'But wasn't the jacket put in the laundry?' Zoe screwed her eyes up as she tried to get the details straight in her head.

'Not at first, and again this is thanks to Kay – a girl at the hotel wanted to stop her boyfriend from getting into trouble for being down on his laundry count so she looked for the jacket, found it in the rubbish and moved it to the laundry bins. Fran could never have envisaged this happening and must have thought that the jacket was long gone until Kay ruined her plans by finding it.'

'You said it was revenge against married men, so why choose Eric? And how did she even know if someone was married or not? Did she just take a chance, or what?' Engrossed, Alex's eyes were fixed on Sasha.

'This is where Eric's mates helped me, as well as a barman at Bar Simone. Fran made up fake escort agency cards to look similar to Elitely Discreet, an agency used by her husband, so perhaps she saw it as some kind of poetic justice, calling her fake agency Discreetly Elite, and acquiring a second mobile phone number for the purpose, writing promotional codes on the back as she gave them out – special codes for married men. Single blokes who called the number would just be told there were no escorts available, unaware that they'd narrowly escaped death. She'd get the blokes chatting and have a laugh with them about who was married. The lads teased Eric about being spoken for – that's because the idiot implied that he and I would be getting back together – so he ended up with one of Fran's killer cards. As did Dillon the barman's friend, when Dillon found one of the cards on the table and used it to book an escort for his mate – Fran's next male victim – Rick Turner – who she murdered at Freedom Chelsea.'

'The night we were there,' breathed Zoe. 'We saw the escort enter the foyer when we were leaving.'

'Yep.' Sasha nodded. 'Fran would call the real agency to book the escort and give them her specific requirements. But before she killed Rick, she decided to take advantage of her mistake in killing Lisa, as well as all the media coverage started by poor Kay, telling us all that there was an escort killer on the prowl, to murder Roberta, or Pippa Robbins, to use her real name, at the Duck Palace. I'm guessing she thought it would detract from her murders of the men, which it kind of did for a while.'

'And then she killed your friend, Kay,' said Alex sadly.

'She did. She wanted to destroy the chef's jacket, knowing it would implicate her, so she lured Kay to her death at The Ballroom. She retrieved the evidence from Kay's flat and destroyed it, planting her handbag and some other bits with the homeless guy, for the cops to find.'

'And it worked. No one was looking for a murderer anymore, and certainly not for a chick who was killing blokes, were they? So how did you know?' James scratched his head, perplexed.

'Well, you helped me with a comment that you made when I was telling you and Zoe about a small case involving an older woman and the younger men who she became fixated on. You said something like, we tend to think that only men can be predators. That stayed with me, but until earlier today, I still thought we were looking for a man. When Kay lay dying, she managed to utter a few words, which I mistook as referring to someone else. She said something about not understanding, about it being the same person from the hotel, and it was only when I listened to her voice notes today that I understood.'

'There was all that confusion outside The Duck Palace when we heard that bloke laughing, then Kay said she recognised someone,' threw in Zoe.

'Bloody Rowan,' added Alex immediately.

'Yes, that was him, and she, as well as some of the girls, had also made mention of a man with dead, grey, eyes...'

'Max,' breathed Zoe, shuddering.

'Max Penrose, who turned out to be The Cutter and who will no doubt receive his own kind of justice... so first of all I thought she meant Rowan, then I changed my mind to Max, but I was wrong on both counts. When I listened to her voice notes, she mentioned a Mr Penrose, with dead eyes, coming to the hotel while she was disguised as a Laundry King employee – that was obviously Max pretending to be Rowan, presumably wanting to check the hotel rooms for any lingering evidence of his time spent there on the same night as Eric, in a room where he abused and tortured a poor escort called Lilly. But then she mentioned a woman called Fran who had popped in to look for her glasses and was going to search for them in the kitchen – all this at the same time that Kay was retrieving the chef's jacket. Fran was there looking for the jacket, but Kay beat her to it.'

'But you still haven't explained how you figured out that men were the intended victims.'

'It was one of those light bulb moments, I suppose, brought about by a number of incidents. The crime scene photos always showed just the hair of the victim above the duvet; I watched a mother leaning over her baby in its pram on The Serpentine Bridge and all I could see was its head, just like when I was in hospital and one of the nurses commented about all the babies in the baby unit looking like peas in a pod; then, when I was looking on my phone, I came across a photo of Eric, taken on our holiday while he'd been sleeping, and all you could see was his blonde hair above the duvet. When Fran entered the room to murder Eric, she saw Lisa Pennington's blonde hair and thought it was him, and once I considered the possibility that it was all the wrong way round, I looked back at other identical murders of men and found the pattern. Then it all began to make sense.'

'But how did you tie Fran to it all?'

'Oh, that was a bit of luck, of course. I went to her home to ask her about the cameras in the foyers, and I happened to see her post on the server in the hallway. One of them was addressed to Mrs Harking, which I thought nothing of until I went back through Kay's Killer Blog and spotted the name of the March victim.'

'Adrian Harking...' Alex nodded, impressed.

'And then you had your interview at Elitely Discreet, for an escort job,' Zoe piped up.

James's eyes widened in surprise as they grinned.

'Yeah, and they told me they had a booking for tonight with the same requirements as the night of Lisa Pennington's murder. And the rest, as they say, is history, thanks to you all, and Sorbet and the girls.'

'The dream team.' Alex beamed. 'That's us. I can already see our first advert for the agency – *Need an investigator? Call the dream team.*'

'Slow down,' laughed Sasha, 'I need somewhere to live and an office for us to work from, not to mention some cases to pay the bills before we start placing adverts about dream teams.'

'You just said *us*.' Alex grinned from ear to ear. 'Have I got the job then?'

'Why not?' Sasha's face broke into a huge smile. 'Let's get Sasha Blue Investigations on the map.'

'We need some champagne,' said Zoe, hugging James delightedly as she smiled at her best friend.

EPILOGUE

Four months later

'Do I really have to cut the ribbon?' Sasha held the scissors awkwardly, looking around at the small group clustered in Gin Alley in front of the Victorian shop front.

'Just get on with it, the champagne will be getting warm in there.' Zoe held her phone poised to take a photo of the big moment.

Pausing, Sasha looked up at the sign above her head, *Sasha Blue Investigations*. 'Alright, here we go.' She snipped the ribbon and turned to grin at her friends. 'I hereby declare Sasha Blue Investigations officially open.'

'Hold up, I want a picture of the two of us,' squealed Alex, shoving her phone at James. 'And make it a good one, I'm in charge of social media.'

'Me too.' Zoe joined the two women as James performed the role of photographer and passers-by stopped to smile at the laughing group.

They piled into the office, the old bell above the door jingling, the smell of fresh paint still strong, and looked around the small space approvingly as Alex proprietorially took charge. 'This is my desk and this is the seating area for clients. Sasha's office is through here.' She led the way to the small rear office, followed by the others, to all appearances a tour guide and her party at a historic country house. 'This used to be the map-making room,' Alex informed her party proudly as she waved her arm around, 'Sasha's desk is really old– look, it's bolted to the floor. Cool innit?'

Sasha pointed to a door. 'This leads up to my flat so I've got no excuse for being late for work and that door leads to the kitchenette and the loo.' She ushered them back to the front office. 'We kept the old bell above the door, and the wooden unit with the old map drawers absolutely had to stay.' Her hand stroked the old wood lovingly.

'It's all gorgeous,' breathed Zoe as James whistled.

'Must have set you back a bit, it's amazing,' he said.

'Eric was extremely generous.' Sasha smiled. 'I still can't quite believe it, I have to keep pinching myself.'

'I can't believe he sold up everything and left the country.' Zoe took the champagne from its bucket and handed it to James.

'At least he saw Sasha right,' Alex nodded approvingly. 'Without her, he'd be in Wormwood Scrubs right now.'

'You all played a part, for which he's very grateful.'

'That's us – the dream team at your service.' Alex clapped her hands delightedly.

'What about that bloke you called *The Cutter*? Any news? I'd like to get my hands on him after what he did to some of the girls and the way he threatened you two.' James scowled in recollection.

Shaking her head, Sasha sighed. 'After they found him and took him to hospital, he disappeared. At least Sorbet and the girls gave him a taste of his own medicine so that's something. Tony reckons he's pretty sure he murdered the prostitute Sonia Clark in June – the murder that got poor Kay talking about a serial killer. They're still looking for him...'

'And you're fully recovered from your op and ready to start working? You're sure, babes?' Zoe's protective instinct kicked in as she studied her best friend solicitously.

'I'm great, honestly. Malcolm Bailey removed the monster from inside me and I feel free for the first time in years. No more endometriosis, no more pain, none of that crap, I've never felt more relieved in my life.' *No need to mention her private pain and the sense of loss that consumed her in her weaker moments.* She eyed the bottle in James's hands, grinning. 'Are you going to open that today, James?'

Laughing, James popped the cork and filled the glasses as Zoe passed them round.

Sasha held her glass up and looked around at her friends. 'Here's to you guys, for everything you've done, for all your support, and for your friendship.'

'To Sasha Blue Investigations.' James held up his glass.

'To the dream team.' Alex beamed, holding up her glass.

'Now all you need is your first official case to get you started in your new office. Cheers.' Zoe held her glass up and they all threw back their champagne as the bell above the door jingled. Four heads swivelled to stare at the woman standing in the doorway.

'Oh good, you're open. I was given your new address by a member of our book club, Dolly Pringle, in Parva Crossing. I'm Rosemary Routledge, the novelist. I think someone's copying the murders from my books and I'm scared that I'll be next. Which one of you is Sasha Blue?'

'I am.' Sasha stepped forward with a smile. 'Come through to my office, Rosemary, and tell me all about it.'

This sounded interesting...

DON'T MISS THE NEXT SASHA BLUE MYSTERY

Book Club Lies

'I'm Rosemary Routledge, the novelist. I think someone's copying the murders from my books and I'm scared that I'll be next.'

The Parva Crossing Book Club proudly boasts among its members the best-selling murder mystery writer, Rosemary Routledge, and since her arrival in the village some six months earlier the number of members had swelled quite dramatically. Where once it was a sedate group of only five ladies of a certain age enjoying a chat about their latest read over tea and biscuits, it had grown to fourteen members of varying ages, quite a few of them from the new estate, the hot beverage had been superseded by wine, the group now included some men, and minor hostilities were not uncommon.

The first death occurred during a book club picnic, an outing suggested by one of the members although no one could quite remember who, and had been ruled as accidental death. The second incident had occurred during a book club trip to a book fair in nearby Rentham and had been, according to Rosemary Routledge, an attempt on her life and one which she had narrowly escaped. Again, no one in the book club could recall quite who had suggested the outing to the book fair.

When the third death occurs, Rosemary Routledge seeks the help of Sasha Blue, Private Investigator.

Sasha packs her bags and heads back to Parva Crossing, checking into The Spotted Dog and reuniting with old friends, and tries to find out who wants Rosemary Routledge dead.

Book Club Lies is the fifth book in the Sasha Blue Mystery Series. Each book may be read as a standalone although there are ongoing connections between the stories which might make them more enjoyable when read as a series.

Follow me on your favoured social media platform for book release date info.

REVENGE PLAN

Also by Linzi Carlisle is the standalone domestic psychological thriller, Revenge Plan.

'I never thought that anyone would end up dead.'

Abigail. Lauren. Emma. Hayley. Fiona. Jenna. Claire. Seven best friends. But one night something bad happened... and they made a bad plan...

'It was just another drunken girls' night, one of so many over the years, but that night was the catalyst for everything bad that happened afterwards. As we threw back shots, laughed, and posed for photos, we had no idea what was about to happen in the near future, or how our lives would be changed forever.

'We'd met at the school gates, young mothers dropping off our kids outside the local primary school, but fast forward a couple of decades or so and we were empty nesters with too much time on our hands.

'We were bored housewives attempting to recapture a youth that existed only in our memories, desperate to show the world that we were still relevant, still attractive, still worthy of attention – which we sought with every photo posted by one or the other of us on our various social media pages.

'It was around this time that someone mentioned a dating app they were on. I suppose that's when it all really started...'

A character-driven, slow burn, domestic psychological crime thriller that picks up the pace as events begin to spiral out of control, with devastating consequences.

The first-person narrative is told from Abigail's perspective, and is written in British English.